ALL THAT WE ~~OWN~~ KNOW

SHILO KINO

MOA
PRESS

Published in New Zealand and Australia in 2024
by Moa Press
(an imprint of Hachette Aotearoa New Zealand Limited)
Level 2, 23 O'Connell Street, Auckland, New Zealand
www.moapress.co.nz
www.hachette.co.nz

A catalogue record for this book is available from the National Library of New Zealand.

ISBN: 978 1 86971 823 7 (paperback)

Cover design by Rachel Clark
Cover illustration by Antonia Rayne Tangatakino-McIntyre
Author photograph by Chase Hauraki
Typeset in 11.75/18 pt Minion Pro by Bookhouse
Printed and bound in Australia by McPherson's Printing Group

The paper this book is printed on is certified against the Forest Stewardship Council® Standards. McPherson's Printing Group holds FSC® chain of custody certification SA-COC-005379. FSC® promotes environmentally responsible, socially beneficial and economically viable management of the world's forests.

For my Grandma Hilda,
who helped me see the world differently

For taking away the land from people who live as people of the land is not simply some passing land 'loss'. It is an ongoing rupture that fractures the essential spiritual and practical ties to identity and belonging.

MOANA JACKSON (1945–2022)

THE GATEKEEPER

Māreikura recognised her in an instant. The woman guarding the event. She was in her fifties, wearing an orange vest and scanning media passes. She had all the nuances Māreikura was familiar with. The judgemental flicker of the eye. The eye roll. Looking at anything but Māreikura. Māreikura handed the woman her pass. *Please don't talk to me in te reo. Don't talk to me in te reo.*

'Nō hea koe?' the woman asked, skimming her pass.

'I'm from Gretton College.'

The woman shook her head, clearly exasperated by Māreikura's incorrect response. 'Nō. Hea. Koe?'

'Oh, my iwi? Ngāpuhi.'

'Ki hea?'

'Um. My mum is from Parua Bay.'

The woman handed her pass back. 'He aha te take kei konei koe?'

Blank stare.

'He aha te take kei konei koe?'

She repeated the question, though it was obvious Māreikura didn't know what she was saying. The woman blinked, her arms folded like she was waiting for Māreikura to magically pull te reo Māori out of her ass.

'Sorry,' Māreikura said. 'I can't speak. Well, I'm learning.'

The woman shook her head again and clicked her tongue. She pointed at the pass. 'You part of the media.'

'No, just visiting for a school trip.'

She pointed to the bag Māreikura was holding.

'I'm taking photos of the marae,' Māreikura told her. 'For school. I have to present about the story of Waitangi.'

The woman's eyes glazed over her. 'How you different from any of them?'

By 'them' Māreikura assumed she meant the Pākehā media. There were cameras dotted over the Waitangi Treaty Grounds and white journalists standing near them.

'Because I'm Māori,' Māreikura said. But it was more like a tiny squeak. When she uttered the word Māori, her voice was small, like a child saying their name for the first time.

The woman smirked. There was satisfaction and a hint of superiority in her smirk. No empathy or understanding of a shared colonised past. It told Māreikura, *You are less than me. You are not enough.*

And then she looked Māreikura square in the eyes. 'You can't tell our stories if you can't speak our reo. Tē taea e koe, tē taea e koe.'

She ushered Māreikura through the gate. Māreikura slunk through, her shoulders burdened not by the camera equipment but by what felt like daggers coming out of that woman's mouth.

What gives her the right to speak to me like that? You think I haven't tried hard enough to learn my language?

Māreikura was standing on Waitangi Treaty Grounds for the first time in her life. This is where her whānau were from. This is where she was supposed to belong. Where her ancestors stood on the very same whenua and signed Te Tiriti. Her ancestors, who envisioned a future far different from the present day. The field was overflowing with brown faces, and Māreikura should have felt safe around her own people, comfortable on grounds tied to her ancestry. This was not how she imagined coming home for the first time.

Māreikura hated the privileged smirks of people like the gatekeeper, who made her feel like there was something inherently wrong with her. Who made her want to recoil in a ball or scrub her brown skin off so she could camouflage. Who made her feel ashamed for being unable to speak a language beaten from her grandparents. She hated the fact she sometimes felt more comfortable around woke Pākehā than her own people. *Be careful of Māori who like being the only Māori in the room*, she had heard so many times. *Well, who can blame me when this happens?*

Māreikura had a job to do, so she took her camera out and started taking photos. She didn't care what kind of photos she took. The camera was on automatic so she just clicked the shutter button randomly. She wanted to leave as soon as she could. She did not care about being here. It did not feel like home. Where did she belong if not on her own land?

Māreikura stood in front of Te Tii Marae and held the camera up to her face. The sad part of all of this, she thought, is that this woman was the reason why Māreikura was scared of learning her ancestral language in the first place. The shame, the embarrassment of being reminded she couldn't speak, through no fault of her own. But maybe the greatest irony was that gatekeepers like this woman were the most colonised of all.

PART ONE

CHAPTER ONE

Māreikura sucked her puku in and squeezed her legs into her tights. First her left leg and then her right. The black tights she bought from Save Mart three years ago were not fitting like they used to. They were stuck on her thighs, so she jumped a few times and squeezed into them until she got them past her waist. She chucked on her black Nike shirt with the little holes and found her shoes under the bed.

'What are you up to, girl?' her nana commented from the couch, eyeing up Māreikura with suspicion.

'Going for a run,' Māreikura said like it was normal, like it was something she always did. But it wasn't normal, and do you know what else wasn't normal? Her best friend leaving to go on a colonising mission to Hawai'i.

Her nana said nothing and turned her head back to the TV. Māreikura sat on the doorstep, jammed her feet into her Nikes and checked her phone for the time. 8.20 a.m. She said bye to her nana and fast-walked past the Johnsons' house, trying not to look, but she did look, and their black Range Rover was still parked outside their home. She wondered what Eru was up to, if he'd locked himself in the bathroom, which is what he usually did when he had an anxiety attack, even though he denies having anxiety. He also denies that he is gay and says he has 'same-sex attraction', which is the term his church uses instead. Māreikura told him it was the same thing and he should just say he's gay, but Eru asked Māreikura to please respect his journey so she didn't bring it up again except for that time they went to Piha. But they don't talk about Piha.

Māreikura started running and it was not as bad as she expected. When she was young and forced to do cross country, she used to imagine Edward Scissorhands chasing her and it would make her run the whole track without stopping, even if she had a bad stitch. She'd hated that movie ever since she was little and snuck out of her room and watched it while her nan was asleep. The white skin and scissor hands gave her nightmares so now she had an extreme phobia of scissors and white men.

Māreikura ran until she was bent over in front of Splitz Cafe holding her stitch just like in her cross-country days. She tugged at her shirt, which was sticking to her skin, and realised the little holes were supposed to be for air. She wanted to collapse on the footpath.

Māreikura checked her phone. 8.25. It had only been five minutes. She had been running for five minutes.

'Mōrena.'

The Pākehā guy with a man bun and a cross earring dangling from his left ear was wiping down the table outside.

'Oh, mōrena,' Māreikura said. She raised her arm in the air, pretending to stretch.

'Kei te pehea koe?'

'Yeah, good,' she said, wiping her forehead.

She'd walked past this cafe so many times and the Pākehā guy was always there, always waiting to pounce on Māreikura so he could practise his Māori with her. Last time, he'd told her he was doing a te reo course and Māreikura did a thumbs up and kept walking. Wasn't there another Māori in Ponsonby he could harass about his new-found love for her culture?

Today was a different day and Māreikura was feeling adventurous. She walked into the cafe and skimmed the menu. Mrs Bell taught Māreikura how to skim read when she was seven, and it was her superpower. She could read anything fast. The menu reminded Māreikura why she never ate out.

Smashed avocado on hand-cut sourdough bread with grilled tomatoes: $23.50. Ridiculous, Māreikura thought. Especially when you can get two avocados from Pak'nSave for $2 and a loaf of bread for $1.19.

'He aha māu?' The bun man grinned at Māreikura as if waiting for her to compliment him on his incredible language skills. When she didn't, he cleared his throat.

'Ah, what can I get you?' He had a nice smile. Not as nice as Eru's but still nice enough.

'Flat white, please,' she said, like she always ordered coffee.

'Small, medium or large?'

'Large, please.'

'And is that takeaway?'

'Yes, please.'

'That's $6.80.'

Māreikura flinched at the price but handed over her card anyway and decided it was Eru's fault for her decision that morning to buy an overpriced cup of coffee she didn't even want.

The man-bun guy made her coffee while she scrolled through her Instagram stories. It was November and nearing summer so it was boring videos of Takapuna Beach, gym selfies and girls in bikinis.

Hailey Simpson posted a photo of her and Chris Campion kissing and Māreikura cringed at the caption. *Love doing life with this one.* Everyone knew, Hailey included, that Chris cheated on her almost every weekend, and Māreikura felt second-hand embarrassment for Hailey. She clicked on Hailey's profile and muted her posts and stories.

'Large flat white?' Man-bun guy asked but it wasn't really a question because he handed her coffee over, knowing very well it was her order. She said thank you and walked to Western Park.

Māreikura sat on a bench. 8.45. She blew on her coffee that was too hot to drink, and wished she'd got water instead. She was thirsty after her run and forgot to drink water. Have they left yet? She clicked through her Instagram stories again and it was still boring people seeking validation, so she went on the 'Nowhitesaviour' Insta page and found a quote from John Henrik Clarke that she thought about sending to Eru.

'Religion is the organisation of spirituality into something that becomes the handmaiden of conquerors. Nearly all religions were brought to people and imposed on people by conquerors, and used as the framework to control their minds.'

She really wanted to send it. It would be her final statement. Her goodbye. A bold ending to their friendship. But he'd never listened to her before so why would he start now? Plus, she didn't want to look desperate, like she didn't want him to leave, even though she couldn't care less. And why should she have to message him first? He knew where she was. All he had to do was walk through her door and apologise.

She sipped on her coffee and it was warm now so she sculled the rest back in less than a minute. 9 a.m. Why was time going so slow? She wandered back down Ponsonby Road and noticed she looked like every basic girl on that Saturday morning wearing active gear and sipping takeaway coffee. She chucked her cup in the rubbish bin in disgust. A girl in denim shorts whizzed past on a Lime scooter.

His flight leaves at 1.40 p.m., Māreikura. There's space in our car if you wanna jump in.

Eru Senior had texted Māreikura last night and Māreikura hadn't replied because she didn't know how to respond to a text like that. Her best friend was leaving the country for two years. Ex-best friend. It's weird when you break up with your best friend. It's not really a thing you talk about. No one ever says, 'I broke up with my best friend.' It just happens. It's part of life. You get on with it.

He was gone. The Range Rover was gone. Māreikura was standing in front of Eru's house. Eru was gone. She would not see him for two years. She breathed what she thought was a sigh of relief but it felt more like the beginning of an anxiety attack.

'What are you watching?' Māreikura asked her nana, even though it was the same thing her nana watched every Saturday morning.

She looked Māreikura up and down. 'You okay, girl?'

Māreikura kicked her shoes off. 'Did anyone come around?'

'Not that I know of. You expecting someone?'

Māreikura said nothing. She went into her room and lay on her bed in her sweaty clothes. This was how Māreikura knew she was not okay. Wearing outside clothes on a bed you sleep on is absolutely vile. It was Eru's fault. It's not like Eru going on a mission was a new thing. It had always been Eru's dream to serve. All young men in the Mormon Church were expected to go on a two-year proselytising mission from the age of eighteen. It was optional for women in the church.

But they were older and educated now. The world had changed. Times had changed. She thought he would change. Māreikura didn't care that Eru was Mormon. She always went along to his church things to tautoko him. She went to his baptism when he was eight and watched him get dunked under the water. Afterwards, Eru's face was all glowy and he was smiling heaps and then they all went into the next room and ate cupcakes. She was at his priesthood thing where he was 'ordained a priest'. Even though Eru had explained so many times that no, he wasn't the new bishop because he was only twelve, Māreikura still didn't really get what was meant by 'priest'. He said he was able to pass out bread on Sunday and she asked him when he was going to be bishop of his own church and he said when the Lord decides and it wasn't up to him.

Māreikura used to go with the Johnsons to church sometimes. One time all the young men and women were in Sunday school and Sister Ferguson held up a photo of a mum, dad and five kids and told them it was the ultimate goal to be with your family together for all eternity.

'How do we achieve this goal?' Sister Ferguson asked, and someone yelled out, 'Be obedient,' and someone else said, 'Be kind to your siblings,' and Māreikura put her hand up and asked, 'What if I don't want to be with my family forever?'

Sister Ferguson paused for a moment. She wasn't expecting a question like that. Then she chuckled and said, 'Oh, sweetheart, I know sometimes we fight with our parents but it's our goal, isn't it, kids? To have an eternal family,' and Māreikura said, 'My mum gave me away when I was a baby.'

Sister Ferguson gasped, trying to find the right words. The other young men and women stared at Māreikura with wide eyes. After class, Sister Ferguson gave Māreikura a big hug. 'God loves you,' she said, then she handed her two pieces of chocolate.

Afterwards, Eru and Māreikura sat on the basketball courts waiting for Eru Senior, who was the bishop, and Eru's mum Eden, who was the church librarian. Eru stuffed his chocolate wrapper in his pocket and started twirling his basketball with his finger. He stared at the basketball hoop longingly. He wasn't allowed to bounce the ball. It was the Sabbath. No sports on the Sabbath day.

Then he asked Māreikura if it was really true, if her mum gave her away.

'She gave me away to my nan when I was a baby,' Māreikura said. 'Before she died. She left me.'

'I will never leave you,' he told her. And she believed him.

Mission, marriage, education – that was Eru's life plan, in order. The missionaries were his superheroes. He had a pretend name badge stuck to his mirror that said 'ELDER JOHNSON' and two little stick-figure missionaries on his desk – two men in white shirts and a black tie. Sometimes Eru would dress in a white shirt and put his badge on and he would role-play with Māreikura. 'Hi, I'm Elder Johnson, and I'm a missionary. Can I share a message with you?' and Māreikura would pretend to be the investigator and listen to his message. He would teach her the lessons from the beginning.

Once he was teaching her about the plan of salvation and Māreikura threw food at him.

'Why did you do that?' he asked, pulling mashed potato out of his hair.

'Because that's what might happen on your mission,' she said. 'Atheists on the street might not like your message. They might abuse you. I'm trying to prepare you for the real world.'

Eru had opened up his mission call three months ago and read the words, 'You have been assigned to serve your mission in Honolulu, Hawai'i.'

Eru Senior cheered and his mum Eden cried and so his sister Erana started crying too and his brother-in-law Matt had a big smile on his face and Māreikura didn't know what to do. She was really bad at hiding her emotions so, after everyone hugged him, Māreikura just patted his shoulder and said congratulations in her most cheerful voice.

Hasn't Hawai'i been colonised enough? Now you wanna go and colonise the Indigenous people over there more with your colonised God? How can you honestly preach something that forcefully converted Indigenous people all around the world?

It was like Eru could read her mind because after that things started to get weird between them.

Māreikura was lying on her bed now thinking of the worst-possible-case scenarios. What if she never saw Eru again? What if the plane plummeted into the water on the way to Hawai'i and he died? Or what if he got to Hawai'i and the locals killed him for spreading a false, white, patriarchal message? Her greatest strength was overthinking.

The book *From a Native Daughter: Colonialism and Sovereignty in Hawai'i* was sticking out of Māreikura's shelf, as if begging to be opened. Māreikura had borrowed it from the Auckland City Library two years ago and she loved it so much she never gave it back. She opened to page 2.

'Our country has been and is being plasticized, cheapened, and exploited. They're selling it in plastic leis, coconut ashtrays, and cans of "genuine, original Aloha". They've raped us, sold us, killed us, and still they expect us to behave . . . Hawai'i is a colony of the imperialist United States.'

Māreikura underlined the quote and decided Eru needed to read this. It would be her final farewell. It was her duty.

'Bye, Nan,' she yelled before her nana could ask her a million questions and make her late.

She scooped up the keys hanging above the shoe rack on her way out the door and got into her car. The petrol dial was just above E and she had no money to fill it up but it added to the adrenaline rush. Was she going to make it to the airport or would she run out of gas in the Waterview Tunnel and never see Eru again? Time would tell. She felt like she was in a movie and chasing after a love, even though he wasn't actually her love because Māreikura hated him, so it was more like she was chasing after a hate, driving 110 kph on a 100-kph motorway and dodging through cars like a dominoes game, trying to make it in time, even though she'd checked the time and she would definitely make it.

She parked at the McDonald's down the road from the international airport and fast-walked to the terminal, still in her active gear and still buzzing from her coffee.

HONOLULU DEPART 1.50 p.m. GATE 21.

She followed the international departure sign and practised her speech to Eru in her head as she went up the escalator.

Hey, e hoa! Just wanted to say all the best and here's a book that might help you on your mission. And then she would hand him the book and leave quietly.

The top floor was swarming with Mormons. Māreikura could tell because the men were all freshly shaven, baby-faced and accompanied by their wives, usually women way out of their league.

Eru was standing under the departure sign talking to Mrs Sorenson from his church. Māreikura didn't like her because she'd once asked Māreikura, 'If Māori want to hear their language, don't you have your own channel for that? Why do we have to hear it on *1News*?'

Kayla Tairua was there too. She was hanging around Eru like an annoying fly and Māreikura instantly felt a pang of jealousy.

'Māreikura!'

Eru waved her over so she pretended to be interested in the departure sign so she didn't have to make eye contact with him while she slow-walked over. HK: 1.38 p.m. LA: 4.45 p.m.

'Hey,' Māreikura said. 'Hi, Mrs Sorenson.'

'Hello, dear.' She peered at Māreikura. 'Glennis's granddaughter? Is that you?'

'Yup.'

'Oh, lovely,' she said, then she turned her attention back to Eru because that's what people always did.

'Now, dear, my daughter Kimberly is in Lā'ie, only two roads down from the temple. I've written her address in the card – go and see her when you get there, okay? She's looking forward to meeting you, so whenever you feel hungry or need a break, you go and see her, okay?'

'Aw, thank you, Sister Sorenson.' Eru placed his hand on her shoulder. 'Sister Sorensen, is it okay if I talk to Māreikura for a minute? I haven't seen her in a while.'

'That's fine, dear.'

Mrs Sorenson scurried off to where Eru Senior was standing. Eru watched her walk away then he turned back to Māreikura, eyeing up her active gear.

'You look different.'

'You look different.'

'I shaved,' he said, rubbing his chin. 'Does it look weird?'

Usually Māreikura would mock her best friend and say something like, *There's nothing on your face to shave*, but they didn't have that friendship now. It was kind of awkward. Māreikura studied his face and wondered how a person could be born with a perfect nose that wasn't too big or too small, just perfectly pointy and with no blackheads. Then she thought about how he had nice skin with no acne and how it wasn't fair and that made her hate him again, because he got everything good in life. Good skin, good nose, a good family.

ELDER JOHNSON. His new name was pinned to his white shirt.

'I got you something.' She rummaged through her bag and found the Whittaker's Peanut Slab that was still in there from the day before.

'Thanks.' Eru ripped open the wrapper with his teeth and then did the thing where he chewed with his mouth open and Māreikura saw bits of chocolate in his teeth. It used to gross her out but now she missed it.

'Not that.' She showed him the cover of *From a Native Daughter*. 'This,' and then dropped it in his shoulder bag before the Mormons tried to confiscate it.

'Thank you,' he said, swallowing another bite.

A hand touched Māreikura's shoulder. Eru Senior.

'Hey, girl, I'm glad you came. You okay?'

Māreikura nodded.

'Son, you have to board soon.'

'Okay, Dad.'

Māreikura watched Eru Senior walk away and then she turned back to Eru.

'What's your number?' she asked him.

That's how they checked up on each other. They never asked how they were doing, they asked for the number: 1 meant really bad – that was Te Pō: darkness, doom, depression. Number 10 was Te Ao Mārama: the light – ecstatic, blissfully happy, content. Sometimes they wouldn't even say any words, they'd just send a text with a number. There had only been a few times that Māreikura had sent a text with the number 1, and Eru had come straight over to pick her up and they'd driven to McDonald's in silence until Māreikura was ready to talk.

'I'm at a 9.5,' he said. 'What's yours?'

'I'm a 10,' she lied. 'I've never been happier.'

He was giving her that stare. At school when she'd had to stand up and say a speech in front of the whole assembly, she'd look at all the faces in the crowd and his would be lit up watching her, like all the people in the room didn't matter and all he could see was her.

'You're a bad liar.'

'Not as bad you, Elder Johnson.'

'Love you.'

'Make sure you read the book,' she said to him. 'Don't colonise the Hawaiian people even more.'

And those were the last words she said to her best friend before she heard Eru Senior yell the opening line of the haka and Eru and Māreikura turned to watch. The feeling of dread, of loneliness latched onto her like an unwanted peril so she crept over to the escalator and then, when she was out of shot, she ran. She was pretty sure it went against tikanga leaving during a haka but Māreikura hoped her ancestors would forgive her. She couldn't be there any longer. The caffeine from earlier that day sparked her feet all the way down the escalator and onto the footpath until she was back at McDonald's, hyperventilating in her car.

Māreikura wanted to run back to the airport and grab Eru by his stupid tie and drag him out of there and away from the Mormons and stupid Kayla Tairua, who had been in the corner of Māreikura's peripheral vision staring at them the whole time. Māreikura wanted to go back to how things used to be, before the blackface incident and when it was just the two of them walking to Gretton College eating mince and cheese pies from the bakery and arguing over whether *Police Ten 7* was racist.

Love you, he'd said, so casually cruel.

Eru wasn't going to die in a plane crash or get ravaged by the Hawaiians. But he was going to come back a completely different person. God took away her mum. God took away her culture. And now God had taken away her best friend. Eru was now dead to her.

PART TWO

ONE YEAR LATER

CHAPTER TWO

I'm here.

So sorry! I'm on my way.

Māreikura was definitely not on her way. She was still at home, her head in the fridge looking for something to eat. Māreikura was supposed to meet her Bumble date at 6.30 p.m. at Pacific Inn but she got distracted looking at the menu online and realised it did not align with her budget and now it was too late to cancel or change the venue. The mains were around $38 and the cheapest food on the menu were the chive dumplings: $23 for three. Māreikura could buy twelve dumplings from Mount Eden Noodles for half that price. She decided she would order the dumplings and eat something now to satisfy her hunger. She was looking in the fridge but couldn't find anything and then she'd looked at her phone and Kat was already there. *I'm here.* She even used a full stop, which definitely meant she was pissed at Māreikura for being late and not respecting her time. Māreikura did respect her time but her lateness was a combination of anxiety, self-diagnosed ADHD and poor time-management skills.

Māreikura took one last look in the fridge and spotted the apple on the bottom shelf, next to the bag of brown carrots she bought a week ago when she told herself she was going to eat only carrots for snacks, which she did not end up doing. She grabbed the apple and glanced in the mirror on the way out. She was wearing the green dress Eru's sister Erana had given her. It was long and flowy and slipped past her knees and everyone always gave her compliments when she wore it. Māreikura said bye to her nan, put on her white sneakers and headed towards Ponsonby Road.

Sorry I'm late, Māreikura practised in her head over and over again. Being late was a symptom of ADHD. Māreikura had diagnosed herself from TikTok and other unreliable sources. She couldn't afford the psychologist appointment to prove she had the disorder. In her notes app, she'd typed out her symptoms, which were, in no particular order:

- overthinks
- always late
- finds it hard to meditate
- can't sit still
- hard time regulating emotions
- overly sensitive
- impulsive
- procrastinates and always leaves things to the last minute
- doesn't shut cupboards
- doesn't put lids on bottles properly

The last one was because one time she did not put the lid on Eru's Sprite bottle and it fell over and spilt on the floor of his car. *Ma*, he'd said, in his non-angry passive way. *You always forget to put the lid on properly.* And he was right, he had told her so many times.

Māreikura didn't know it was a symptom of ADHD until a girl on TikTok told her.

Māreikura reached the top of the street and saw Kat through the window of Pacific Inn, sitting down at the table. She recognised her from the Bumble photos, and looking at her from afar, from the outside, she was clearly out of Māreikura's league. Māreikura went through phases where she was wildly confident and had the audacity to match with girls on Bumble who were a solid 10 when Māreikura was a solid 6, 7 at her best. The conversations on the dating apps always died out, though – it was always the same questions. *What do you do for fun?* and Māreikura wanted to say *Decolonise wbu* but instead she would lie and say hiking because that seemed more attractive and also she had a hiking photo on her profile from three years ago when she did the Tongariro Crossing with Eru and almost died. Then the girl would ask if she wanted to go for a hike and Māreikura would panic and block her.

Kat was different. Kat's first question was, *Nō hea koe?* and then *What do you think our country would look like if it was Indigenous-led and Te Tiriti was honoured?*

Māreikura had to think for a while and then she replied, *Our whole country would look different. We would honour the environment. There would be no homelessness. Our people wouldn't be in prisons. No child services. Everything would change.*

They sent long paragraphs back and forth and then it moved to voice memos and then they followed each other on Instagram where Kat's bio was 'be kind' and a link to her business.

Kat was thirty-two years old, the CEO of a tech company that had a net worth of $20 million. She was Sagittarius, was once married to a white man, and had her own TED Talk about re-indigenising technology. Māreikura found out this information on Google. She's a 10 and a CEO? Māreikura almost cancelled the date from extreme whakamā. But then she told herself she would simply eat her dumplings and then call it a night. Tell Kat she had to get up early the next morning and maybe they could be friends. Someone told Māreikura she had imposter syndrome once but she was 100 per cent sure that was a dumb term Pākehā invented because her tīpuna most definitely did not have 'imposter syndrome'. They navigated the most expansive oceans in the world and discovered Aotearoa. She could not imagine her tīpuna ever looking at the ocean, sighing and saying, 'No, sorry, I can't do it because I have imposter syndrome.'

Kat spotted her and waved and Māreikura waved back and then remembered she was holding her apple in her hand so she hid it behind her back until Kat was out of sight. She took a few bites of the apple and dropped it in the nearest bin.

I am my ancestors' wildest dreams, she told herself as she approached the very pretty and intimidating white woman at the front of the restaurant.

'Welcome to Pacific Inn,' the woman said. 'Have you got a booking?'

'Yeah, for Kat? She's already here.'

The woman nodded and Māreikura followed her in. She always felt a weird discomfort walking into places like this – rich, white spaces where one night of eating could feed a family for a week. It was a mind-fuck when she'd just passed George, the man who lives at the park, on the way here and Māreikura said hi and sorry she didn't have any cash on her and he said it's okay, and Māreikura felt guilty because if she really wanted to, she would get cash out and carry it with her, but it was always her excuse – 'Sorry, I have no cash on me' – and now she was about to drop a whole lot of money on food that could feed George for a week.

'Here we are.'

The waitress stopped in front of the table and Māreikura's mouth dropped slightly. Up close, Kat was the most beautiful woman Māreikura had ever seen. She was effortlessly beautiful, like she'd just thrown on a dress from her wardrobe minutes before the date, shook her hair out of her ponytail and made her way over to Pacific Inn. Māreikura wasn't sure if that's what Kat did exactly, but she looked like the kind of woman who could do that, like she didn't have to try to look pretty, unlike Māreikura, who spent two hours trying on ten different outfits and putting on shitloads of concealer to try to cover her forehead acne.

'Kia ora, Māreikura.'

'Sorry I'm late.'

'Maybe we should get you a watch, babe.' She paused and then burst out laughing. 'I'm kidding, I'm kidding. Sit.'

Māreikura sat down. There was a very expensive-looking bottle of champagne sitting in the middle of the table.

'Was that an apple you were eating?' Kat asked.

'What?'

'When you were walking. Were you eating an apple?'

'Yes.'

'You couldn't wait for dinner?' Her eyes flicked on Māreikura. 'I love that dress. You look beautiful.'

'Thanks.'

'You are beautiful.'

'You are too.'

The waitress interrupted them and asked if they wanted any drinks and Māreikura said, 'Just water, thanks.'

Kat handed Māreikura a brown paper bag. 'I got you something.'

'What? You didn't have to.'

'It's a maramataka journal,' she said as Māreikura unwrapped it. 'I saw on your Insta story you were wanting to follow the moon cycle? This is really good for tracking the maramataka. It's been life-changing for me.'

'Thank you. I didn't get you anything.'

'That's okay.' She waved her hand. 'I get them for free. Perks of my job.' She smiled. 'Shall we order? You're clearly starving.'

Kat handed her the menu and Māreikura scanned it like she was reading it for the first time.

'The dumplings look quite good,' Māreikura said.

'Mmm, they are. Why don't we get a couple of dishes and share?'

'Okay,' Māreikura said, but when the waitress came back, Kat did not order a couple of dishes. She ordered the market fish, the chao broccoli, the steamed buns and the stir-fried tofu.

'Oh, and you want the dumplings?' she asked Māreikura. 'What flavour?'

Māreikura went to say the vegan ones, but then Kat said, 'Let's just get both,' then she winked at Māreikura.

'Do you want a drink, babe? I got us champagne but do you want something else?'

'I don't usually drink,' Māreikura said. 'I'm decolonising my whakapapa.'

'Oh?' Kat raised her eyebrows. Māreikura thought she would ask her questions about it but she didn't. There was a silence and Māreikura wanted to add, *My tīpuna became alcoholics after they were colonised and alcohol has single-handedly destroyed Māori families since colonisation yet we pretend like alcohol is okay*, but she would save that one up for later. If Kat really wanted to know, she would ask.

The waitress left and now they were both staring at each other.

The music playing in the background was seductive, the kind of music that lures you into a false sense of reality.

'What are you thinking about?' Kat asked. She had a little smile on her lips and Māreikura looked down, fumbling the champagne glass in front of her.

'Do you know if the owners are Pasifika?'

'Huh?'

'Just because of the island theme here,' Māreikura said, looking around the room at all the flowers on the wall. 'And the name. It's a bit of cultural appropriation, don't you think?'

'Oh, right. Pretty sure the owner is Samoan,' Kat said. 'Do you want me to check?'

'No, it's okay.'

'Well, in that case, cheers.'

Kat poured champagne into Māreikura's glass. She raised her glass and Māreikura raised hers and they both took a drink. Māreikura felt a pang of guilt, like she was betraying her tīpuna.

'So,' Kat said. 'When do you start kura? That's what you're doing this year, right? Studying te reo Māori?'

'Yeah,' Māreikura said. 'I start on Tuesday.'

'How did you get in?' She leaned forward. 'I heard there's a five-year waiting list.'

'I submitted a late entry,' Māreikura said. 'So I have no idea.'

'Your tīpuna must really want you there,' Kat said, sighing. 'I wish I could take a year off and learn my language.'

'Well, you could,' Māreikura said. 'There's always a way. It just takes sacrifice.'

Kat looked at her. She kept eye contact when she talked and Māreikura wondered if this was a skill you learn over time. Being able to talk to someone and look them directly in the eye.

'Well, I have a confession.' Kat cleared her throat. 'I recognised you from that amazing head girl speech.

'I was so moved,' she carried on. 'You basically told the racist, white school to go screw themselves, and I remember thinking, *Wow, this young wahine is formidable.* What happened to that racist girl who did blackface?'

Māreikura picked up her fork and put it back down again.

'I don't know. I ended up dropping out after she left. I heard she can't find a job anywhere but I don't know if that's true or not.'

Kat scoffed. 'I'm sure she'll be fine. So many people saw your video. It was doing the rounds on social media, wasn't it?'

'Yeah.'

'What was that like for you? Must have been a crazy time.'

Crazy was an understatement. Māreikura had no idea Alexandra Minogue was recording from the third row and that she would upload it onto her Instagram page and that more than sixteen million people from around the world would see her speech on YouTube and social media and that she would be thrust into the spotlight, interviewed by media all across the world; even the Prime Minister weighed in and announced that the government would be reviewing protocol when it came to racism and racial discrimination in schools. Gretton College came out with a public apology but by then it was too late. Māreikura stood her ground and refused to go back.

Months passed and everyone forgot about it, they forgot about her. She was left with the damage, the aftermath, the shame and disappointment she felt from her nana every single day. *Now what?* her nan had asked her, tight-lipped. And so she got a part-time job at the local Countdown while trying to monetise her Instagram following, which had climbed to thirty thousand. She began posting commentary on all issues concerning Māori and she started calling people out on

Twitter. Māreikura refused to call it by its new name. Soon she grew tired of it, tired of finding things to get angry about, tired of fighting with trolls who came for her online and tired of feeling alone. She went on antidepressants and then deleted her Instagram permanently.

Kat squeezed Māreikura's arm.

'I can only imagine how hard that must have been for you. I don't think I know anyone who's brave enough to dismantle the racist education system the way you did. Māreikura, it was incredible. We are all lucky to be in a world with powerful, strong wāhine Māori like yourself.'

Māreikura said nothing. She was chugging down the champagne now. Kat's eyes narrowed in on Māreikura as if trying to make sense of her.

'What do you think of imposter syndrome?' Māreikura asked.

'What about it?'

'Do you have it?'

'No,' Kat said. 'I know who I am.'

'But do you ever feel like you don't belong in some spaces? Like in the tech space – it's filled with old white men, isn't it?'

Kat just shrugged. 'I don't have a reason to doubt myself. I'm good at what I do.'

'Is it because you're white-passing?'

Kat looked slightly offended so Māreikura quickly said, 'Oh, sorry, I mean, you know . . . Is it because you're white-looking?' which wasn't much better.

'Do I not look Māori to you?' Kat asked, and Māreikura told her she did, even though she didn't really. She could definitely pass for a white woman with a tan.

It got awkward and Māreikura took another sip of her drink. She wondered if that was part of her ADHD, blurting things out without thinking and offending people. She wanted so badly to go on a rant about how she didn't believe in imposter syndrome. We are all imposters, aren't we? she wanted to say. We are born into a world we blindly accept. The world we live in is a white world, it's not our reality.

But it was only the first date. The food arrived and the waitress laid all the kai out on the table. Kat picked up a dumpling with her chopsticks and put it on Māreikura's plate.

'Eat, babe.'

They talked about colonisation and racism and LGBTQ+ issues and everything they were passionate about while they ate dumplings and sipped on champagne. Kat told her why she started Kaha. She'd had a dream in which her ancestors appeared to her and told her she needed to revolutionise data and Māreikura thought that was out the gate. They discussed problematic issues like the ACT party and David Seymour and the trauma of learning Māori, and Kat just listened and nodded and Māreikura thought it was quite refreshing that she didn't have to explain anything to her, that Kat just got it.

A few times, Kat put her hand on Māreikura's and said, 'Aw, honey,' and it did something to Māreikura that no male touching her had ever done before. The more time Māreikura spent with Kat, the more attractive Kat became. Up close, Māreikura could tell she wasn't even wearing makeup. Imagine having skin so flawless that you don't even need to wear makeup. Māreikura thought the only woman who could pull that off was Alicia Keys. Māreikura tried to wear no makeup once but then she went outside in the revealing Grey Lynn sun and some Karen stopped her on the street, pointed to her forehead acne and asked if she had thought about giving up dairy and gluten. Māreikura put her head down and said nah but now she wished she'd told the lady not everyone was in a privileged position like her to afford gluten-free food. To be honest, Māreikura probably did have some hidden food intolerance but she liked cheese and noodles too much.

After dinner, they went to the counter and the Pākehā group in front of them were calculating the costs and dividing the bill by the items they ate. 'I had half the wine so I'll pay for half of that, and for my main and one of the sharing plates,' the guy in front of them said.

Māreikura and Kat just looked at each other. When it was their turn to pay, Kat stood guard over the EFTPOS machine.

'I'm paying. You're a student.'

'So? I can pay my own way.'

In the end, they agreed to halve the bill and when $120 appeared on the screen, Māreikura said, 'Oh, we're going halves,' and the man looked at her like she was stupid. He pointed to the receipt on the counter.

'The full bill comes to $240.'

Māreikura scanned the bill and saw the champagne was $80 on its own. She had never spent so much on dinner before in her life.

'You okay?' Kat asked from behind.

'Yeah,' Māreikura squeaked. She quickly transferred money on her phone and then inserted her card. The $120 would send her into overdraft but Māreikura decided it was worth it. Tonight was a special occasion. She was on a date with a hot woman.

Kat insisted on dropping Māreikura home but Māreikura said she would walk – the streets were safe because it was 'Ponsnobby' and Kat giggled and Māreikura liked the feeling of making Kat laugh. The alcohol seemed to give her permission to say things out loud she would usually keep in her head, which made her appear funnier and more confident.

Māreikura looped her arm into Kat's. 'Did you ever play basketball?' she asked. 'You're really tall.'

Kat said no but she had played netball and Māreikura felt dumb for asking such a basic question.

Both were too drunk to drive and Māreikura didn't want to go home. Then Kat asked her in a presumptuous voice, 'Wanna come back to mine and drink tea?'

•

'Welcome to my whare,' Kat said as they stumbled out of the Uber.

She swiped a card and the gate opened to a villa with a spa on the front deck, perfectly mowed lawn and big palm trees.

'Woah,' Māreikura said, staring up at the palm trees. 'It feels like I'm in Fiji.'

'When did you go to Fiji?'

'I haven't,' Māreikura said, and Kat laughed and said, 'You're so funny'.

Māreikura slid her shoes off and flopped on the couch. Kat handed her a book, *Goddess Muscle* by Karlo Mila.

'Have you read this?'

'I love this book.' Māreikura clutched it to her chest and glanced up at Kat who was hovering over her.

'Read me your favourite poem. I'll make tea.'

'Kay.'

Māreikura sat up and pushed her shoulders back. She felt a surge of responsibility, that this could be the deciding moment when Kat would decide if she wanted to see her again based on her choice of poem.

'Found one yet, babe?' Kat called from the kitchen.

Māreikura heard the jug boil and the opening and closing of a drawer. 'Have you read page 52? "Lonely"?'

'Hmm, probably, but I can't remember right now. You'll have to read it to me.' She paused for a moment. 'Are you lonely? You've said that a few times tonight.'

'Um, sometimes. I'm not alone but I do feel lonely sometimes. If that makes sense.'

'Yeah,' Kat said, coming into the lounge to look at her. 'It does.'

For a moment, Māreikura thought she was going to bend down and kiss her, but then she turned away and walked back to the kitchen.

'I like your house. I love that,' Māreikura said, pointing at a painting of a Māori woman with a moko kauae. 'The painting, I mean.'

'Oh, thank you. That's my tipuna – her name is Hinemoa. She's ātaahua, eh.'

Kat placed a cup in front of Māreikura.

At the restaurant, the lighting had been dim and Kat was sitting at the table so Māreikura could only see her face and chest, but now she could see everything – the shape of her hips behind her tight maxi dress. Māreikura tried her very best not to look at the split that travelled up her thigh, but she was very drunk so it was very obvious to Kat that Māreikura's eyes kept dropping, and when they made eye contact again, Kat asked her, 'Are you okay, love?' but with that same smirk on her face from earlier, so Māreikura nodded and quickly looked down at Karlo's book on her lap and flicked through the pages like she was really interested and not distracted by the goddess that was sitting in front of her. She then looked at the title of the book, *Goddess Muscle*, and thought it was a tohu from Kat's tipuna Hinemoa, who was still watching her from the wall, confirming to Māreikura that her descendant Kat Harrison was in fact a goddess.

'Read me the poem,' Kat said, and when Māreikura turned the page, Kat slid across the couch and next to Māreikura so that her left thigh was touching Māreikura's right thigh. Māreikura pretended she wasn't flustered and turned to page 52. She cleared her throat and read aloud, channelling the goddess of Karlo Mila.

I am lonely
This truth seeks out the hollow,
Finds its mark,
Rests inside me

It fills the curve of my ache,
More than the question of
Who loves me

I am lonely
And do not have
A circle of women
To sit around me,
Share
And meditate
Their conscious will
Into the world

How I crave minds,
Like mine
The tapa of connected talk
Beating singular thoughts
And shame
Into the symmetry
Of company

Māreikura knew that if she was to look up, Kat would kiss her, but her head was still screaming with anxiety so she tried to take in the words of Karlo and thought just maybe she had found her tapa cloth she was craving – a mind and energy that could match hers. Māreikura thought about how on all the dates she'd been on with men, she felt like someone had got a vacuum and sucked all her energy out and so she was always tired after the date and wanted to go home and wipe her makeup off and collapse on the bed. Oh, how different it felt now. Now she felt like someone had zapped her with one of those things that electrocuted you and she was overflowing with life, and she didn't know if it was the champagne or Karlo's poem, or the fact Kat was a woman and everything she had been looking for.

Māreikura moved her head slightly, just in time to see Kat put the mug she was holding on the table in front of them very gently and then move her way back to Māreikura so their thighs were touching again. Her eyes flicked down to Māreikura's lips then back up to her eyes.

'I really liked the poem,' she said, then Māreikura nodded and said, 'Me too,' then Kat's eyes switched and said something else so Māreikura closed her eyes and breathed in the scent of her perfume and the smell of champagne and the lavender essential oils coming out of the diffuser on the floor and then she felt Kat's lips pressed against hers, her hands cupped around Māreikura's chin as she pulled her in closer. Māreikura couldn't get over how soft her lips were and how nice she smelled and all she could think about was lying back on the couch and letting this woman devour her, but at the same time she wanted to pull off Kat's dress and push her onto the couch and see and touch everything, and now she was confused because she didn't know which one to do or even how to do it, but then Kat stopped kissing her and pulled away slightly.

'I really like you, Māreikura.'

She opened her eyes. 'I really like you too.'

'Do you still feel lonely?' Kat asked, breathing warm air into Māreikura's mouth.

How I crave minds,

Like mine

The tapa of connected talk.

Māreikura's eyes closed again, her hand resting on the front of Kat's dress.

'No,' she said. 'I don't.'

CHAPTER THREE

Māreikura was never meant to see the photo of Dylan Stowers doing blackface. She sat next to Selena and Caitlin in PE class one day and Caitlin asked Māreikura to take their photo.

Māreikura had reluctantly taken Caitlin's phone and tapped the red button a dozen times while they did their dumb poses by the bleachers. Then they came rushing over, scrolling through the photos.

'Ew, I look tragic today,' Caitlin had said, fixing her hair in the reverse camera. She puckered her lips and did a fake smile.

'Whatever,' Selena said. 'I wish I had your lips.'

'You can, for nine hundred dollars.' Caitlin giggled.

'So it's not that I'm ugly,' Selena said. 'It's just that I'm poor.'

Selena pushed her lips out and stared at Māreikura's mouth.

'Where'd you get yours from?' Selena asked.

'My what?'

'Your lips.'

'Um, my parents?'

'Aw, lucky.' They both stared at Māreikura in a fetishising way so Māreikura turned her back to them. She studied her lips in the reflection of her black phone screen. She used to hate her big juju lips growing up. The kids at school used to mock her and now suddenly it was a trend. Now society got to tell her that her lips were beautiful.

'Can you take another one?' Caitlin asked, holding her phone out.

'Hurry, S,' Caitlin said. 'Come here. Let's do a standing pose like this.'

Māreikura tapped the red button again and then Caitlin took the phone from her and swiped through each photo.

'Ooh, this one's cute! We are so cute. Might upload it to my story or—'

But she had swiped too far – what was on her phone Māreikura wasn't supposed to see. A photo of a white girl doing blackface. Caitlin immediately swiped back the other way.

'What was that?' Māreikura asked.

'What was what?'

'Go back to where you were before.'

Caitlin swiped right. 'That's the end of the photos.'

'No, the other way.'

Her reluctance made Māreikura even more suspicious. She saw Selena glance at Caitlin.

'It's nothing.'

Māreikura snatched the phone from her.

'Hey, give it back—'

It was too late. Māreikura had seen it. 'What is . . . is that Dylan?'

'No, it's—'

Māreikura pinched the screen so it zoomed in on the face. 'That's Dylan Stowers doing blackface.'

She glanced up at both the girls, who were looking at each other wide-eyed. 'Where did you get this?'

'She sent it to me,' Caitlin said.

'When?'

'I dunno. Can I have my phone back?'

Māreikura quickly sent the photo to her own number. She handed back the phone, her head spinning. 'Do you even know how deeply racist this is?'

'Of course I do,' Caitlin said quietly. 'That's why I screenshot it.'

'And what were you going to do about it?'

'It was just a joke,' Selena quickly said. 'I don't think Dylan even knows what blackface is.'

'What are you going to do?' Caitlin asked, tugging at her hair. 'I just, like, don't want Dylan to get into trouble, or like cancelled or anything.'

'She should have thought about that before she decided to be racist,' Māreikura said as she typed out something on her phone.

Ladies and gentlemen, your head girl of Gretton College, she wrote, then she posted the photo of Dylan in blackface to her followers on Instagram.

•

The photo of Dylan had gone viral and Māreikura had expected the school to punish Dylan. To take away her head girl role. Mr Buckley looked at Māreikura like she was speaking a foreign language when she asked him what the school was doing about it. *It's a private matter*, he told her. *It has nothing to do with Gretton College.*

Eru didn't seem to care either. *Everyone deserves a second chance*, he told her. *There's power in redemption, in learning from our mistakes*, and then he started talking to her about grace. *We should offer grace*, he said. To offer grace is to offer forgiveness and Māreikura told him she did not believe in forgiveness because when does accountability come in to play? It places a moral burden on the victims. It takes white guilt away. It's an easy way out for perpetrators. Where is the justice? She wished Eru would be on her side for once but he never was, he always hid behind his church-speak, so she told him he was an embarrassment to his ancestors and then stormed out of the house.

Then Mr Buckley asked Māreikura to be deputy head girl. Māreikura didn't turn it down at first. She wanted to see the look on her nan's face when she told her.

'What's that mean, girl? It's a big deal, is it?' her nan asked.

'I guess. I mean, I got chosen out of a hundred Year 13 students? I sit up front with the principal at assembly?'

A smile formed on her nan's lips. 'See? Told you that school was the best thing that could have happened to you. I told you, didn't I? When you didn't want to go there, I said you would be stupid not to take this opportunity. Now pass me the phone, at least let me tell Gale the news. Go on.'

Māreikura handed her the cordless phone from the kitchen counter. Theirs was probably the only house in Auckland that still had a landline.

'Hi, Gale!' her nan shouted. 'What's that, you can't hear me?' She lowered the phone and squinted at the buttons. 'Mine's working, must be yours . . . Turn your volume up louder! Hold on, no it's your phone, Gale . . . Yes, that's it. Well, guess what my granddaughter just told me . . . She's the head girl of the school . . . Yes, that's right . . . Yes, of Gretton College.'

Her grin was wider than ever now.

'Oh, hang on. Let me ask her.' She held the phone to her chest. 'When do you start?'

'This year. And Nan, it's deputy head girl.'

'Yes . . . This year, Gale . . . Well, I can't take all the credit.' She laughed. 'I always said, Gale, we must lead by example. That's how I was able to teach her . . . always let her choose . . . Mmm. Yes. I will pass on your congratulations . . . Now how about your granddaughter Sophie? Hmm.'

She cupped her hand over her mouth.

'Well, prefect is good too, Gale, I suppose. It's not quite head girl but I'm sure she tried her best.'

•

Mr Buckley had given Māreikura clear instructions. A two-minute speech on her aspirations on how she was going to serve in her role as deputy head girl. When Māreikura stood at the podium, she gazed out at the unsuspecting eyes of sixteen hundred students staring back at her. She could feel Eru's eyes burning into her, wondering why she hadn't told him she would be sitting up at the front of assembly today. They had not spoken for three days, since he tried to gaslight her into forgiving Dylan Stowers. She intended never to speak to him again.

While she was giving her speech, Mr Buckley was standing next to her the whole time, inching closer, trying to take the mic from her, but Māreikura held it tightly with both hands as she read aloud.

'When I was asked to be deputy head girl for Gretton College, initially I was honoured,' she said. 'I received top marks at school for English and I will be studying law at Auckland University part-time next year. However, I cannot stand here today and accept the position of deputy head girl while ignoring the underbelly of racism that exists within Gretton College. Using me as a token Māori face to tick off a quota box while not bothering to do anything about the systemic racism that exists in the education system will not fix anything.

'Your head girl, Dylan Stowers, decided not only to do blackface but she also used the N-word. Yes, the N-word. A derogatory, offensive and ugly slur that should never ever come out of the mouth of anyone who isn't black. It has been nearly two hundred years since white performers first started painting their faces black to mock enslaved Africans in the United States. It was racist and offensive then, and it's still racist and offensive today. As tangata whenua, I stand with my black brothers and sisters who are fighting for freedom, fighting for sovereignty, for mana motuhake. We are fighting for the same things here in Aotearoa.

'To Mr Buckley, teachers and fellow esteemed students, you must reprimand Dylan Stowers for her actions. I speak up for all victims of racism, I speak up for my people and I speak up for my ancestors who were beaten at school for speaking my native tongue, te reo Māori. My name is Māreikura Pohe and I refuse to be quiet.'

No one clapped. Not even one person. The auditorium was silent.

Mr Buckley pushed her aside gently, took the mic and said, 'Thank you, Māreikura. We take your accusations seriously and will talk further today.'

She walked past the gawking eyes of students and out of the auditorium. She knew it would be the last time. She would not be welcome back.

Eru had followed her outside and was knocking on the car window. 'Open the door, Ma. Please.'

Māreikura unlocked the door. She felt him place his hand on her back until her breathing slowed down. Then she pushed his hand away. She hated him so much. *As if he thinks his stupid touch can just make everything better.* Make everything magically go away.

'You didn't tell me you were deputy head girl,' Eru said quietly. 'Why didn't you tell me?'

Māreikura felt her rage boil up. 'Did you even hear my speech up there?'

'Yes,' he said. 'That's why I wanted to see you if you're all right.'

'Stop asking me if I'm all right, God damnit.'

Eru winced.

'Sorry,' she said. 'I didn't mean to say the G-word.'

'It's okay.' He paused as if thinking of what to say. 'It was really brave what you did up there.'

She buried her face in the steering wheel and then took a breath.

'It's not brave, Eru. I didn't have a choice. I've probably lost my law scholarship now and the title of deputy head girl, and for what? I don't need you to ask me if I'm all right or tell me that I'm brave. What I need is for you to stand with me. So that I'm not so alone.'

'Ma.'

'Not making a choice is a choice,' she told him. 'You and every other person at this school is enabling racism by choosing not to stand up to Dylan's actions.'

He was giving her the look. It was a weapon he had used in the past to dismantle her. Calm her down. But now he looked pathetic.

'Eru, how long have we been friends?'

'Uh, why?'

'We've been friends for ten years.'

He nodded as if trying to understand her point.

'Ten years and yet you still refuse to say my name properly.'

His mouth dropped open. Māreikura raised her hand before he could say anything.

'My name is not Ma. Or Maaa. It's Māreikura. Mā-rei-ku-ra. Say my name properly.'

Māreikura shut the car door and Eru didn't try to stop her. She turned the engine on and reversed out of the car park. It was the last time she would speak to him until he left for his mission.

CHAPTER FOUR

The woman at the door was not wearing any shoes. She had wild hair and was in a fluoro-coloured dress. Her toenails were covered in faded red nail polish.

'Am I at the right place?' Māreikura asked.

'Were you expecting something else?'

Māreikura didn't know what she was expecting but it was not this. The outline of the full-immersion te reo Māori course said students would be learning the way of their ancestors, but it was like she had stumbled into a kindergarten. The walls were plastered with the English and Māori alphabet. A is for Apple. Āporo. B is for Banana. Panana. This wasn't how she'd envisioned her ancestors had lived.

'I guess not. I'm Māreikura.'

'I know who you are.' The woman leaned forward and Māreikura thought she was going to kiss her on the cheek, but then she tilted Māreikura's face with her hand until their noses were pressed against each other.

'I'm Whaea Terina, your kaiako. Now, hā ki roto,' she said, taking a deep breath. 'That's it, and hā ki waho, big breath out. You are here now. You are here. Come in.'

There was a man in blue overalls sitting closest to the door. He glanced at Māreikura standing at the doorway.

'Well, don't just stand there.'

'I'm Māreikura,' she said, sitting down next to him.

He leaned over and gave her a kiss on the cheek. 'Call me Koro Ian.'

Koro Ian had a full crop of grey hair, had big circles under his eyes and looked like he was in his sixties. He had an exercise book and pencil case already laid out on the desk.

'Did you just finish mahi?' she asked him.

'No,' he said. 'I just like wearing my work clothes inside.' He chuckled, smacking Māreikura on her back. 'Only joking with ya. I just got off night shift.'

'How can you work full-time and study?'

'It's not too bad,' he said. 'I figured it out, you see. I get home from school at around five and then I can start my shift at twelve and then come straight from work to school at seven.'

The curriculum outline had strict instructions – the course required a high level of intensity and students should not be working.

'I wish I had the money so I could pay for you,' Māreikura told him. 'So you could just focus on learning te reo. You shouldn't be working.' Then she paused. 'None of us should be working. None of us should even be here learning our own language.'

Māreikura received a weekly student allowance of $240.19 a week from the government. It wasn't much but it was enough to pay $29 a week for power and water, $120 for food for her and her nana, $40 for public transport, and the rest went on her phone bill, toiletries and petrol. There wasn't much left after that. Koro Ian probably had a family to support, a mortgage to pay.

'Can I sit here?' a girl asked. She was chewing gum and smelled like sage.

'Yeah,' Māreikura said.

'I'm Jordana.'

'Māreikura. That's Koro Ian.'

Jordana dropped her bag on the floor and kissed Koro Ian on the cheek.

'Kia ora, Koro.'

'Tēnā koe, girl.'

'So what brings you here?' Māreikura asked.

'Colonisation,' she said, and they both laughed. Māreikura liked her immediately.

'I've always felt this gap in my life.' Jordana shrugged. 'And then I went to India on a yoga retreat but I realised it was dumb being in a foreign country trying to find myself so I came home. I gave all my shit away and ended up living in a van.'

'Were you a minimalist?'

'Nah,' Jordana said. 'Just suicidal.'

There was silence, then they both laughed again, not because it was remotely funny that Jordana once wanted to kill herself but it was their way of dealing, making humour out of trauma. Koro Ian did not laugh but maybe he didn't hear. A guy from the other table gave them both a weird look.

'Yeah,' Jordana said, continuing the conversation even though Māreikura did not ask. 'I was giving my stuff away because I was planning to die. That's what happens when you're in a toxic relationship, bro. You get yourself into a dark place. I pretty much woke up every day wanting to die.' She smoothed out her hair.

'And now you're here.'

'Te reo Māori is keeping me alive. I just want to live off the grid and be a green fairy.'

'What is a green fairy?'

'It's someone who makes cannabis oil for sick people,' she said. 'Since dope is illegal. They are doing the Lord's work.'

Whaea Terina stood at the centre of the room and there was a quiet hush.

'You are not here by accident', she said, scanning the room, stopping to look into the eyes of every person.

'To all the Māori in the room, I want to tell you this – I'm sorry for what happened to you. I'm sorry for what happened to your whānau. Te reo Māori was your birthright, it should have been your first language but it was beaten, stripped away from you, your grandparents, your great-grandparents. That should never have happened and for that, I am sorry.'

Later, Māreikura would tell Jordana it was the first time she had heard that.

'Heard what?' Jordana asked.

'Heard someone apologise,' Māreikura said. 'For what happened to us.'

•

Whaea Terina was from Ngāti Pāoa and te reo Māori was her second language. She cried a lot in class and always rested her hand on her chest whenever one of the students spoke. 'Kore kau ngā kupu,' she would say, like she was out of breath. 'I have no words.' But she did have a lot of words because she would end up speaking for another ten minutes after saying she had no words. Sometimes she would even break into a waiata.

Whaea Terina reached for the paper on the desk and called the roll. 'Māreikura?'

It was the first time a teacher had pronounced her name correctly. Māreikura. No one could say her name right. Ma-ray-cobra, her teachers would call her. Next to her name, they wrote '(Ma)' and suddenly her name was Ma. They gave her a new name without her permission. Eru called her Ma. Her nana called her girl. No one called her Māreikura.

'I'm here,' Māreikura said.

Whaea Terina locked eyes with her. 'Do you know what your name means?'

'A nobly born female,' Māreikura said, like she was reading the definition straight from Google.

That's what she had been told, anyway. That her name Māreikura meant a noble-born female. A term of endearment. A treasure, a darling.

Her mother gave her the name after their tipuna Māreikura Pohe, a warrior who fought alongside men in war. Her mother prophesied that Māreikura would follow in her footsteps. *She will fight the war for us*, her mother had told the midwife and the doctor at Whangārei Hospital. *My daughter will change the world.* They both exchanged a look and then smiled at the young and mentally unstable woman, both knowing that soon the baby would be taken from her arms. They had seen it all before. They were all the same.

Whaea Terina had not taken her eyes off Māreikura.

'There is power in a name,' she said. 'This is why you must correct them when they say your name wrong.'

She glanced back down and finished the roll. Afterwards, she nodded to the baby-faced guy in front of her.

'E tū.'

He stood up.

'Introduce yourself.'

'Ah, my name's Alex.'

'Thank you, Alex. E noho.'

Whaea Terina drew a squiggly outline of a mountain on the whiteboard.

'When we meet someone for the first time, we don't ask, "What is your name?" or, "What do you do?" We ask, "Nō hea koe?" – where are you from? And through our river, our mountain and our iwi, we tell a story and weave our connection to each other through our ancestral lines. Our job status or "what we do" doesn't define who we are. It is our whakapapa, our genealogy, our connection to the land that does. Because when we disappear, the land remains.'

'Do you know your pepeha?' Māreikura whispered to Jordana.

'Yeah,' Jordana said. 'On my mum's side, I'm from Taranaki.'

In Year 11, Gretton College had a guest speaker and Māreikura was one of the only Māori in the room. The woman pointed to her and asked, 'Nō hea koe?' Māreikura just stared at her. She didn't even know what 'nō hea koe' meant back then. 'Your pepeha,' the lady said. 'What's your pepeha?' She waited, and everyone turned to look at Māreikura until finally she said, 'I don't know. I'm a plastic Māori,' and she fake-laughed so everyone else would laugh too, and they did, and then she regretted saying she was plastic because she hated that stupid colonised term.

'Why else would a pepeha be important? Anyone?' Whaea Terina asked.

'Because,' a guy wearing a backwards cap called out, 'it's a way of making a connection, to know if you're whānau or maybe you have another connection to them. That's why when I'm at the Solid Bar, I always have to ask the wāhine their pepeha in case we cuzzies.'

Whaea Terina cackled at his joke and Māreikura could already tell he was her favourite.

'Āe, Troy. It's to make a connection. But also remember, when we are saying our pepeha, they are not just words. It is how we connect to our whānau, to our past generations and to our future generations.'

She held out the whiteboard marker.

'Now, I'm going to pass the rākau to you all. Tell me your pepeha, your connection to the land. Or if you don't know it, just say your name. Speak as long as you like.' She glanced at the clock. 'Well, if you go over twelve, then you're buying me lunch. Tell me why you're here.'

But isn't it obvious why we are here? Māreikura thought. Somewhere along the way, the language was stolen from our families. People think te reo Māori was 'lost' but that's not true, it was stolen. Forcefully beaten out of our grandparents at school after the Native Schools Act was enforced by the government. And now we are here, taking a year out of our life to learn how to be Māori.

'Māku e tīmata.' Troy stood up. 'I te tipu ake au ki te ao Māori. I went to a full-immersion school when I was young,' he explained. 'But I can't remember a whole lot so I'm here to relearn.'

He spoke beautifully, like a fluent te reo speaker, and it made Māreikura want to shrivel up. She naively assumed everyone here didn't know any te reo Māori, like her.

A Pākehā girl with blonde hair stood up. 'My name is Sarah, I'm from Christchurch,' and then she sat down again.

It was Koro Ian's turn. He rummaged around his pocket and pulled out his phone.

'This is my moko, Matariki,' he said, his face beaming with pride at the little girl on his screensaver.

'She just started going to kōhanga reo, you see, and now she only speaks Māori and it's got to the point I can't even understand what she's saying. I thought to myself, *Well, old bugger, you better get your A into G and go and learn your language. If your moko can do it, so can you.* I thought, *Better late than never, eh?* We were always told speaking Māori wouldn't get you a job anywhere, that it was useless, a waste of time. That was my generation anyway.'

He shook his head in disbelief. 'Now look at the world. Who would have thought? Who would have blimmin' thought? Now you got Simon Dallow on the TV news speaking more Māori than the rest of us!

'I'm a happy man,' he said. 'I have a good life. I love my family. But I've lived sixty-nine years without my language. I have everything but my reo.'

A sadness washed over the room. Māreikura thought about her nana who was the same age, who would probably never get the opportunity to relearn her language in this life. It was a realisation for many in the classroom that this was more than just a hobby, an extracurricular activity or something to tick off the bucket list for Māori. It was reclamation. It was restoration. Te reo Māori was intergenerational healing.

After Koro Ian spoke, a pale-white girl with short, brown hair stood up. She wore big, dangly, koru-shaped earrings and a huge pounamu around her neck, as if to overcompensate for her whiteness.

'Ōwairaka is my mountain. Ngāti Kahungunu is my tribe.' She beamed with pride and Māreikura felt guilty for assuming she was Pākehā.

'My name is Chloe and I love the Māori culture and that's why I'm here. I grew up in Hastings, my aunty Jan married my uncle who is from Ngāti Kahungunu, so I've always had that connection to the people of Ngāti Kahungunu. But for myself, I'm Ngāti Pākehā.'

'Hang on,' Māreikura said. 'You just said your iwi is Ngāti Kahungunu?'

'Yes.'

'So are you Māori or not?'

'I'm Pākehā.' Chloe smiled. 'But I grew up around Ngāti Kahungunu and the marae. Ngāti Kahungunu is like my iwi.'

'But it's not your iwi. You can't claim it. You don't whakapapa back to Māori. So you can't say Ngāti Kahungunu is your iwi.'

Now everyone was looking at Māreikura. Chloe sat down.

Māreikura's body was shaking and Whaea Terina said, 'Nau mai ngā roimata. Let the tears come. That's how the healing starts. Nō hea koe, Māreikura?'

'I don't know,' Māreikura said. 'I don't know where I am from. That's why I'm here.'

Jordana patted her on her back and then she got to her feet.

'Auē, whānau, this is intense. Drinks at mine after this. K Road.'

Then everyone laughed.

•

'You shouldn't say K Road,' Māreikura told Jordana after class. 'It's Karangahape Road. You should say the full name.'

'Aroha mai,' Jordana said. 'It's a bad habit.'

'Don't be lazy,' Māreikura told her. 'No one calls Ponsonby Road, P Road.'

Once, when Māreikura was walking with Eru, an old white woman stopped them for directions to get to 'K Road' and Māreikura corrected her.

'It's Karangahape. Ka-rang-a-ha-pe. Don't be lazy,' Māreikura told her, knowing very well Eru was full-on staring at her.

After she left, Eru said, 'She was just asking for directions, Ma.'

'Yeah, and she just got a free education,' Māreikura shot back. 'I should have given her my bank account details while I was at it.'

Memories of Eru came back often, sometimes good, sometimes bad, and most of all a reminder of why Māreikura never wanted to see his stupid face again.

Māreikura asked Jordana if she wanted a ride home and she said yes. They got in the car and Jordana had a smile forming on her lips, like a joke was about to come out.

'"Ngāti Kahungunu is my tribe."'

Māreikura started laughing and then they both sat in the car laughing.

'It's not funny, though, is it?' Jordana said after the laughter died down. 'It's actually serious.'

'Who claims to be from an iwi when you're not even Māori?' Māreikura shook her head. 'I didn't know this still happened. Are people that clueless?'

Jordana wound the window down. 'I think people just don't know,' she said. 'You don't know what you don't know. Can I vape in here?'

'Yeah, all good. It sucks trying to learn your language with a bunch of white people who treat it like a hobby.'

'Sarah seems cool, though.'

'She's still Pākehā,' Māreikura said. 'Still taking up space when there's so many of our people who want to learn our language.'

'Yeah, but she's a good Pākehā,' Jordana said.

They were at the intersection of Ponsonby and Karangahape roads.

'What is a good Pākehā?' Māreikura quizzed her. 'They're all the same, bro. All those Pākehā who go to reo classes and get a bit of reo? They're the ones who are the most racist. They'll use our culture and weaponise our reo and take more from us behind our backs. You watch.'

Māreikura could feel Jordana giving her the side-eye.

'What? That's what they did when they colonised us, didn't they?' Māreikura asked. 'They learnt our reo so they could soften us up, indoctrinate us with Christianity and then take our land from us. How is today any different? We spent most of the class teaching Chloe and the other Pākehā, did you notice that?'

'What did you think about Troy?'

'He's whakahīhī,' Māreikura said. 'I don't like his āhua.'

Whakahīhī was a new word they learnt that day. It means arrogant. Kaue e whakahīhī, their kaiako told them. Leave any arrogance at the door. Be humble. E waka eke noa. We're all in the same boat. We're all trying to learn our language together. We are all equal here. And when one of us fails, all of us fails.

Jordana pointed ahead. 'See that white car? Turn left down here and my house is the one where that white car is parked.'

Māreikura slowed the car outside an apartment block.

'I can come pick you up tomorrow if you want. It's on the way.'

'Sweet, e hoa,' Jordana climbed out. 'Wanna come up?'

•

Jordana lived in a 'New York loft-style' apartment. Māreikura had never been in one before but she had seen them advertised on Trade Me when she went through delusional episodes thinking she could move out of home. She would search city apartments in Auckland and fantasise about staying in bed for three straight days without her nan knocking on her door and asking if she was depressed again. Or bringing a girl home and not having to be quiet knowing her nana was in the next room. Māreikura wasn't into one-night stands, or maybe she was? What if she met a nice girl and decided she liked the look of her and did the thing Kat did, *Hey, wanna come back to mine?* It was about having options.

But most of all, she wanted to wake up every morning and not have to look across the road at the eyesore that was Eru's house. A constant, daily reminder of her ex-best friend's betrayal of leaving her. And if that wasn't enough, the Mormon missionaries had started knocking on her door since he left, which resulted in Māreikura hiding out in her room until she heard them leave. One time, they 'heart-attacked' the front door, which in Mormon terms is putting up little sticky hearts with notes all over the door. Māreikura was on the other side pretending not to be home and had to sit and not make a noise for a good fifteen minutes. Her nana said next time to just call the cops.

No matter how many times Māreikura wrote a budget plan or made a 'manifestation' board, there was no way she could afford her own place or overcome the intergenerational guilt of leaving her nan alone to live by herself. Whānau come first! Back in the day, her ancestors lived in communities! Even if your mental health is suffering! Imagine putting her nan in a rest home and visiting her once a week for an hour. Pākehā were ruthless like that.

Jordana handed Māreikura a bright-coloured can of drink that looked like a kid's fizzy drink, except for the tiny fine print that said 5 per cent alcohol.

'Nah, I'm good,' Māreikura said.

'Oh, they're sugar-free,' Jordana said, as if that would change her mind.

'I don't drink,' Māreikura said. 'I'm decolonising my whakapapa.'

'Oh. Cool.'

Jordana placed it on the bench.

'You want anything else?' She burrowed her head back in the fridge. 'Hmm, there's water. Red Bull.' She picked up a purple drink. 'Er, I think this is a brain drink. Helps you focus or something.'

'Water is good.'

'Ka pai.' Jordana reached into the top cupboard and handed her a glass. 'Make sure you get it from the fridge. Who knows what the government put in the tap water?' She pointed to the ice dispenser at the front of the fridge. 'You hungry? I can order us some kai.'

'Nah, I'm going to dinner soon,' Māreikura said, filling up her cup. 'Thanks, though.'

Jordana flopped onto the couch, popping the cap of her drink. She took a sip and made a satisfied sound. An overgrown, leafy, green plant that was kind of ugly brushed the top of her head.

'Tēnā koe, e Anahera,' Jordana said, talking to her plant. She shuffled to the left. 'I know, I know. Māmā needs to propagate you so you can have a pēpi.'

Jordana had a lot of plants. They were scattered all over the apartment. Vines falling from the roof, huge palm-looking plants in the corner. She had names for all of them, which she told Māreikura but Māreikura forgot as soon as she told her. Aside from the fact Jordana lived in an apartment that would cost probably $1200 a week, the plants were an indicator that Jordana had money. When Māreikura was at a plant shop in Ponsonby once, she saw a little tiny pot plant for $30 and she couldn't believe how much people would pay for plants. Her nan would say it was daylight robbery. Plants were a trend among Gen Zs and millennials. Māreikura wasn't sure why – maybe it was to fill the empty void in their lives. Maybe it was a lazy attempt to go back to the days of their ancestors, live among the forest and be connected to the environment without having to leave your city apartment or damp Ponsonby villa. Kat didn't have any plants in her house. Māreikura made a note to ask her why. Maybe because she was the older end of millennial and didn't believe in plants? Maybe there was a bigger reason.

'Do you think houseplants are a form of colonisation?' Māreikura asked.

'What?' Jordana put her drink down. 'Shit. Do I need to get rid of them?'

'Nah, you good. I was just wondering.'

'Thank God,' Jordana said. 'Please don't cancel my babies.'

She took another drink then she said, 'We should be speaking te reo, eh? What's the kupu for remote? Hmm, homai te remote.'

Māreikura picked up the remote. 'Anei te remote.'

'Kia ora!'

She pointed the remote to the massive flatscreen hanging on the wall. 'Look at us, almost fluent already. What music do you like, e hoa?'

She pressed a button and Tom Misch came on the speakers. Jordana leaned back on the couch, nodding her head. There was a coolness about her, even the way she sat back on the couch with her drink in one hand, her head cocked to the left. She made Māreikura feel like she could be herself.

'I like your whare,' Māreikura told her, looking around. 'It's nice.'

'Yeah, it's okay.' Jordana shrugged. 'I thought about getting a flatmate but my therapist said I need to learn to be by myself.' She pointed at the surfboard leaning against the wall that looked like it had never been used before. 'That's why I started surfing. You surf?'

'Nah.'

'It's so good for the wairua. I like meditation too.'

'I can't meditate.'

'Have you heard of the Headspace app?'

'Nah.'

'It's a meditation app – you should try it. I never used to be able to be alone in my own thoughts but I do ten minutes in the morning. Bro, life-changing.'

'I'll download it,' Māreikura said, even though she had no intention of downloading it. 'How long you been at therapy?'

'I've been going for the last two years,' Jordana said. 'Highly recommend.'

'Yeah, well, some of us can't afford it.'

'Yeah, I know,' Jordana said. Her tone softened. 'I heard Hinemoa Elder say once that te reo Māori is like rongoā. Medicine. Maybe it can be that for us.'

'Why do you have so many plants?'

'The same reason why people have so many children.'

'A distraction?'

Jordana snorted. 'Nah, it's more like taking care of someone other than yourself, you know?'

Māreikura did not know. She picked up a book from the table. The title read *Healing My Child Wound and other stories.*

'Such a good book, e hoa,' Jordana said. 'You can borrow it if you want. It's helped me understand why I'm in toxic relationships.'

'Because of your parents?'

'Yeah, my dad.'

'What did he do?'

'What didn't he do?' She sat up straight with a look of excitement as if she had been waiting her whole life for someone to ask.

'The last time I saw him, we were at my aunty's house at Christmas. It's the only time I go there 'cause it's like walking into an extreme right-wing meet-up. Anyway, we were playing charades and my aunty was doing the thing with the eyes, you know, the racist thing people do to describe Asian people? I was like, Aunty, cut that out, and she was like, "Why? Nothing wrong with describing people and how they look." And I was like, "No, actually, there is, Aunty, you racist cow."

Then we started going at it and then my dad was like,' she put on a deep voice, '"Jordana, why do you have to ruin everything?"'

She made a face, taking another drink.

'Like I'm deficient or something. Anyway, what was my point? Oh yeah, my dad doesn't want me learning te reo. Said it's a waste of time.'

She kept the sour look on her face and then sculled back the rest of her drink.

'Sounds like my nana,' Māreikura said.

'Is she white too?'

'Nah, Māori.'

'Oh.'

'That makes it worse. She was beaten for speaking the language but she never talks about it. We never go back home either. She doesn't talk to any of her siblings.'

Jordana shook her head. 'That's like my mum's side. I'm the first one in my family to learn Māori. My nanny's dead now but she and her siblings were so traumatised by colonisation, they became alcoholics. So my mum did her best to make it in the white world, married my dad. But it sucks now because every time we go back to the marae or see my mum's family, they look at me and my brothers like we're all privileged and treat us different, like we're not even Māori, like we're guests on our own marae. Like what the hell, we have the same nana, bro. Why are you talking to me like I don't belong here? Or even worse, like I'm a five-year-old?'

Māreikura didn't say anything and Jordana said, 'Aroha mai, e hoa. I could go on and on about this shit.'

'Ka pai,' Māreikura said. 'Talking about colonisation is my love language.'

Jordana cracked up. 'This is why the first thing I ask a guy on Tinder is, "Nō hea koe?" So at least I know they are Māori. Like, bro,

I don't care if you go to the gym and lift. Just tell me where you're from and then take me to your marae and show me what you're doing to give back to your iwi and your hapū.' She jumped to her feet. 'You want a drink while I'm up?'

Māreikura said no thanks but Jordana was already in the kitchen. She filled a jug with water and started watering the big plant in the corner of the room like Māreikura wasn't there.

CHAPTER FIVE

Māreikura peeled the remote from her nana's grip and switched the TV off.

'Hey!' Her nan jolted awake. 'I was watching that.'

'You were asleep.' Māreikura sat down on the couch.

'Was I? Must have drifted off.' She looked around for the clock. 'What's the time? Hey, pass me that remote back.'

She fiddled with the buttons and turned the TV back on. Her favourite show *The Chase* was playing.

'I'm waiting for the news about the house prices in Auckland. Apparently they're at their highest.'

'You know you can just go on your phone and read the news, Nan?'

She waved her hand. 'I can't work those blimmin' things. Anyway, we know who's buying all the houses – the foreigners! Rhona told me her son went to buy a home and someone else got it instead, a Chinese family! Bet you they'll knock the house down and build those ugly-looking unit things, you watch.'

'How do you know the Chinese family isn't from here?' Māreikura asked. 'You can't just assume they're foreigners because they look

Asian. And anyway, Nan, if we don't build those units, where is everyone going to live? Would you rather our people are homeless on our own land?'

Her nan grunted something under her breath and turned back to the TV. It's not her fault she's colonised, Māreikura told herself. Her favourite politician was Winston Peters. *He's quite a handsome man, isn't he*, her nan said once. *That's not a reason to like a politician*, Māreikura replied. *What about his morals?* Her nan replied, *Well, he's a straight shooter, tells it like it is. Gets the job done and he's promised to do something about immigration.* Māreikura had to leave the room before she said something she would regret. The other day, her nan said Māori shouldn't expect handouts and Māreikura just about lost it. 'If you weren't lucky enough to buy your house thirty years ago and your husband didn't leave you money, you'd be needing help from the government too,' Māreikura had snapped. Her nana went real quiet after that. She didn't like it when Māreikura brought up her dead husband.

'My gosh, you stupid lady. What were you thinking?!' Her nan was yelling at one of the contestants on the TV.

'You know they can't hear you, Nan.'

'Yeah, well. If they just thought about the questions a bit more carefully,' she said. 'The problem is they let anyone on this show.'

'You should go on the show, then.'

She glanced over at Māreikura. 'What's wrong with your hair?'

Māreikura brushed her fingers through her curls. 'I'm decolonising my hair.'

'What you mean? Is that another word for not brushing it? Looks like a rat clawed its way through it.'

'Nan, I'm trying to live like our ancestors did. I'm just letting it be natural and not straightening it anymore.'

'You think your ancestors were dirty?' She turned back to the TV. 'They still brushed their hair.'

Māreikura stopped straightening her hair after seeing television host Indira Stewart wear her natural, curly hair on breakfast TV. She realised not only had her language been colonised, but so had her hair. Māreikura had an unhealthy addiction to straightening it so she sold her straightener on Facebook Marketplace for $15. She promised her ancestors she would never burn her hair ever again.

'Big Eru came over looking for you,' her nan said. 'Gee, he can talk, can't he? Couldn't get a word in.'

She nodded at the roof. 'He fixed the light and the fan in the bathroom. 'Bout time. I did mention it to him a few weeks ago. Said he's been busy. I said, funny that, not too busy to go running. Saw him run past every day this week and he could have stopped in. Gee, he's a handsome man, though. I bet his church is full of ladies with their bums on the seats. Not like back when I used to go to church – the pastor looked like he was already knocking on heaven's door, if you know what I mean? No wonder I didn't stick around. Anyway, he said he's tried calling and texting you. Your phone broken, girl?'

Māreikura had ghosted Eru Senior and the Johnson family. At first, it was unintentional. Eru Senior had texted multiple times and she told herself she would reply later but then later turned into a few hours and then a day and then a week had passed and it was too late.

How's your car? You checked your oil?

This scripture reminded me of you (insert scripture about Jesus).

Come over for dinner. Kei te pehea? You hungry?

Eru Jr emailed this morning, I sent it to your email!

And the one that always got Māreikura teary: *We miss you, girl. When you coming home?*

She used to spend every day at their house but now she couldn't bring herself to see them. It hurt too much.

He sent her memes too. Eru Senior loved memes. 'You seen this?' he'd grin, shoving his phone in front of Eru Junior's face. Eru would nod and say 'Cool, Dad' in his monotone voice. 'Well, it's not cool, it's supposed to be funny.' He would do the same thing to Eden and she would say, 'Hold on,' then take two minutes to find her glasses, then when she finally found them, she would put them on, point to the phone and say, 'Who is that, Eru?' And then Eru would say, 'I dunno, hun, just look.' But Eden didn't get it. 'What am I looking at exactly? How do you know these people?' and Eru would shake his head. 'I don't know them! Oh, never mind.' So he would wait for Māreikura to come over and then he would hold his phone in her face, trying not to laugh. 'Is this you?' The last one was a meme of Frodo from *The Lord of the Rings* when he completed his mission saying, 'It's done,' and then the caption: *Introverts after making it through an entire phone call.* She laughed hard at that one.

'Well, I told him you're busy at school anyway. He said that boy's doing good in Hawai'i, said he's—'

'Nan, I have to do my pepeha at kura.'

'What?'

'My pepeha. You know, our mountain and river.'

'I know what a pepeha is. I'm not stupid.'

They both sat in silence watching the Chaser answer the trivia questions. Māreikura knew it wasn't the right time to bring it up but she didn't want to hear another word about her ex-best friend.

'Can you help me?'

'You'll have to ask my sister, your Aunty Lois,' her nana finally said. 'She lives in Hokianga. Look up her daughter Kris on Facebook, probably faster. Kris Hohepa.'

'Okay.'

Māreikura waited for her to say more but she didn't. She hated asking Nana about home. She always got funny about it. The news headlines came on and Simon Dallow said, 'Kia ora, good evening.'

Māreikura found Kris on Facebook and sent her a message.

Kia ora, cuz, I'm Māreikura, Glennis's moko. Do you have Aunty Lois's phone number?

Within a minute, her cousin replied. *Kia ora, cuz! Hope you and Aunty are good. Yep, give her a call! 02-3920302.*

Māreikura was scared of calling her Aunty Lois. The image of the gatekeeper at Waitangi came into her head and she imagined her Aunty Lois yelling at her.

Where have you been? Why you haven't you come home? Why haven't you called?

Māreikura said a silent karakia, imagining her ancestors navigating the expansive oceans on a waka. She could do this. She could make this phone call. She pressed the call button. She heard heavy breathing and then, 'Kia ora?'

'Aunty Lois?'

'This you, Maia?'

'It's Māreikura.'

'Hold on.' More heavy breathing and movement. 'Who?'

'Māreikura? Glennis's moko.'

'Oh, hullo, moko! It's nice to hear from you. I haven't seen you since you were little. Kei te pehea koe, darling?'

'Kei te pai, Aunty.'

'How's my little sister doing? She healthy and looking after herself?'

'Yeah, she's good, healthy as.'

'Well, at least one of us is.' She laughed. 'My sis wouldn't recognise me now. The food too good up here, that's why. Now is everything all right, dear? I thought something might have happened to that sister of mine. Almost gave me a heart attack hearing your name.'

'Everything's all right, Aunty. I'm ringing because I'm at kura this year studying Māori and I need help with an assignment.'

'You're not at rumaki reo with Pāpā Sean are you?'

'Yeah, that's the one.'

Her aunty bellowed with laughter and Māreikura had to hold the phone away from her ear.

'Next time you see that old bugger, you tell him he still owes me a beer. Blimmin' heck, what a small world.'

'I will.' Māreikura cleared her throat. 'Aunty, I'm trying to learn about my pepeha. I need to know about my mountain, my river and all that. Can you tell me the names?'

Silence. Dead silence. Māreikura knew she shouldn't have asked yet. It was too soon. She should have waited. Made small talk for half an hour at least. She waited for the growling. She was expecting it. She would simply say sorry and tell her aunty she was poor and had no gas – did she know the price of petrol these days? Plus she was busy with school and also had severe mental health problems and that's why she hadn't been to visit.

'Well, I can, dear,' her aunty said finally. 'I can tell you all of that. But what happens then? You'll write them down and they will just be some words on a paper. But they won't mean anything to you.'

Māreikura said nothing because she didn't know what to say. Her aunty was right. Of course she was.

'Can you drive?'

'Yes, Aunty.'

'Well, you need to come home and stand on your mountain, touch your river, stay at your marae. No use me telling you over the phone. You might as well read out the Bible. Will mean nothing to you.'

'Okay, Aunty. I'll come up soon,' Māreikura said. But it was more like a croak. Then she hung up the phone.

CHAPTER SIX

Māreikura had heard the story so many times. When Glennis and Philip Pohe bought their small villa on Franklin Road thirty years ago, it was $130,000, which was quite a bit of money in those days. They lived next door to a Tongan family – the Faletaus – who at first Glennis didn't really like. She shook her head at the seven kids all cramped up in the three-bedroom house. She wondered if she should get the children's services involved but Philip told her to stop being so nosy, and plus she thought they must be all right because the kids were all getting fed well by the looks of it. On Sundays, the Faletau men and boys dressed in nice lavalavas and the girls wore beautiful floral dresses from the islands with little flower headbands. Glennis saw it all from her kitchen window. She was quite impressed by their Sunday outfits and began to like the Faletaus, especially the young boy Anjelo.

Then one day, Glennis saw Mr Faletau holding a cardboard box while sweat dripped from his forehead. 'The landlord is selling,' he said. That was the beginning. Apparently the housing market in Auckland was rocketing, which explained the number of flyers

Glennis got in her mailbox talking about a 'free evaluation'. The truth was they were trying to move out all the Māori and Pasifika people so they could gentrify Grey Lynn and Ponsonby and bring all the rich Pākehā in. Glennis could smell the truth. She was never going to sell her house and she was sick of the darn pesky real estate agents knocking on her door. *Get out of here!* she screamed once at an unsuspecting Pākehā agent who showed up at her door. It wasn't Glennis's finest moment but it did stop the agents from bothering her for a while. She wanted to write in big bold letters 'NO JUNK MAIL' above her letterbox but she liked the feeling of receiving mail, even if it was just a Warehouse catalogue or Burger King vouchers.

Franklin Road was different now. The state homes were freshly painted white villas all owned by wealthy Pākehā families with big Range Rovers parked half on the road, half on the footpath. The footpath was also overridden by skinny mums in tight exercise pants holding a little glass cup in one hand and their little dog in the other. Glennis always wondered why they smelled like a duty-free shop when they walked past. Who sprays expensive perfume just to go for a walk? Perfume was for special occasions and not to parade around your little fluffy dog and tight behind. And where did all the Pākehā families come from anyway? It was like they were all brought over in a shipping container.

Glennis was the longest-residing resident on the street – an honour she didn't take lightly. She took it upon herself to make sure everyone was looked after. Everyone. She often went to war with the Auckland Council and had a reputation for winning, like the time she fought hard to keep their water rates down. 'Never Give in Glennis' someone nicknamed her. She quite liked the name as it did fit her persona. She dealt with concerns very quickly. Like when the Stevenses moved in last year. They were causing all sorts of problems. They had two little yappy dogs that barked all hours of the morning. Glennis couldn't hear them mostly because she was deaf in one ear, but Gloria and Dale from number 27 mentioned it to her in passing. She decided to leave a polite letter in their mailbox.

Hello, Stevens family, she wrote. *Your dogs are barking at ungodly hours of the morning and it's upsetting the residents of Franklin Road. Please get them under control. From a concerned neighbour.*

After that, the dogs never made a sound again. Gloria and Dale thanked her for speaking up. 'You're welcome,' Glennis told them. 'It's my duty as one of the longest-standing residents here to keep this street orderly.'

But the Stevenses just wouldn't stop causing problems. The ditzy mum Alison was always letting her friends park their cars in front of Glennis's house. One day, Glennis 'bumped' into Alison when she was getting ready to hop in her Range Rover and go to work. Glennis joked to her, 'I should send you and your friends a bill for my rates since they're always parking outside my house.' Even though Glennis didn't drive, that wasn't the point. It would be nice if they asked her, that's all. Glennis was kind enough to leave pamphlets in their mailbox about local family events, and a few times she took it upon herself to give their hedges a trim as they were looking worse for wear, and she didn't even get a thank you. They left a letter in her mailbox asking her to not enter their property or they would call the police, and then they built a big fence so no one could see inside. The nerve!

Living on Franklin Road also meant they were in the best area for schools. Glennis had wanted Māreikura to go to Gretton College, the most prestigious and well-known school in Auckland. They were in zone so Māreikura was eligible but she also had to pass a test to get a scholarship. Of course her granddaughter got in. She'd always been smart, even when she was a little girl. She used to study the *Women's Day* magazines and make her own books.

Glennis did not want Māreikura to study te reo Māori. What the hell for? It was not like Glennis not to say what was on her mind, but she had to these days. She was always tiptoeing around Māreikura, making sure she didn't hurt her feelings. Her moko was sensitive and she didn't know what Māreikura would do next. Glennis tried to tell herself that times had changed, it wasn't the same as when she was younger when she was told 'being Māori will get you nowhere'. Glennis remembered when Naida Glavish had to fight to say 'kia ora' when she was working at the Post Office. That was almost forty years ago. Now it was different. Now it was 'cool to kōrero'.

Sometimes it did catch her off guard. The other week, the young girl at the checkout at the Countdown in Grey Lynn started speaking to her in Māori, and Glennis didn't know what to do so she just looked down at their groceries and said, 'Just these, thanks'. The girl must have been Māreikura's age, maybe older.

Glennis made sure to avoid that counter the next time she was shopping. She didn't mind the odd chat, in fact she quite liked it, but she didn't like the way people spoke Māori to her. It felt intrusive, when Glennis simply wanted to go about her day.

CHAPTER SEVEN

Kat's fridge was scattered with magnets of all the countries and places she'd visited. Great Wall of China. Switzerland. Tokyo. Rome. Philippines. Thailand.

'I've never been overseas,' Māreikura told her and she felt embarrassed, like she had just confessed she was poor.

Kat kissed her on the top of her head. 'We've got plenty of time to go overseas, my love.'

Kat was overly affectionate with both her physical touch and words. It was like she had never experienced rejection before. Or maybe they were her love languages. They were not Māreikura's love languages.

'Why do you like travelling so much?'

'I think when you travel you realise there's a world that exists outside of your own,' Kat said. 'It's like when you go hiking up a mountain, you feel insignificant.'

'Why do I need to travel or climb a mountain to feel insignificant?' Māreikura said. 'I wake up every day feeling that way anyway.'

Kat burst out laughing. 'Why are you so funny?'

She liked making Kat laugh, even though she wasn't meaning to be funny. If it was Eru, he would look at her with sad eyes and say, *I'm sorry to hear that. Do you want to talk about it?*

'Do you like cooking?' Kat asked and Māreikura shook her head. 'I'm not really good at it.'

'Oh, babe,' Kat said. 'It's so easy.'

She finished rolling the dough and then pointed to the funny-looking machine on the bench. 'Spaghetti or fettuccine?'

'Fettuccine.'

Kat put the dough through the machine until it turned into long and stretchy pasta.

'The secret to pasta is to keep it simple,' she said. 'Westerners always try to complicate things. This is just pasta, fresh tomatoes from the garden and spices. I learnt it in Italy on my OE.'

When the pasta was done boiling, Kat twirled some onto her fork and tasted it.

'Mmm, try some,' and she held the fork out in front of Māreikura. The pasta was the best Māreikura had ever had, although she didn't have much to compare to. She only ever ate pasta at the cheap Italian place down the road and it always gave her a sore gut afterwards.

'See,' Kat said. 'Cooking is easy.'

'Cooking requires a lot of self-confidence,' Māreikura said. 'And time. What if no one likes the food you make? What if you spend hours cooking something for it not to work out?'

'You are the funniest and cutest little human I've ever come across. It's only cooking, babe. Don't read too much into it.'

She touched Māreikura gently on the waist and then moved her to the side.

After they ate dinner, Kat lay back on the couch and stretched her arms out and Māreikura crawled on her chest. Māreikura loved her smell. She inhaled it with every breath. They watched the Tainui wars documentary, bonding over past trauma and a shared history. It was Māreikura's idea to watch it. She was from Ngāpuhi and it was new information they were learning together. The war invasions and the re-enactment of Māori taking sanctuary in churches and soldiers coming to order them out and then kill them. A ten-year-old boy ran out and was shot dead. The British set fire to the church. It was worse seeing it on Kat's giant plasma screen, rather than just imagining it.

•

'You are so beautiful', Kat said, her eyes scanning Māreikura's body with a hunger Māreikura had not seen before. 'Look at you.'

'You are,' Māreikura said.

'What?'

'Beautiful.'

'I am? Tell me more about that,' Kat replied, her hand grazing Māreikura's skin. Māreikura would later realise this was a common thing for Kat to do – ask 'Am I? Tell me more' every time Māreikura complimented her, forcing Māreikura to repeat herself. Māreikura was the worst at giving compliments – she would think nice things about someone but never say it out loud, always in her head. Kat would force her to say what was on her mind.

'You are the most beautiful woman I've ever seen,' she said in a confident voice and Kat giggled, taking delight in her words. She leaned over and lightly fingered Māreikura's arms and kissed the freckles on her left cheek and then tapped her shoulder with her lips. An Ecoya candle flickered in the corner.

'Cuddle me,' Kat said softly and Māreikura wrapped her arms around her while she lay her head on Kat's chest.

'Why do Pākehā take up so much space?' Māreikura asked.

Kat brushed Māreikura's hair with her fingers. 'What happened?'

'There's a girl in my class, Chloe, who claimed she was from an iwi but she's not even Māori.'

'Oh.'

'Yeah, and I blew up at her and now everyone thinks I'm the crazy girl.'

'Oh, honey,' Kat said. 'You're not crazy. You're just from Ngāpuhi.'

'Stop. I'm being serious.'

'So am I.' Kat smirked. 'It's sexy.'

'Why do they have to come to the one place where I need to feel safe? Learning my ancestors' language. They don't have the same trauma as us, they treat it like a squash lesson or something. There should be a separate class for them to learn. Also, I heard Chloe speak reo and it's real good and it just makes me feel ashamed that it's better than mine. It's my language, I should be the one who's able to speak it, not her.'

'Oh, but your reo is good,' Kat said. 'It's helping me so much when I hear you speak it. I want to do full immersion next year because of you. That's how much you inspire me.'

'Really?'

'Yes,' Kat said, leaning over and kissing Māreikura on her head. 'I find it such a turn-on when you speak Māori.'

It was the first time Māreikura had been told this. That it was attractive being Māori. Kat had given her a love for herself that was new. A love for her Māoritanga, her curly hair, her brown skin, her reo Māori. In a world where the dominant race would swipe left on her Tinder profile or look right through her as she walked the street, here was the most beautiful woman telling Māreikura she loved her for being Māori. Her culture was now working for her and not against her. It made Māreikura feel more confident, like it was curing her internalised racism, the parts she used to resent about herself.

CHAPTER EIGHT

Māreikura was the descendant of the greatest navigators in the world and now she was sitting in a classroom learning basic colours in a language that should have been her birthright.

Mā is white. Whero is red. Kākāriki is green. They were learning the words for colours in te reo Māori in the form of a kindergarten song and then taking turns pointing to each rod and saying which colour it was.

'Māreikura, homai tētahi rākau parāone?' Sarah asked her, and even though Whaea Terina had repeated the colours so many times, it wasn't registering in Māreikura's brain what colour Sarah had asked for. She hovered her hand over the brown rod and Sarah nodded. Māreikura picked it up and handed it to Sarah.

'Ka pai,' Sarah said.

Shut up, Māreikura wanted to scream. *Don't ka pai me. It was your ancestors who put me here in the first place.*

Whaea Terina clapped her hands together.

'For our first assignment. Hoki atu ki tōu maunga', she announced.

'Go back to home. Go back to your mountain. Learn your pepeha, where you come from, and then report it back to class.'

Chloe put her hand up.

'Yes, Sarah?' Whaea Terina asked.

Chloe glanced behind her and then back at Whaea Terina. 'Oh. It's Chloe.'

'Auē. Sorry, Chloe!'

Māreikura snorted. Sarah and Chloe were the only two Pākehā girls in the class and they looked nothing alike. Sarah was tall with blonde hair and really quiet, Chloe was short with mousy brown hair and had a big mouth. Neither Sarah nor Chloe probably ever experienced being mistaken for someone else just because they shared the same skin colour.

'For Pākehā, how do we say our pepeha?' Chloe asked. 'Can I still, um . . .' Her eyes shifted in Māreikura's direction. '. . . use Ngāti Kahungunu's maunga but not claim it? Since I grew up around it.'

Sarah turned to Chloe. 'I think,' she said, 'the obvious answer is we don't have the same spiritual connection to the land because the land is not ours. So we would use our ancestral mountain, is that right, Whaea?'

'But what if we have been here for generations?' Chloe asked. 'I feel a connection here more than I do anywhere else. I haven't even been to England.'

'Why do we even have to explain this?' Māreikura piped up. 'Our pepeha isn't yours to steal. Your maunga isn't in Aotearoa. Your mountain is in England or wherever your ancestors come from. You have no connection to the land.'

'How should Pākehā say their pepeha then?'

'Google it.'

Chloe sunk in her seat and for a moment Māreikura felt guilty, but she shook it away. White guilt was not her burden to take on.

•

Whaea Terina placed a photo of her marae up on the whiteboard. She pointed to the pole in the middle.

'Does anyone know what this is called?' and Alex put his hand up and said, 'The poutokomanawa.'

'Yes, and what is that, Alex?'

'It is the main support of the marae. Without the poutokomanawa, the marae would collapse.'

'Tika! And if you break that word down further, toko is what?'

'Support.'

'And manawa is the . . . ?'

'Heart,' the whole class chanted back.

'Exactly. So the pou is the pole, the toko is the support, and manawa is the heart. Pou-toko-manawa. The poutokomanawa can also be the person in your whānau who holds it together – who holds you together – and without them you would fall.'

She stuck a photo on the whiteboard with Blu Tack. It was of a Māori man who looked like he was in his fifties.

'This is my poutokomanawa. My tāne, my whaiāipo, my husband of twenty years. Most of the time, he's a pain in the bloody backside.' She laughed at her own joke. 'But I wouldn't be here without him. Now I want you to all think for a minute. Who is the poutokomanawa of your whānau?'

'What if,' Jordana asked, 'I am the poutokomanawa?'

The class laughed and she said, 'I'm serious. Without me, my whānau would fall apart.'

'That's a very individualistic way of looking at it,' Whaea Terina said.

'By individualistic, I think she means Pākehā,' Māreikura whispered.

'Did you get to where you are on your own?' Whaea Terina asked.

'Got to where?' Jordana asked. 'I'm just existing.'

The class laughed again and Jordana shrugged.

'Probably my sister then – even though everything about her annoys me. But when I need help I call her and she's always there.'

Whaea Terina nodded. 'What about you, Māreikura?'

'Oh, I didn't realise it was sharing time.'

'It's always sharing time around here.'

'My nana then,' Māreikura said. 'She raised me.'

Whaea Terina waited, as if coaxing Māreikura to say more.

'And she's been through a lot in her life. Made lots of sacrifices for me to get a good education.'

'Ka pai.' Whaea Terina turned to Claudia. 'Ko koe, Claudia?'

'My grandfather. He came on a boat from our village in Guangzhou, came here with nothing and opened up a fruit shop for our family to be here today.'

Whaea nodded and then clasped her hands together.

'The next assignment, class, is to share about our poutokomanawa and talk about them, their life, and their impact on us. We will each share not in class but at the end-of-year graduation. But we are going to do it a bit differently.'

She reached for the upside-down bucket hat on the desk and shook it.

'I've put all the names in the hat and each of you is going to pull out a name and pair up with that person, and then you are going to spend the year interviewing their poutokomanawa. If their poutokomanawa is not alive or unavailable, then you need to conduct your own research, talk to a family member of that person. Does that make sense?'

She shook the hat again. 'Claudia, let's go with you first.'

Claudia put her hand in and pulled out a tiny piece of folded paper. She unfolded the paper and did a fist-pump. 'Koro Ian.'

A few people in the class groaned and Koro Ian sat on his chair, like the king he was.

'Damnit,' Māreikura said quietly. 'I wanted him.'

Jordana put her hand in the hat and pulled out a paper. She read the name, closed her eyes for a moment too long, and then opened them again.

'Troy.'

Māreikura would mock her about that later, but for now it was her turn. She rummaged her hand around, getting a good feel. Anyone but Chloe. *Please*, she prayed to her tīpuna and anyone who would listen. She grasped onto a piece of paper and pulled it out. She unravelled the paper and stared at the name. For a moment, she thought about quickly putting it back and swapping it but she could feel Whaea Terina breathing behind her.

Jordana looked over her shoulder. 'Who'd you ge— Oh.'

'Chloe,' Māreikura said out loud so everyone could hear. 'I got Chloe.'

•

Whaea Terina raised one finger in the air.

'One minute, Māreikura,' she said. 'Let me just finish typing this. Okay . . . yes . . . here we are . . . Okay, kei te pai.' She gestured at a chair.

'It's okay,' Māreikura said, standing by the door, her hands fidgeting with the clasp on her backpack. 'I don't have a lot of time. I'm just quickly letting you know I can't do the assignment with Chloe. Just seeing if I can swap.'

Whaea Terina stared at her, a smile curving her lips. She pointed to the chair for the second time. Māreikura sat down.

'He aha te raru? What's the problem?'

'I don't want to be partnered with Chloe, Whaea. I'm asking if I can swap.'

'Māreikura, do you know how many people apply to come to this school?'

'A lot.'

'Thousands,' Whaea Terina emphasised. 'We have waiting lists for five years, that's how in demand this school is. We have celebrities paying money to try and get a place or bump their name higher up the list.'

'Celebrities? Like who?'

'Well, you know what I mean, people in high-up places.' She waved her hand. 'Well, they think they're famous anyway. They do everything they can to get in or get someone in their whānau in. This school is the only place in the world where you can learn these types of skills. And now more than ever before, everyone wants our culture. Our culture is a commodity, that's why we have to be careful about who we let in – we don't want just anyone coming in and tokenising our culture, do we?'

What's your point? Māreikura wanted to ask, but she bit her tongue and waited for Whaea Terina to continue.

'So the process of choosing the classes is a spiritual experience,' she said. 'You think anyone can just walk through those gates? What, you think we just put a bunch of names together and throw them in a class and hope for the best like Pākehā schools do?' She shook her head.

'Our leadership is very, very clear. We choose based on ā-wairua. We karakia over all the names and if we feel that a name of a person is meant to have a spot, we move them based on that feeling. That's how the Māori world works. Everything has mauri. Everything has purpose. Everything has whakapapa. We leave the pesky politics out of it.'

'Okay, if this is true,' Māreikura said, 'you're saying that the wairua thinks a Pākehā should take a place over Māori to learn our own language?'

Whaea Terina shrugged. 'Some things we will never be able to understand. Some things logically might never make sense, when we follow ā-wairua.'

'Well, our people should be the priority, no exceptions,' Māreikura told her. 'If Māori are missing out on a spot here to learn our own language, that's not a wairua-based decision. That's the continuation of colonisation.'

She thought she might have said too much like she always did, accidentally offending people or hurting feelings, but Whaea Terina's expression didn't change.

'You applied last minute, Māreikura. And you got a place, straight away. Why do you think that is? Why were you placed before all of the names on the list?'

'I don't know.'

Whaea Terina's eyes wandered around as if they weren't alone in the room.

'Let me ask you another question, what's the definition of a tohu to you?'

'It's like a sign.'

'There's a word I'm looking for. What do Pākehā call it again? A miracle. That's it, that's what I believe tohu means. A miracle. And a tohunga is someone that recognises miracles in their life. They see the signs. They don't just look for miracles, they go where miracles are. Even if at first they aren't clear what the miracle is.'

Eru always talked about miracles. Everything was a miracle to him. Once, Māreikura brought over his favourite pie from the local bakery – mince and cheese – and he looked at her and said, 'Ma, I was praying about a pie this morning and here you are.' He was so ridiculous sometimes. Children are dying all over the world but it was a miracle he got his pie. Whaea Terina was a bit wīwī wāwā – not making sense – and it irritated her. If she wanted a church sermon, she would go to the Johnsons' house and ask Eru Senior for one.

'The point I'm trying to make, Māreikura, is that your tīpuna have a plan for you.'

'Or maybe they're all laughing at me.'

Whaea Terina's head fell back and she cackled.

'What?' Māreikura said. 'Feels like they're all having a laugh up there watching me fail, and then putting me with the most annoying girl I've ever met in my entire life. That's not cool and it's not my job to educate her.'

'No,' Whaea Terina said. 'It's not your job. And it's not her job to educate you either.'

'I don't want her to educate me,' Māreikura said. 'I have nothing to learn from her. I'm not interested in white saviourism and learning about the history of her colonising ancestors, and I don't have anything to learn from her poutokomanawa. What she gonna teach me? How her ancestors drank tea and colonised the land?'

Her voice was doing that thing where it was getting shaky and words were tumbling out of her mouth with no control.

'I know what you're trying to do, Whaea. You think if you put me with Chloe, it's going to change my mind about white people. You think if I get to know her, my heart will soften or something. It's not going to happen. I don't care about her or her colonising ancestors. I'm just here to get my language.'

'Interesting,' Whaea Terina said. 'You say you are here to get your language. Your reo is not lost. It's not something that you get or you come to collect, like a Pak'nSave click and collect or going through a McDonald's drive-thru.'

'You know what I mean, Whaea,' Māreikura said. 'I mean, to learn. I've come here to learn my language and that's all I am interested in.'

'You will find, Māreikura,' Whaea Terina said as she shut her laptop and stood up, 'language is the least of what you will get out of this place.'

CHAPTER NINE

There was once a time when Māori owned all the land, and now Māreikura's only asset was her cheap Japanese import car that she bought for $900 on Facebook Marketplace, with its old radio that only played one music station.

Jordana was sitting in the passenger seat on her phone googling Kat. 'Bro, she's hot,' Jordana said under her breath. 'She has a Wikipedia page and a TED Talk?'

Māreikura felt Jordana's eyes on her for far too long, as if asking, *How did you get her?*

'Maybe I should date wāhine,' Jordana said.

'Why don't you?'

'Because I like men,' Jordana made a gagging sound, 'and no amount of decolonising is going to change that.'

Jordana showed Māreikura her Tinder profile.

'Do you think the photos are too basic? I'm not matching with any hot Māori guys on here.'

Māreikura took her phone and scrolled down. A photo of Jordana doing a yoga pose in the sunset. Another one in front of Mission Bay in a bikini holding an acai bowl. A close up of her smiling. The last one was of her wearing denim shorts on a skateboard. Her bio read: *Looking for my Scotty Morrison*, followed by the two eyes emoji.

'Hmm,' Māreikura said. 'Maybe change it to Māori Scotty Morrison and put a photo of you by your marae or something. Might filter out the racists.'

'This girl, eh, thinks she's the dating tohunga 'cause she had some dates with a hot wahine.' Jordana put her phone back in her pocket. 'The psychic lady I see reckons I will meet my baby daddy this year. She said he's Māori, has long hair and plays the guitar.'

'Wow, that's very specific,' Māreikura said. 'I don't know any Māori guys who have long hair and play the guitar.'

'I can give you her number if you want. I found her on Instagram.'

'Why don't you date Alex? He seems nice.' Alex was a quiet guy in the class. He was taking a hiatus from law to study te reo.

'Yeah, too nice,' Jordana said, puffing her vape. 'Not enough trauma for me. What do trauma-less people even talk about? Oh God, I'm so toxic.'

She scanned Māreikura's face. 'I want a brown guy like your colour. Man bun, plays the guitar and we have little Māori babies running around on our pā in Taranaki. But he has to be Ngāti Porou.'

'Why?'

'All the good-looking boys are from Ngāti Porou.'

'That's debatable.'

'Have you even been to Gizzy?' Jordana sucked in her lips. 'They all have green eyes, surf and speak reo.'

'What's wrong with brown eyes?'

'Nothing,' Jordana said. 'It ain't that deep.'

'All the pretty girls are from Ngāi Tahu.'

'What about the guys?'

'I don't know. I don't look.'

Jordana sighed. 'All I want for Matariki is a Ngāti Porou boy who doesn't play up.'

'Is that what happened with your ex?'

'Yeah,' she said. 'I was looking through his phone one night when he was asleep and he wasn't just texting one girl, he was texting like ten and arranging to meet up with all of them, and then I woke him up and confronted him.'

'What he did say?'

'He was like, "Oh, sorry, I'm polyamorous and I just forgot to tell you."'

•

Every morning, school started with a karakia, a mihi and a waiata. It wasn't a religious prayer but a Māori prayer to enter into a different realm, another world. Sometimes the multitude of voices singing was so loud it felt like there were hundreds in the room and Māreikura began to think that maybe all of their ancestors were singing too. Māreikura did not know the meaning of the words she was singing and yet she felt the mauri, the life force, of each word, and she began to cry, thinking of her nana who was beaten for speaking the language, and now she was here, trying to learn for her, even though her nana didn't want her here.

Pāpā Sean was the principal of the school and he was considered royalty in te ao Māori. Yet he was quiet and meek, usually dressed in his infamous red Hunting & Fishing jacket and Red Band gumboots, often observing the students and never saying much. His voice boomed through the microphone, stern but crisp.

'You are at the bottom of the mountain and you haven't even started climbing yet.'

Māreikura heard someone say 'wow' and then a hushed silence fell over the room.

'The snowball is coming down the mountain and it will get bigger and bigger. Don't get left behind.'

Students were typing into their notes apps on their phones, the older students scribbling into their notebooks.

After the karakia, a man from each class would get up and give the whaikōrero or speech.

Troy was the first to speak. He paced towards the centre of the room, his shoulders upright. Something changed in Troy as soon as he started speaking. It was like he was a chief, standing on the marae, harnessing the powers of heaven. All the girls were eyeing him like he was prey, like they wanted to take him home and demolish him.

'It's hot in here.' Jordana was tugging the collar of her shirt.

Māreikura was about to tell Jordana to stop thirsting over Troy but then she saw a notification pop up on her phone.

From: erujohnson@ldsmail.net
Subject: 7

I miss you

CHAPTER TEN

Eru Junior and Māreikura had been best friends since they were five years old. Māreikura couldn't remember her first time meeting Eru but her nan liked to tell her the story. Fifteen years ago and three years after Philip's death, Glennis dressed Māreikura in her Ponsonby Primary uniform and walked her to school, like she normally did. She stopped by the mailbox to fix Māreikura's hair and then she heard a 'Kia ora!' and she looked up and a man was walking across the street towards them, two little ones clinging on to both of his hands.

'Hello.' Glennis eyed him up and down.

'I'm Eru. We just moved here from Tauranga.' He pointed behind him. 'We moved only this weekend, meaning to come around and introduce ourselves. Aroha mai, Whaea.' Then he bent over and kissed Glennis on the cheek.

'Who are you calling Whaea? I'm Glennis, and yes, I've seen you around. Was that you running late last night? Wearing those big headphones while you're running at night-time? How you gonna hear if a car comes when you got those things in your ears?'

Eru Senior just smiled. 'This is my girl Erana and my boy Eru Junior. Say hi to Whaea – sorry, Glennis.'

'Hi Whaea Glennis,' Eru and Erana said in unison.

Eru Senior knelt down until he was face to face with Māreikura. 'And what's your name?'

'Her name is Māreikura. She's shy around men,' Glennis said. 'She's not been around many men since my husband Philip died, you see.'

Māreikura peeked from behind Glennis's legs.

'Well, you're welcome to come over any time,' Eru Senior said. 'Nice to meet another Māori whānau.'

'Well, we're all the same colour at the end of the day,' Glennis said. 'Black, blue, yellow. It doesn't bother me.'

The following Sunday after church, there was a knock on the door and it was little Eru holding a yellow rose. A rose he stole from the property of Mr and Mrs Madison who lived on the other side of Glennis. Glennis knew this because she watched him pluck the rose from her kitchen window.

'This is for you, Whaea Glennis.' He grinned, handing her what was now a scrunched-up version of what was once a stunning rose. She didn't have the heart to scold him, though. When she took the rose from him, she noticed he had taken all the thorns off.

The next Sunday at the same time, Glennis watched Eru run out of the family truck, dart his way to the Madisons', scan the garden for roses, sneak a glance at the house then pluck one and run over to Glennis's door. She could hear him singing 'Popcorn popping on the apricot tree' while plucking the thorns off, and Glennis thought what a peculiar church song that was. The next time he showed up at her door, Glennis put a small chocolate in his little hand. His eyes popped up. 'Thank you, Whaea!' he squealed. Then his little feet ran across the footpath and back to his siblings. Glennis had a bit of spare time so she thought she might as well start making treats for little Eru. Sometimes it was banana muffins. One Sunday, it was double chocolate-chip cookies.

Now Eru Senior was the bishop of his local congregation and had been for the last eight years. It was a volunteer position – he wasn't paid but he was 'called' to the role. Being the bishop was like being the keeper of secrets, Eru Senior told Māreikura once. He knew everything about every person in his congregation and sometimes he wished he did not. He was no trained therapist; he owned and ran a security firm and he reminded his members of this constantly. Yet many of them looked to him like he was a messenger of God and everything that came out of his mouth was from God himself. Secrets make us sick, he told Māreikura. That's why we come to church. We're all injured or wounded in some way. No one knew about each other's problems. One of the biggest lies we tell ourselves is that we are alone, that we should suffer alone, that no one understands us. But that is not true. If each person could only know what the person next to them was going through, the world would be a different place.

His wife Eden was a professor of law at the University of Auckland. Māreikura started spending almost every day at the Johnsons' house. She went along to church on Sunday, to youth-group nights, to camps, and would help bake muffins for the service activities they held once a month. The Johnsons were always looking for opportunities to serve. 'When you are in the service of your fellow beings, you are in the service of God' was a quote stuck on their fridge door. Māreikura had memorised it because she was always looking for food every time she was at their house. The Johnsons were rich so they went on family vacations and skiing trips and Māreikura tagged along until they just always assumed she was coming.

The Johnsons seemed to have a certain ease about them. It was like they never had to worry. It's a rich-person thing that rich people don't know they have, where money doesn't dictate your life. Contentment. Peace. It would frustrate Māreikura seeing her nana live week to week, writing her budget in a little notebook even though she was sitting on a goldmine. Her house was worth over $3 million. Māreikura knew this because real estate agents would drop by every other week asking to buy or the mailbox would be overflowing with flyers informing them of the value of the property. 'Over my dead body,' her nana would mutter, tearing up the papers and going back inside her home that definitely would not pass the government's Healthy Homes evaluation because Māreikura and her nana were wearing long pants and extra layers to bed in the middle of summer. Her nana would rather have mince on toast and two-minute noodles for dinner and live in the poorest house on the richest street in Auckland than live in a nice home that didn't have mould on the walls and feel like Antarctica.

Eru was a year and a half younger than Māreikura but he acted like a hundred-year-old man trapped in a young person's body. When they were older, Māreikura told him this and he said, 'Well, yeah, my spirit is older than my body,' and he started teaching her about the plan of salvation and how we were all spirits before we came to Earth. He was so serious all the time and sometimes Māreikura wished he would just take a joke. *Live, laugh, love, Eru*, she would tease him and he would give her the same dorky smile – the famous Eru smile. He was also the most selfless person she knew and maybe there was a rule that you could either be really funny or really selfless and it was impossible for both to co-exist.

One time, they picked up a hitchhiker who stunk like bourbon and Māreikura lowkey thought he was going to murder them both. Eru insisted on driving him all the way to his home in Hamilton even though Hamilton was two hours out of the way. The whole way down, the guy talked about conspiracy theories and how Earth was flat, and Māreikura wanted to drop him back on the side of the road but Eru acted like it was the most interesting conversation he had ever heard, nodding and asking questions like, *True, bro, what makes you think that?*

After they dropped him off, the man gave Eru a hug and said, 'God bless you, bro,' and then stumbled inside.

'You don't believe all that stuff, do you?' Māreikura asked him and Eru told her, 'Sometimes people just want to be listened to,' and then they drove through the McDonald's drive-thru and Eru ordered two caramel sundaes.

Eru seemed to have a connection with lonely old ladies and even though Māreikura mocked him relentlessly for it, she secretly loved this side of him. He usually visited Mrs Baker, who was the kind of lady who sold black golliwog dolls on Facebook Marketplace despite everyone telling her they were racist. Māreikura was pretty sure Mrs Baker would break something just so Eru would come around and fix it. Māreikura would eat the concrete-hard cookies Mrs Baker made and think about how her house smelled like the moth smell that lingered in op shops and she wondered if that was a Pākehā smell and then she sniffed herself and wondered if Māori had their own smell too. Holding Mrs Baker's hands, fixing a flat tyre on the side of the road, driving a possible murderer home even though it was a two-hour detour – this wasn't Eru showing off; it was a natural part of him.

Another time, they went to visit a whaea from Eru's church – a short Māori lady named Janey who wore big, round glasses. Earlier that day, Eru had picked flowers from the side of the road. Whaea Janey opened the door and looked Eru up and down.

'How did you know it was my birthday?' And then she saw the flowers in his hands and burst into tears. 'And how did you know sunflowers are my favourite?'

She invited them in and they ate carrot cake and celebrated her seventy-ninth birthday.

'How did you remember her birthday?' Māreikura asked him when they got back in the car. 'You have the worst memory.'

'I didn't know it was her birthday.'

It freaked Māreikura out when he said that. But that was Eru. He always seemed to be at the right place at the right time. Even when Māreikura was feeling low, he would call at the exact right time. No one was allowed to just randomly call Māreikura – it was so intrusive to call and not text – but when he called, Māreikura always picked up.

Before he left on his mission, Eru told her they should go no contact.

'I just want to focus on doing the Lord's work,' he explained. 'I don't want to be distracted. I'll probably just write a mission email and send it to everyone,' he'd told her.

'What's a mission email?'

'You know, like a weekly update. Miracles I've seen on my mission, people that I've helped baptise. That kind of thing. It's what missionaries do.'

'Oh, well, don't send that to me,' Māreikura told him. 'I want to know all the important things, like what you ate that week and if you spoke to any Indigenous Hawaiians about land confiscation.'

He told her that he would get one hour on Mondays to email.

'I think we can call home now the rules have changed but it depends on my mission president and what his rules are,' he told her.

She started typing I miss you and I hope you are okay but then she closed the app and put her phone away. She missed him and was physically yearning for him, a pain she had not felt for a long time, but contacting him wouldn't help either of them. She closed her eyes and said in her head a prayer to a God she did not believe in.

God, if you're listening. Please look after Eru and keep him safe. Ngā mihi.

CHAPTER ELEVEN

Since being at school and learning te reo Māori, Māreikura had become obsessed with the phases of the moon and how her ancestors used to live. She imagined them walking barefoot on the whenua, living their best lives according to the moon and the environment and not imposed by the colonial construct of time.

'One day you'll get to the point where you don't have to check your Instagram for the moon phases,' Kat told her. 'You'll be so connected that it'll be exactly how our ancestors did it. You'll just be able to feel it.'

They were lying on the mattress out on the deck staring up at the sky. It was Whiro, the first day of the new moon and the darkest day of the moon calendar.

'I can't wait for that day,' Māreikura said. 'I'm scared of Whiro. It always brings up trauma. The moon makes me feel like I'm a werewolf and I can't control my emotions.'

'I used to be like that,' Kat said, stroking Māreikura's hand. 'But if you recognise Whiro as a time for new beginnings, it will change the way you see it. Whiro just magnifies emotions that are already there, so you need to do the work all year round. I try not to work on Whiro.'

'And you don't work when you have your menstrual cycle either?' Māreikura said.

'Nope.'

Kat was so incredible and smart and it made Māreikura fall even more in love with her. Māreikura decided she was in love with Kat the other morning when Māreikura woke up with blood-soaked undies. The blood had gone right through to Kat's Egyptian cotton, 1000-thread-count white sheets. Māreikura was embarrassed and kept saying sorry but Kat pulled the covers back and bent down and kissed the blood on the sheet.

'My queen is bleeding,' she said and Māreikura thought that was absolutely wild.

Kat told Māreikura about how periods have been colonised too and that our ancestors were never whakamā about bleeding.

'When wāhine used to get their period, it was a celebration,' Kat told her and then she gave her Ngāhuia Murphy's book *Te Awa Atua* to take home.

They spent every weekend together. Friday night they would watch a movie at home and Saturday morning they would go for a walk, and Kat would order a coconut chai latte and a hot chocolate for Māreikura and then go back to hers. Kat would make scrambled eggs and they would study Māori together. Māreikura had cue cards and Kat would test her on the new words she learnt that week – every time Māreikura got a word right, Kat gave her a kiss and sometimes more. Kat would tell her over and over again, 'Babe, your Māori is good. I'm so proud of you,' and it made Māreikura feel invincible, like she was smashing school even though she had the fluency of a three-year-old.

On Saturday night, they would go out for dinner or watch a play. Kat really liked theatre and afterwards she'd ask Māreikura what she thought and Māreikura would say, 'Yeah, good,' but usually it was boring – she didn't mind sitting through the boringness, though, because of the way it made Kat happy. Māreikura liked the way Kat looked over at her during the show, a look reserved only for her.

When they were out together, Māreikura felt like everyone was looking at them. Kat didn't seem to notice and maybe it was normal for her. Maybe when you're beautiful you're just accustomed to being looked at all the time. Māreikura liked the feeling of people staring at them, walking next to Kat, being in her presence. It made her feel important.

One morning, Māreikura woke up sweating under the duvet. She reached her arm out to Kat.

'I just had a dream.'

'What happened?'

'My great-nana,' Māreikura said. 'My nana's mum. She was talking to me in te reo but I couldn't understand her.'

Kat pulled her in for a hug.

'I think she was trying to tell me something. Like she seemed really worried but I couldn't understand her. She seemed disappointed in me. Maybe she was trying to warn me, I don't know. I didn't feel good when I saw her, Kat. I thought that when I dreamt about my great-nana it would be a beautiful feeling and she would be proud of me for being the first one in my family to learn my language and break all the intergenerational curses. But she was scary.'

'Are you sure it was your great-nana?'

'Yeah, it was her.' Māreikura said. 'I was always told she was a hard woman. But in the dream she was even hard to me, like I thought she would be happy to see me and give me a hug or something. But she just stared me down and told me to stop being a tangiweto.'

'A what?'

'A crybaby.'

Kat clasped her hand over her mouth.

'It's not funny.'

'I'm sorry but she came to visit you from the spirit world just to tell you to stop being a tangiweto?'

'Yeah, well, I've been waiting my whole life to talk to my great-nan and that's all she has to say.'

Kat reached over and stroked her hair. 'It's probably her way of telling you she loves you. You know what kuia are like.'

'I think she just wants me to go home.'

'Back up north?'

'Yeah, to my marae.'

'You should go.'

'I don't know how.'

'Well, the first thing you should do is get into your car and drive.'

Māreikura just looked at her.

'I get it,' Kat said. 'It's not that easy.'

It was silent, then Kat said, 'Māreikura, you never talk about your family.'

'It's late,' Māreikura said, reaching over to her phone and checking the time. 'You have sunrise yoga in the morning.'

'So? We're connecting. It's my love language.'

'Everything is your love language.'

'Why are you getting defensive?' Kat asked. 'You never talk about your mum. Just your nana. Where's your mum?'

'Where's yours?'

'You know where mine is. In Matakana, with my dad. I told you you're welcome to come up with me any time.'

'Yeah, and I said I will one day. School is just full-on at the moment.'

'Yup.' Kat sounded annoyed.

Māreikura moved the pillow and turned around to face the wall.

Sometimes she dreamt of her mother. *Māreikura, Māreikura.* She could hear her mother calling for her. But she knew it was just a dream because why would her mother cry for her when she didn't want her in the first place?

Māreikura put her hand on Kat's hand and pulled it over her waist so Kat was cuddling her from behind. They didn't say anything for a while and then Kat said, 'Pō marie,' but Māreikura didn't want to say goodnight yet. She didn't want to end this conversation. She wanted Kat to keep asking her questions, to keep prodding, to keep talking to her about her mother even though she didn't want to talk about her mother.

'See, this is why I hate Whiro,' she said finally. 'It always brings up stuff with my mum.'

Kat ran her finger over Māreikura's arm.

'Tell me everything.'

•

There was a recurring dream Māreikura had of her mother. She is on her mother's back, riding through the waves at Ocean Beach. Her mother was happiest in and near the water and, even though the ocean was wild, her mother knew how to tame her. That's what it felt like anyway. That her mum could harness the powers of the ocean. Her mum would ask, *Kua rite?* and Māreikura would squeal and wrap her arms even tighter around her mother's neck as they dived under the waves. Māreikura wished she could stay in the moana with her mum forever, where they were safe. But eventually they would have to go back to shore, back to the land, back where her mother was no longer free.

'How did she die?' Kat asked.

'Car accident,' Māreikura said. 'I was only a baby. I don't remember her. I don't remember any of it.'

CHAPTER TWELVE

'I have an idea,' Jordana said. 'I think it's why our tīpuna brought us together.'

'What?'

'We should start a podcast.'

'That's the worst idea I've ever heard,' Māreikura said.

'Bro, come on,' Jordana said. 'It would help others who are trying to learn te reo too.'

'Haven't you seen the memes about friends starting podcasts when they should just keep the conversation between themselves?' Māreikura asked. 'I don't want our faces to be on a meme.'

Māreikura hated podcasts. Maybe she wasn't listening to the right ones. Maybe she was too much of a hater. She cringed at the self-love podcasts and the white feminists talking about themselves for thirty minutes straight. Wasn't it all a bit self-serving? *I want to be famous and I've exhausted all other platforms so I'm going to record myself talking with my friends.* No one cares. Anyway, talking was a gift Māreikura did not have. She would listen to radio announcers fill in gaps between songs played and marvel at how they were able to just talk for a living. In conversations when Māreikura had nothing to say, she would simply say nothing. She did not fill in gaps or talk for the sake of talking. She also did not like being around people who did that. People who were uncomfortable with silence and talked nonstop should all hang out together in a place far, far away from Māreikura.

'C'mon', Jordana said. 'Being at kura is a safe space. Imagine if we could replicate it on a podcast? Help people feel like they belong. Do it for your tīpuna. You are your ancestors' wildest dreams.'

'It is not my ancestors' wildest dream for me to be at school learning my own language and then dealing with severe language trauma. And they definitely did not envision we'd make a podcast about it.'

'Okay then, it will be more of us sharing our journey.'

'I hate that word.'

'What word?'

'Journey. It was Eru's favourite word. *It's part of my journey, Ma. I'm not gay, please respect my journey. She's not racist. She's on her journey.*'

'Okay, well I won't say that word again. I have a name for it, though.'

'What?'

'*Wahine Chats.* And I was thinking our first topic could be: should Pākehā learn te reo Māori?'

•

Jordana had no shame and asked Whaea Terina if she would make an important announcement before class.

'Māreikura and I are going to start a podcast, e te whānau. It's called *Wahine Chats*,' she announced proudly. 'Out soon on Spotify, Apple Podcasts or wherever you get your podcasts.'

And then she invited everyone back to her house for drinks to celebrate the launch of their podcast that they had not even started yet. Jordana bought Pals and beers for everyone and chucked them in huge buckets of ice. She was generous like that – not asking anyone to bring anything except themselves. Māreikura felt bad for showing up empty-handed because it wasn't the Māori way but Jordana insisted. Māreikura told herself she was doing Jordana a favour anyway, now that her time was limited with school and a new girlfriend. Jordana was always asking on the group chat if anyone was keen to hang out. 'Who's hungry? My shout!' or 'Anyone wanna come over for a drink?' She was left on seen most of the time but Māreikura love-hearted her messages to show her some support. Jordana must be one of those psychopaths who get energy from being around other people. Māreikura was the polar opposite.

When Māreikura arrived, 'Kōrero Māori anake' was scribbled on a chalkboard outside Jordana's house. Fairy lights stretched along the footpath to the back of the house where there was a marquee and a karaoke machine set up. Tui, who was the best singer at kura and had been a finalist on *Australian Idol*, was singing The Temptations' 'My Girl' and Troy, Jason and Rāwiri were all pretending to be his back-up singers, and everyone was cracking up.

Jordana gave Māreikura a Pals and reminded her for the hundredth time they were sugar-free. After a few songs, Tui passed Māreikura the mic and Māreikura told him, 'I can't sing,' and he said, 'C'mon, oi, you're Māori,' and so she snatched the mic and went full-on Beyoncé. Everyone stopped what they were doing to watch her and then when she was done, she said, 'See? Told you I can't sing. Now can we please normalise Māori not being able to sing?' And everyone cracked up laughing. There was no way she would have done that sober so whatever was in that Pals was making her feel some kind of way and Māreikura liked the feeling.

Sarah was walking around with a platter of crackers and cheese.

'Where's your other half?' Māreikura asked.

'Who?' Sarah asked.

'Chloe. Where she at?'

'She's at home,' Sarah said. 'I think she has social anxiety.'

'You sure?' Māreikura said. 'She doesn't seem to have social anxiety in class. She's got all the confidence.'

Sarah said nothing. Māreikura told her she should sit down and have a drink and Sarah looked surprised for a moment and then said, 'Aw, that's okay, I don't drink.'

'Me neither,' Māreikura said. 'I'm decolonising my whakapapa.'

Sarah stared at the half-drunk Pals in her hand.

'Well, it was your ancestors who came over to my country and brought alcohol with them,' Māreikura said. 'They got my ancestors drunk and stole the land from under them.'

'Māreikura!' Troy said in a loud and shouty drunk voice. He was sitting down on one of the camping chairs next to Alex.

'Come sit, oi.' He patted the chair next to him. 'Want another drink?'

'Nah, I have one,' Māreikura said, holding up her Pals.

Troy looked quite handsome tonight, which annoyed Māreikura because she was in love with Kat. Māreikura sat down on the fold-out chair and her bum sunk low.

'Oi, I really liked your kōrero i tēnei rā. Your reo is getting real good. When you started talking about your tīpuna, it was like the heavens opened. Phew, pai rawa atu.'

'Thanks. You were all right too.'

'Just all right?'

'Kāore te kūmara e kōrero mō tōna ake reka,' Māreikura said, and then she blinked. 'Woah, did I just say that whakataukī off by heart without having to google it? Holy shit!'

She did a fist-pump and clinked her can of Pals against Troy's Corona bottle.

'My dreams are coming true.'

'Ooosh,' Troy whistled. 'The next Stacey Morrison.'

'What about you?' She punched his chest and noticed it was hard. 'Why are you even at kura? Your reo is so good. Are you just trying to find your wahine?'

Troy laughed and rubbed his chin. 'Nah. Girls don't like me.'

'Shut up. You know they do.'

'Like who?' He put his empty beer bottle on the ground. 'Well, I know it's not you. You hate me.'

'What? No, I don't.'

'Don't lie,' he said. 'I saw you giving me pūkana eyes on the first day.'

'Yeah, 'cause you were being whakahīhī.'

'You mean confident?'

'Nah, I mean whakahīhī.'

'Maybe you're just not used to seeing a Māori male with the confidence of a white man, Māreikura.' He tapped the side of his head with his finger. 'Maybe you need to decolonise your whakaaro.'

'Nah,' Māreikura said. 'You were just being whakahīhī.'

Troy raised his shoulders. 'Well, you can blame my mum for that. All four of them.'

'What does that mean?'

'My two mums divorced when I was eight and both got remarried to two women and so I was raised by four women.' He said it in a way that he had recited over and over.

'You were raised by four Māori women?'

'Well, kinda,' Troy said. 'Three of them are Māori but Māmā Leah has a ngākau Māori.'

He showed her a photo on his phone and Māreikura pointed to the woman in the middle and said she was lowkey hot and he said, 'Can you not? That's my mum.'

'Sorry,' Māreikura said. She looked closer. 'Wait, is that Jaz Te Huia? Is your mum Jaz Te Huia?' and Troy said, 'Yeah, do you know her?'

'Do I know her? You mean, the Jaz Te Huia who went on live TV and told the whole country our Prime Minister doesn't care about Māori? The Jaz Te Huia who led the occupation at that golf site? The Jaz Te Huia who wrote the book *Aroha Mutunga Kore: a protest to the colonial systems*?' Māreikura took a deep breath. 'I knew she had a son but I did not realise he was you.'

Troy was grinning like he was enjoying watching Māreikura get flustered over his mum.

'She loves you too.'

'What? Jaz Te Huia knows me?'

'Yeah, my little sister looks up to you. You're like her hero.'

'Okay, well, your little sister has really good taste,' Māreikura said. 'How old is she?'

'Okay, kūmara. She's like fifteen now? She's at Epsom Girls Grammar. She said that head girl speech you did changed her life or something. But yeah, when she found out you were in my class, she was jealous. Haha.' His eyes were glistening. 'I was like, calm down, sis. She ain't all that.'

He elbowed Māreikura playfully.

'Kāore te kūmara e kōrero mō tōna ake reka. Eh?'

Troy reminded her of Eru. They had the same boy smell and a similar smile, but they weren't alike at all. Troy was a lot more dominating and he also knew he was hot. Eru pretended like he didn't own a mirror and was unaware of his looks. Māreikura took another drink until her can was empty and then she crushed it with her fist.

'Woah, settle down, girl,' Troy said.

He changed his tone and asked her how she was finding kura, and she said it was hard and she had a lot of trauma but sometimes she couldn't tell if it was language trauma or just trauma in general, or maybe a combination of everything. Troy nodded like he could empathise and said he also struggled. He said he felt a lot of pressure having to do the whaikōrero every week and people kind of just expected him to do it.

'Well,' Māreikura said, 'maybe you should just pretend your reo is bad. I can give you lessons on that.'

He shook his head. 'Cut it out, oi, your reo is good. Don't be hard on yourself.' Then he said, 'Maybe they should let the wāhine speak so we can actually listen to some quality kōrero in the mornings.'

It surprised Māreikura when he said that. He asked her if she had listened to *Getting Better: A Year in the Life of a Māori Medical Student* by Emma Wehipeihana and Māreikura said, 'Nah,' and he said she should because it talked about the disparities of Māori in health and that's the reason he was doing medicine. He told Māreikura he actually hated blood and fainted in front of everyone when he was eight years old and got the flu shot, but he wanted to give back to his people so being a doctor was his way of doing that but the hardest part was getting over his phobia first.

Māreikura told him she had a phobia of Edward Scissorhands and Troy looked confused and asked, 'Do you mean Johnny?' and

Māreikura said, 'Yeah, but not Johnny, I mean his character, you know, with the scissor hands.' And then Troy made scissors with his hands and pretended to chop Māreikura's hair and she screamed, 'Don't you dare or I'll stab you and make you bleed.'

'Okay, okay,' he said, putting his hands up in the air. He was looking at Māreikura with flirty eyes now but she wasn't sure if she was imagining it or not.

'I have a girlfriend,' Māreikura blurted out.

Troy shuffled in his seat. 'Who?'

'Kat Harrison. She's the CEO of the tech company Kaha. Do you know her?'

'Nah, show me a photo.'

So Māreikura showed him Kat's Instagram and he whistled and said, 'How old is she? I'm pretty sure she's friends with my mum.'

'Like thirty-two?' Māreikura said. 'She knows all the wāhine rongonui.' She put her phone away. 'I still can't believe you grew up with four wāhine. You're so lucky.'

Troy told her that when he was seventeen, he worked a part-time job in construction and couldn't believe how the men spoke about women, and he came home crying to his mums and they sat him down and told him that unfortunately this was what the world was like. Then they taught him about how he had to be a disabler and not an enabler and call other men out because it wasn't a woman's job to do that.

'I have tried to speak to Pāpā Sean about changing the tikanga so wāhine can speak,' Troy told her. 'But he's set on his own iwi and their ways, it's almost impossible. I'll keep trying. Tikanga should be adaptable.'

Lucy, a pretty Māori girl in their class from Kāi Tahu, stumbled over and waved her phone in their faces. 'It's a video,' she screeched.

While she was videoing, a police helicopter hovered over and Troy said, 'Ah, I hope they find the dangerous white woman they're looking for.'

Māreikura snorted a little too loudly and everyone at the table looked at her. Lucy started singing a waiata and so everyone stood up and they all put their arms around each other's shoulders and sang it together: 'E kore au e ngaro' – 'I am not lost.' And Māreikura declared her love for everyone, because in that moment she loved every single one of them.

CHAPTER THIRTEEN

They were at Muriwai Beach – Kat's favourite place – and had picked up a salad from Ripe to have dinner and watch the sunset. They were walking along the beach holding hands when Māreikura saw the worst possible person imaginable walking towards them. Kayla Tairua. Māreikura tried to pretend she didn't see her but Kayla was already running over.

'Māreikura, oh my gosh, girl, you look so good,' she exclaimed. 'And I love that colour on you.' She pinched Māreikura's green shirt.

'Welcome home,' Māreikura said in a tone that was not welcoming at all. 'How long have you been back?

'Aw, thank you! I've only been back two weeks,' Kayla said. 'I've missed the New Zealand air so much! It's so good.'

She had an accent. An American accent. How do you get an American accent in only eighteen months?

'Oh, sorry! This is my mum, Kelly,' she said, glancing at the woman next to her, a middle-aged, slightly rounder version of Kayla.

'This is Māreikura, Mum. You know Eru? This is his friend.'

Best friend, Māreikura wanted to correct her, but then Kat coughed and Māreikura found her voice.

'This is Kat,' she said.

'Her girlfriend,' Kat said.

A flicker of surprise came over Kayla's face. It was only for a split second and anyone could have missed it if you weren't looking for it.

'Cute!' Kayla clapped her hands. 'How long have you two been together?'

'Like two months?' Māreikura looked at Kat and Kat nodded and said, 'Yeah, two months. Two and a half? Feels like forever, though, eh, babe?'

'Oh, cute,' Kayla said. 'Are you still doing law? I remember the last time we spoke you had a law scholarship?'

'Nah, not anymore. I'm at kura now learning te reo Māori.'

'Oh, ki hea? Pai rawa atu, e hoa.'

'You speak Māori?' Of course she did.

'Āe.' She smiled. 'I went to a kura kaupapa when I was little. So, where are you from, Kat?'

Kat started talking about her business and Māreikura zoned out, studying Kayla's face in a way while trying not to be obvious about it. Eru thought Kayla was pretty. Māreikura knew this because Eru said all the pretty girls went to the Salt Lake City Temple Square Mission and that's where Kayla had gone. Eru never called girls pretty; he always said something about their personality or how they were smart or kind-hearted or had a nice spirit, or were – as he liked to call Māreikura – brave. But he called Kayla pretty. Once Eru told her he 10 per cent liked girls and 90 per cent liked boys. What does that even mean? she wanted to ask him. Then she wondered if she was in the 10 per cent. Now all Māreikura could think was how Kayla Tairua was in the 10 per cent club of women he was attracted to. It made perfect sense that Eru would end up marrying her. She believed in God and was chirpy and wore long floral dresses and had acne-free skin and she was always so happy, like a real-life Disney character. It drove Māreikura crazy – how could someone be so happy and bubbly all the time? She was everything Māreikura was not.

'Have you heard from Eru?' Kayla asked.

'Who's Eru?' Kat asked.

'Um, not really,' Māreikura said, ignoring Kat's question.

'Oh, I'll tell him you say hi. We've been emailing a bit.'

'Cool.'

'Sounds like he's been having some amazing spiritual experiences over there, eh. He's always been really spiritual. I always made this joke that there are Christians and then there was Eru. He's the type of Christian that will get transported to heaven, eh, Mum? A lift straight up to Jesus while we're out here still on the sixth floor climbing the stairs.'

Kayla cracked up but Māreikura didn't laugh. She didn't get the joke.

Then Kat asked, 'Are Mormons Christian?' and Māreikura looked at her and Kat said, 'What? I'm curious.'

Kayla's smile widened. 'Well, of course! We believe in Christ, we are Christians.'

'Yeah, but what's the difference between you and Christians? Why do you call yourself Mormons?'

'Because,' Māreikura said, 'Mormons have their own book. Mormon is actually the name of the prophet in the Book of Mormon. But Mormon is not the name of the church.'

'What's the name of the church then?'

'The Church of Jesus Christ of Latter-day Saints,' Māreikura, Kayla and Kayla's mum said all at the same time.

Kat said, 'Woah, you all recited that like a cult.'

'Kat,' Māreikura said in a low tone.

'If you want to know more, I'll be happy to answer any questions,' Kayla said. 'Although Māreikura probably knows just as much as me.'

'Are you a Mormon, babe?' Kat asked with a slight smirk. 'I never would have guessed.'

'Not yet, eh.' Kayla laughed, elbowing Māreikura.

'I'm not but Eru is.'

'Who's Eru?' Kat asked for the second time.

Kayla stared at Māreikura, waiting for her to answer, and when she didn't, Kayla said, 'He's our friend from church.'

'Are Mormons the ones who don't celebrate birthdays?' Kat asked.

'Nah, that's Jehovah's Witnesses,' Māreikura answered.

'Oh. Are they the ones who don't give blood?'

'Um, I think that's Seventh-day Adventists.'

Kayla and her mum were standing there awkwardly watching them talk about religion that neither Māreikura nor Kat believed in, so Māreikura said, 'Well, I better let you both get back to your walk.'

'Ka pai kōrua, kia pai te hīkoi,' Kayla said, giving Māreikura and Kat a tight hug. 'Let me know if you need anything! You have my number, eh?'

'Yup,' Māreikura said. She did not have Kayla's number.

'She seems nice,' Kat said as they walked away.

'She's all right.'

'So how do you know her again?'

'Through Eru.'

'And Eru is?'

'A friend from school.'

She paused and then said casually, 'He's actually on his mission now in Hawai'i,' as if it hadn't been on her mind every single day, as if Eru going to Hawai'i wasn't the most devastating day of her life.

'Oh, wow,' was all Kat said, and she didn't bring it up again.

•

It's a Mormon thing, Māreikura had learnt, to get married young and have lots of kids. You go on a mission and have a companion and then when you come home, your next mission is to get married, except this time you get to choose your companion. 'What if you don't get married?' Māreikura had asked, and Eru had said he had strong faith that the Lord would provide. 'My patriarchal blessing says I will marry a woman,' he told her. Māreikura did not really understand what a patriarchal blessing was. All she knew was that it was a piece of paper folded in Eru's scriptures that told him how his life would end up. 'Is it like a fortune blessing?' she asked him once. He'd looked offended. He told her it was like a letter from God. Every area of the church had a Stake Patriarch who was ordained or called by God to give each member of the church a blessing. Māreikura was not allowed to read it because it was sacred.

'I trust God,' he'd said. 'I know there's a chance. Even though I have same-sex attraction.'

'Why do you call it same-sex attraction? Just say you're gay.'

'Ma, please respect my journey.'

'Do you really want to go on a mission?

'There are so many people who want to know God but have never had the chance.'

'What, your colonised God?'

Eru flinched.

'Sorry,' Māreikura said, though she was not sorry at all.

'I've had experiences with God,' Eru said. 'I've seen him in my family. I've seen him in my life. Once you know, you know. Once you experience something, you know. You can't unknow something. Everything after that – you are just betraying and lying to yourself.'

'You can have both', Māreikura said. 'You can believe in God and be gay.'

And you don't have to shove your beliefs down everyone's throat, she wanted to say to him. Especially in Hawai'i. They don't need your saviourism.

Once, Eru told her he would never be able to forgive himself if he broke his temple covenants.

'I would be separated from my family for time and all eternity,' he told her.

'What? Your family would disown you?'

'I mean in heaven. We won't be sealed together.'

'I don't get it.'

'My family are sealed in the temple for time and all eternity, for generations. If I break it, then I break it for generations before me. We will only be together for this life but not for eternity.'

'How do you break covenants?'

'Not living up to God's standards.'

'Eru, you're the most holy person I know.'

He didn't answer, though she knew what he was thinking. The most holy person except for the fact he was gay. That's what made her angry. That's what made her want to storm down to all the churches, kick down the front doors and rescue all the queer people who had been indoctrinated and told they weren't allowed to be themselves. It's what made her protective of her best friend. She didn't want him going on a mission, not just because she didn't agree with the colonising message, but because she couldn't be there to protect him. To keep him safe. She knew when he got anxiety. She could feel Eru tense up when Eru Senior started teaching the family proclamation where the first paragraph stated that marriage between men and women is ordained of God. Eru went to the bathroom and when he came out, his eyes were red and he told everyone he had hayfever so Eden handed him some medicine from the cupboard.

'Look at my parents,' Eru used to say, using Eden and Eru Senior as the Mormon trophy of marriage success. They were married a month after Eru Senior came home from his mission. Eden grew up in the same ward as him but she was never interested because he was 'immature', but then he went on a two-year mission.

'He left as a boy and came back as a man,' she would tell Māreikura. 'A mission does that to you. It changes you. Wait until you see when Eru Junior gets home.'

Now Eru Senior and Eden were in their forties and both looked like they were in their thirties. When Eru Senior went on his morning run, all the Ponsonby mums perved at him. Once, Māreikura was getting her hair cut when Eru Senior popped his head in the door and Māreikura suddenly saw dimples on both the hairdresser's cheeks she didn't see before. 'Girl, is that your dad? He single?' She raised her eyebrows and then did this annoying little giggle. 'Nah, but what makes you think you have a chance?' Māreikura asked. The hairdresser stopped giggling and then Māreikura tried to be nice to her in case she gave her a crooked haircut but she kept giving Māreikura sour looks in the mirror and yanking her head when she was cutting her hair, so Māreikura never went back.

Māreikura would marry Eru if he asked her. Then she could be in the Johnson family forever and Eru Senior and Eden would become her parents. Erana would be her big sister. Even though they told her she was part of the family, this would seal the deal. She would get to experience what almost everyone else in the world got to experience. A family. She wanted Eru Junior to look at her like Eru Senior looked at Eden, like she was the most beautiful woman he had ever seen. And sometimes there were glimpses of it, when she would catch Eru looking at her, a crinkle in his forehead like he was buried deep in thought, like he loved her.

CHAPTER FOURTEEN

Chloe Simpson was at Māreikura's front door in a black chequered dress and pointy, white, lace-up shoes. Her shoes looked like they were her grandma's but they were probably from that expensive vintage op shop on Ponsonby Road Māreikura walked past and never bothered going into because it annoyed her that rich white liberals were trying to make 'op-shopping' cool when poor people had no choice.

Chloe pulled out a loaf of warm rēwena bread wrapped in a tea towel from her bag and handed it to Māreikura.

'Who made it?' Māreikura asked her suspiciously and Chloe, with a tiny smirk on her face, said, 'Māku te mahi.'

Chloe bent over and untied her laces carefully. Māreikura never understood why people did that; why not just kick your shoes off? It saved time.

'Where did you park your car?' Māreikura asked. 'There's a sixty-minute time limit around here.'

'I don't drive.'

'Are you a climate justice warrior?'

'No, actually,' Chloe said. 'I'm blind in one eye.'

She slipped her shoes off and placed them neatly on the porch. Māreikura almost felt bad but Chloe still had a dumb little smirk on her face.

'Make sure you call my nana Whaea,' Māreikura told her. 'She likes being called that.'

'Is that rēwena?' Glennis was standing at the door now, eyeing up the bread in Māreikura's hand. 'Can smell it from here.'

'Āe,' Chloe said. She leaned forward and gave Glennis a kiss on the cheek. 'I'm Chloe. Nice to meet you, Whaea.'

'Whaea?' She looked at Chloe, disgusted. 'I'm not your whaea, I'm just Glennis.'

'Oh, aroha mai, Glennis.' She snuck a dirty look at Māreikura. 'Well, thank you so much for this opportunity. Māreikura has told me so much about you and I'm looking forward to hearing more about your story.'

'Huh?' Glennis squinted at Chloe and then glanced at Māreikura. 'What she on about, girl?'

'Oh, yeah, Nan, I forgot to tell you,' Māreikura said, ignoring Chloe's side glare. 'It's for an assignment for school, Nana. Chloe just wants to ask you questions. Is that okay?'

'You make that rēwena, girl?' Glennis pointed to the bread, ignoring Māreikura's question.

'Āe,' Chloe said.

'Far out. How'd you know how to make that?'

'A whānau taught me. The Ripeka whānau, do you know them? They're from Ngāpuhi.'

'Hmm,' Glennis said.

'You have to try it,' Chloe said. 'He tino reka.'

'All right then, hurry up. Come on in, make it quick. My show starts in twenty minutes.'

Glennis motioned for Chloe to sit down on the couch and Māreikura took the bread and placed it on the chopping board. She cut it up in slices and smothered butter on.

Chloe pointed to the framed black-and-white photo of a younger Glennis in a ball gown. 'Wow, is that you, Glennis?'

'Yes, that's me,' Glennis said, as if she got asked the question a lot. 'Back in my modelling days.' She cackled as Māreikura placed the bread in front of them on the small table in the lounge. 'I know what you're going to say, that I should have been Miss New Zealand, and, well, I did think about applying back then, but I just never got around to it.'

Glennis took a bite of the rēwena bread. 'Hmm.' Her hand lazily covered her mouth while she chewed. 'This good, girl. Good.' She swallowed. 'Where'd you say you got this from again?'

'The bug? The Ripeka whānau. It's been in their whānau for generations. You know them? They're from the Hokianga.'

'No.' She studied Chloe suspiciously. 'Now what you want from me, eh? Why you trying to sweeten me up?'

'You know how it is, Nana,' Māreikura called out from the kitchen. 'First they learn our language, then they learn how to make our favourite kai. Then when we're not looking, they take our land.'

'Māreikura,' Glennis said in a low tone. 'Cut that out.'

Māreikura took a bite of the rēwena.

Chloe cleared her throat. 'I heard rēwena is your favourite, Glennis,' she said. 'Do you get to make it often?'

'No,' Glennis said. 'I don't make it anymore, ever since my so-called sister took our whānau bug and didn't share it. I don't talk to her now so what's the point? I was going to make my own bug, but I thought, stuff it. If I can't have our bug from my mum, what's the point?'

'Uh huh,' Chloe said. 'So why don't you talk to your sister?'

'Excuse me?'

'Sorry,' Chloe quickly said. 'You just said you don't talk to your sister. I was just wondering why you didn't.' She paused. 'You don't have to answer.'

'I'll be in my room if you need me,' Māreikura said, holding her plate with two pieces of rēwena. 'That's if I don't die from being poisoned.'

'Gee,' Glennis said after Māreikura shut the door. 'You let her talk to you like that, do you?' She shook her head. 'And that's why that girl doesn't have many friends.'

'Really?' Chloe asked. 'She seems really popular. Everyone loves her at kura.'

'Well, just between you and me,' Glennis said, 'she's only ever had one friend and that's that boy. Has she told you about him yet?'

'No,' Chloe said with a huge smile on her face. 'Who's this boy then?'

'Well,' Glennis said, lowering her voice, 'I think they had a bit of a riff. Not that it's any of my business. Eru was his name, yeah. Handsome boy too. Mormon. The family live just across the road in that big house. The dad's the pastor, ah, bishop, the mum's a university teacher, nice family. Bit too squeaky clean for me.' She screwed her nose up. 'Don't like how the parents have all these rules. When Eru turned eighteen, I asked him if he wanted a beer and he said no. What eighteen-year-old boy would refuse a beer? You see, that's why I don't agree with those rules. So on his way out, I slipped a beer into his bag. Why not? And I said to him, "Look, it's between you and your God if you have a drink of that tonight, but I won't be telling anyone. It will be our little secret."' She sniffled with laughter. 'Nice boy, he was. He used to always come over for a chat. He would bring me over rēwena too. Yours is better, though. Oh.'

She stopped suddenly, remembering there was rēwena bread on the table, and leaned forward and grabbed a piece, then took a bite. 'Hmm, yes, yours is better. Where was I? Oh yeah, that's right. So the boy was always Māreikura's only friend. They did everything together. I think that girl finds it hard to make new friends. Too much in her head, you see. Always going off to these protest things and getting angry. I think she'll grow out of it. That rebellion stage. I did that in my twenties too, but eventually you realise it's easier to just settle down and not get caught up in the hoo-ha. Anyway, I saw her kissing a girl the other day too – you know anything about that? Not that I was watching, but I just happened to pull the curtain and I saw her with a girl in a nice-looking Jeep. I was thinking maybe it was you, but she looked a bit older, now that I think about it. Not as pale as you and a bit taller, yeah. Anyway, don't know if she's gay or if it's part of her rebellious stage. You know anything about that?'

'Oh, I don't know, sorry, Glennis. Have you asked her?'

Glennis waved her hand. 'The way I see it, if she wants to tell me, that's up to her. She knows where I am. It's not like I go anywhere.' She laughed but it was a sad laugh. 'She doesn't talk to me much. Anyway, it's nice she found you, Claire. She needs a good friend. She's had a tough life, that girl.'

'Oh, it's Chloe.'

'Huh?'

'Oh, um, my name's Chloe.'

'Chloe, sorry.' She examined Chloe as if seeing her for the first time. 'Gee, you're skinny and too pale. Eat some bread. You want a drink? I should have asked you earlier.'

'No, I'm okay, I'm okay,' Chloe said. 'Just happy listening to you, Glennis. Is it okay if I record this, I forgot to ask?'

'And where is this going?'

'For our presentation at the end of the year at graduation.'

'Oh, okay,' she said. 'And why do they wanna know about me?'

'Because you're Māreikura's poutokomanawa.'

From the confused look on Glennis's face, it was obvious she had no clue what Chloe was talking about.

'For our assignment, we have to choose our poutokomanawa – do you know what that is?' Chloe felt guilty for having to ask a Māori woman in her sixties if she knew the meaning of a Māori word. A language that was her birthright.

'I know what it means,' Glennis said. 'I used to speak Māori. Now, I didn't know she chose me. You sure about that?'

'Yes, Glennis, that's why I'm here.' Chloe said.

Glennis glanced at the clock. 'Well, I suppose I've missed my show now but that's okay. I can catch up another time. What do you want to know then?'

Chloe pointed to a picture, a black-and-white photo of Glennis holding a baby in her hands. 'Is that your daughter?'

'Yes,' Glennis said.

'Should we start there then?'

•

Māreikura came out of her room to a sight she hadn't ever seen before, a sight that filled her with envy. She didn't recognise the feeling at first because she had never really felt it before when it came to her nana. Her nana was sobbing into Chloe's arms, her hands pressed against Chloe's back.

'It's okay, kei te pai koe,' Chloe said softly.

Māreikura cleared her throat and they both looked up. Glennis let go of Chloe and straightened up, like she had just been caught out.

'All good, Nan?'

'Yes,' she said. 'Gee, was getting carried away there.' Her voice was muffled from behind a tissue.

'Okay, well, are you done? It's getting late.'

'Yeah.' Chloe got to her feet. 'Thank you so much, Glennis. Tēnei te mihi ki a koe. Thank you for sharing your story with me. Nōku te hōnore. I am honoured.'

Glennis nodded. 'You come over any time, you hear?' Then she turned to Māreikura. 'Drop Chloe off home, would you?'

Before Māreikura could make up an excuse, Chloe said, 'It's okay, I was just about to call an Uber.'

'Uber? Don't be silly, girl, Māreikura will take you. Hurry up, girl.'

•

They were both sitting in Māreikura's car now. Before Māreikura started the engine, she turned to Chloe. 'I changed my mind. I don't want you to do my nana for our whakapuaki. I'm going to get you to interview someone else.'

'Umm . . . okay?' Chloe sounded confused.

Māreikura started driving, then Chloe asked, 'Why?'

'Because,' Māreikura said.

'Māreikura,' Chloe said, 'your nana is so beautiful. You should ask her more about her life. You could write a book about her experiences – they are really powerful.'

'Oh, here we go,' Māreikura said. 'Of course you jump straight to thinking about writing a book – profiting off my nana's trauma. Why am I not surprised?'

'It's not what I meant.' Chloe sighed. 'Don't worry.'

The silence was awkward so Māreikura put on Mai FM. A misogynistic rap song was playing and Māreikura hated listening to that sort of music but she left it on; she would rather listen to it than have to talk to Chloe.

'Who's Eru?'

Chloe saw Māreikura's face switch and she said, 'Oh, sorry. Your nan mentioned him. Just wondering if he's an old boyfriend or something.'

Māreikura didn't say anything for a while, letting the music fill the silence, then she turned to Chloe.

'Are you autistic?'

'What?' Chloe folded her arms to her chest. 'Why would you even say that?'

'Because you blurt things out without thinking and ask questions that you have no business asking and I'm sure that's what people with autism do. Have you looked up the symptoms?'

'Of what?'

'Autism.'

'I don't have autism.'

'You should ask your doctor about it.'

It was quiet for a moment and then Chloe said, 'You can just drop me off here.'

'It's dark.'

'I'm fine.'

She didn't sound like she was fine. The car had barely stopped moving at the traffic lights before Chloe reached for the lock as if she was being kidnapped. She jumped out and before she shut the door, she turned and looked back at Māreikura.

'No offence, Māreikura, but you can be a bitch sometimes,' and then she slammed the door.

CHAPTER FIFTEEN

Jordana rummaged in her pocket for her vape. She was always looking for her vape when she was nervous, always misplacing it even though it was usually right in front of her or somewhere obvious. They were at her apartment waiting for Jordana's Tinder boyfriend to pick her up. Māreikura took one look at his Tinder profile and decided she didn't like him. Too many gym videos and selfies. She didn't like his name either. It was a douchy sounding name. Chris.

'Does he read?' Māreikura asked and Jordana said she saw a book on his night stand.

'What book?'

'*The Seven Habits of Highly Effective People*.'

'That doesn't count,' Māreikura told her. 'It's probably there for decoration. Like your surfboard.'

Jordana told her to shut up and that at least he could speak te reo Māori.

He was late. Ten minutes late. It was 6.10 p.m. Jordana told her it's because he had never been to her apartment; she always went to his. 'Does he not have Google Maps?' Māreikura asked and Jordana hit her on the back of her head and sculled back the rest of the glass of Pinot in her hand.

'Chloe called me a bitch yesterday.'

Jordana started cackling and Māreikura elbowed her.

'What did you say to her?'

'I asked her if she was autistic.'

'Bro, what the hell? You don't just ask a person that. You're not a doctor.'

'I never said autism was a bad thing,' Māreikura said. 'But she just says anything that comes to her mind, like blurts it out with no filter.'

'Yeah, well, so do you. Anyway, you need to sort your raru out with Chloe. It's giving me bad vibes and I ain't here for it.'

'She asked me about Eru.'

'Ohhhhhhh,' Jordana said. 'Your ex. Why didn't you say that at the beginning? Touchy subject. I know the feels.'

'He's not my ex.'

'Mm hmm.' Jordana said, clearly not believing her. 'So you don't think about him at all?'

Māreikura looked out the window and saw that Jordana's Tinder date was here. Māreikura didn't like to stereotype but it was very hard not to stereotype the man getting out of his white BMW. He was exactly what his Tinder profile suggested. Muscly, broad shoulders, nice teeth and an air of arrogance about him.

'Isn't he cold?'

Jordana, who was in the kitchen probably refilling her wineglass, ran to the window. Māreikura heard her suck in her breath.

'He's so hot.'

Their faces were against the window watching Chris stupidly looking for the front door even though it was right in front of him.

Jordana was in a state of hypnosis and Māreikura wondered how women found this type of guy attractive. It was one of those life mysteries she could never understand. There was a knock on the door and then Jordana brushed her hand through her hair, smoothed her top and opened the door.

'Hey,' Jordana said, in a weird voice Māreikura hadn't heard before. 'Come in. Do you want a drink? I've got beer in the fridge.'

'And Pals,' Māreikura said. 'It's zero per cent sugar.'

'Ka pai, I'll just have water.' Chris was standing in front of her. 'Kia ora, I'm Chris.'

'I'm Māreikura.'

He kissed her on the cheek and Māreikura could smell his cologne. It was too much. She coughed and he let go.

'You surf?' He pointed behind her at the surfboard.

'Jordana does.'

'Impressive.'

'Thanks,' Jordana called from the kitchen. 'I'm still learning. Māreikura, want a drink?'

'I'm decolonising my—'

'I mean non-alcoholic.'

'Just water, please.'

Jordana came out of the kitchen holding a glass of water in each hand.

'You know alcohol is bad, eh?' Chris asked her like he was asking a child if they knew lollies were bad for your teeth. 'Alcohol in Māori is waipiro. It directly translates to dirty water.'

'Āe,' Jordana said, handing him a glass. 'That's why I've started drinking less. I've been thinking of giving up for a while.'

Māreikura snorted and wanted to ask, since when? But she kept her mouth shut. She couldn't understand why Jordana was entertaining such a douche. She didn't like the way Chris was talking to her friend, like she was less than him.

Chris nodded at Māreikura. 'You don't drink?'

'It's a form of protest,' Māreikura said. 'I hate what it's done to Māori families and communities. It's been destroying us for years but now suddenly it's a trend to not drink because white people are saying zero per cent alcohol is cool, yet we've been screaming out for help for years.'

He gave her a weird look. They stood there not saying anything and then Māreikura asked, 'Aren't you cold?'

He was in a singlet and it was eleven degrees outside. He smoothed his hand over his left bicep.

'Nah, sis, I'm like a hot-water bottle. I don't get cold.' He leaned towards Māreikura. 'See, feel.'

She touched his arm. 'Wow,' she said. 'What a talent.'

Māreikura wanted him to leave already. She didn't like his energy. He seemed to look through her and not at her. He was the opposite of Eru.

'Should we head out then?' Jordana came out of the kitchen.

'Yeah,' Chris said. 'You wanna come, sis?'

'Nah, I'm good.'

They left and then Māreikura pulled out her phone. She was thinking about Eru. Being around someone like Chris made her miss Eru. She opened her email app.

To: erujohnson@ldsmail.net

Subject: 8

I miss you too.

CHAPTER SIXTEEN

Whaea Terina thought it would be a great idea to do a 'surprise test'.

'It's just an indication to see where you're all at,' she said. 'Kaua e āwangawanga. Don't be worried.'

She handed out the papers and Māreikura flipped through the pages. All the questions were in te reo Māori. She was sitting next to Koro Ian who looked like he was about to pass out. If Māreikura didn't know any of the questions, he definitely didn't. Māreikura made a lazy attempt at answering, knowing that the results were not an indication of her worth. It was the mantra she repeated to herself in her head over and over again.

'Remember whānau,' Whaea Terina said. 'There's no fail. It's just an indication of where you're at so if you might need some help, I'm here. Or someone who maybe got a higher score is there to help you. He waka eke noa. We're all in the same boat.'

We are not in the same boat, Māreikura wanted to scream.

Afterwards, they passed around the test papers and Whaea Terina read out the answers. Māreikura ended up with Lucy's paper. Jordana got Sarah's. As Whaea Terina read out the answers, Māreikura saw that Sarah got almost every answer correct. Lucy got over half right. Whaea Terina asked everyone to share their score. Māreikura failed. Chloe only got one question wrong.

And then as each person read out another's score, it dawned on Māreikura.

All the Pākehā in the class got the highest scores.

She said it under her breath but Jordana heard her and said, 'Damn, you're right.'

When it was Māreikura's turn, she got to her feet and read out Lucy's score, then before she sat down, she said, 'All the Pākehā got the high scores'.

'Kia ora, Māreikura,' Whaea Terina said softly.

'Don't you see how wrong that is?' Māreikura asked. 'Tell me how it's fair Pākehā have better te reo Māori than Māori?'

'So do you think it's better if we just don't learn te reo?' a small voice asked from the back of the class. Chloe. Of course it was Chloe. Who else would it be?

'I'm just asking,' Chloe said quickly, scanning the eyes of everyone staring at her.

'Understand your privilege,' Māreikura said, her voice trembling. 'You studying my language is an entirely different experience from me studying my language. You have no connection to it. But you will get praised for being able to speak a little bit of te reo because it makes you special. For the majority of Māori, we're ostracised for not being able to speak it.'

'I understand, but what is better? What do you want us to do?'

'You being here is taking up a Māori person's place. Did you know te reo Māori classes are booked out everywhere so my own people can't even learn their own language if they wanted to?'

'I didn't know that,' Chloe said quietly. She was fidgeting with a little toy cube in her hands.

'If I'm spending all my time decolonising, then it's white people's jobs to break down oppression in their family history.'

'That's what I'm – we—' she said, pointing to Sarah, 'are trying to do.'

'Do it more quietly.'

'Sorry.' She put the cube in her pocket.

'No, I mean breaking down oppression. You don't need to be so loud in class, so opinionated. You can study te reo Māori but don't even pretend to have the ability to understand, because you will never understand what it's like to be Māori. How can you advocate for change when you are fundamentally part of the problem?'

No one else said anything. Māreikura wished someone else would speak up and it wasn't always her. But everyone was looking at her like there was something wrong with her, like she should just shut up.

Māreikura shoved her paper in her bag and walked out of the classroom. She was at the car park when she heard a voice.

'Māreikura, hold up.'

She turned around to see Troy running towards her.

'Don't look at me like that.'

He was squinting at her, his hand on his forehead blocking the sun. 'Like what?'

'Like I'm crazy.'

'I don't think you're crazy. I'm just worried about you.'

'Why? 'Cause I just had a mental breakdown in front of the class?'

He shook his head. 'You need to look after yourself. Ko te mea nui, nē?'

'It's easy for you to say. Your reo is good. Do you not have trauma or something? What's wrong with you?'

Troy scrunched up his face and it made Māreikura even more angry because he was still handsome even with a wrinkly forehead.

'Nothing is wrong with me,' Troy said. 'And nothing is wrong with you.'

'I'm quitting.' She shrugged. 'I just don't think te reo is for me. I'm not getting it, I'm slow, everyone's better than me. I got a two on that test. I can't blame my ADHD and intergenerational trauma anymore. Nothing is sinking in. I think I'll just go back to the Pākehā world and be a well-respected Māori who can say a karakia at meetings and that's enough for me.'

'You don't need to do that, Māreikura. That's not your true self.'

'Yeah, well, what is my true self? Who decides that? What if that's who I want to be?' She felt her pockets until she pulled out her keys. 'Maybe I want to be colonised. Happily colonised. Like all the other Māori living their best Pākehā lives. Like Eru.'

'Who's Eru?'

'No one. Anyway, I have to go.'

'I'll walk you to your car.'

They walked side by side without saying anything. An older man Māreikura hadn't seen before walked in their direction and Troy nodded at him. 'Kia ora, bro.'

Māreikura shook her head.

'What?'

'You just remind me of someone.'

'Who? Taika Waititi?' He shrugged. 'I get that a lot. It's my handsome Ngāti Porou looks.'

'Why are you so whakahīhī?'

'Why do you sound like my mum?'

'Does your mum cry in her Māori class and scream at all the Pākehā too?'

'No, but you both have that same mana wāhine energy.' He had a smile on the verge of his lips. 'You know, the scary mana wāhine energy,' and Māreikura pushed him. He held his hands up in the air and Māreikura found herself noticing for the second time how handsome he was. She wiped the smile off her face and looked away.

'I mean, Mum's been where you've been. She's struggled with her reo, with her identity. You're not the only one. And even though she's well known in the writing world, she still struggles.'

'Okay, well, I'm no Jaz Te Huia,' she said. 'But thank you for the compliment. Tell your mum I love her.'

'Tell her yourself,' he said. 'Why don't you come over to Mum's for dinner tonight? You two can talk about wahine things. We can go over our assignment if you want. Mum would be keen to help. My sis would be excited to meet you.'

'Really?'

'Yeah,' he said. 'I'll message you the addy.'

He went to open the car door for Māreikura but it was locked so she fumbled her key and unlocked the driver door and he opened it and she climbed in.

'I can't tonight,' she told him. 'Me and Jords are doing our podcast.'

'Tomorrow night?'

'I can't.'

'Ka pai, just let me know when you're free,' he said and then he shut the door.

CHAPTER SEVENTEEN

Kat insisted Māreikura go to yoga with her. It would help with Māreikura's stress levels so now they were driving to a yoga class somewhere in Ponsonby. The thought of going to a yoga class in Ponsonby with rich, white mums added to Māreikura's stress levels so she was unsure how it was supposed to help.

'You'll be fine, babe,' Kat said. 'It's an easy class.'

'I'm just not that flexible.'

'Could have fooled me,' she said, reaching over and rubbing Māreikura's thigh. 'Just go at your own pace, okay? You don't have to actually be flexible to do yoga.'

They parked outside the yoga studio. 'Liberated' flashed on the front window. Two white women wearing Lululemon activewear walked past with yoga mats tucked under their arms, their blonde ponytails swinging in sync with each other.

Kat saw Māreikura's reaction and leaned over and kissed her on the lips. 'Babe, you'll be fine.'

The yoga studio was softly lit and had a nice ambience. There were eight other women there already stretching on their yoga mats.

'Hey, hun! How are you, babe?' Kat greeted everyone as she passed them.

A blonde woman who looked slightly older than Māreikura came up to them. Her face seemed nice and she had a thick Australian accent.

'Kat! How are you?'

'I'm good, babe. This is my partner, Māreikura. It's her first session.'

'Wonderful. I'm Tessa. It's nice to have you here. There's blocks in the cupboard and blankets over there. I'll keep an eye out for you but raise your hand if you need anything, okay?'

Māreikura nodded and followed Kat to the corner. There was a woman already there rolling her mat out but when she saw Kat approaching, she rolled her mat back up and moved to the other side. People seemed to do that, Māreikura noticed. Get out of the way for Kat. It was only obvious if you witnessed it repeatedly like Māreikura did. The other night, they had gone to the Italian place on the waterfront and a man held the door open for them even though they were far away. That had never happened to Māreikura before and she analysed it in her head and decided it must be because Kat was beautiful and white-passing. So she had double the privilege – white privilege and pretty privilege. Something Māreikura did not have. It's not as if Māreikura was ugly. After a while, people would tell Māreikura, 'You're quite pretty,' like they had to get used to her face. Kat was a bombshell, aesthetically pleasing to the eye – the type of face and body you see in the media, so society was accustomed to rating her beautiful in one glance. The type of beautiful where you click your fingers and things happen for you. You get the best spot in the yoga studio. You get the best table in the restaurant. You become the CEO of a million-dollar company. You get a TED Talk.

The class started and Tessa's voice was hypnotic – it made Māreikura want to sleep. She lay on her back with a blanket on top of her and her arms stretched out. She was definitely relaxed. She tried to focus on the instructor and wanted to be present but she kept thinking about what they were going to have for dinner and if Kat was going to make the yum tofu dish. Māreikura loved Kat's cooking. It was her second favourite thing about her. Her cooking. Food was definitely the way to Māreikura's heart. She glanced over at Kat. Her eyes were closed and her body was stretched out. Māreikura found it widely attractive witnessing her in her element. She really loved Kat. She liked being Kat's girlfriend. She liked going along to events and holding her arm and feeling important. She liked how Kat introduced Māreikura as her 'partner' and not her 'girlfriend'. It made her feel more grown-up, like they were in a serious partnership even though they had only been dating for two months. Māreikura was becoming more fit and boujee since she met Kat. She exercised more, went for walks, drank green smoothies in the morning, liked organic food from Farro, and had even given up gluten to support Kat. Miraculously, the Karen in Grey Lynn had been right and Māreikura's acne cleared up after giving up gluten. She realised that she was actually gluten intolerant and now the bloated tummy and headaches after eating dumplings made sense.

She scanned the room at all the hot women doing yoga and felt a surge of jealousy. The thought came into Māreikura's mind that Kat might leave her for another woman. The idea of another woman being in the proximity of Kat made Māreikura want to curl up in a ball and scream. If she found a woman in Kat's bed, she would pull her out with her bare hands and strangle her. Or maybe she wouldn't. Maybe she would shut the door and leave quietly. You never really know until you're in that situation. That's why there're always stories on the news of scorned lovers murdering their ex-partners or the lover of their husband or wife. They were probably just ordinary people at first and then they had a whole heap of unresolved trauma and then fell in love, and next minute, they're sitting in a jail cell wondering what the hell just happened.

The class was over and Māreikura had spent the whole time overthinking. She was sure it was her ADHD. How do ADHD girlies do yoga anyway?

The lights came on and Kat's eyes slowly opened. She made a murmuring sound. She glanced over at Māreikura and smiled.

'How did you find it, babe?'

'Good.'

'Really?'

'Yeah, it was nice. I feel more relaxed.'

'Baby, that's amazing.' She moved closer and kissed her on the cheek. 'I can't wait until we can do more yoga together.'

Māreikura went to put the blanket and blocks away while Kat did a quick stretch. When Māreikura came back, two women had now joined Kat and they were talking about their kids and other uninteresting things. Māreikura sat down silently and pulled out her phone.

'Oh, this is my partner, Māreikura,' Kat told them. 'This is Kasey and Amy.'

'Kia ora,' Māreikura said.

'Hey.' They both smiled and one of them, the blondest one, asked, 'What do you do, Māreikura?'

It was such a weird question to ask someone what they do instead of where they are from, Māreikura thought.

'I'm studying.'

'What are you studying?'

'Te reo Māori.'

'Oh, okay.' They seemed bored with her answer.

Kat leaned over and grabbed Māreikura's phone. She typed something and then turned the phone to landscape and Māreikura heard her own voice blaring over the speaker.

'Māreikura is an activist too.' Kat beamed, holding up the phone.

Soon there were five white women huddled around Kat, watching the speech while Māreikura sat there awkwardly. If there was ever a time Māreikura wanted to unalive herself, it was now. Right now.

'I remember this.'

'You were so brave.'

'That must have been so hard.'

'You are so inspiring.'

The video came to an end and Kasey, hand on hip, asked, 'Where's the girl now?'

'I don't know.'

'Did she know blackface was racist?'

There it was, the comment Māreikura had been waiting for.

'Um, she used the N-word,' Māreikura said. 'So, yes.'

'It would be interesting to see how this affected her,' a woman with badly tattooed eyebrows and overbearing fake eyelashes piped up.

'That's the problem with viral videos, you never know the impact on the other person.'

Māreikura didn't say anything until afterwards in the car. She climbed in, put her belt on then asked Kat, 'Are they really your friends?'

'No,' Kat scoffed. 'We just do yoga together. They're not my friends.'

Māreikura waited until she had reversed out of the car park and onto the road, then asked, 'Why did you have to show everyone the video?'

'Babe.' She put her hand on Māreikura's thigh. 'Because I'm proud of you. I want to tell the whole world about you.'

'It just felt weird,' Māreikura said, looking out the window. 'Like a show and tell or something. You know when you're a kid and you bring your object into class for show and tell? That's what it felt like.'

Kat took her hand away. 'If you feel that way, then that's on you.'

'It just felt like I was being tokenised by a bunch of white people.'

'A bunch of white people?' Māreikura felt Kat's eyes drilling into her soul. 'Are you including me in the bunch of white people?'

Māreikura didn't say anything and Kat made a huffed sigh. 'So this is what this is really about. You don't think I'm Māori enough.'

'I didn't say that.'

'Is this going to be a problem, Māreikura? I'm not Māori enough for you?'

'I never said that.'

'Okay, fine,' she said in a low tone. 'I won't say anything next time. I can't even be proud of my own girlfriend.'

They were sitting in Kat's driveway now. She pressed the remote controller and the gate opened. She turned the engine off and looked at Māreikura.

'Why haven't I met any of your family yet?'

Māreikura felt a rush of anger, like Kat expected her to have a normal family. *Who did she want to meet? My imaginary dad? My dead mum?*

'They are not in Auckland.'

'What about your nana? Your friends?'

Kat got out of the car and slammed the door behind her.

•

Later that night, Māreikura said sorry and Kat said it was fine.

'We're in the final phase of Whiro', Kat told her. 'We're both highly emotional.'

They read an Instagram post about healthy communication in relationships and the first step was recognising triggers.

'What is your trigger?' Kat asked.

'White people. What's yours?'

'Not meeting your family.'

Māreikura didn't say anything then she asked Kat if she knew that yoga was colonised.

'It originated in India, did you know that?'

'Of course, darling,' Kat said and then she rolled over and gave Māreikura a kiss.

CHAPTER EIGHTEEN

'Kia ora e te whānau,' Jordana said, her hands holding on to the mic in front of her.

'Welcome to the first ever podcast of *Wahine Chats*! I'm your host Jordana Hawke. He uri nō Te Kāhui. I'm from the tribe Te Kāhui. And I'm here with my co-host Māreikura. Ko wai koe?'

'I'm Māreikura, ko Māreikura tōku ingoa. I'm from Ngāpuhi, and we are two wāhine reclaiming te reo Māori this year who want to share our journey with you. We love that Māori and all Indigenous people around the world are reclaiming our ancestral languages, our ancestral knowledge, our ancestral power. But we also know it can be hard and often lonely.'

'We don't want you to feel alone,' Jordana said. 'which is why we have started this podcast, e hoa mā. So no matter if you are old, young, just starting out, or have been on the reclamation path for years, or even if you are a Pākehā or non-Māori, we hope we can help you in any way. Just a reminder, though, we are both simply sharing our experiences; we are not experts. Anything we share is not a reflection of te ao Māori or the school we attend, but based on our own individual experiences. They aren't a reflection of all Māori. Just like when you listen to a Pākehā podcast, it's not a reflection of all Pākehā.'

'Āe,' Māreikura said. 'We also want to acknowledge all of the te reo Māori champions and pioneers who made it possible for us to be here today. Like Ngā Tamatoa and Te Rōpū Reo Māori who delivered the Māori language petition, with over thirty thousand signatures, to parliament. The petition demanded for te reo Māori to be taught in schools. Our reo almost became extinct. I can't imagine how hard it was back in the day for our pioneers. Te reo Māori wasn't cool back then. You lost jobs for signing a petition, you were threatened with violence. They were called radicals.'

'And now they are our heroes. We wouldn't be here without them today,' Jordana said. 'Kei te mihi, kei te mihi, kei te mihi. So let's get on to the topic. Should Pākehā learn te reo Māori? Now this is a huge ongoing debate that is talked about in all spaces. Here's a whakataukī commonly used for te reo Māori: "Whiua ki te ao, whiua ki te rangi, whiua ki ngā iwi katoa." That translates to: "Spread the language to the world, spread the language to the sky, and spread the language to all people." Māreikura and I are learning te reo Māori in a class with Pākehā and I would say it has been an interesting experience.'

'Interesting or traumatising?' Māreikura asked. 'I would say learning my mother tongue alongside Pākehā is the single most traumatising aspect of reclaiming my language.'

'Before we get into that,' Jordana said, 'I want to read a quote from Doctor Will Flavell, who said, "In order to maintain and grow te reo Māori, both Māori and non-Māori must be involved in the ongoing revitalisation and further development of the language." So, Māreikura, I want to go back to what you said about how it has been traumatic for you. Trauma – intergenerational language trauma – is real, e te whānau, and it affects so many Māori. How has it impacted you?'

'People think te reo Māori was "lost" but that's not true. It was stolen,' Māreikura said. 'Forcefully beaten out of our grandparents after the Native Schools Act was enforced by the government, which effectively banned te reo Māori being spoken at schools. And now we are here, taking a year out of our lives, to learn Māori. And not only do we have to deal with the actual learning, we have to deal with the trauma that comes with it, the fact we are all out here trying to work and survive. It's traumatising when you have to leave class because you failed a test – an actual test on your reo – but the Pākehā in your class got 100 per cent. They get the best marks, they pass with flying colours, while the Māori in class are struggling, trying to reclaim a language that should have been ours in the first place. Traumatising is paying money, money to learn your *own* language. Let me spell that out again. You're paying money to learn your own language. So what should cost us nothing ends up costing us everything. Who's paying for my trauma? Who's going to pay for my therapy? So spread the language to all people – but at what cost? How many Māori can speak our own language?'

'Uncle Google says as of 2022, 23 per cent.'

'So 23 per cent of our people can somewhat speak our reo while Pākehā are filling up all the classes and our own people are missing out. What about the other 80 per cent? What about the māmā of three who has been on the waiting list for three years to learn her language but can't get a spot because of Pākehā? Give our language back to us first. We don't need Pākehā to revitalise our language. We never did. Maybe that's the biggest colonising lie – that we need them. We don't need them for anything.'

'So you really think we should gatekeep Pākehā from our culture?' Jordana asked.

'When we get to 50 per cent of fluent Māori speakers, I think that's when Pākehā can learn. But not right now. There's too much mistrust. It's so painful for me to have to sit next to a Pākehā in class who is getting the reo better than I am. My reclamation of my language isn't a hobby. It's not a nice thing that I'm doing. I'm unlearning hundreds of years of trauma. I'm the first in my family. It's painful. Let me learn with my own people so it's a safe place and we can make mistakes and not feel deep shame when a Pākehā has better reo than us.'

'It is the same for me, being the first in my whānau. I get the mamae, I feel that too,' Jordana said. 'But gatekeeping is extreme, e hoa. I disagree with you on that. I think we need to take a step back and ask how Pākehā can support Māori. Rather than just banning them. I agree with Doctor Flavell, we need everyone to be on board. What about Pākehā advocates like that New Zealander of the Year lady, Jennifer Te Atamira Ward-Lealand? John Campbell? What about Pākehā teachers who teach te reo? We need them.'

Māreikura shuffled in her seat and said nothing. Jordana paused. 'What is it that you would like Pākehā to know?'

'There is a grieving process when you come to the realisation of what you've lost, what was taken from you. I wish Pākehā understood that.'

'Explain that.'

'The grieving process? The first part of the process is anger. How can I not be angry? Do you mean to tell me I've spent my entire life living as a diluted version of myself, because who I was meant to be and what was meant to be mine – my reo, the mātauranga of my ancestors, the very essence of who I am, a whānau and community that once thrived on my land – was destroyed before I was even born? And now I am meant to spend the rest of my life looking and searching for what was lost – trying to reach some kind of reconciliation – until the day I die, knowing deep down I can't go back to an imagined and idealised past? But I keep trying until the reclamation of my culture becomes who I am and my identity? Because it is my identity. My trauma is now an object lesson for Pākehā to all learn from, to make the world and this country a better place for our descendants. But maybe part of that grieving process is realising I won't ever see the fruits of my labour while I am alive. Just like those who came before me, some with names I do not know. My whakapapa is just broken, fragmented pieces, filled with gaps and pain, and maybe there's good stories woven in there too, but how am I supposed to know? What makes me angry is how I can't just live my life like Pākehā get to. I'm picking up the broken pieces of my whakapapa except I don't know where to look, how to look, how to become part of a world I don't belong in.'

'And for you, this all comes up as you learn te reo Māori?' Jordana asked.

'It's not just the language you learn when it's your own ancestral tongue. The cost of learning reo is less about the monetary value and more about unravelling parts of ourselves and trying to dismantle colonisation, unlearn lessons of internalised racism and overcome trauma, both intergenerational and individual trauma from learning a language beaten from our ancestors.'

'For me, the experience has been different,' Jordana said. 'You might not like this but I actually don't mind learning alongside Pākehā. We have a girl in our class named Sarah who is a really good ally. I think if more Pākehā were humble like her, kind, willing to take a back seat in class and not shout out all the answers, then everyone would have a good experience. Maybe it depends on your trauma, your whakapapa. I'm not sure.'

'You know, it is really hard for me to say my pepeha,' said Māreikura. 'I say a mountain I don't even know, that I've never visited, and I claim it as mine. It brings up the trauma of being uplifted as a baby by child services and it reminds me of how broken my family is.'

'E hoa, I'm sorry.' Jordana gulped. 'I didn't know about that.'

'I guess that's what you call intergenerational trauma. So when I sit in class, yeah, I'm angry. Who is to blame? Do I put all the blame on my mum who neglected me as a baby? Do I blame my nan who wasn't there for my mum? Or do I blame my great-grandmother who I've never met and only heard a few stories about, but apparently she was nice and spoke only te reo to the kids and was a good mum?'

'But then you don't know what happened with your grandmother?'

'I know what happened. What happened between my great-grandmother and grandmother is colonisation. And now here I am dealing with the consequences.'

'People are going to ask what does this have to do with te reo Māori?'

'Don't you get it?' Māreikura asked. 'Who are we without our language? Where do we belong if not on our own whenua? That's how they tried to destroy us.'

•

On Monday morning, Jordana ran to the car and opened the door squealing. Māreikura had never heard Jordana squeal before.

'What's wrong?'

She waved her phone in Māreikura's face. 'We got twenty.'

'Twenty what?'

'Twenty streams.'

'Is that all?'

'What do you mean, "is that all"? She slid her belt across her chest. 'We got our first review, wanna hear it?'

She didn't wait for Māreikura to answer.

'Dear Jordana and Māreikura, after listening to your podcast it made me think. Why haven't I started learning my own language yet? I am forty-six years old and I have been embarrassed for so many years. I have tried everything. When I am the only brown face in a room, I am always scared they will ask me to do the karakia. I live in fear even when I go back to my marae and my cousins speak to me in Māori. Now I feel inspired to take the leap. I have enrolled in a class and I know if I remain committed, my language will come. I feel like te reo Māori is the missing piece in my life. Thank you for being vulnerable and I am looking forward to following your journey. I am proud of you both.'

'Aw, that is nice,' Māreikura said. 'Who's that from?'

'My mum.'

'Seriously.'

'I talked to her last night and she was excited,' Jordana said. 'She's inspired by us, oi. And twenty streams is better than nothing. I'm proud of us. By small and simple things great things are brought to pass. I learnt that on my silent retreat.'

Jordana had once told Māreikura her life had been changed after going on a silent retreat where she couldn't talk for a month.

'What do you mean "can't talk",' Māreikura had asked her. 'Like not at all?'

'Not at all,' Jordana said. 'You learn to control your thoughts and sit in silence. It changed the way I seek validation.'

Maybe that's why Jordana was handling the failure of their podcast so well.

'I still think we can do better,' Māreikura told her.

'Nah, it's hard to go viral these days,' Jordana said. 'We gotta join TikTok and do some dumb dance.'

Māreikura pulled her phone out and typed 'Māreikura Pohe speech' into Google. Hundreds of links came up immediately. Māreikura clicked on the first link, which took her to the original YouTube video. It was now up to 21 942 920 views.

She passed the phone to Jordana, trying not to cringe at her voice blaring through the phone speaker.

'Wha'?' Jordana's mouth dropped open. 'Nah, hold up – is that you?'

She turned the audio up to full volume, glancing at Māreikura then back at her phone and then back at Māreikura and then back down to the phone. She kept doing this until Māreikura said, 'Can you stop?'

'Bro.' Her mouth was still hanging open. 'That's why you seem familiar, I thought we just knew each other in a past life.' She carried on watching the video while Māreikura looked out the window.

'I remember seeing this and thinking, *Shit, this wahine toa. I wouldn't wanna get in a punch-up with her.*'

She cracked up laughing.

'How did you end up here with me? Holy shit, the universe is a crack-up.'

She stopped laughing.

'Is that twenty million views, what the fuck?' She looked at Māreikura again. 'You are literally famous.'

'I am not.'

'Does anyone from class know?'

'Know what?'

'That you're famous?'

'I'm not famous.'

'Can I post it in the class group chat?' Jordana asked.

Māreikura wrested the phone out of her hand.

'Um, okay, I won't then. Bro, that speech was the modern-day version of "I have a dream". If I did a speech like that I would feel this responsibility to change the world.'

Māreikura didn't say anything and Jordana slowly nodded.

'Ohhh, I get it. Why that would be traumatic. Now everyone is looking at you to change the world.'

Māreikura turned the car on and reversed out of the drive.

'That's why I don't understand why we don't have more streams,' she said. 'The podcast industry is saturated with white men. I thought we would be refreshing. Like, why listen to Joe Rogan when you can listen to us?'

'We need to crack TikTok.'

'We're too old for TikTok,' Māreikura said.

'How did you even go viral?'

'I don't know, Jords,' Māreikura said. 'Quit high school and fuck up your education prospects and have your nan not speak to you anymore because you flushed all her money and dreams down the drain, because in her mind you were going to be the cycle-breaker in your family, the first to get a white colonial education, but instead you get a viral video and called brave?'

Jordana didn't respond. She was checked out, looking down at her phone.

'Oh, sorry. I just got a text from my mate. He's going down a spiral – saying he wants to end his life.'

She was furiously texting.

'Gazza', she read out loud. 'You are worthy. You deserve to be here. You are loved.' She slipped her phone into her pocket. 'What were you saying?'

'Nothing, is your friend okay?'

'Yeah, he's fine, just spirals out sometimes.' She clicked her tongue and she was back again. 'I could start us a TikTok.'

'Um, okay. But you're not very good at social media.'

Jordana had 158 followers and was following 298 people on her Instagram. She recently posted a plant on her feed with no caption.

'I have a photographer mate who can take our photos,' she said. 'So at least we'll have a cool cover photo for our podcast? He owes me a favour anyway.' She got her phone back out. 'I'll see if he's free.'

•

Māreikura found out Jordana was a trained makeup artist while she was painting Māreikura's face with a foundation that looked five shades too white to be her colour but Jordana said it was all about the blending. She also told Māreikura she'd worked at the Farmers beauty department, applying makeup whenever someone spent $70 or more on beauty products. She quit after two shifts because she said she didn't like the vibe.

Jordana smeared eyeshadow on Māreikura's eyelids and then patted some blusher on her cheek.

'Look up,' she said, applying mascara to her eyelashes. 'Okay, now look down.'

Her mouth was so close that Māreikura could smell her raspberry-peach breath from her vaping. She sprayed Māreikura with some kind of magic mist and then stepped back, inspecting her face in the bright and revealing light. Māreikura had never felt more insecure about her pores.

'Okay, perfect.'

Māreikura turned and looked in the mirror. 'I look like a clown.'

'Trust me,' Jordana said, 'It might seem extreme but you'll come out looking flawless in the photos.'

'Okay, ngā mihi.'

'Wear anything from my wardrobe if you want,' Jordana said.

Jordana had a walk-in wardrobe, so Māreikura walked around and touched every dress in there, just because she could. In the end, Māreikura stuck with what she was wearing – her ripped jeans, black shirt and denim jacket with the tino rangatiratanga flag sewn on the back.

They went down to one of the alleyways on Karangahape Road and Jordana's mate Jawson took their photos. He was lanky and wore big-framed glasses and a beret on top of his head. He kept doing this dopey grin every time Jordana talked, like he was under hypnosis or something. Jordana seemed blissfully unaware. Maybe she was used to guys fawning over her.

Jawson showed Māreikura the photos on his camera.

'Woah, these are really good,' she told him and he said, 'Yeah, it helps when the models are beautiful.'

He then explained about lighting and aperture and different functions of the camera to Māreikura for a good five minutes and Māreikura nodded politely, pretending she was interested, but the whole time she was thinking about what she was going to eat for dinner, and when he was done talking, she pulled out her phone to message Kat.

Jawson packed up his kit and asked if they wanted to get a feed but Māreikura had a date night with Kat so Jordana went to Coco's Cantina alone with him. Jawson looked pleased. When he turned the other way, Māreikura whispered to Jordana, 'He's kinda cute.'

She scrunched up her nose. 'Is he, though?'

CHAPTER NINETEEN

The first episode of the podcast began to gain attention after a popular girl on TikTok shared a snippet of what Māreikura had said.

'Who are we without our language? Where do we belong if not on our own whenua? That's how they tried to destroy us.'

Someone commented, 'Is that the girl who did the head girl speech?' Māreikura did not have TikTok but her followers went up to five thousand on Twitter. Hēmi Kelly and Stacey Morrison both endorsed the podcast on their social media platforms. Māreikura received about twenty messages, mostly Pākehā allies who were inspired and touched by her thoughts. The podcast got their first sponsor and they were offered $400 each in advance for the next episode. Māreikura used the money to buy Kat dinner and put her account back into the positive.

'See?' Jordana told her. 'Told you it was a good idea. We're helping heaps of people reclaim their Māoritanga.'

Popular right-wing radio host Matthew Hart called Māreikura a 'brat' after someone shared a video of her saying 'Ban Pākehā from learning te reo Māori'. A Twitter storm erupted. Left-wing commentator Crystal Haywood chimed in and accused him of bullying. 'When is it okay to bully a young woman?' she asked. #pakehaandreo and #standwithMāreikura starting trending on Twitter. On his breakfast show the next morning, Matthew Hart, who refused to even say the Māori word for hello on his show, asked his white, conservative, sixty-five-plus audience, 'How can they keep the language alive if people like her are set on putting white New Zealanders down for simply trying?' Coincidently, the same day, Māreikura received her first hate mail from an older Pākehā man named Graeme who told her she was a waste of space, te reo wasn't even a real language and Māori weren't the first people to reach New Zealand and it was actually a race called Moriori. He even linked to several histories of New Zealand, all written by white men.

Māreikura was asked to appear on the biggest morning television show in the country. She didn't want to do it but Jordana said it would be good publicity. *The more publicity, the more people will listen to our podcast and the more people we can help*, she told Māreikura. Kat agreed and said she had been trying to get a spot on *Breakfast* for her business because it was a prime slot and everyone watches *Breakfast*. They just have it on in the background in the mornings, Kat explained. That was true. Her nan always had *Breakfast* on in the morning.

The morning show producer asked Māreikura to be at the studio by six thirty.

'Umm, a.m.?' Māreikura asked.

'Yes, a.m.,' the producer said on the other end of the phone. 'Your makeup and hair is booked for six thirty and you'll be on air at seven fifteen.'

'Oh, okay. That's a lot of time just to do makeup and hair. I'm not that ugly, am I?'

She laughed at her own joke but she actually had her hand in a fist from crippling anxiety. The producer told her not to worry.

'The questions will be easy – about your reo journey, about your upbringing. You'll be fine. We'll brief you when you get here,' and then she hung up. Māreikura told her nan she was going to be on *Breakfast* and her nan said, 'What for? Oh, for your radio show? Pass me the phone. I'll let everyone know.'

Kat let Māreikura borrow her green Kiri Nathan dress. When Māreikura put it on, Kat clasped her hands to her mouth. Māreikura sat on Kat's lap and Kat told her she was proud of her. For what? That was always the first thing that came to Māreikura's mind when people said they were proud of her. Eru used to tell her that all the time and she never understood why. There was nothing to be proud of.

'We better go,' Kat told her. 'Don't want you to be late, do we?'

Māreikura was on time for the first time in her life. Kat wanted to come in but Māreikura said she was too whakamā, and Kat rolled her eyes and said she would wait in the car park then or maybe go and get a coffee from across the road. Māreikura told her there was no need and she could catch the bus back. Kat said she hated when Māreikura did that, refusing her help, shutting her out. Kat just wanted to be more involved in Māreikura's life, how hard was that to understand? Māreikura said sorry and asked if they could fight about this later. She kissed Kat on the cheek, got out of the car and walked into the TVNZ studio.

The lady behind the desk said hi and asked her to sign in, pointing to the iPad-looking thing stuck to the desk. Māreikura entered her details and a label came out with her name on it. She stuck it on her chest but it wasn't sticking well enough so she put it on the back of her hand.

A lady appeared out of nowhere in black pants, a white shirt and loud shoes. She stuck her hand out.

'You must be Māreikura,' she said and then shook her hand. 'I'm Courtney. Glad you found the place all right! Come on through.'

Māreikura followed her in.

'Did you get a park okay?'

'Oh, I got dropped off,' Māreikura told her.

'We do have guest parking but maybe you can use it next time.'

Courtney's boots thumped along the floor as she pointed to everything like she'd done it many times before.

'This is where the *1News* journalists sit. Over there is the *Breakfast* team. That's Simon Dallow's chair. This is the radio team.'

'Where's the *Māori News*?' Māreikura asked.

'Oh, they sit over there. I can take you there if you want. Maybe after, if we have time.' They stopped at a brightly lit room. 'And here we are. Chelsea will take good care of you.'

'Hi, I'm Chelsea. Take a seat.'

Māreikura sat down. She stared in the mirror and Chelsea played with her hair for a bit. She examined her skin and pursed her lips.

'Sorry for my bad skin.'

Chelsea laughed. 'Honey, I've seen worse. Trust me. Makeup is a miracle worker in this building.'

She studied her makeup kit and then studied Māreikura. 'Is your face bare? Have you got anything on?'

Māreikura shook her head.

'Great.'

Chelsea rubbed moisturiser on Māreikura's face and then started applying makeup. She asked her questions like, 'Is this your first time on TV?'

And Māreikura said, 'Yeah, it is.'

'It will be over before you know it,' Chelsea told her. 'Trust me. Five minutes. Blink and you'll miss it. Plus Tristan is a pro. He looks scary on TV but behind the scenes, he's a gentle giant.'

Māreikura opened her messages. *Good luck babe.* From Kat.

Kei te pai koe? Jordana messaged.

Māreikura glanced up at the mirror and already looked like a different person. Holy shit. She opened her camera app and took a photo and sent it to Jordana and Kat. *Kua rite. Ready.*

Kat messaged back *Marry me* with heart emojis.

Chelsea reached for the straightener but Māreikura told her she wanted to wear her real hair.

'Good thinking', she said. 'I love your natural hair.'

She put some product in Māreikura's hair and then turned Māreikura's chair around and tilted her head to the left.

'What do you think? Do you like it?'

'Yes.'

For the first time, Māreikura liked what was looking back at her in the mirror.

Courtney popped her head in the room and then took Māreikura to the green room. 'Wait here and we'll come and get you when they're ready.'

Māreikura took another selfie and then Courtney came back in.

'We're ready for you, Māreikura.'

•

Tristan O'Larry was shorter in real life and had a lot more wrinkles up close. He said hi to Māreikura in his famous booming voice she and the rest of the country had come to know and love.

'Big fan,' he said, grinning at her, and then he said, 'Copy that,' to his earpiece, shuffled some papers in his hand and Māreikura took a quick sip of water even though she wasn't thirsty at all. She actually wanted to throw up. She touched her hair and then someone yelled they were rolling and O'Larry turned towards the camera.

'Kia ora and welcome back to *Breakfast*! We have a remarkable young woman on the show with us right now. She is doing a full-immersion te reo Māori course and has a new podcast out that has caused quite the stir, but that's not all. You also might remember her from this.'

A snippet of Māreikura's head girl speech played on the screen.

'I speak up for all victims of racism, I speak up for my people and I speak up for my ancestors who were beaten at school for speaking my native tongue, te reo Māori. My name is Māreikura Pohe and I refuse to be quiet.'

'Here to talk about her journey is Māreikura Pohe. Kia ora, Māreikura.'

'Kia ora, Tristan.'

'Now, that head girl speech, every time I watch it, it gives me goosebumps. Goosebumps! Look at them.'

He held out his arms to the main camera so the audience at home could see.

'Can you zoom in on that, Mark? There you go. That's how affected I am by that speech. Look, what's going through your mind watching that clip? What would you tell the girl in the clip, your old self?'

'I would tell her it's going to be okay,' Māreikura said. 'I would tell her that although she feels alone, she really isn't and there are many Māori wāhine and rangatahi watching and feeling the same way, and that it is going to be hard, but to stay strong.'

'Excellent,' he said, nodding. 'Now you dropped out of school because you felt so passionately that the school wasn't taking racism seriously, is that right? That's a daunting but courageous act.'

Māreikura nodded. 'Yes, that's right, and honestly, it was a really lonely time. I felt like I was standing alone up there. I didn't say what I said hoping to go viral, hoping for fame, to get clout, to blow up on social media. I didn't know any of those things would happen. I said it because I knew I wouldn't be able to live with myself if I let it go. And so I had to speak up and I was prepared to take on any consequences.'

'Right, of course,' O'Larry said. 'I've listened to the first episode of your podcast *Wahine Chats* and it's incredible. Let the people at home know why you decided to study te reo Māori full-time?'

'Well, Tristan, imagine having someone else's culture and language forced on you from the moment you were born. That's what it's like for me and every Māori in this country. So, really, it's not a decision of mine to learn te reo Māori by full immersion – I felt like I had no choice. English is not my language. It is not my ancestors' language. Do I want to spend the rest of my life speaking this foreign language? No, I don't. So why was I forced to speak it? This is enduring colonial violence. And do you know how much it costs me to learn my language full-time? Seven thousand dollars plus living costs. I have a classmate who works night shifts to pay for his course. Can you imagine? He comes into class every morning with bags under his eyes needing sleep, but he and so many other Māori are making sacrifices.'

'How can we solve this? What can we do as a country to change this?'

'Make learning the reo more accessible. Pay Māori teachers what they are worth so they can help Māori reclaim our language. Did you know it takes one generation to lose a language, but three generations to restore it? Te reo changes lives and it saves lives.'

O'Larry nodded furiously. 'Right. One last question. There've been calls for Lindsay Williams to stand down as CEO of Oranga Tamariki.

I heard on your podcast you were uplifted as a baby, taken from your mother and put into another home until your nana adopted you. Tell us your thoughts. Should she stand down?'

Māreikura froze. O'Larry was looking right at her, his eyes scanning her face, waiting for an answer. She did not expect this question. She did not expect them to ask her about her fucking childhood trauma. She looked at the producer Courtney, who'd promised to keep her safe. None of this was in the questions she was sent.

'Yes,' Māreikura said finally. 'She should.'

'Why?' O'Larry leaned forward with a slight smile as if he was enjoying the moment. There was a glisten in his eye, like he knew this was it. This was the gotcha moment he was looking for.

'Because.'

'Because why?'

'If she doesn't, then children who have been through the system will end up like me.'

'And how's that?'

Māreikura gulped.

'Broken.'

O'Larry turned away from her and looked straight to the camera. 'A special thank you to our guest Māreikura Pohe for coming on the show. Māreikura, ngā mihi. We'll be back in two, see you after the break.'

•

O'Larry got to his feet and placed his arm on Māreikura's shoulder.

'Māreikura, you are exceptional,' he said. 'Just a bloody exceptional young woman. I'm so proud of you.'

Māreikura said nothing and then O'Larry bellowed with laughter, startling her.

'Speechless, are you? I tell you what, our viewing numbers are going to go through the roof. Your family at home must be so proud.'

Māreikura wondered again why people always said they were proud of her. She smiled and said thank you and that her nana was a big fan of his.

'What're your plans after your reo course?' he asked.

'I'm not sure,' Māreikura said. 'I was going to do law but I'm not sure now.'

'I can see you in politics. I can see you in journalism. Heck, I can see you doing many things. The world is your oyster.' He reached into his pocket and handed her a card. 'Give me a call if you ever want to do an internship here at TVNZ or if you need a reference anywhere.'

'Thank you,' Māreikura said.

I'm waiting outside for you. It was a text from Kat. A lady Māreikura hadn't seen before showed up and walked her out of the building and to the front entrance where Kat was waiting.

'Did I do all right?' Māreikura asked as she got into Kat's car. 'I wasn't sure if I answered the questions properly. I just said whatever came out of my mouth.'

'Babe, of course. You did amazing. And you look so good.' She leaned over and kissed Māreikura on the lips.

Afterwards, Māreikura typed her name into Google. *OT Baby Calls for Lindsay Williams to Resign* came up at the top, the headline of a *Stuff* article with quotes pulled from Māreikura's interview on *Breakfast*. Then Māreikura searched her name on Instagram. Social activism account @decoloniseyomind shared soundbite clips of Māreikura's interview.

'English is not my language. It is not my ancestors' language. Do I want to spend the rest of my life speaking this foreign language?

No, I don't. So why was I forced to speak it? This is enduring colonial violence.'

When Māreikura checked back later that day, the video had gone viral with over 600 comments and 200 000 views. *Wahine Chats* went number one on the Spotify charts in New Zealand. The Māori Language Commission asked Māreikura and Jordana to be in a video series where they would be paid $2000 per video.

'I'm so proud of you,' Kat said that night as she read through the articles on her phone. She kissed Māreikura on the cheek.

'My little star.'

CHAPTER TWENTY

Chloe was waiting outside the front gate dressed in a long black coat, black jeans, black Chucks, and holding a cigarette in her hand. Māreikura could smell the anxiety – or was it fear? – from four metres away. Māreikura recognised the anxiety because she had the same symptoms. Her hands were shaking like someone with an extreme coffee addiction. They were meeting so Māreikura could interview Chloe's grandmother, her poutokomanawa. Māreikura couldn't think of anything worse, but if she didn't do the assignment, she would fail the course.

Chloe spotted Māreikura walking towards her and she threw her cigarette on the ground, squashed it with her shoe then straightened up.

'Kia ora,' she said, acting like she didn't call Māreikura a bitch the other week. 'Kei te pehea koe?'

'Kei te pai,' Māreikura said with no expression. 'Didn't know you smoked, thought you were smarter than that. Anyway, should we take my car? I parked over there.' She pointed to Tōtara Avenue.

'Oh, we can walk,' Chloe said. 'Grandma only lives over there.' She pointed past the mall and all the way down to nowhere.

'I would rather not walk,' Māreikura said. 'And I have cake in the car.'

'Okay.'

They walked in silence and when they got to the red Toyota hatchback, Chloe tried to open the passenger door but it was locked. She fumbled it again awkwardly.

'It's locked,' Māreikura said, jiggling her keys. 'I have to unlock it through the driver's door.'

'Oh.'

'One day I won't be poor and I'll have a car where I can just press a button and all the doors will unlock,' Māreikura said.

If it was Jordana, she would have laughed or said something like, 'Fuck capitalism,' and if it was Kat, she would have at least fake-laughed, but Chloe was awkward and didn't get Māreikura's sense of humour so she said nothing. She struck Māreikura as someone who took everything personally and couldn't take a joke.

Māreikura turned the engine on. 'You'll have to direct me.'

'Go straight ahead and then left at Passenger Way, and it's the little red granny flats.'

Māreikura started driving and thought about turning the radio on but it was a short distance and there would be no point. When they got to the give way sign, she turned her head to check for any cars, subtly sneaking a glance at Chloe. Her right knee was bobbing and she was staring out at the street like the houses were the most interesting sight in the world.

'Is there anything I should know about your nana?' Māreikura asked.

'Call her Whaea, I'm sure she'll like that,' she said coyly, and Māreikura turned her head to the right so Chloe wouldn't see her laugh.

•

An elderly woman wearing a bright purple, woollen cardigan was peering through the holes of the screen door.

'Is that you, Chloe?'

'Yes, Grandma, it's me,' Chloe said. She was pretty much shouting and it gave Māreikura a headache. 'I brought a friend. Remember I told you yesterday?'

'Oh, yes, hold on, let me put my face on.'

Māreikura heard loud laughter and then, minutes later, the door opened and a woman with glassy eyes and a huge smile appeared. She was wearing blusher on her cheeks, her lips also streaked with light pink lipstick. Her hands were gripping onto a walker but she moved it aside, brushing Māreikura's hand.

'Why, hullo sweetheart!

She was only tiny, almost half the size of Māreikura, bundled up in a woollen vest. Her sparkly eyes were peering out from behind her glasses, almost like a child's. She had adoring eyes for Chloe – like she was a beautiful thing – but she had the same adoring eyes for Māreikura even though she didn't know her. She was in her nineties, Māreikura guessed, but once old people reached seventy, Māreikura honestly couldn't tell the difference. Chloe's grandma held her arms out and Chloe said, 'Grandma, this is Māreikura. Māreikura, this is my grandma, Molly Simpson.'

Chloe's grandma placed her hand on Māreikura's cheek. 'Gosh, you're a beautiful girl! And call me Grandma, will you?'

'Grandma,' Chloe said slowly, 'remember we can't just touch strangers. We have to ask for permission first.'

Grandma Simpson took her hand away and it stayed hovering in the air, like she didn't know what to do with it.

'May I give you a hug?'

Māreikura nodded, and she squeezed Māreikura tight.

'See.' She giggled. 'I've only ever been refused a Grandma Simpson hug once and I've never forgotten it! He was a young man delivering the mail, and I said to him, *May I give you a hug?* and he said no. To this day, I have never forgotten it, dear.'

She pulled away and asked, 'And what did you say your name was? Māreikura?'

'Yes,' Māreikura said.

'Ah, beautiful, dear.'

She patted Māreikura's cheeks a few more times. A tūī flew past and Grandma Simpson laughed.

'Do you like birds, dear? I love birds. I like to sit out in the garden there,' she pointed to the front yard, 'and listen to the birds. If you close your eyes, you can hear the birds singing. Sometimes they have little messages for you. I actually have some photos somewhere of the morepork, I'll have to show you. Will you remind me? Actually, I don't know where they are. You'll have to write your number down for me so I can give you a call when I find them, would you do that?'

'She will after, Grandma,' Chloe interrupted. 'Māreikura is here to ask you questions, remember I told you on the phone?'

'Yes, of course, that's why I put my face on,' she winked, turning to Chloe.

'How's my favourite granddaughter?' She hugged Chloe like she hadn't seen her in a long time. 'Thank you for coming all the way here, dear. I know you're busy with your studies. Thank you for making time for me.'

She turned back to Māreikura and squeezed her hand.

'Woah, you're strong,' Māreikura told her and Grandma Simpson laughed.

'Now, what are you going to ask me, Māreikura ?' She hung her head shyly. 'I have had such a boring life, I'm no big deal.'

'I bet that's not true,' Māreikura said, surprising herself.

Grandma Simpson grinned. 'Well, you'll have to come in and see, won't you?' She paused and glanced at the bag Māreikura was carrying. 'Oh, and what do we have here?'

'It's a cake,' Māreikura said. 'Chocolate.'

'How did you know? That's my favourite flavour!' She elbowed Chloe. 'Think we'll keep her on, eh, Chlo?'

Grandma Simpson reached for her walker and Māreikura pulled it so it was easier for her. Grandma Simpson said, 'Thank you dear, thank you.' She pushed the walker inside. 'I have your favourites, Chloe, on the bench there. Help yourself.'

'Ooh, yum. Thanks, Gran,' Chloe said, and she took a handful of brown toffee lollies and put them in her pocket. 'Want one?' And then when her grandmother was out of earshot, Chloe whispered, 'They're not actually my favourite but Grandma thinks they are so I just let her believe it, and now I don't know how to tell her they aren't.'

Māreikura popped one in her mouth. 'Ew,' she said, then Grandma Simpson turned around and she said, 'Yum.' Chloe sniggered.

'Gran, sit down.' Chloe proceeded to take away the plate her grandmother was juggling in her hand. 'Sit down.'

'I just need to—'

'I'll do it, you sit down and answer Māreikura's questions, and I'll cut the cake.'

'Okay, dear. I made some custard slices too, in the pantry. Will you get those out as well? And make us a hot tea, will you, dear? The jug's just been boiled.'

She reached for her walker and made her way to the armchair, across from where Māreikura was sitting.

'Chloe is stubborn like her father,' she said to Māreikura, her hand cupped over her mouth like it was a secret, and Chloe yelled out from the kitchen, 'I heard that, Grandma. And where do you think we get it from?'

'Gosh, not me, that's for sure!'

'You're the one who refuses to move into a rest home,' Chloe muttered under her breath. Māreikura heard her but her grandmother did not. She was still staring at Māreikura with adoring eyes.

'So you go to school with Chloe? That's nice,' she said. 'Do you enjoy it?'

'Um, yes and no,' Māreikura said.

'Oh? What don't you enjoy about it?' Her face was inquisitive, and Māreikura could tell she asked not to be polite, but because she genuinely cared. If it was anyone else who asked that question, Māreikura would have said something sarcastic about colonisation and language trauma or probably would have gone off on a rant. But there was something about Grandma Simpson that made Māreikura feel protective of her – she wanted to guard her from anything negative. She didn't want to hurt her.

'It's hard learning my own language,' Māreikura said gently. 'It's my ancestors' language so there are a lot of layers to it. A lot of pain.'

'I'm sorry to hear that, dear,' she said. 'I do remember when I first came here with my husband Dave, I was shocked at how the native people were treated. I think when we got here, the language was banned at schools. I'm so happy when I hear Māori on TV, even though I can't understand it. I hope you have good support around you, dear, do you?'

'Kind of,' Māreikura said. She shifted in her seat.

'Oh, no, I can tell that look,' she said. 'Looks like boy troubles! Well, who is he?'

'Oh, it's a she.'

'How rude of me to assume.' Grandma Simpson looked horrified. 'Are you pansexual like Chloe?'

'Gran.' Chloe placed a platter of cake and slices on the table in front of them.

'What? I'm just asking if she's pansexual like you are, dear?' She gave Māreikura a sweet smile. 'Chloe's been teaching me all of the different sex names. The way I remember pansexual is I think of a frying pan and then I just add the word sexual – it really isn't that hard.'

'Tea's ready, Grandma,' Chloe said and she mouthed *sorry* to Māreikura, although Māreikura didn't mind at all. Grandma Simpson was cute. Chloe went into the kitchen and came back with a white teapot and little cups. It reminded Māreikura of a doll's house.

'So which one are you, dear?'

'I thought I was supposed to be asking the questions,' Māreikura said and Grandma Simpson laughed. 'I'm takatāpui.'

'Oh, that's a new word,' Grandma Simpson said. 'Will you write that down for me?' She passed Māreikura a piece of paper and pen. 'What does that mean?'

'It means queer in Māori,' Māreikura said, writing it down on the paper. 'There isn't really a label. I like whoever I fall in love with.'

'I like that,' Grandma Simpson said. 'Say that again for me, dear?'

'Ta-ka-taa-pu-i. Takatāpui.'

'Ta-ka-taa-pu-i.'

'The way I remember words is through a pūrākau or a story,' Māreikura said. 'Hinemoa and Tūtānekai are gods and it was a typical heterosexual forbidden love story, like *Romeo and Juliet*. But Tūtānekai was also in love with Tiki, who he called tāku hoa takatāpui, which means my intimate same-sex friend and that's where takatāpui comes from.'

Grandma Simpson was nodding intensely like it was the most interesting story she'd ever heard. Māreikura saw in the corner of her eye Chloe playing with dishes, her ears perked up and also listening intensely.

'This is the most beautiful part. There's a quote from Tūtānekai about Tiki. He says: Ka mate ahau i te aroha ki tōku hoa, ki a Tiki. I am dying for love for my friend, for my beloved, for Tiki.'

'Oh dear.' Grandma Simpson clutched her chest. 'That is beautiful. How beautiful, isn't it, Chlo? I would love to come along to one of your classes and learn.'

'There's always a whakapapa or an origin of where the word comes from in Māori. That way, you'll never forget.'

'Absolutely beautiful.' Grandma Simpson leaned forward and cupped her hand around her mouth. 'Do you know any nice girls for Chlo?'

'Grandma!'

'I was just telling Māreikura I can't wait to try this cake.' She winked at Māreikura. 'What flavour is it again, dear?'

'Chocolate.'

'How did you know? That's my favourite flavour! Now, you might need to teach our Chloe to cook – you remember that time you almost burnt the house down?'

Chloe groaned, pouring tea into the tiny cups. 'We don't need to talk about that.'

'No, I want to hear,' Māreikura said. 'Tell me, please.'

'Well, since you asked,' Grandma Simpson smiled gleefully. 'Chloe asked me for a recipe for – what was it? I think it was shepherd's pie, wasn't it, darling? Yes, that's right, it was my shepherd's pie. You see, it's an old family recipe. Best shepherd's pie you'll ever taste, Māreikura. I'll have to make it for you next time. Don't ask Chloe to make it.' She laughed. 'Anyway, to cut a long story short, Chloe asked for the recipe and I said it to her on the phone for her to write it down, and she was like yes, Gran, okay, Grandma, and was following the instructions. And then an hour later I got a phone call. I could hear the smoke alarms going off, and Chloe told me in a heated panic, "Gran, Gran, something went wrong and the house almost caught on fire," and I said, "What on earth? How did you do that?" You see, it's a simple recipe. And so after she calmed down, I said talk me through what you did. She said, "Well, I turned the oven on," and I said yes. "And then I put the potatoes in the pot and put it on high." And I said, "Yes . . . wait – hold on a minute. Darling, you did add water, right?" And Chloe said, "Oh, no, I didn't, Gran. You didn't tell me that part." And I said, "Chlo, that's what I meant when I said put the potatoes on to boil. Don't tell me you just put the potatoes in the pot and didn't put any water in it for them to boil?" And she said, "Well, yes, Gran, you didn't say anything about water?" And I said, "Chloe, dear, that's what boil means. Add water."'

Both Māreikura and Grandma Simpson were laughing.

'How old were you?' Māreikura asked, looking at Chloe.

'I think it was last year, wasn't it, Chlo?' Grandma Simpson piped up.

Māreikura howled with laughter and Grandma Simpson said, after she caught her breath, 'Yes, Chlo was always our special grandchild.'

Māreikura was wheezing from laughing so hard. She took a sip of tea and swallowed.

'Glad you think it is funny,' Chloe said.

'Wait, how did you make the rēwena bread?' Māreikura asked.

'I know how to cook now,' Chloe said. 'Gran is exaggerating, it wasn't last year. I was like fifteen. Anyway, we better get asking questions. I'm not able to be here for the interview, Gran. Will you be okay? I'll be in the other room.'

'Are you sure about that? I hope it's not because I was giving you a hard time. You know I'm only teasing.'

She went to get up but Chloe ushered her to sit back down. 'No, Gran, it's okay. It's just part of the assignment, that I can't be here.'

'Well, take some cake with you.'

Chloe showed her an almost empty plate. 'I had some already, Gran.' She grabbed a handful of the toffee things. 'I'll take some of these, is that okay? Yum.'

'Yes, take them all,' Grandma Simpson said. She got to her feet and Māreikura held her arm out and she grabbed onto it. 'Thank you, dear.' She stretched her arms out and gave her granddaughter a hug. 'Okay dear, love you so so so so much.'

'To the moon and back.'

'To the moon and back.'

Chloe blew her a kiss as she closed the door behind her. Grandma Simpson shook her head as she sat back down.

'I do worry about that girl,' she said and then she placed her hand on Māreikura's. 'She's very lucky to have a friend like you.'

Māreikura wanted to tell her that they weren't actually friends and she actually hated everything about Chloe, but she liked her gran and she didn't want to hurt her feelings.

'She's been through a lot, that girl,' Grandma Simpson sighed. 'It's hard for her to make friends.'

Māreikura put on her best surprised face. 'Oh, really?'

'Yes, dear. I can't see why. She's such a lovely girl, Māreikura. She has such a big and beautiful heart. I remember when she was little, maybe five, and I gave her and her brothers and sisters $20 each to go to The Warehouse and they could buy whatever they wanted. Cam, her brother, came back with one of the water-gun things, and the other kids came back with, well, I can't remember what, but Chloe had bought a little stuffed toy and some of those toffee chocolates and a rose, and I thought, that's strange, and after we went through the checkout, she turned around and said, "Here you go, Grandma," and it just took my heart away, Māreikura, because she could have bought anything she wanted, but she used all the money to buy me a gift, and that just describes Chloe perfectly. That's who she is.' She reached out to get some tea and Māreikura poured her a cup.

'Thank you, dear.' She was looking at Māreikura when she spoke but Māreikura felt she was thinking about something else.

'Do you mind if we turn the radio off?' Māreikura asked, looking behind her at the radio. 'Just so I can record this.'

'Oh, okay,' Grandma Simpson said, looking down at her hands. 'I do like to keep it on, it reminds me of my David.'

'Who's that?'

She reached out next to her and passed a framed photo to Māreikura.

'This is my David,' she said. 'Isn't he handsome?'

It was a black-and-white photo of a young man in a Royal Navy uniform. He was white, with a pointy nose and a nice smile.

'Oh, I never thought he would go for someone like me – I was always so plain and I thought he would go for my friend. She was always the pretty one.' She laughed.

'He passed away ten, no, eleven years ago? Yes, it was sad. Very sad, dear.' She closed her eyes then opened them again.

'You know, dear, we were married at seventeen years old in the ruins of a church when the world was a very scary place. And the world is still a scary place, Māreikura. So when you find your love, it is important they make you feel safe, just like David did for me. I can tell you, when you find the right one, you will feel the heavens rejoice and light enter your life, that is how you will know they are for you.'

'I don't think I've ever felt that before.'

'Well, you're still young, dear. Plenty of time.'

Māreikura shook her head. 'I mean, safe. I don't really know that feeling. With anyone.'

Grandma Simpson leaned forward and squeezed Māreikura's hand. Māreikura cleared her throat and pointed to the framed photo, changing the subject.

'Who's the baby?'

'That's my son, Hugh, that's Chloe's dad. If you look closely, you can see the resemblance.' She laughed again and then her voice softened. 'I suppose she told you about what happened. Yes, it was a very sad time in our life. You should never have to bury your own child, Māreikura. I wouldn't wish that upon anyone.'

Her eyes closed again and Māreikura felt bad for asking.

'I'm so sorry,' she said. 'Chloe hasn't told me, but that's really sad.'

'Oh, I guess I shouldn't be surprised she hasn't told you,' she said. 'She doesn't talk about her father too much. Seems to shut down when we mention him. It was a horrible time, Māreikura. He passed away in a boat accident – it was just so unexpected. Chloe must have been about ten when it happened.' She shook her head.

'Anyway, dear, there's a lot to be grateful for, isn't there? So let's count our blessings.' She squeezed Māreikura's hand again. 'I can see why Chloe has taken such a fondness towards you. You're such a sweet girl.'

'I've never been told that before.'

'Well, I don't believe that for a second. If I was to poke you with a stick you would be filled with goodness and it would ooze out like jelly.' She giggled. 'Your parents must be so proud.'

She squeezed Māreikura's hand tighter. 'Did I say something wrong, dear?'

'No,' Māreikura said, rubbing her eyes. 'It's all right.'

'Well, I tell you what, dear, Chloe talks about you all the time. She said you were the one in class everyone looks up to, always brave and speaking your truth. Chloe said to me, "Gran, I wish I was able to do that, speak my truth." And so I can see why she has taken such a liking to you.'

Grandma Simpson looked concerned. 'Now, you haven't touched your food. Are you not hungry, dear?'

'I've been trying to give up gluten,' said Māreikura.

'Oh, yes!' She put her finger up in the air. 'I have some biscuits in the cupboard that are gluten-free, hang on, dear. Will you pass me my walker?'

Māreikura wanted to say no but Grandma Simpson looked determined. She furiously manoeuvred her walker to the kitchen and then a minute later appeared with a packet of Mint Slice biscuits.

'These are gluten-free, you see.'

She opened the packet and put the biscuits gently on the plate. Māreikura saw the packet said 'vegan' and definitely not gluten-free, and she would have brain fog and cramps from one bite of those deadly biscuits, but Grandma Simpson was worth it so she ate them anyway.

'Sorry, dear, I talk so much and I know it's getting late.' She laughed to herself. 'You'll have to come back, won't you?'

Māreikura promised she would. It was 9 p.m. so she kissed Grandma Simpson goodbye. Chloe came out and Māreikura offered to drive her home but she said her flatmate was picking her up.

Grandma Simpson insisted on standing at the door and then she called out, 'I love you so much, dear' and Chloe said, 'I love you too, Gran.'

'You too, Māreikura!' Grandma Simpson called out. 'I love you, sweetheart.'

CHAPTER TWENTY-ONE

Tinder Guy ghosted Jordana and Māreikura pretended to be shocked.

'I just didn't see it coming,' Jordana said.

I did, Māreikura wanted to say. She put her hand on Jordana's back. 'Ka aroha, e hoa.'

'I thought we got on really well,' Jordana said. 'He invited me to his brother's birthday next weekend but then he just stopped replying to my messages. He still likes my posts and watches my stories but he doesn't message me back.'

'Is that still ghosting if he likes your Insta posts?'

'My therapist said it's called orbiting,' Jordana said. 'It means it's not quite ghosting.'

'I never liked him anyway, e hoa,' Māreikura told her. 'You're way out of his league.'

She sighed. 'He must be an avoidant.'

Jordana always diagnosed men who weren't interested in her with an avoidant attachment style. Apparently, she was an empath with secure attachment and everyone else was avoidant with a narcissistic disorder.

'I thought he was love-bombing you anyway,' Māreikura said. 'He seemed intense at the beginning.'

'The problem is, Māreikura, if someone doesn't love-bomb me then I think that's a red flag. I deserve to be love-bombed.'

Jordana scrunched her nose up as she bit into an apple.

'I can taste the pesticides. Where did you get these from?'

'Pak'nSave.'

Jordana looked at Māreikura like she had committed the worst crime possible, though Māreikura knew it was not about the apple and all to do with the Tinder guy.

'I'm going to have to settle for a white guy,' Jordana said. 'Oh well, at least they're stable and good with finances.'

'Do you believe in past lives?' Māreikura asked. 'Chloe's grandmother feels familiar, like I've met her before. I can't explain it. How I feel around her.'

Jordana took another bite of her apple. 'I believe you,' she said. 'I had the same feeling with my ex. Then he cheated on me and ruined my life.'

'How's Troy's poutokomanawa?' Māreikura asked.

'Good.' Jordana shrugged. 'Except his poutokomanawa is his grandmother who is dead so I'm just reading old journals.'

'I thought it would be his mum.'

'He actually doesn't talk about his mum,' Jordana said. 'Like, at all.'

•

Chloe's smell lingered in the lounge when Māreikura got home from Jordana's house.

'Has Chloe been here?' Māreikura asked her nana.

'Who?'

'Chloe from school.'

'Oh, yeah,' Glennis said. She gestured towards the shelf behind her. 'She dropped off something for my legs.'

Māreikura picked up the jar. It was kawakawa balm. She immediately googled the brand name to check if the owners were Māori. They were.

'What's wrong with your legs?'

'Nothing, don't worry 'bout me.'

Māreikura pulled a chair from the dining room and put it in front of her nan. She told her to put her leg up and rest it on the chair. She pulled Glennis's trousers up and her nan groaned. Māreikura opened the balm and rubbed it on her leg and then her feet.

'If it's not better tomorrow, I'll take you to the doctor's.'

She sent Chloe a message: *Send me your bank details so I can transfer for the kawakawa*

Chloe: *It was a koha*

Māreikura: *thank u*

Māreikura: *You can still interview Nan if you want. It's too late to change anyway.*

Chloe: *Ok*

•

The next day, her nan's leg was still not better so Māreikura took her to the doctor. Glennis refused to see anyone except for Doctor Wang because he was 'Chinese' so he was 'legitimate'. She used to see Doctor Yan but he told her she needed to lose weight and to stop eating white bread and red meat so Glennis changed doctors. 'I just didn't like his tone with me,' she told Māreikura.

An hour sitting in the waiting room and $50 later, Doctor Wang told Glennis to go home, rest and take Panadol. Exactly what her nana did anyway. Māreikura took the day off from school and stayed with her, mostly out of guilt for not being around much since she was always at Kat's or Jordana's house. Her nana had told the whole street Māreikura was on *Breakfast* and was now a 'famous' radio host.

'I'm not a radio host,' Māreikura told her over and over again. 'I have a podcast. They're different.'

'Same thing,' her nan said, waving her arms in the air. 'Now, Gloria down the road wants to know how to download it – you'll have to show her, she has one of those smartphones. Will you show her? She asked what it's about. I still don't get it.'

'It's about learning te reo Māori,' Māreikura said.

Her nan said nothing. Māreikura set up her work on the table while her nan was in the lounge watching the horrors of daytime television.

'You need anything, Nan?'

'No, I'm good. Don't know why you took the day off. Nothing wrong with me.'

She watched Māreikura walk back and forth, mouthing words.

'What you doing, girl?'

'Learning new kupu hou. New Māori words.' Māreikura sat next to her on the couch. 'Can you test me? Ask me the time and I'll try answer in Māori. If you want to say, What's the time? you say, He aha te tāima?'

'Say that again.'

'He aha te tāima?'

'He aha te what?'

'Te tāima.'

Her nan shook her head. 'He aha te wā, not te tāima. Te wā.'

It was the first time Māreikura had ever heard her nan speak Māori.

'Don't know what they teaching you at school, what the hell is tāima? That's not even Māori. That's just a translation from English.'

Māreikura scribbled out tāima on her notes and wrote wā in big letters. 'Okay, how do I say two thirty then?'

'He rua karaka te hāwhe.'

'And two forty-five?'

'That's enough,' she said coldly.

'Nan,' Māreikura said, trying to hide the excitement in her voice, 'do you still remember how to speak Māori?'

'A little bit.'

She was staring in front of her, not looking at Māreikura.

'Can you teach me?'

'Teach you what?'

'Te reo.'

She pursed her lips. 'I taught your mum. What good did that do? Look where that got her.'

'I'm not her,' Māreikura said quietly.

'Exactly,' her nan shot back. 'Waste of time.'

Māreikura went into her room and closed the door behind her.

CHAPTER TWENTY-TWO

David Seymour was on the news again. Something about Māori having special privileges.

'Shut up, David,' Māreikura yelled at the TV. She made a gagging sound and stuck two fingers into her mouth.

Māreikura was at Kat's house; they were curled up on the couch watching the news. The story changed to a group of Pākehā outraged about te reo Māori being added to street names and how the language was being 'forced' upon them.

The next day, Māreikura would explain on her podcast how English was once forced on Māori, how the Native Schools Act impacted Māori in the present day and how adding te reo Māori to street signs is really the bare minimum.

'We don't have time to explore our intergenerational gifts because we're too busy explaining and justifying our reason for being,' Māreikura told Kat.

'Think about it. We want to fill our lives with te reo Māori and mātauranga and stories of our tīpuna, but how can we when we are constantly distracted by having to watch our existence be debated over and over again like it's a debate over whether pineapple belongs on pizza?'

Kat picked up the remote and turned the TV off.

'Why don't we do something happy?' she asked in a cheerful voice. 'How about a walk?'

Māreikura did not feel like going for a walk. She felt inexplicable rage and she did not know where to direct her anger. It was not really David Seymour she was angry at. He did not deserve to live rent-free in her head. It was not even the system she was enraged at. It was the world and the way colonisation had seethed and gnawed its way through every aspect of her life.

'We are being constantly gaslighted by politicians who hold power over decisions that directly impact Māori,' Māreikura said. 'Politicians in power who have Māori heritage and yet their deep internalised racism means they refuse to acknowledge our colonial past so they can be applauded in a Pākehā world, and in turn they end up denying their own existence at the cost of our own people.'

Kat sighed. 'When does it end?'

'It doesn't,' Māreikura answered. 'It will never end until colonial violence is uprooted from within our systems. It will never end until Pākehā break the intergenerational curse of racism within their own families and within the walls of their homes. Maybe one day I can do a podcast about puppies and romantic love but until then, I will have to keep using my platform to justify our very existence.'

CHAPTER TWENTY-THREE

'Māreikura, hey!'

Eru's tall and lanky white brother-in-law Matt was standing outside of the gate waving. One time at the dinner table, he asked Māreikura, 'Aren't we all Indigenous?' She'd never liked him after that. Māreikura had done a good job over the last year avoiding their family. Sometimes she wouldn't leave her house until she saw the black SUV was gone and the windows were shut. She was spending most of her time at Kat's or Jordana's so maybe that's how she managed to avoid them.

Matt jogged over to Māreikura. 'How are you doing? You good?'

'Yeah,' she said. 'I've been busy with school.'

She'd forgotten how tall he was. Had it been that long? He was towering over her. He had a little stubble and he was balding now. Māreikura still couldn't make sense of it. A guy like Matt being able to claim any kind of space next to Erana, who was an older, female version of Eru, with dewy skin and big brown eyes and a perfect symmetrical face.

Erana told her once that Matt loved Jesus and that was the most important thing and Māreikura asked her, 'Is it, though? Like is that his whole personality?'

Erana laughed and then Māreikura asked her, 'So all the guys in the church just have to love Jesus and they get all the pretty girls? Is it that easy? Maybe I need to find Jesus?'

And then Erana hit her playfully and said, 'Why are you so funny, girl?' even though Māreikura was serious.

'Hey, you wanna come inside?' Matt asked. 'It's just me, Erana and baby Te Atarangi home. Erana will want to see you.'

He smiled and Māreikura remembered the warmth in his smile, that even though he was annoying, he always meant well.

'I can't,' she said. 'Sorry, I'm really busy with school and stuff.'

'Okay, Ma. That's okay.'

'Tell everyone I said hi, yeah?'

'I will. We miss you.'

Māreikura turned around and went inside. Once she got in, she peered out from behind the curtain and watched Matt wheel the rubbish bin in. Erana came out, and Matt said something and then Erana mouthed 'Where?' looking out, and Matt pointed and for a split second, Māreikura saw sadness come over Erana's face. Then they went inside and shut the door.

•

Later that night, there was a knock at the front door. Māreikura could usually tell who it was by her nana's footsteps. If it was someone her nan didn't like, there would be no movement and the person would be ignored. Like Mrs Donaldson from number 56, who usually came over unannounced. 'Nosy old bag,' her nan would say. 'Always sticking her nose into my business.'

If it was someone her nan liked, there would be a, 'Hold on, hold your horses, I'm coming,' followed by loud, thumping footsteps. Like Eru Senior or Eru Junior.

This time, Māreikura heard soft footsteps and her nan almost whispering. She heard Chloe's voice and then her nana telling her to sit down. Then she heard Chloe say, 'Are you sure, Glennis?'

Māreikura moved closer to the bedroom door to listen.

•

Sometimes, when Glennis Maipihi saw a blackboard, she remembered being stretched over, hanging over the desk, and being hit from behind. The supplejacks hung to the left of the blackboard. After the teacher beat her, she would hang the supplejack back up.

'All because I needed to go to the toilet,' Glennis told Chloe. 'I didn't know the English word for toilet so I said, "Kei te pīrangi au i te mimi". I spoke Māori and we weren't allowed to. If we did, we got punished.'

The first time it happened, Glennis went home and told her mum. Later on, she heard her parents arguing, and the next day they only spoke English to their kids.

'I learnt that when you speak te reo Māori, it's dangerous,' Glennis said. 'Not just at school but even on the streets, you wouldn't dare say kia ora.'

This is why her nan never goes home, Māreikura realised. It's easier to disconnect. The pain is unbearable. The truth doesn't always set us free. Truth can feel like betrayal. If we are not careful, truth will destroy us.

Māreikura opened her bedroom door. Her nana was huddled on the couch, the photo of her mother close to her chest. She glanced in Māreikura's direction.

'You ask me why I didn't teach you,' she said. 'I was trying to protect you.'

CHAPTER TWENTY-FOUR

Māreikura left to go to Kat's house. When she arrived, Kat was lying on the couch scrolling on her phone. Even in a baggy shirt, fresh-faced and with her legs dangling over the side, she was beautiful. She scrolled down and then scrolled up. Māreikura managed to just read the headline over her shoulder: *'I'm a White-passing Māori in Between Worlds.'*

'Not another one,' Māreikura groaned.

'What?'

'Aren't we done with this narrative?' she asked. 'I'm so sick of reading opinion pieces about white Māori, like I'm so sorry it was hard for you. I'm sorry that you benefited from your white skin. How many stories do we need to read like this?'

Kat dropped her phone and made a noise with her mouth – an exaggerated noise Māreikura was now familiar with that told her she was pissed off.

'I'm sorry,' Māreikura said. 'I'm not talking about you.'

'Well, you are.'

'I'm just sick of reading about how hard it is for white Māori. I was born disconnected from my culture too but guess what, I didn't get to camouflage like white Māori did and receive all the benefits from white skin, did I? Like that gatekeeper lady – if I was white, she wouldn't have stopped me at the gate and made me question myself for not being able to speak te reo. Now all these white-passing Māori are taking up space and repeating the same narrative year after year. It's 2024. If you are Māori, you whakapapa Māori. The end. Stop giving colonisers what they want.'

Kat's arms were folded. For a while, she didn't say anything. And then she said, 'I didn't get any benefits.'

'You did.'

'Like what? I've worked hard my whole life.'

'You're palatable,' Māreikura said. 'You're just the right amount of Māori that isn't deemed threatening to white people.'

Kat's mouth dropped.

'What?' Māreikura asked. 'You're a hybrid, you get the best of both worlds. You can blend in when it matters. Do you think brown-skinned women would get the same seat at the table? I don't think your company would be successful if you weren't white.'

The silence was deafening. Māreikura was afraid to look over at Kat. But the words had flown out of her mouth and she meant what she said.

'That is so unfair of you to say, Māreikura,' Kat said finally, gritting her teeth. 'I work hard.'

'I'm not saying you don't work hard,' Māreikura said. 'But we experience the world differently. I can't camouflage but you can. You can take off your pounamu earrings and go into a board meeting and use your whiteness to get ahead. Your whiteness affords you so many privileges.'

'You're being judgemental,' Kat said. 'You don't know what it's like to have to prove your Māori-ness because of having whiter skin.'

'Right, and that's probably the biggest discomfort you will face – having to prove your Māori-ness. Whereas for me and other dark-skinned Māori, our discomfort is lateral violence. Our discomfort is racism. Our discomfort is that we are more likely to be stopped by the police, or followed in shops, have fewer job opportunities, or face discrimination. I have to try twenty times harder than you. So your discomfort is nothing in comparison to what many of us experience on a day-to-day basis.'

Kat pulled the blanket over her so Māreikura couldn't see her face. How could someone be so blissfully unaware of their own privilege? Māreikura found herself questioning their relationship for the first time.

Māreikura messaged Jordana.

I have an idea for our next podcast episode.

The three small dots appeared and then Jordana messaged back. *What?*

Colourism and privilege in te ao Māori. Why are Māori so scared to talk about it?? And why are white Māori in denial??

•

Wahine Chats became the number three most-listened-to podcast in the Pacific with over two hundred reviews on Spotify.

'Refreshingly honest' and 'Māreikura dives into issues many are afraid of.' 'The voices of our generation!!' someone else wrote.

Māreikura was soon asked to speak at sold-out shows and as a keynote speaker at conferences and workplaces. The Pākehā lapped up her words – oh, how they loved her, applauding from their seats, their heads nodding furiously as Māreikura spoke and then shaking when Māreikura talked of her father who was in a gang, a man she did not know. Afterwards, they would go home and have a dinner party and invite their rich white friends and discuss Māreikura's story over expensive Marlborough wine and olives and canapes, except they wouldn't quite remember Māreikura's name – it was too difficult to pronounce. They will talk of her as the nice Mowry girl whose father was in a gang and whose mum is dead and they will sigh and say, 'How very unfortunate,' and then Susan will say, 'Well, that's the world we live in and there's a consequence for every choice.' 'Good on her,' someone else will say. 'It just shows, when the odds are against you, you can beat them.' And then someone will make an offhand comment about gangs being the scum of the earth and everyone will nod and agree and then they will change the subject and talk about the stock market and about Janis's grandchildren coming to visit from London and eventually about how they hate the Labour Government and it was all Jacinda Ardern's fault because they were forced to put the prices up for their five rental homes since the taxes were getting higher. Susan will wipe her hands clean and serve dinner and they will never speak of Māreikura again.

Māreikura spent her childhood yearning for the approval of Pākehā, and now she had it, she did not want it. It didn't matter to her anymore. Deep down, what she really desired was the approval of Māori, but when she scanned the audiences she saw no brown faces, and when she scanned the social media comments she saw a Māori name write, *This girl needs to go back to school and learn her reo lol.* It brought back the feelings from when she met the gatekeeper – feelings of hatred and helplessness, not for this person she didn't know, but for herself. The pain was so much worse when it came from your own people.

Soon Māreikura became a poster child for Māori. She felt like she was profiting off her trauma as a form of entertainment for Pākehā – held up as an example of a Māori person who could make it in the white world, despite New Zealand's history, despite accusations of a racist system that was supposedly set up to work against Māori. Says who? Māreikura was uplifted as a baby; were there any more stereotypes she could tick off? Yet here she was, proving you can make it despite the circumstances you're born into because we're all equal and we all deserve equal rights. Oh, you don't know your language? No worries, go back to school and get your reo – it's that easy. It just takes a year. What's a year out of your life anyway? Māreikura did it. Oh, you were taken from your family as a baby? You can still succeed because look at Māreikura. Deputy head girl and a law scholarship. A walking, talking advertisement that if Māreikura can make it, so can you. There's no excuse. Now Māreikura could add LGBTQ+ to the list because she happened to fall in love with a woman. Now she was Māori, a woman and queer. Tick tick tick. She was part of the even more marginalised and oppressed community. It gave her a pass, permission to speak to LGBTQ+ issues because now she had lived experience. Although when Māreikura was asked about gay rights, she really had nothing to add to the conversation and she didn't know what to say except to quote Elizabeth Kerekere. Thank God for Elizabeth Kerekere.

And as she purchased her first Doc Martens for $350 and a pair of AirPods for $369 with the money she made from talking about her trauma, she felt a pang of guilt that she was a sell-out – buying into capitalism and colonialism and everything that was very wrong with the world and what put her where she was in the first place. But man did she love her AirPods. Not having a wire from her phone to her ears was life-changing. This was how rich people lived. Minor things stop being an inconvenience, like not having a wire dangling from your ears. Leaving them in her ears when she was listening to nothing, when someone tried to talk to her, she would simply point at her ears and they would get lost. It gave her a new-found power.

She started to enjoy money appearing in her account, often in chunks, like a magic trick, coming out of nowhere until Māreikura remembered it was from the performance she did two months ago where she was paid three grand to 'share her story'. Then the guilty feeling would come again. She was getting paid money that a construction worker would spend a month earning, but she pushed it away because she liked going to a boujee cafe and not having to look at the price on the menu for once. Ordering what she felt like. *Is this what it feels like to be rich?!* She liked the feeling of saying to Kat, 'I'll get it,' and actually meaning it, slipping her card to the person behind the counter without the anxiety of her card declining. And she loved her Docs. They gave her a new sense of identity, a coolness that she'd always craved, and every time she put them on, she was edgy and hot and slipping into her queerness. Kat would look Māreikura up and down and tell her, 'You're so hot in those,' and sometimes she would make Māreikura leave them on when they were in bed.

Māreikura started a new Instagram account and soon her follower count reached 60 000. Her page became the go-to source for news, although she didn't mean for it to be, so she made sure to post something daily. It was usually something that was trending and to do with colonialism, Māori or Indigenous people around the world. She reshared a video of a group of white nurses performing the haka on a boat. *THIS IS WHITE COLONIAL ENERGY* she wrote and it went viral. She scanned Twitter for updates and started screenshotting them and posting them on her page. One time, she posted about Pasifika and someone wrote, *Please don't speak for our community*, and she wrote back, *I AM TANGATA WHENUA AND THIS IS MY LAND*, and then she blocked them. The more people came at her, the more she would simply block them. She didn't have time to deal with haters. There was too much work to do.

CHAPTER TWENTY-FIVE

No one had seen Koro Ian for weeks and then he appeared at the door in his blue overalls and muddy boots. Māreikura got to her feet and gave him a big hug. He seemed to cling on to her tighter today.

'Kia ora, girl.' His smile wasn't as bright as usual, his eyes lined with dark bags. He scanned around the room and then tapped the table with his hands.

'He pānui,' he said and then he pulled out an A4 piece of lined paper from his pocket. 'Dear whānau, my time at the school of Māori has been wonderful,' he read aloud.

'By far the most wonderful part of it has been meeting you all. Thank you to you, Whaea T., and to all of you who have supported me. Unfortunately, all good things must come to an end. I have tried everything to learn te reo Māori and I really thought getting into this school would be the answer. But I cannot juggle full-time work and take care of my dear Maureen, spend time with my mokos and do all the hours that Māori requires of me. I have to give up something, and recently I have been diagnosed with diabetes so I need to look after my health. I realised I don't have many years left and I need to spend them with my family. I have made amends and have come to peace with the fact I will never get my language in this life,' he read.

'However, I know I have done my best and I am most proud of being able to speak more Māori than I did before. When I die, I hope my tīpuna will forgive me and that they will teach this old goat in heaven.' Then he paused and added, 'Because I bet ya te reo Māori is the only language spoken in heaven. The language from the heavens.'

'You can't quit,' Māreikura said. 'You can't. We all need you. We can help you.' She looked around, waiting for someone else to say something. 'Can't we, whānau? We can have tutorials and do other stuff to help you.'

'Āe, Koro,' Jordana said. 'We're here to help you.'

'Thank you, everyone,' he said. 'But I've made my choice.'

One by one, the class went up to him and hugged him. When it was Māreikura's turn, he took both her hands and said, 'You make sure you stay the course, girl. You promise? Don't you dare quit, you keep going for me.' And Māreikura nodded and promised she would.

Afterwards, she went to the bathroom and sobbed in the toilet cubicle because she hated that Koro Ian was leaving, that he had tried everything but it still wasn't enough to learn his own language. It wasn't fair. Then, she went to Whaea Terina's office. Whaea Terina's face was buried in her hands, and it felt like Māreikura had intruded on an intimate moment she wasn't supposed to see. She never thought about how hard it was for Whaea Terina to be a teacher, responsible for thirty students, many who came in with unresolved trauma. She wondered how Māori teachers dealt with language trauma, especially if they're second-language learners themselves and dealing with their own problems.

Whaea Terina, without even looking up, said, 'Come in, Māreikura.'

'Aroha mai, Whaea. I can come back.'

'No need.'

Māreikura walked in and shut the door.

'Auē, such a tangiweto, nē?' Whaea Terina said, reaching over to the box of tissues. 'You know, Māreikura, sometimes being Māori has to come second to surviving. Some Māori don't have time like you and me to sit around and think, "Ko wai au?" – Who am I? – and twiddle their thumbs and think about it for the rest of the day, week, years. Some of us are just trying to feed our kids, survive in this world.'

'Like Koro Ian.'

'Like Koro Ian,' she repeated. 'I'm telling you this because you have all the time now, girl. You must do everything to get your language back. To hold on to your identity. Everything.'

'I am, Whaea. Language trauma stops with me.'

'Māreikura, you must speak te reo Māori to gain the language,' she said. 'Surprisingly enough, that's how it works.'

'I know. I just get whakamā speaking it.'

'Well, here's a tip. If you're starting out playing tennis, you'd never go straight to playing with Serena Williams, would you? Same with te reo Māori. Best to practise with someone who's a bit better than you.'

'I want to speak with the Māori in the class but they have their own stuff going on. You know, language trauma and all that.'

'Mm hmm. What about those in the class who might not have trauma?'

'What? Pākehā? I'm not asking Pākehā to help me learn my own language.'

'I'm just say—'

'I'm not asking Pākehā to help me learn my own language.'

Whaea Terina glanced out the window and then back at Māreikura.

'When I was a little girl, I was swimming at Waipū Cove and a rip had taken me out. It was the scariest moment of my life. I was praying to God, the father, the son, and his mother too. Thought I was gonna die. There I was, gasping for air, ready to let go. You know the Māori word for immersion is rumaki, nē? Rumaki also means to drown. So you could say "rumaki reo" or full-immersion reo also means to drown in reo. So there I was in the middle of the ocean, flapping my arms out, thinking I was gonna die. Then I saw something. Can you guess what it was?'

'Jesus?'

'It was a rope. I saw a rope, and I grabbed onto that thing like my little life depended on it and it pulled me all the way back to shore. Me maumahara koe, ina ka toromi koe, kaore koe i titiro ki te tai te kara ō te taura e whakaora ana i na koe. When you are drowning, it doesn't matter what colour the rope is.'

CHAPTER TWENTY-SIX

Jordana told Māreikura they should go for a drive after school even though she did not own a car. *Did you know car pollution is one of the major causes of global warming?* she once asked Māreikura as she hopped into the passenger seat and stretched her feet out, putting her dirty Jordans all over the glove box. Māreikura wanted to tell her to get out and walk then. Jordana Ubered everywhere and drank from plastic bottles so Māreikura did not believe the environment was the sole reason she didn't own a car, but more to do with the fact she was used to being a princess and liked the idea of being driven around. Māreikura cared about climate change, because how could you be Indigenous and not care? She just had a different way of showing it.

They parked up at Point Chev beach and Jordana said, 'This is the saddest beach I've ever seen.' Then she scanned the water and said, 'How come the water's brown?'

'If you wanted a nice beach you should have stayed in Bali.'

'The moon really must be in a mood today.' Jordana cackled and then picked up her flask. 'This will help you connect with your divine self. Straight from South America.'

She poured the cacao into two mugs and handed one to Māreikura. She didn't know what cacao was until Jordana introduced it to her. It was after drinking cacao that Jordana felt the prompting to move back to Aotearoa and learn te reo Māori. 'It's trippier than drugs,' she said. 'But there's no comedown.

'There's been studies, did you know?' Jordana was now talking about the moana. 'It's scientifically proven that if you just look at the moana every day, it will lift your wairua.'

'That's nice,' Māreikura said, taking another sip. 'Do you ever think about what happened on these shores all those hundreds of years ago?' She opened the door and touched the sand. 'Or that our ancestors could have touched this very sand that runs between my fingers? Or was blood shed here by the hands of our colonisers? Sometimes I feel the brunt of my tīpuna's pain, their heartache.'

Māreikura shut the door. 'One day, every Māori is going to have to wake up to what colonisation has done to us. How racism is engraved in every fragment of society. But most of us are in a deep sleep.'

Jordana was looking down at her phone, her right thumb swiping through Instagram, her left hand still gripping her mug. She sucked in her breath. 'He's so hot.'

'Who?'

'Brad Ahiwawa,' she said, as if expecting Māreikura to know who she was talking about. 'You know, "thatMāoriguy" on Instagram.'

'Is he that douchey guy that shares his hot takes that aren't actually hot takes?'

'What? Nah. This is him.' Jordana flashed her phone at Māreikura.

'Yeah, he's the guy who writes a tweet that gets two likes on Twitter then uploads it on his Instagram.'

'So? He teaches Māori too.'

'He looks whakahīhī.'

'I thought we don't use that word anymore.'

'Sorry, I mean he looks like a very confident young man.'

'Yes, he is.' Jordana held up a photo of a shirtless selfie at the gym.

'What's that got to do with te reo Māori?' asked Māreikura. 'He does the bare minimum. Says a few things to the camera in Māori and everyone thinks he's all that. You just think he's hot.'

'Well, yeah,' Jordana said, as if it was obvious. 'He's dating Shona Hohaia anyway.'

'Who?'

Jordana looked at Māreikura like she was stupid. 'The singer Shona Hohaia? You know that waiata, "Ka Aroha"?'

'Oh,' Māreikura said, even though she did not know.

'She's like the queenie of Māori music.'

'No, she isn't. Maisey Rika is.'

'You just have a crush on Maisey.'

Māreikura didn't say anything.

'What if we got Brad on the podcast?' Jordana asked. 'I think it would be good to get a kura kaupapa kid on the show to talk about what it's like growing up in te ao Māori.'

'Why? So he can talk about how he got handed his language on a silver platter?'

'So? Why are you jealous of kura kaupapa kids?'

'It's not jealousy, it's an acknowledgement.'

'Acknowledgement of what?' Jordana gave her a look.

'Acknowledgement of the class system that exists in te ao Māori that kura kaupapa kids belong to – a certain sector of the class that you and I, through no fault of our own, will never belong to.'

'What? There is no class system. Someone in their whānau had to do the exact work we are doing, e hoa. It was harder back then. Kura kaupapa was radical back in the days.'

'Yeah, but te ao Māori is still divided,' Māreikura said. 'It's like a class system. Māori who have support from their whānau and are handed their language on a platter. And then the struggling, who are trying to reclaim a stolen language while working through intergenerational trauma with limited to no support and extreme whakamā.'

Māreikura heard Jordana take a deep breath in, count to three, then breathe out.

'If you don't think there's a class system then what about nepotism?' Māreikura asked.

'What's that?'

'Google it.'

Jordana brought her phone aggressively to her face and typed into Google. After a while, she looked up from her phone. 'You really think that exists in te ao Māori?'

'All I know is that te ao Māori is full of ego and it doesn't matter how much we learn the language, we'll never belong.'

'Colonisation really did a number on us,' Jordana said. ''Cause you're angry at the wrong people.'

Jordana fumbled around her bag and pulled out a lighter and a sage stick. She lit the sage and waved it over Māreikura.

'This will help with your raru but it ain't no miracle worker.'

Māreikura coughed dramatically and opened the car door like she was dying. She stuck her face outside. 'Don't do that again.'

'What?'

'Wave your sage over me. That shit is colonised and you didn't ask for my permission. I feel violated.'

Jordana tapped her nails on the side door. 'I was just trying to help.'

'I'm not a project.'

Jordana dropped her head and scrolled on her phone. Māreikura finished off the rest of her cacao and waited for something to happen. Nothing happened. No prompting, no connection with her divine self. She started the engine and drove Jordana home.

CHAPTER TWENTY-SEVEN

Suffering is the place where your faith is tested, Eru told Māreikura once. *What do you know about suffering?* she asked him. She liked interrogating him about his privilege. She wondered how he knew suffering when he seemed to get everything in life. *Job had everything taken away from him*, Eru told her. Job was a fictional character from the Bible that had no relevance to Māreikura's life. *But it was in his suffering he felt God the most*, Eru said. *It is in our suffering we feel the love of God.*

Sometimes it would get on her nerves when Eru went on about his faith, but now she wished she could hear his voice again. She wanted him to take her by the hand and pray for her. She could use that right now. She secretly liked it when he did that, when he would ask God to watch over her, to pour over his blessings. Even though she rolled her eyes and pretended she didn't like it, she always felt better afterwards. Maybe somewhere out there in the universe there was a God who loved her. Not a white, Mormon God, but an Indigenous, woman God who heard Eru's prayers and poured down blessings. Māreikura was beginning to change her mind. Not about God, but about the idea of suffering. Eru came from a different world. A world she could never comprehend, but maybe everyone knew what suffering felt like – it just looked different on each person.

Māreikura hated the feeling of suffering. It comes and goes, an emptiness, Te Kore, like a hole in her chest that is infinite and eternal. If Eru was here, she would message him with a big *ONE* and he would come to her rescue. But he wasn't here so she drove around the city wishing she could just drive without having to think about how much money she was wasting on gas, and then she thought about how rich people don't have to think about that – they can drive for as long as they like and not worry if their car will break down because it's making funny noises or if it will run out of gas on the motorway.

Māreikura drove to Grandma Simpson's house. It was a stupid idea. They had only met once and Grandma Simpson was probably just being polite when she said Māreikura could visit any time. People always say things like that when they don't really mean it. *Come over any time, call me any time.* It's all lies. People just say it to make themselves feel better, to make themselves look good. But it always comes with rules, with hidden expectations. *Come over any time* – so what if Māreikura showed up at 3 a.m.? People never say what they really mean. Grandma Simpson would probably take one look at the unhinged brown girl on the doorstep with bloodshot eyes and a snotty nose and either call the mental health services or the police.

The front door clicked open and Māreikura could see Grandma Simpson's fuzzy hair in between the cracks.

'Grandma Simpson,' Māreikura said. 'I don't even know why I'm here.'

Māreikura was crying. Grandma Simpson put her hands on Māreikura's face and then hugged her.

'I do, dear,' she said. 'I know exactly why you're here.'

•

Grandma Simpson told Māreikura that God told her she was coming.

'I was thinking what to make for dinner and a little voice told me to make a shepherd's pie,' Grandma Simpson said. 'Not just any shepherd's pie, but the one that has been in my family for generations. Isn't the Lord wonderful? He does that, you know, shows us little pockets of love just when we need it. You will stay, won't you?'

Māreikura nodded and Grandma Simpson rubbed her hands together, pleased.

'Oh, I'm so glad. My mother taught me it when I was young, even younger than your age now. It was actually one of the last meals we made before my mother died. That's why it's so special, you see, it always reminds me of her. I think that's what makes cooking so special, because it reminds me of a time and place and a memory.' She reached into her sleeve and pulled out a handkerchief and wiped her nose. 'Do you have a favourite food, dear?' she asked, then she blew her nose. 'Excuse me, dear.'

'I like rēwena,' Māreikura said. 'My nan makes it on special occasions.' She scanned the wall. 'Do you have any photos of your mum?'

'No, dear, she died when I was fifteen. But I can tell you exactly what she looked like – I can remember her as if she was standing right in front of me. Oh, Māreikura, she was absolutely stunning. She loved people and she loved God. And do you know what, if she met you she would absolutely adore you.' She touched the tip of Māreikura's nose.

'Do you know about the history of Ireland and how we almost lost our language?' Grandma Simpson asked. 'Padraig Pearse, the Irish revolutionary leader, famously said, "A country without a language is a country without a soul." So now Gaelic has been revitalised just like te reo Māori has been here. Though I know the struggles are very different; there has been a lot of struggle, but I don't know much. You see, we left Ireland and moved to England during the war.'

'The war?' Māreikura asked. 'What war?'

'World War II, dear.'

Her mouth started trembling and Māreikura reached out and grabbed her hand.

'Thank you, dear.' She squeezed Māreikura's hand back. 'I still remember the sound of bombs dropping,' she said. 'That was the most frightening part, Māreikura. My mother and father would gather us children together and we would huddle by the fire and pray. We didn't know if we would live or die, or if I would see any of my friends or neighbours the next day. We were waiting for it to be over. For Hitler to stop.'

She was still clutching Māreikura's hand tight, their fingers now laced together.

'You were alive through the Holocaust?'

'Yes,' she said, her voice quiet. 'Many people, including some of my friends, worshipped Hitler like he was God.'

The oven timer went off and Grandma Simpson was back in the present day again.

'How are you so happy?' Māreikura asked, following her into the kitchen. 'When you've had so much suffering.' Then she paused. 'Don't you get lonely?'

'I get very lonely, dear,' she said. 'But eternity is a long time, and one day I will be reunited with my David, my mother, my family, with God. That's what brings me hope.' She smiled.

'I always begin my day with gratitude too. As soon as I open my eyes, I tell the Lord all the things I am grateful for, and then I see the awe and wonder of what the Lord has given me. Because I have been given much, I too must give. So I always look for ways to give, although in my old age I can't give like I used to. I pray to love His children the way He loves them, and so now when I look at every person I meet, I ask God to show me who they truly are and He gives that to me, to see people in all of their fullness. Relationships and connections might seem random but they are orchestrated by God. I always ask God, *Well, what is the divine purpose of this event? Why has this person come into my life?* And that's what I asked God when you showed up to my door with Chloe. I thought, *How lucky am I? Why did the Lord bring this beautiful girl into my life?* I believe He is in every detail of our lives and that He brought us together. Perhaps there is a lot we can learn from each other. Or perhaps you have simply come into my life to be a blessing, to be the light that you are.'

'I don't feel like a light,' Māreikura said. 'But thank you.'

'The truth you speak into the world is light,' she said. 'And the more you speak truth, the more light will radiate from you.'

She stopped and looked again at Māreikura, both hands on her cheek.

'Māreikura, dear, I'm so glad you're here.'

CHAPTER TWENTY-EIGHT

Chloe was sitting at the library, her eyes scanning the open book on the desk. The book was *Māori Made Easy*, with pink Post-it notes sticking out from the pages. Her right hand was fidgeting with a cube on her lap.

'Why are you always playing with that?' Māreikura asked.

Chloe glanced up. 'It helps with my ADHD.'

'I think I have ADHD.' Māreikura put her bag on the floor and sat across from Chloe.

'I can see why you would think that,' Chloe said.

'Um, okay.'

'I mean, because ADHD is commonly undiagnosed in women.'

'What are your symptoms?'

'I can't sit still,' Chloe said. 'I procrastinate, I overthink. I experience extreme sadness but also extreme joy.'

'That sounds like bipolar.'

Chloe just looked at her. 'Why did you want to meet again?'

'Grandma Simpson—'

'Oh no.' Chloe sucked in her breath. 'What did she do? I know she gets touchy. I did tell her to stop that. Sorry, I—'

'What? Your grandma is a literal angel.'

Chloe exhaled. 'Oh, thank God, I thought you were gonna cancel Grandma.'

'I was with her last night,' Māreikura said. 'We had shepherd's pie.'

'Shepherd's pie?' Chloe said. 'Can't remember the last time she made me that.'

'I can't believe she was alive when Hitler was around? She has some cool, I mean, interesting stories. You're lucky.'

'So are you,' Chloe said. 'Glennis is the funniest person I've met, like I am actually in tears when I leave the house. And she's really wise. I always think about the generation who lived during the Native Schools Act, how that part of our history is so recent.'

'Yeah, she doesn't talk about that a lot,' Māreikura said. 'To me, I mean.'

'Grandma doesn't talk about Hitler a lot to us kids either,' Chloe said.

Māreikura saw the word 'ADHD – Aroreretini' in big letters on Chloe's textbook. 'Is that the Māori word for ADHD?'

'Āe! Ātaahua, nē?' Chloe said. 'ADHD has always been such a negative term in English but in te reo Māori, it's "attention goes to many things" so it's seen as a superpower. It changed the way I see myself.'

'Why did you come here? I mean to school to learn te reo.'

'My Uncle Rob.'

'Your uncle from Ngāti Kahungunu?'

'Yeah,' she said. 'The day I said my iwi was Ngāti Kahungunu, I was so embarrassed. I didn't know you weren't meant to. But yeah, he's like a dad to me. When I used to go stay with him and my cousins, it just felt different, you know? Being around a Māori family, I dunno,

I don't want to sound tokenistic. My mum had depression growing up so it was nice to get a break from that. We used to go out on the boat for kaimoana, go to the marae. Last year, I was studying biology but I felt like, I dunno, like it had no meaning, so I applied to the Māori school and I got in. I'm not trying to be Māori, I just don't know where I fit in. Coming here I felt like it might help me. But I realise now there's a lot that I don't know.'

'About yourself?'

'About my privilege,' she said. 'Whaea Terina teaching us about our history – I didn't know any of it, any of what happened. It's embarrassing.'

'It's even more embarrassing when you're Māori and you don't know,' Māreikura said. 'It was my first time learning about it too. But I know about Te Tiriti, not because I've read a book but because I've experienced the pain of the Treaty not being honoured on both sides of my family. The impact it has on my whakapapa. Sometimes I feel like it's just a history lesson for non-Māori, like you can treat it like biology, and you can go home and never have to think about it again. For me, I have to experience it.'

'I never thought about it like that.'

'It's yearning for something that's been lost. I lost my language, the mātauranga, knowledge, my culture.' My mum. She didn't say the last part but she wanted to.

'I don't know how it feels to lose a language but I know the feeling of grief,' Chloe said.

'Are you talking about your dad?'

'Yeah.'

'Grandma Simpson told me he passed away.'

'He did not pass away,' Chloe said. There was anger in her voice. 'He died. I don't like the term "pass away". Or when Grandma says she lost her son. He's not lost. Lost implies he'll be found again. He died and that's the end.'

'You must miss him, though.'

Chloe tucked her hair behind her ears and straightened up.

'I'm gonna go over what we learnt today. Stay if you want.'

Māreikura stayed for two hours. They went over the words they learnt in class. Afterwards, they walked to the car park together and Māreikura asked if she wanted a ride but Chloe said she liked catching the bus, plus she wanted to finish her book anyway.

'What are you reading?'

'*The Parihaka Woman.*'

'Witi Ihimaera?' Māreikura asked. 'You should really read *Bulibasha.* That's my favourite book of his. I'll bring it next time.'

Chloe walked to the bus stop and Māreikura sat in the car and checked her phone. There was an email from Eru.

From: erujohnson@ldsmail.net
Subject: 3

CHAPTER TWENTY-NINE

Eru had never gone below 4 on the scale and Māreikura didn't know what to do. The lowest Eru had ever gone was 4 and that's when he was having an anxiety attack because he had to teach Sunday school and the topic was how marriage is between a man and a woman. Māreikura went over and sat with him until he started breathing normally and calmed him down. What if he was having an anxiety attack on his mission? Who was there to help him? She thought about contacting Eru Senior but instead she emailed back.

You are the strongest person I know, I'm here if you need me. Just call.

And then she put her phone away, because she was at school, in a different world – a time and place far away from Eru.

•

Jordana told Māreikura they needed Troy on the podcast and Māreikura told her that was a stupid idea.

'I remember one of the first things we said about Troy was that he was whakahīhī and we didn't like him,' Jordana said. 'And then I was thinking, *Why don't we like him?*'

'Because he is whakahīhī,' Māreikura said. 'And we didn't like him.'

'Is he, though?' Jordana asked. 'Or is it that we are not used to Māori men who are confident? Think about it. Think about how confident white men are. There is another privilege white men carry and that's a belief system that we have lost through colonisation. White men one hundred per cent believe they can do anything, run a country, run a business. Look at the studies of how many white men apply for jobs they're underqualified for. They have this insane belief in themselves.'

Māreikura was listening but still wasn't convinced.

'The name of our podcast is literally *Wahine Chats*. Um, why do we need a man on our show?'

'Look at all the Māori men in our country who know our reo, our language, our culture. They're not the ones who are filling up our prisons, are they? We're so used to seeing Māori men who are colonised shrink into the Pākehā world.'

'I get what you're saying,' Māreikura said. 'But an important part of being Māori is being humble.'

'Our tīpuna were humble but they never wanted our mana to be trampled upon. Our tīpuna had a belief that has been lost through colonisation. Confidence in themselves, in te ao Māori. We should hear Troy's whakaaro.'

•

Troy agreed to be on the podcast on one condition – he didn't want to talk about his mothers.

'Please do not bring them up,' he said. 'I'm my own person.'

Māreikura agreed and so they arranged to meet at Jordana's apartment on Māwharu, a high-energy day of the moon cycle.

Troy showed up fifteen minutes early in a cap, shorts and his grey I Love Ugly hoodie.

Jordana handed him a Corona. 'It will calm your nerves,' she told him.

Troy took a sip and sat down at the table. Māreikura was sitting at the other end.

'Kia ora.' She put her phone in her pocket. 'Did Jords send you the questions?'

'Yeah,' he said. 'I'm nervous, though. I'm not a good public speaker.'

'I can help you.'

'Okay, kūmara,' he said. 'Teach me how you go viral on social media.'

'What?' she asked. 'I'm just being a confident Māori man.'

'Are you guys ready?' Jordana interrupted. 'We should start.'

'Āe,' they both said, and Jordana put her headphones on and pressed the record button.

'Testing, testing. Okay, kia ora everyone! We have an awesome, hearty kōrero for you all but first myself and Māreikura just want to thank everyone for listening to our podcast. We've reached thousands of listeners around the world, we're number three on the podcast charts and we've even been on TV. So thank you, everyone. The most important reason we are doing this is to help Indigenous people continue to reclaim language and identity.'

'Tika,' Māreikura said. 'In this episode, we want to talk about the term whakahīhī. It means to be vain, conceited, arrogant, smug. But is "whakahīhī" a colonised term? Should we stop saying the famous whakataukī? Kāore te kūmara e kōrero ana mō tōna ake reka? The kūmara doesn't talk about its sweetness? And the reason we want to talk about this is because our classmate and guest Troy is a very confident Māori man. Kia ora, Troy.'

'Kia ora,' he said.

'Ko wai koe?'

'I'm Troy and I am Ngāti Porou on my mum's side. On my dad's side I'm Pākehā – Scottish and English whakapapa to be exact. A bit about me – born and raised here in Tāmaki. I have one little sister, Tasmin. I graduated from med school last year and now I'm here at reo Māori school with these two. What else do you want to know?'

'Why did you want to be a doctor?' Jordana asked.

'And how did you overcome your fear of blood?' Māreikura added.

'Okay, I'll answer the first pātai. I was really close to my nan growing up but she died when I was maybe five, six? She was probably only fifty. It broke my little heart. One day she was here, the next day she wasn't. I don't remember my nan being obese or even eating anything that bad, but I would ask my mum, *How did she die?* It was either heart problems, or diabetes, cancer . . . but no one really knew. As I got older, it became clear that the health system failed her. My nan was another statistic of Māori dying young. Māori die at twice the rate of non-Māori from cardiovascular disease, Māori are more likely to be diagnosed and die from cancer, and Māori die on average seven years earlier than non-Māori. The health system has been failing Māori since colonisation and I knew I had to do something about it.

'I also think about how so many of us Māori missed out on knowing our grandparents. The loss of our grandparents means missing out on so much mātauranga or knowledge, our reo Māori. How many of our Māori grandparents or great-grandparents are still alive? I can't help but think this was all orchestrated swiftly by the colonisers.'

'What was?' Māreikura's ears perked up.

'Our grandparents dying young. Because if you kill them off, you kill our language. If you take the patriarch away, everything else crumbles too.'

Māreikura had never thought about this before and now her brain was spinning from what Troy had said. Orchestrated swiftly by the colonisers. Her nana was alive, yes, but all Glennis's siblings except one had died. Māreikura's great-nana died in her fifties.

'Um,' Jordana said, 'so you have a phobia of blood?

'Yeah, just like Māreikura hates scissors.'

He pretended his fingers were scissors and started cutting Māreikura's hair.

'I remember when I had to get my first injection. I just remember being in the school hall paralysed by the sight of needles. Then my mums came in and I was able to get it done with them there. So how did I get over that fear? I love my whānau. I love my culture. My people. I'm driven by a higher purpose. That's the only way to overcome a phobia.'

'So the reason we got you on the podcast,' Jordana said, 'is because of the question we have. Is "whakahīhī" – to be arrogant – is it a colonised term? Should we stop saying the whakataukī? Kāore te kūmara e kōrero ana mō tōna ake reka – the kūmara doesn't say how sweet it is? The reason we have asked you on here is because you have strong opinions on this, on what it means to be a Māori man and that it isn't being whakahīhī, but just being confident. Can you explain?'

'When I was younger,' Troy said, 'I went to America for a basketball camp and the American kids there are all like, "One day, I will be the president of the United States." They are confident as! I realised I never hear Māori speak like that, and then it got me thinking. When a Māori man says, "I'm great and I want to achieve this," people don't like that. I'm a taonga. I know who I am. I come from a line of chiefs. I'm proud of who I am. I can achieve anything. I'm not afraid to say it. I have big dreams and aspirations and people call me crazy, cocky, arrogant. But a white man can do the same and no one bats an eyelid. I believe Māori who have high self-esteem, it's hard for us to find a place in the world. I think of Tame Iti. White people hate him because he doesn't fit the good, safe Māori module. He was called a radical, a terrorist. Whereas people like Simon Bridges? White people love him. He's a safe Māori.'

'Is it tall poppy syndrome?' Jordana asked. 'We love to downplay achievements here in Aotearoa.'

'No,' Troy and Māreikura answered at the same time.

'Because,' Māreikura said, 'tall poppy syndrome doesn't take into account racism and colonisation. It's just a term white people made up. Like imposter syndrome.'

'Māreikura is right,' Troy said. 'I personally believe that the whakataukī of the kūmara was coined by our tīpuna when the belief system was there. Because think about our tīpuna back in the day. They were 100 per cent connected. They were whakahīhī and proud. They were uncolonised. They had the language, our gifts, the land. They were warriors, explorers, navigators, scientists, and so that whakataukī made sense. They didn't need to speak of their sweetness because it showed who they were as people. But it becomes problematic when that belief system is no longer there among our people. So then that whakataukī can almost become disempowering.'

'Moana Jackson said the worst thing colonisation did to us is mess up our belief system,' Māreikura said. 'And I think that's what it's done to me anyway.'

'That's why what you're doing here at school is so important,' Troy told her. 'You're unlearning everything you've been told or taught. All

Māori need to do that – believe in who we are again. We have grappled with self-esteem since colonisation.'

'How can we have high self-esteem when we are raised in a world set up for us to fail?' Māreikura asked. 'We live in a Pākehā world; of course we're going to have low self-esteem when we aren't white. It's why I hate the term imposter syndrome. I'm an imposter. The English language is not mine. The school system is not designed for me. The stories I read are not mine. The dominant culture of this country is not mine.'

'It isn't ours, no, and that's why we get our self-esteem through reclaiming who we are,' Troy said. 'Learning who we are. Not just as Māori, but for me I know who I am as a descendant of Ngāti Porou. That's where my confidence comes from.'

'And being at kura,' Jordana said. 'It feels like I'm taking my power back being at school and learning my reo.'

'Because you're learning who you are,' Troy said. 'We could be making all the money in the world, getting degrees from top universities and still lack the internal and real self-esteem if we don't know our whakapapa. If we don't know who we are.'

'Have you always been this confident?' Jordana asked.

'Yes,' Troy said firmly. 'Although the world tried to tell me I should be otherwise. You don't think I grew up with the narrative, the same news and stories about Māori telling us we were destined to fail or go to prison or be drug addicts? The greatest thing my mothers did for me is instil a belief system that can never be shaken. That I'm a seed down from greatness. He kākano āhau, i ruia mai i Rangiātea – it's something I repeated every day since I was a child. And that's where my validation comes from. My whakapapa and who I am.'

'So how do we get over the whakamā?' Jordana asked. 'The shame of not knowing our language. The shame that so many of us are born with as Māori. Intergenerational shame. Shame for our appearance – our hair being too frizzy, our noses too flat, our skin too black.'

'Like I said before, knowing who we are. But we need to stop being victims. What happened to us was horrific but now we need to step into our power and take individual responsibility.'

'That's easy for you to say,' Māreikura said. 'You had a good upbringing, a supportive whānau.'

'I know but—'

'No buts,' Māreikura said. 'You still speak from a privileged position. Not just as someone with a good upbringing but as a male. You haven't mentioned anything about Māori women.'

'It's not my place to say—'

'Oh, but it is,' Māreikura said. 'You called me out for saying you were whakahīhī – arrogant – and said it was a colonised term. And I actually agree with you and appreciate your kōrero. But what about Māori women? A confident Māori woman isn't called whakahīhī or arrogant. We get called much worse. We get called angry, crazy, narcissistic. We get told we're too much, we're out the gate.'

'I get what you're saying,' Troy said. 'I love the whakataukī "Mā te wāhine, mā te whenua, ka ngaro te tangata" – By women and land do our men perish. Without women, we would be nothing. I've always acknowledged that.'

'What about your privilege, in that you were raised by four women. Not just any women, though', Māreikura said. 'Māori women, feminists and lesbians. Your mum is Jaz Te Huia – well-known activist, writer and scholar. Is that right?'

Troy looked confused and then shocked. He didn't answer and then Māreikura said, 'That must have had a big impact on your whakaaro – the way you think, who you are today?'

'It did.'

'What was it like growing up with Jaz Te Huia as your mother?'

He glanced at Jordana and then back at Māreikura. 'It was good, yeah,' he said, his voice emotionless. 'She definitely helped shape who I am today.'

'She literally led the protest of the golf course and was prominent in the Waitangi Tribunal cases that have led to the empowerment of Māori today. I mean, surely that made you who you are today.'

'Okay, well, let's get back to the kaupapa—' Jordana started but Māreikura spoke over her.

'So on the scale of privilege in this country, it goes Pākehā men, Pākehā women, Māori men and at the bottom of the heap it's Māori women. Would you agree?'

Troy glanced at Jordana again. 'Yes.'

'So what are you doing about it?'

'Huh?'

'What are you actively doing to fight for Māori women?'

'Um.' Troy scratched his chin. 'Sorry, I don't know how to answer that.'

Yeah, I thought so, Māreikura wanted to say. She could feel Jordana's eyes burning through her, so she said nothing.

'Okay, well our time's up,' Jordana said.

'Hold on,' Māreikura said, reaching for her phone. 'I would like to finish this episode with a quote by Ani Mikaere. Because throughout this kōrero today, I am reminded of how Māori women are neglected, forgotten about, erased from important conversations. It is my belief that tāne Māori were part of the process of colonisation, and in fact sexism is still rampant in te ao Māori today. So here's the quote: "It is indeed as if the colonisers understood that throwing the hearts of our women to the ground was and is vital to the success of the colonisation project." Kia ora.'

Jordana pressed the stop button. Troy took off his headphones and walked out.

•

'That went well,' Jordana said, yanking a wire from the recording machine.

'I thought it went quite good,' Māreikura said.

'We must have been recording two different podcasts.' She yanked another wire out. 'I mean, I'm going to have to spend the whole night editing your parts out.'

'Don't edit my parts out,' Māreikura said. 'If you do, then that's not genuine. We never agreed to edit any part of the podcast, Jords. And you know my kōrero will go viral.'

'You need to apologise to Troy.'

'Apologise for what?'

'Māreikura.' She gritted her teeth. 'You disrespected our guest. He said he didn't want to talk about his mothers. You brought up shit that wasn't even relevant to the kaupapa.'

'I was speaking my truth.'

'It might be your truth but it's not everyone's truth.' Jordana paused. 'And not all truth needs to be spoken out loud. That's why we have journals and therapy.'

She turned back to the machine and now Māreikura was raging that Jordana cared more about Troy than what was right.

'Troy deserves to be called out,' Māreikura said. 'He's still a Māori man benefiting from the dispossession of women. I just want him to acknowledge that he is part of the problem. And you are too if you're going to put his feelings before our podcast.'

Jordana spun around, grasping the mic in her hand like she was strangling it to death.

'You know, Māreikura, you're so busy trying to cancel everyone around you that you can't look at your own shit. Your trauma isn't a personality. No one owes you anything. Fucking deal with it like the rest of us are.'

She went to turn around and then stopped midway and turned back again.

'You know, for once it would be nice for you to ask me how I am. This whole time I have known you, not once have you ever asked me about my family. This whole time I've set up this podcast – I do the editing, I do the social media. All you do is just show up and take, take, take. And you talk about that lady who made you feel shit about not speaking te reo? But guess what, you're just as bad, if not worse. You make people feel shit for being Māori. For being who they are. You're the gatekeeper now.'

CHAPTER THIRTY

It was Saturday morning and Kat and Māreikura were doing their usual morning walk to their local cafe Riz to get a coconut milk chai latte and mocha. Riz, the owner, had short spiky hair and always complimented them every time they came into the cafe. 'How's my favourite couple?' she'd ask, then she would hand over their drinks in their KeepCups and add, 'Extra sweet for my favourites,' and then pop a marshmallow on top of Māreikura's cup.

Māreikura had not heard from Jordana, although they would see each other soon at the podcast awards. After they released the episode, the backlash had been immediate, though Māreikura expected it.

Intergenerational trauma? More like intergenerational privilege.

So sick of these little activists that think they know shit but don't know anything.

Go and touch some grass, sis.

When you go against the norm, you'll always get opposition. It's what the te reo pioneers had to go through. They were once radicals and now they were national treasures. They suffered and sacrificed for the next generation. What Māreikura didn't expect was the backlash from her own. It hurt more when it was your own.

Māreikura asked Kat if they could go for a bushwalk and Kat said, 'Babe, we're in Ponsonby. If you want to go for a bushwalk, we have to get in the car and drive somewhere.'

So they walked to the Viaduct instead, staring at the expensive boats bobbing up and down in the water and the people in the restaurants across from the boats who were probably the owners. Māreikura was about to make a joke and then Kat said, 'Aren't they beautiful? Which one would you want?' And Māreikura said, 'I wouldn't want any of them.'

There was no grass to touch so Māreikura put her hands in the air to feel the wind instead, then she held on to Kat's arm. 'Just hold my hand like a normal person,' Kat would tell her, but Māreikura didn't like how every creepy man stared when they held hands.

'You all good?' she asked a balding guy who looked at Kat for way too long. He grunted something and Kat closed her eyes and opened them again like Māreikura was an annoying kid.

'You need to calm down.'

'Well, I wanted to go for a bushwalk but you brought me here instead.'

She heard Kat sigh, the same sigh that came out of Jordana only two days ago.

'I don't know if that podcast is good for you,' Kat said. 'For your mental health.'

'I'm trying to help other Māori by sharing our journey.'

'Yeah, but at what cost?' she asked, then she unlinked her arm from Māreikura and sat on a bench.

'There were some good messages too,' Māreikura said.

'Oh yeah, like what?'

She pulled out her phone and showed Kat.

Omg, thank you, sis, someone had written. *You've put into words everything I've been thinking but didn't know how to articulate.*

'Someone else asked for my PayPal too,' Māreikura said. 'So I put a link in my bio. I feel guilty taking people's money but—'

'But nothing. You deserve it,' Kat said, then she put her arm around Māreikura and they leaned back and watched the world go by. A kid in front of them skateboarding, a mother pushing a pram and walking a little white dog at the same time.

'I need a holiday,' Kat said, pushing her sunglasses on to the bridge of her nose. 'Desperately. If you could be transported anywhere in the world right now, where would you go?'

'You go first.'

'I would go somewhere hot, tropical, where I can lay down and read,' she said.

Kat was so predictable. Māreikura knew she'd say that, although she wasn't sure what Kat would read because she had never seen her pick up a book the whole time they had been dating, even though she claimed to love reading and had a whole bookshelf of books. Maybe she had Audible and listened to books on her phone.

'I would turn back time,' Māreikura said.

'That wasn't really the question.' Kat sighed. 'But that's a Māreikura answer. Where would you go?'

'To the 1980s.'

'What's so great about the 1980s?'

Māreikura shuffled in her seat and said, 'It's when my mum was born.'

Kat said nothing and then the guy on the skateboard fell on his bum and swore and then he pulled his pants back up and carried on.

•

Later on that night, when they were home, Kat said to Māreikura, 'Have you thought about seeing a therapist?'

'For what?'

'You know, for your mum. You're still grieving your mum.'

'I'm not grieving her,' Māreikura said. 'She gave me away.'

'Well, I think you need to forgive your mum,' Kat said. 'She didn't give you away. You were whāngaied, that's different. In te ao Māori, we have more than one mum, you know?'

It pissed Māreikura off that Kat said that, as if it was easy. As if it was a switch you could turn on and off. Forgiveness was a concept Māreikura didn't agree with. One time, Eru Senior told her, 'It's one of the hardest but most rewarding things you can do,' as if he was talking about a marathon race and not forgiveness.

Māreikura once read a tweet that said: *Unforgiveness is like drinking poison yourself and waiting for the other person to die*, and Māreikura tweeted back: *My people and I are drinking the poison that is a white colonised patriarchal society and you expect us to just forgive?* The original poster, a Pākehā woman, deleted her tweet and tweeted again moments later, *Apologies for my last tweet, I'm still learning.*

Māreikura could feel Kat's eyes on her now.

'I don't think you realise how much you benefit from having stable parents,' Māreikura said.

'My parents are not rich.'

'I'm not talking about money.'

'I just think,' Kat continued, 'you have so much trauma. I just wonder, where does it all go?'

Māreikura just stared at her. 'Well, I know where yours goes,' she shot back. 'Your trauma went on this $3 million house.'

Kat switched the TV off and turned so her whole body was facing Māreikura. 'What did you just say?'

'Being Māori bought you your house.'

'And what's wrong with that?'

'How many Māori are employed at Kaha?'

'What are you talking about?'

'I'm just asking, how many are employed?'

'This is ridiculous—'

'It's just a question, Kat. But I know the answer. The answer is zero. You have a hundred and fifty employees and none are Māori. How is that upholding Te Tiriti?'

'You know nothing about running a business.'

'No, but I can smell cultural appropriation from a mile away. You can't sell your business as Indigenous and yet not hire any Māori employees.'

'Māreikura,' she said, her tone stern. 'Stop this right now. You have no idea what you're talking about. You did one year of full-immersion te reo Māori and you think you're an expert.'

'I didn't just do one year,' Māreikura said. 'I sacrificed my education for te ao Māori, I'm doing a podcast to help Māori. I've dedicated my entire life now to the revitalisation of my language.'

'*Your* language?'

'You know what I mean.'

'No,' Kat said, her arms crossed. 'I don't know what you mean.'

'We come from two different worlds.'

'Two different—' Kat began to ask. 'Oh, you mean, you're now in some elite Māori world while I'm over here slumming it in the Pākehā world?'

'I didn't mean it like that.'

'How did you mean it then?'

She was glaring at Māreikura, as if testing her, waiting for her to back down. But Ngāpuhi never ceded sovereignty and Māreikura was not about to concede defeat.

'Your business isn't Māori and it does nothing for the benefit of Māori,' Māreikura said. 'When you started your reclamation journey in te ao Māori, your first question should have been: how can I give back to my culture? But instead it was and has always been: how can I take from my culture? I didn't know that it was possible Māori could tokenise our own culture until I met you.'

Māreikura knew she had gone too far. The look on Kat's face was terrifying, like she was inches from smacking Māreikura to the ground. Her eyes were steel coal.

'Get the fuck out of my house.'

CHAPTER THIRTY-ONE

The cross-earring guy from Splitz Cafe was waving at Māreikura like they were best buddies.

'Kei te pēhea, e hoa?'

She pretended not to hear him but he carried on waving like the confident white man he was.

Māreikura stopped, turned to him and said, 'I am not your friend, stop calling me e hoa.'

'Sorry, Māreikura.'

She had not told him her name.

'My name's Matt, by the way.'

'When?'

'When what?'

'When did I ask?'

He laughed. 'Should have known that was coming. Hey, I listen to your podcast. I love it actually. I'm learning a lot.'

'Are you really?' she asked. ''Cause if you were, you would stop abusing me on the street with your te reo.'

She immediately felt guilty and wanted to take it back, knowing very well that was uncalled for. Her anger had nothing to do with him and everything to do with Kat.

She heard him yell 'sorry' but she carried on, bolting past the unhinged lady on the corner who was always asking for money. Once, she was with Eru and this same woman came up to them and waved sunglasses in their faces. 'Wanna buy my glasses? They're Ray-Bans. I'll give them to you for $100, they're worth $200. If you have cash right now, $50.' She was scratching her face.

'Nah, we good', Māreikura told her. Then the woman moved closer and Eru went to give her money but Māreikura pulled him away in the opposite direction.

'Why'd you do that?' Eru said. 'She must have been desperate for money. Maybe she needs food.'

'It's called meth addiction,' Māreikura told him. 'Didn't you see the sores on her face?'

'Oh,' he said. 'I thought she just had really bad acne.'

He was so naive and that's why Māreikura loved him, because of his 'I won't hurt anyone, I'll make you feel safe' vibe, except he never truly made her feel safe. He made her feel like she was too much. Too out the gate. And then he left. And now Kat had left her too.

•

Jordana was waiting outside Māreikura's house in an Uber the next morning. *Wahine Chats* had been nominated for 'Podcast of the Year' at the official media awards in Wellington and they were on the way to the airport. They had not talked since Jordana yelled at her and called her a gatekeeper.

'Sorry I'm late,' Māreikura said, climbing into the back seat. 'I've got my menstrual.'

'All good,' Jordana said. 'We should still be able to make it. The domestic airport, please,' she said to the driver.

'I've got bad cramps and I had a fight with Kat last night.'

'Sorry to hear that,' Jordana said, though she did not sound sorry at all. 'I've got Panadol in my bag. Want some?'

'It's okay, I took some already.'

They drove in silence to the airport and when they arrived, Jordana said, 'We better walk fast before we miss our flight.'

They got to the gate just in time and once they were sitting on the plane, Māreikura said, 'What if I don't go and just wait at the Airbnb for you? And if we win, you can collect the award on behalf of me too.'

'I'm not going if you don't,' Jordana said. 'Anyway, no one cares about me. Everyone wants to see you. The podcast would be nothing without you.'

'That's not true,' Māreikura said, although it was very true. 'Don't you think it's weird that we get flown to Wellington to get free food and alcohol and schmooze with slightly famous people just for talking shit?'

'No, I don't,' Jordana groaned. 'Do you think white men have this conversation? Do you think they talk like this when they get flown to places and get free kai and alcohol and are nominated for stuff? Do you think they are ever like, "Oh, I don't want to go"?'

Māreikura said nothing.

'So what was the fight about with Kat?'

'It doesn't matter,' Māreikura said.

'Well, it does, because look at the state of you, bro.' Jordana shook her head.

Māreikura had her phone out, which she had carried around everywhere that morning, subconsciously waiting for Kat to text her.

Jordana put her AirPods in her ears, an indicator that the conversation was over. It annoyed Māreikura that Jordana was not more empathetic. She'd listened to Jordana rant about stupid guys she matched with on Tinder all the time. One was a married man who they nicknamed 'Bad Dad'. The other was a personal trainer with big muscles and no personality. So many times, Māreikura had wanted to tell her, *Have you thought that maybe you're the toxic one? Maybe you're the problem?* But she hadn't. Jordana had a family who supported her and funded her lifestyle and here she was, sitting in her little seat with her AirPods in and her $300 puffer jacket, thinking she was Zen and chill and judging Māreikura for her bad decisions when really her obsession with plants and surfing and meditation was just a cover-up for her trauma and unhealthy alcohol dependency.

Māreikura checked her pockets for her AirPods and they weren't in there, so she looked in her backpack. Nothing. She tapped Jordana, who took the AirPod out of her right ear with a look that was scarier than the face her nan used to give Māreikura when she would drink straight from the milk carton and not from a glass. 'Have you seen my AirPods?'

'Nah,' Jordana said.

Māreikura checked her pockets again. Nothing. Now she would have to sit with no internet, no headphones for the entire flight. She turned her phone on airplane mode and wrote a message in the notes she would send Kat.

I'm really sorry for hurting you. I love you and I don't want us to break up over this.

The plane landed and Māreikura and Jordana caught an Uber to the Airbnb. When they got to the house, Māreikura punched in the pin and opened the door, took her shoes off, then ran in with the excitement of someone who would never be a homeowner. At least she could live vicariously through an Airbnb owner. There were dead flies on the sink and the house had a weird mouldy smell.

'I'm leaving a bad review,' Māreikura announced.

'Cool.'

Jordana walked into the bedroom on the left.

'The owners aren't even on the Airbnb site,' Māreikura said, scanning her phone as she strolled down the hall inspecting the rooms. 'It's just a property manager. Landlords hijack everything.'

She came back to the bedroom. Jordana was on the floor with her suitcase open, sorting through her clothes.

'The downfall of Airbnb will be when landlords just Airbnb their multiple properties out and hire a manager and cleaner to take care of the house without any obligation. Greedy people, rich people, consumerism. It's all a joke. You go to an Airbnb now and it's just a landlord's property with cheap furniture and dead flies everywhere.'

Jordana just stared at her. 'Are you coming tonight or not?'

Māreikura put her phone down and started hunting through her suitcase. She threw her clothes on the bed. 'I don't have anything to wear. I don't like any of my clothes.'

'You can wear something of mine.'

'We're not the same size.'

Jordana sized up Māreikura's body with her eyes. 'We are.'

'No, we are not. I have big boobs.'

'Do you?' That sounded like a dig.

'Yeah, that's why I wear baggy clothes,' Māreikura said. She pointed to the skimpy black dress Jordana was holding. 'If I wore that, I'd look like a female video-game character designed by a man. It just wouldn't look right. Or human.'

'Okay, so let's not go then.'

'I didn't say I didn't want to go.'

'Make a choice already. Bro.'

•

Māreikura ended up wearing Jordana's black dress. Her boobs were popping out and there was a cold breeze coming through because of the stupid and unnecessary split on the side that came all the way up her thigh. What was the point of the split in dresses except to attract the male gaze? Although the split reminded Māreikura of the first night she met Kat, and to be fair it had attracted Māreikura's gaze so she couldn't really talk.

Jordana wore a short, body-hugging red dress and bright red lipstick. They got ready quietly to Jordana's Spotify playlist called 'Bipanic', and then Jordana said, 'I wish we went to the alcohol shop beforehand.'

When they got to the awards venue, they were escorted to a table with champagne and wine in the middle and little dishes around the side. As Māreikura predicted, Jordana headed straight for the wine. She poured herself a glass and then took a sip.

'I'll just pour my own then,' Māreikura joked, though it wasn't really a joke because she did pour her own.

'I thought you were decolonising your whakapapa,' Jordana said and Māreikura didn't laugh. She actually felt like turning around and punching Jordana in the face. She poured her glass of wine, said cheers to herself and took a drink.

There were random people sitting around the table who looked over the age of forty. They were probably famous but Māreikura had no idea who they were and she didn't have the energy to make small talk and stroke their egos pretending to be interested in what they did for a living or ask about their kids when she didn't care.

'Kia ora,' the woman next to her said. She had short brown hair and was quite pretty. 'I'm Mereana.'

'I'm Māreikura.'

'I know who you are,' Mereana said. 'I love your podcast.'

'Oh? Thank you.'

'Is that your friend, or your *friend* friend?' She gestured towards Jordana.

'What?'

'You know, girlfriend. I heard you mention her on your podcast.'

'Um, this is Jordana. She's the co-host of the podcast.'

'Oh.' Her eyes widened. 'Jordana!'

Jordana turned around.

'Holy shit, girl, you're stunning,' Mereana said, leaning forward.

'Huh?' Jordana asked, although Māreikura was sure she'd heard Mereana the first time and just wanted to hear her repeat it.

'You're stunning!'

Jordana smiled and said thanks. Māreikura sculled the rest of her wine.

'Wow, you go, girl, the night hasn't even started.' Mereana laughed.

'Don't worry,' Jordana said. 'She doesn't drink. She's decolonising her whakapapa.'

'Fuck off, Jordana,' Māreikura said, and she meant to lightly elbow her but she ended up knocking Jordana's glass over. The wine spilled on Jordana's lap before the glass fell to the floor, smashing into pieces. It was made worse by Mereana's gasp, which made everyone at the table turn to stare at Māreikura, who was now on her knees making a flimsy attempt at picking up the broken glass, hoping a waiter or someone would come and help clean it up. No one came. She picked up the pieces one by one while Jordana watched. She put them in a paper napkin and then shoved them under the table. Māreikura stood up and now the Mereana lady was looking at her, horrified. Jordana had her back turned, dabbing her lap with napkins, distracted by some guy who wasn't there before but had now conveniently shown up.

'Jordana.'

She ignored her. Māreikura tapped her on the shoulder.

'Jordana!'

'What?'

'I'm going.'

Māreikura turned around and walked out. She ran down the stairs, stopped and thought about turning back, but it was too late now. She ordered an Uber on her phone and cried all the way to the Airbnb. The driver handed her a box of tissues so when she got back to the Airbnb she gave him a five-star review.

•

Māreikura accidentally ate gluten but she had no one to tell. That's the hard part of breaking up with someone. No one cared about the insignificant details of your life anymore. No one cared that you accidentally ate gluten and now you're paying for it with severe constipation and stomach pains. You could text your friends and tell them but they would just message back *Ka aroha*. Just like Jordana would. Māreikura could easily look on Reddit for solutions, or for a community to find belonging, but it wasn't the same. Kat would say something like, *Aw, babe, that's not nice*, and she would tell Māreikura what exactly to take. She would make her a hot water bottle and give her a shot of apple cider vinegar and give her cuddles. Maybe this was the point of mothers. She'd heard Jordana talk to her mum on the phone the other day and her mum was asking heaps of questions about what she was eating and what she was learning, and Jordana kept answering back with 'Mm hmm' and 'Yeah' like it was the most boring and uninteresting conversation. Māreikura wanted to tell her she should be more grateful.

Māreikura live-streamed the awards from bed, eating Hell Pizza, her laptop balancing on her stomach. She wished Kat was with her so they could laugh at the really bad dad jokes the MC was saying.

Māreikura laughed out loud at one but then she remembered she was sad so she stopped laughing. She opened and closed all of her apps, hoping Kat would have messaged by now. She hadn't. Jordana messaged earlier, *Where are you?* Māreikura left her on 'delivered' and turned her phone to sleep mode.

They didn't win. Podcast of the Year went to two white men called Jack and Jim who gave their opinions on politics and blamed Jacinda Ardern for everything even though she was no longer Prime Minister and wasn't even living in the country.

A relief came over Māreikura when she didn't hear her name called out. She didn't want the added pressure of having 'award-winning' next to her name. She didn't want more expectations placed on her. She still cried, though. She still felt rejected. Life sucked when you were just trying to survive.

Māreikura was asleep when Jordana came crashing through the door at 2-something a.m.

'E hoaaaa, we didn't win.' Jordana turned the light on and ripped the blanket off Māreikura.

'We didn't win,' she slurred. 'Oi, Muhammad Ali, you awake?'

Māreikura stretched her arms out and sat up on the bed. 'You're drunk.'

'And? Sis, you're violent but I'm not judging.'

Jordana made a swing in the air with her fist, her head falling back with laughter. She flopped onto the end of the bed, trying to kick her shoes off. She smelled like a night out – a combination of smokes, beer, bad breath and Dior perfume.

'Can't believe those two basic white men won,' she groaned, kicking her left leg as if her Docs would magically slip off. 'You should be happy you left 'cause they were asking about the letter, all these mother-truckers in my face saying how young people these days need to stop being entitled.'

'Who?'

'Girl, I was about to knock someone out,' she said. 'Talking about "give Māreikura our love" and "no wonder she doesn't want to show her face around here". I was like, these mother-truckers. Ka aroha, e hoa. Probably better you came home 'cause everyone was lit with all the free alcohol and had no filter, so they were asking if we were going to respond and giving me their hot takes I didn't ask for.'

'Bro, what are you talking about?'

'The letter.' Jordana looked at Māreikura as if she should know. 'The letter. The open letter. I messaged you. It's all over Twitter.'

'I haven't been on Twitter.'

Jordana snatched Māreikura's phone before she could get to it.

'Maybe you shouldn't read it. It was about our podcast. Well, they didn't say our names, but . . .'

'They can't stand it when wāhine Māori are successful,' Māreikura said. 'They will do anything to dismantle our power. To bring us down.'

Jordana had a look on her face that gave Māreikura a bad feeling.

'Who wrote the letter? Was it Kat?'

Deep down Māreikura hoped it was – at least it would show Kat was still thinking about her.

'Kāo.'

'Who then?'

Jordana didn't answer.

'I feel sick.'

'Me too,' Jordana said. 'I drank too much. It's my Irish genes.'

'Jordana, give me my phone now.'

Jordana sighed in defeat and handed Māreikura her phone. She opened the Twitter app and saw #openletter was trending. She clicked on the hashtag and the first post that came up was from Māori writer Melanie Ruha.

Māreikura clicked the link.

AN OPEN LETTER

We are a group of Māori professors, artists and writers who are concerned at the growing trend of online activism and, in particular, we direct our thoughts to those who have platformed themselves on social media and weaponised terms such as 'colonial violence' under the guise of activism.

These are the people who preach kindness, who talk of being oppressed when they are the ones actively oppressing others.

These people will throw pitchforks at anyone who does not agree with them. They have built a platform of fear, where there is little room for critical thinking, no space for nuance.

This is not activism.

What we find most troubling is the lack of original thought. What you think is a trailblazing take is in fact plagiarising our work and the work of the many Māori scholars who came before you.

You have centred yourselves as experts with no genuine understanding of our work. This is not only ignorance but it is blatant disrespect. You takahi on all of our mana.

The lack of gratitude, the sense of entitlement is baffling. Activism is not trampling on the mana of your own, all for the sake of attention, likes and validation.

Activism is not cutting people off who do not agree with you under the guise of self-care and boundaries.

Activism is not riding on the back of mātauranga that is not yours.

Activism is not centring yourself.

None of the work you are doing is brave and fearless.

It is, however –

Entitled

Self-centred

Performative

Egotistic

Shallow

One question we have for these activists. One that is missing in all of these conversations. One that we feel is most important.

Does the ahikā at your marae know you? Does your maunga know your face? Can you stand before the world, not just as a Māori but as a proud descendant of your tribe?

If the answer is no, then the work you are doing is redundant. It is smoke and mirrors. You must start within the walls of your own home. Your own whakapapa. You cannot change the world if you cannot look within yourself first. None of what happened in our history is your fault, but what happens from now on is your responsibility.

We urge you to study the lives of activists in our history. Dame Whina Cooper. Kīngi Tāwhiao. Te Whiti o Rongomai and Tohu Kākahi.

We urge you to stop with your podcasts and spreading false information. Everything you are doing is not tikanga Māori. It is something else, and we are concerned we are raising a generation of narcissists.

Haere taka mua, taka muru; kaua e whai.

Signed by:

- Professor Karu Jones
- Professor Mania Flavell
- Professor Joseph Taylor
- Professor Kristin Campbell
- Professor Deb Leslie
- Professor Aroha Joseph
- Professor Nīkau Ahiwaka
- Professor Hōhepa Martin
- Professor Lucianne Barry
- Doctor Jaz Te Huia, activist, author
- Melanie Ruha, writer

CHAPTER THIRTY-TWO

Māreikura's Instagram was flooded with comments and messages.

The presumption of this individual thinking they speak for Māori is out the gate. I am Māori and she doesn't speak for me.

About time these young entitled folk like Māreikura are called out. They say a lot without saying anything at all. Tired of their woke narcissism.

What annoys me is that the media and public in general fawn over her for . . . just being Māori. Yes I know she's a good speaker but what has she actually achieved?? Ultra-woke, left-wing pin-up girl. Get a real job.

You are what is wrong with the world today. You cancelled yourself!!

She literally tries to check off every 'give me attention' box.
– Indigenous? Yes!
– Gay? Probably!

Her head girl speech was inspiring but after that . . . The narcissism came out in full force.

Proud to be Māori? Proud to dwell on something that happened 150 years ago and has no effect on today? Proud to take advantage of the govt? Proud to divide this country and make this place so miserable that people are moving to Aus? Yeah, you should be real proud . . .

You should be ashamed of yourself! You are the racist one!

They were in an Uber on the way home from the airport, Jordana's head resting on Māreikura's shoulder. Māreikura had told Jordana that Kat broke up with her and blocked her. Jordana told her they should light a candle and wish Kat all the best. Māreikura said that was stupid because she didn't wish Kat all the best. She hoped Kat would get hit by a bus and die. The Uber driver side-eyed her in the rear-view mirror and Jordana asked Māreikura in a cheerful voice how her search for a therapist was going. They arrived at Jordana's. Māreikura hauled her suitcase out of the back and slammed the boot of the car down.

They trudged their suitcases up the stairs and Jordana swiped her card.

'I'm home,' she yelled to no one, then she touched all of her plants and turned on the two lamps, one in the corner of the lounge and the other near the kitchen. She stripped down to her underwear and lay on her Shakti mat and told Māreikura to lay down on the floor so they could meditate to Aunty Oprah.

Oprah's voice began blasting through the speakers in pristine surround sound. 'You are a spiritual being having a physical experience.'

Māreikura took off her shoes and lay down on the couch. She closed her eyes and tried to focus on Oprah's voice. 'Remember who you are and who you are meant to be. Honour that in the best way possible.'

Māreikura tried her best but she could not focus.

'I need to go over to Kat's,' she announced.

'What?' Jordana's head popped up.

'I need my jacket back.'

'What jacket? You don't need your jacket.'

'It's my favourite jacket.'

'Your denim one?'

'No, my tan one from ASOS.'

'Never ever seen you wear that one.'

Māreikura didn't say anything at first, irritated by Jordana not understanding.

'I want my jacket.'

'Let it go,' she said. 'What did Aunty Oprah just say? We own nothing. When we die, we take nothing with us. Be free.'

'No one prepared me for this.'

'Heartbreak is normal,' she said. 'I'm still not over my ex and it's been years.'

'No, I mean, losing my jacket.'

'The jacket is just a metaphor.' Jordana shrugged. 'You are grieving the loss of something much deeper. Like your language. Your culture that was taken away from you. A mother you never had.' She paused. 'Said with aroha. You can always get another jacket but you can't get another heart.'

She skipped over to the green leafy monstera plant in the corner. She turned to Māreikura.

'E hoa, I propagated Āiorangi and I want to give you her baby.'

'What?'

'I want to give you her baby,' she said, her fingers in the soil. 'It's my koha to you.'

Māreikura started crying and Jordana sat down next to her and placed a small pot with a tiny leaf growing in front of her.

'Aw, e hoa,' Jordana said. 'Please accept it. It's a koha.'

'It's not that,' Māreikura said, through her tears. 'I try and try my best and it feels like it's never enough, like I'm not enough. Or that I'm too much. I don't see the point anymore. I wish people just loved me for me. That I could simply just exist and be loved without bonds or conditions.'

'You're never too much for the right person,' Jordana told her.

'Is it true?'

'What?'

'The letter.'

'Which part?'

'Are we entitled?'

'We?'

'I mean me. Am I entitled?'

Jordana sat up and rubbed her left eye, smearing her mascara across her eyelid.

'Sometimes, Māreikura, you can be intimidating.'

'I speak the truth. I'm not going to change who I am.'

'And you shouldn't. But you should at least say sorry to Troy.'

Jordana was lying back down, her cheek squashed into the pillow. Māreikura was trying not to cry again. She held a pillow to her chest and rocked back and forth.

'Do you think our ancestors are proud of us?' Māreikura asked. 'Or do you think they're embarrassed? Ashamed of me.'

Jordana eyes were closed, a little smile at the corner of her lips. She reached over and rubbed Māreikura's head.

'You are your ancestors' wildest dreams,' Jordana said. 'But you are also the biggest pain in their ass.'

She gently pushed the small pot towards Māreikura.

'I found Āiorangi when I wanted to die. When you want to die, nothing can hurt you anymore. You can't feel nothing. I walked past a random shop and she was there looking at me and she saved my life. I had someone who kept me alive, someone to worry about, someone to nurture, to be proud of. It's like rongoā – a form of healing, 'cause self-care is being selfless, eh? And now look at her – she's all grown up and now she looks after me.'

Māreikura looked at Āiorangi and saw her through Jordana's eyes. She wasn't just a house plant but a descendant of Papatūānuku. And when Māreikura looked at Jordana she realised what Grandma Simpson was talking about. The feeling of safety.

'You're still here,' Māreikura said.

Jordana looked at her, not knowing what she meant.

'Everyone leaves eventually,' Māreikura said. 'But you stayed.'

•

Māreikura was eligible for free therapy through ACC. She didn't know this until she called the suicide hotline. The world was so cruel, so broken, and it felt easier for Māreikura to leave this world than to stay.

Māreikura requested a Māori therapist but there were waiting lists so it was either talk to a white lady or dig herself a grave. Her therapist's name was Catherine. She had red hair, suspiciously long fingernails and looked like she could be anywhere between late twenties and mid thirties. She asked Māreikura if she had been to therapy before, and Māreikura said no but that she followed the holistic therapist on TikTok.

Catherine asked her, 'What are your expectations?'

Māreikura wanted to tell her, *Honestly, lady, my expectation is that I don't die. I'm holding on. I don't want to be here. That's my expectation.* But Māreikura told her, 'I just need someone to talk to, I guess.'

Catherine nodded, staring at Māreikura's hands that were scratching at her thigh.

'Where should we begin?'

•

When you're in Te Pō, you just exist. You mope around, desperate for validation, for love, for something, anything. You're left with a black hole and memories that play out in your head over and over again. You go for walks because some stupid girl you follow on TikTok says going for a walk outside is good for your mental health, but is it really? You just end up walking around in public with puffy red eyes and blowing into a tissue every time the tears come. You wander around, walking hopelessly, and people just walk past without even noticing, without even caring. If only one person stopped and asked you how you were, maybe you would reconsider living. You never used to like hugs. Now you'd accept anything. No one stops. Except for dogs. Dogs seem to just know. They will jump on you and lick your face and maybe you think you are loved.

You listen to podcasts but it's just mumbling. Nothing is sinking in. You're not really listening. The thoughts still fly around your head. It's never silent. Meditation doesn't help. Fuck yoga. What's it even good for? How do normal people do this?

Since the open letter was published, everyone started acting weird towards Māreikura. Sometimes she would walk into the classroom and it was obvious everyone had been talking about her because they would stop and look the other way.

Troy was still not talking to her. She tried to get his attention in class, smile at him, catch his eye, but his eyes glazed over and it made her want to throw her bottle at his face for being so whakahīhī.

When Māreikura got home from school, the word 'RACIST' was spray-painted on her fence. She called the police and asked for security but they said they couldn't do anything. 'Why don't you install a security camera?' the officer asked. 'Are you going to pay for that?' Māreikura shot back.

Her nana kept looking out the window every five minutes hoping to catch the person. 'It was probably those no-hopers down the road,' she said. 'Those white kids, the Bayers' sons. Those mongrels better watch out. See this is what I mean, girl. You gotta think about these things. You can't just open your mouth without consequences. In my day, we couldn't even say kia ora without the KKK coming for us. That's how dangerous it was.'

How do you fix trauma? How can Māreikura go back in time to when she was a baby, to when she was screaming for her mum and some Pākehā worker pulled her out of her mum's arms? It's a memory made up because Māreikura can't remember exactly how it happened but it's what she imagines. A caseworker by the name of Karen or Helen, who thought they were good-willed people doing social work for a greater purpose, came into her mother's home and pulled Māreikura from her mother's arms and put her in her car seat and dropped her off to some random family, and then Karen or Helen or whatever the fuck her name was went back to her nice three-bedroom home in Westmere with her husband and two kids and a poodle called Rupert. Karen gets to live blissfully for the rest of her life while Māreikura has to deal with the ongoing trauma. You lose before you are even born. Society is structured that way, to make Māori fail. And the people who know this – Eru, Kat, who should understand the most, who have their own trauma interwoven in their own whakapapa – don't care. Māreikura had never felt so vulnerable, so ripped apart. Every single word hurt. And here she was, saying it out loud to a stranger, a white woman she had no business trusting.

CHAPTER THIRTY-THREE

Whaea Terina's hand was on Māreikura's shoulder. Class had finished and Māreikura was trying to run out the door, trying to escape before she had to talk to anyone.

'E whakaaro nui i a koe e te hine,' Whaea Terina said. 'You have been on my mind. Now, tell me why your ancestors are keeping me up late at night. What is going on?'

She motioned for her to sit down and Māreikura sat, her bag still on her back.

'Have you read the letter?'

'What letter?'

'There was an open letter on social media,' Māreikura said. 'Directed at me.'

'Oh, I don't have social media, except for the Facebook to see my mokos' photos.'

'I've been cancelled.'

'What do you mean, cancelled?'

'You know, like when you do something wrong and then you get cancelled in public,' Māreikura said. 'Kind of like in the old days when witches were put on a stake and burnt to death in front of the public, except it's on the internet now and people burn you at the stake that way. People like Jaz Te Huia, Mania Flavell – you might have heard of them.'

'Yes, I am aware of them,' Whaea Terina said. 'What did you do to upset them, e hine?'

'I don't know,' Māreikura said. 'I thought I was doing the right thing but it's hard to know what's right anymore.'

Whaea Terina didn't say anything. She seemed comfortable with silence, with taking in the heavy emotions that were in the room with them.

'I didn't mean to offend anyone, I didn't mean for any of this to happen,' Māreikura said. 'I never had bad intentions.'

'Well, Māreikura, you know what they say,' Whaea Terina said. 'The road to hell is paved with good intentions.'

Whaea Terina's words hurt and Māreikura was crying now.

'Māreikura, here's what I want you to feel with every fibre of your being.' Whaea Terina reached over and gripped her hand. 'There is nothing wrong with you. You are not broken, you are not deficient. They tried to tell us for centuries we are broken people but there is nothing wrong with you.'

'How can that be true?' Māreikura asked. 'My own community, the very people I look up to, have told the entire world that I'm useless, that I'm entitled, that I'm a narcissist? Whaea, this is what I repeat to myself every day – I tell myself, I am my ancestors' wildest dreams. I say it three times in the mirror. But am I really? I think I am my ancestors' nightmare.'

Whaea Terina did not break eye contact as she opened the first drawer and placed a petrol card on the desk.

'Your ancestors are calling you to go home. Have you heeded the call?'

'But what if you don't know how?' Māreikura said. 'Sometimes it feels easier to just stay away.'

'Everyone has felt the calling to go home,' Whaea Terina said. 'It comes in different ways. It's a soft voice. A loud voice. A yearning. A whisper. A conversation with a friend. An inkling. A deeper knowing. We just need to listen to the call.'

'Everything hurts, though,' Māreikura said. 'I can't explain it. The emptiness I feel. The pain. I want to take it all back. I wish I never started the podcast, I wish I never came here. I want to go back to the Pākehā world. I felt safer there.'

'The thing with intergenerational trauma is that often we can't explain it,' Whaea Terina said. 'We can only feel it. Everything will make sense when you go home, e hine – when you fill your wairua up with te ao Māori. The cancellation, the letter, all these things will become insignificant when you stand in your mana, in your power. And on the other end, all the racism, what is hurled at you – it won't hurt you as much because you will be tau, at peace with who you are. Nothing will stick because what is most important will become clear.'

Whaea Terina had a look about her that gave the impression she had been through it all and come out the other end. It made Māreikura warm to her, because it felt like she knew struggle.

'Hokia ki ō maunga kia purea ai koe e ngā hau a Tāwhirimātea. Return to your maunga so you can be cleansed by your whenua, Māreikura. Go home.'

PART THREE

CHAPTER THIRTY-FOUR

Māreikura was six years old, squashed up against cushions in the back seat of her nana's car going around windy roads, trying not to vomit, the door rattling against her head. The McDonald's sign in Wellsford whizzed past and before Māreikura could even ask if they could stop, her nan said, 'There's food at the marae,' and Māreikura groaned.

Earlier that morning, her nan showed up at school, ushering her out of the classroom.

'My brother died, your Koro Pat.'

Māreikura threw her arms around her nan's legs and her nana just patted the top of her head. Why aren't you sad, she wanted to ask. Māreikura would cry if she had a brother and he died. She would even cry if Jenson – the white boy in her class who told everyone she had nits and called her shittykura – died. Why didn't her nan cry?

When they got to the marae, Aunty Lois was standing guard at the entrance. That was her job, her responsibility. She was the kaimataara, the observer, the person who watched out for the guests. She had done this since she was a little girl, raised by her grandmother on the marae. Aunty Lois was her nan's youngest sister but you couldn't tell from first glance. Glennis, with her short frame and wearing her pearl necklace and earrings to match her cream coat, was a striking contrast to Lois who was plumper, darker, and wore shorts, a baggy singlet and gumboots. Aunty Lois spoke te reo Māori unless she was forced to speak Pākehā. She knew nothing else. That was normal for her and maybe that's why there was such a divide between the sisters. One was allowed to be her authentic self while the other had to learn survival techniques that buried her true self, her identity. And with the burial of her identity came deep resentment. Resentment of her sister who appeared to have everything. The best of both worlds. The love of their grandparents and parents. The ease of te ao Māori. She had no idea how hard it had been for Glennis.

'Hullo, Lois,' her nan said.

'Kia ora, sis.'

Aunty Lois hugged her sister and then she turned to Māreikura, who was hiding, camouflaging behind her nana's skirt.

'Kaua e whakamā, e kōtiro.'

It was her nana's marae but somehow they were still outsiders. Not because of the way they were treated, but the way her nana acted, like she was there out of duty rather than out of want. The only tears Māreikura saw from her nana were when they closed the casket. Glennis started wailing. Māreikura would never forget that sound; it was a low shrill that pierced through her. Four out of five of her nan's siblings had died now. Only Aunty Lois was left. They only went home when someone died.

•

Aunty Lois was standing by the mailbox in a baggy t-shirt that was supposed to say NGĀ-PUHI, but Māreikura could only make out the NGĀ. The PUHI was faded, her chest bobbing up and down as she waved.

'That you, girl?' One of her eyes was squinting, the other wide open.

'Hi, Aunty,' Māreikura said, getting out of the car.

'Last time I saw you, you were this high.' Her hand measured above her knees. 'Now look at you! You hungry? Must be after all that driving. Gee, how long did it take you?'

Māreikura did not know what question to answer first. Her Aunty Lois would not stop talking. She squeezed Māreikura, and then she led her into her house, which looked like a garden shed from the outside. Inside, the house felt warm, light streaming through the windows, photos of tīpuna hung up on the walls. Māreikura was mesmerised by a photo of a bride and groom – the groom tall and handsome and the bride petite in a white dress and holding flowers.

Aunty Lois smiled. 'That's your Great-Nana and Koro,' she said. 'Their wedding day. Beautiful wasn't she? That's where we get our looks from. Our famous Pohe looks. E noho, girl, come eat. Must be starving.' She pointed to the scones on the table.

'Oh, um, I'm gluten-free.'

'You're what?' Aunty Lois just stared at her.

'Never mind.'

Māreikura said a silent karakia to her tīpuna to help her stomach handle the gluten, then she sliced open a scone and took a bite.

'These are better than Nan's,' Māreikura told her and Aunty Lois bellowed with laughter, her whole body vibrating.

'Gee, don't you tell my sister that, she'll get mad. You know why these are good? This is what our nan used to make us.'

She spread butter over a scone.

'Gee, these are good. I always outdo myself,' she said, her mouth half open. 'You watch girl, you might leave this whare ten kilos heavier with a full puku but at least you'll have a full heart.' She patted her tummy. 'Kai is rongoā, it's my medicine. Now, your uncle is at work but he will be back later. He's excited to see you. You like kaimoana? Well, of course you do. He will be back later with our kai. Kina, fish. All the good stuff.'

She took another bite. 'Mmm. Your nan know you're here?'

'No.'

'You know, I don't blame my sister,' Aunty Lois said. 'She was the oldest you see, had to grow up faster than the rest of us. She looked after all of us siblings, must have been tough. Then when your mum died . . . well. Well, that would be hard on anyone, wouldn't it?'

'Yeah. Sorry I haven't been up to visit in a while, Aunty.'

Aunty Lois leaned forward and gave Māreikura a kiss on the head, and it took her by surprise, the amount of affection her aunty freely gave.

'Well, you're here now, ko te mea nui, nē?' She buttered another scone and put it on Māreikura's plate. 'There's some jam there, don't be shy. You wanna drink? Hold on.'

She made a snorting noise and got off her seat and went to the fridge. She put a two-litre milk carton on the table and then got two glasses. She poured the milk into a glass and handed it to Māreikura.

'Now at least you're home now, eh? Your tīpuna are rejoicing. They are having a party. Last night, I couldn't sleep 'cause they were excited you were coming home. I said to my mum, "Māmā, I know you don't sleep up there but down here we do, so if you don't mind, can you shush please?" She was always a talker anyway, where do you think I got it from?' She tilted her head back and laughed. 'But I know they're just happy you are here, my girl.'

Māreikura had also never met anyone who could talk so much, her mouth moving faster than Māreikura could keep up with. She was so different from her nana. Her smile was huge and her eyes full of love that seemed to glisten in a familiar way. It felt like no time had passed even though the last time Māreikura saw her was years ago.

'Now, last thing I heard, Kris said she saw on the Book-face you got a law scholarship? You're not doing that any more, bub?'

'Nah,' Māreikura said. 'I just want to learn my language first and then I'll figure everything else out.'

Aunty Lois nodded in agreement then studied Māreikura's outfit – a Kathmandu jacket, jeans and white Air Force 1 shoes – then she wiped her mouth with a paper towel and got to her feet. She waddled into the back room mumbling something and then came out with a pair of gumboots and grey woollen socks.

'These are my spares, they should fit you. Try them on. If not, Kris got some. We can go pick them up.'

Māreikura swallowed the rest of her scone and sat on the stairs. She wiggled her feet into the boots.

'Cool, Aunty, they fit.'

•

Māreikura didn't really believe in miracles but she couldn't help but think maybe it was meant to be that she was here, on her whenua, looking directly at the urupā with her mountain behind her and her marae on the other side.

Aunty Lois raised her arms in the air.

'The wairua, girl, you feel it? All our tīpuna are at the front gate waiting for your arrival, lining up to greet you. This is how long they've been waiting. That's what I could hear all last night. She's coming home, she's coming home. Kua karanga mai te whenua ki a koe kia hoki mai ki te kāinga. Our mokopuna is home.'

Aunty Lois opened the gate and pointed towards the first gravestone.

'Now, we start from this side, of course, with my mother. Kia ora, Mum, hi Mum. Yes, yes, I know.' She kissed her hand and touched the side of the gravestone.

'Mum's happy you're here, girl. She said about time. But she knows you've been busy. Busy restoring and putting our family back together. Auē, that does sound busy.'

Māreikura bent down at the grave of her great-grandmother.

BELOVED MUM, DAUGHTER, SISTER, WIFE.

KIRIANA POHE 1928–1986. DIED AGE 58.

'She died young,' Māreikura said. 'What was she like?'

'Nosy.' Aunty Lois laughed. 'Well, yes, Mum, I'm going to tell her the truth 'cause you were the nosiest in the neighbourhood, always poking your head out the curtains, spying on the neighbours, calling the aunties to have a gossip session. Yes, she was nosy, but she was the most beautiful mother in the world. You know manaakitanga? That word is overused these days especially 'cause people have adopted it and seem to throw it around willy-nilly. But my mum was the epitome of manaakitanga. We used to have all the neighbours' kids staying at our house. We used to cook up big kai for everyone. She had a big heart.'

Aunty Lois moved over to the left.

'Now, Koro, he was the most beautiful father. We grew up here, on the marae. My childhood memories are of being near Pāpā on the marae. He was a kaumātua. Hunting, gathering. We didn't have a lot but there was always love. Te reo Māori was our first rongoā. It's a wairua language, a spiritual language. I was brought up with it. Knew nothing else.'

'Why were you brought up by your nan and koro?' Māreikura asked.

'Mum and Dad had six kids already and they were in the city, caught up in the urban drift. Mum didn't want to give me up but eventually she couldn't afford to have me anymore. I think it was hard on my siblings. I got my nan and koro all to myself, I got all the love in the world. I mean, don't get me wrong, sometimes your nan could be a hard woman when she wanted to, but auē, they loved me. When they died, I must have been your age.' She sniffled. 'I'd already met your koro by then and I was hapū with your cousin Tāmati Junior.'

'That's why you're different,' Māreikura said. 'I mean, different from Nan.'

'The only difference, bub, is one of us stayed on our land and the other was taken from our whenua. Wrenched from our homeland. In other countries, they call that genocide.'

She moved over to the left to Māreikura's mother's grave. There was no photo, just the words engraved.

MĀIA POHE

BELOVED MOTHER, DAUGHTER, GRANDDAUGHTER.

1981–2005. DIED AGE 24.

There was a windmill by her name blowing in the wind. A Jim Beam bottle was leaning against her headstone.

'Why is there alcohol on Mum's grave?' Māreikura asked. 'Alcohol doesn't belong in our whakapapa.' She snatched the bottle. 'And it doesn't belong in our urupā. Especially on Mum's grave.'

Māreikura was surprised at the anger that washed over her. How grief could turn into rage in an instant.

What kind of mother were you? Why did you leave me? What's happened to our family?

'I hear your mum, she speaks to me sometimes,' Aunty Lois said. 'She tells me how proud she is of you.'

'She gave me away,' Māreikura replied.

'Who told you that?' Aunty Lois asked. 'You were whāngaied, that's not the same as giving you away. I was whāngaied as well. Whāngaied means to nurture, it's not the same as adoption. My mother didn't give me away, I always knew she loved me. Your mother loved you too.'

'Why did she drink then?' Māreikura asked. 'She chose to get in the car and drive. That's why I hate alcohol. I don't want any of us drinking that poison.'

'I don't know all the details,' Aunty Lois said. 'Your mum was young, she didn't know any better. I suppose that's one of the reasons why your nana can't come up, too hard. Having to confront what she's lost.'

They stayed at the urupā for another hour, Aunty Lois walking around and cleaning the graves, nonstop talking. It was starting to make sense to Māreikura, her grief for a past she knew nothing about. The gaps of emptiness, the blank spaces. She grieved for her great-grandparents who she'd never met. A life she could have had. A life her nana should have had.

Māreikura pointed to Mount Manaia in the distance.

'One day, I will climb my maunga.'

'Well, not today 'cause ain't no way I can get up there.' Aunty Lois cackled. 'You think these knees will get up there? You'll have to come back.'

They took turns washing their hands under the tap outside of the urupā and started walking towards the marae. Aunty Lois started telling a story about when she was little but Māreikura wasn't really listening. She sighed and Aunty Lois stopped and turned to Māreikura.

'There's already so much pain in the world, e hine. Don't you forget to reclaim your joy.'

'It's hard when I feel so much mamae,' Māreikura said. 'I can't just switch it off.'

'Well, there's a reason you feel this pain so deeply,' Aunty Lois said. 'You are the bridge. You are healing the generations who came before you and the ones who will come after you.'

'What if I don't want to be the bridge?' Māreikura said. 'I just want my biggest struggle in life to be my forehead acne.'

Māreikura had decided that after everything, she did not want to be a pioneer either. She wanted to be the opposite of a pioneer. 'I want to be the last. I want to enjoy the fruits of everyone else's hard labour.'

Aunty Lois laughed. 'You might think learning te reo Māori is for future generations, but it's for past generations too,' she said. 'It's healing my sister. It's healing your tīpuna. E hara koe i te tangata, he momo koe. You are no ordinary person, Māreikura. That's what they want you to know.'

'Who does?'

'Your mum, your tīpuna. Your name was given to you for a reason. A noble-born female who is one with the gods. Ko koe, Māreikura. That is you.'

•

Māreikura followed Aunty Lois into the kitchen of the marae, where a lady with a messy bun and black Kathmandu jacket was viciously peeling kūmara.

'This is cousin Maria,' Aunty Lois said. 'Cousin, this is Māreikura. You know, Glennis's moko.'

Maria did not flinch. She pointed to the peeler on the kitchen bench.

'Well then, make yourself useful.'

Cousin Maria was in her fifties and she peeled kūmara like Māreikura had never seen anyone peel kūmara before. From top to bottom, five swipes as quick as a flash and she was done. Māreikura could tell she was proud of it too, by the curve of her mouth when she chucked the kūmara into the bucket.

Maria used to babysit Māreikura when she was little but Māreikura didn't remember.

'Of course you don't remember,' she sneered. ''Cause that's how long it's been since you've been back here.'

'There's no more land left in the urupā to bury our whānau,' Aunty Lois said, changing the subject. 'So we having a wānanga today, gotta think of the next step. That's what all this kai is for.'

'What about cremation?' Māreikura asked.

'It's not how our tīpuna did it,' she replied. 'Our bodies were tapu, auē, I don't want my body burnt into ashes. No, thanks. And if we get cremated, then my mokos might not come back to the marae and visit since I'll be with them in a little jar.'

'Tika,' Maria said. 'It's already hard enough to get the young ones coming back. When they do come back, he koretake rātou,' she carried on. 'They take a photo for their TikToks, get their fix, and we see them in another ten years or when it's convenient. Never mind all the hard work we do to keep the marae running.'

'There's a lot of reasons for that,' Aunty Lois said.

'Yeah, well, no point making it in the flash Pākehā world when you don't even know your own marae or how to pick up a peeler, nē?'

Māreikura suddenly felt insecure about her peeling. Her name meant she was apparently one with the gods but she couldn't even peel a kūmara properly. She tried to peel faster.

'We harvested this kūmara on our whenua,' Aunty Lois said, picking up the biggest kūmara Māreikura had ever seen.

'Look at them, big and juicy, nē? It was planted where our tīpuna used to tend to kūmara. And it only takes one.'

'One what?'

'One good kūmara to harvest many.'

•

'Should have warned you about your cousin,' Aunty Lois said as they were walking to the wharenui. 'There's a reason all the kids call her a taniwha. She's the ahikā. Well, one of them, anyway. She keeps the fire burning, the marae going. She means well, dedicated her whole life to keeping this marae together. You can see why she gets hōhā, nē?'

They were sitting on the stairs watching some of the kids play. Māreikura shook off her gumboots.

'I don't want to be another one that comes and takes,' Māreikura said. 'But what can I honestly give back? I can't karanga, I can't sing, I can't do kapa haka, I can hardly speak te reo Māori and I'm useless at peeling kūmara. It just feels like I'm useless here and everyone can see it, like all my weaknesses are on show. I want to karanga, I want to know my whakapapa, I want to do all those things.'

'It takes time,' Aunty Lois said. 'It's something you can't learn in one hour, one day, even one visit. Time spent giving, not taking. You peel long enough at the side of your cousin, you'll learn your whakapapa. You spend enough time at the urupā cleaning, you'll learn your whakapapa. You come contribute to the wānanga at the marae, karanga and te reo Māori will come out of you like it's meant to.'

'In the Pākehā world, I am successful,' Māreikura said. 'Here, I am nothing.'

'Me maumahara koe,' Aunty Lois said. 'We are not like the Pākehā world here. We don't put anyone on a pedestal. We are all the same. You'll find our leaders in the kitchen and scrubbing the toilets. No one is better than anyone. You think no one cares about your achievements but they do, except it's the least important thing about you, bub.'

'Do you think this is why so many don't come back?' Māreikura asked. 'It's easier in the Pākehā world than to come here and face what was taken from us. To start again.'

'Probably why your nana stays away.'

''Cause it's too hard.'

'Don't know,' she said, looking away. 'I think about my sister every day. I miss her. I wish things were different.'

'They will be,' Māreikura said. 'I'll bring her back here one day, I promise.'

'If only it was that easy, nē?'

Aunty Lois got to her feet.

'Come on, let's go inside.'

•

The wharenui did not have carvings, and Aunty Lois told her it was because of the strong Catholic presence.

'Wait, what?' This was new knowledge to Māreikura. 'What do you mean?'

'Back in the day, a lot of our people were Catholics,' she said. 'Joined the church when the missionaries came over. They said that the carvings were worshipping a false god, so that's why a lot of maraes don't have carvings.'

Māreikura felt anger build up. What else had colonisation done? It's like every time she stepped into a new place, she was unmasking a new wound.

'How could our tīpuna be so naive?' Māreikura asked.

Aunty Lois pointed towards a photo on the wall.

'You know who that is? That's who you're named after. Māreikura. You were given your name for a reason. Noble, warrior, fearless. Mātauranga, te reo Māori. Matakite. She had many spiritual gifts and fought in wars. I see her in you. You might not be able to see your gifts, but I can. She also prophesied of the missionaries coming over and she was the first to accept God. Many of us followed her. I would call her many things, but the last thing I would call our tipuna is naive.'

Māreikura stared into her eyes, trying to make sense of it. It didn't make sense. She couldn't understand.

'Well, she was misled then, because if there is a God, He is evil,' she said. 'Look what He did to our whakapapa – we don't even have carvings on our wall.'

'Now you say our tīpuna were smart? And then our tīpuna were deceived? So which is it?' Aunty Lois asked.

'How could our tīpuna, who were so connected to themselves, to ā-wairua, be misled? It is Māori today who are more disconnected from ourselves than we have ever been before.'

Māreikura wondered if her ancestors envisioned the trials, the tribulations, the hardships, the grief their descendants would face. Māreikura wondered if they knew all that they had – all that they owned – would be taken. But maybe they were enlightened with hope and assurance that it would be restored. It only takes one.

'E koe, humans have always had a way of taking something pure and turning it into something ugly,' Aunty Lois said. 'Nothing is ever just black and white. In te ao Māori, we see the world in all colours. But remember, te reo Māori comes from God. It's a Godly language. And it is God who made you Māori.'

CHAPTER THIRTY-FIVE

Māreikura desperately wanted to ask her nana why. Why it had taken her nan so long to come home. Why she stopped talking to her sister. Why she cared more about the hedges of the neighbours' lawn than looking after her whenua back home.

As she drove over the Brynderwyns and back towards Auckland, Māreikura felt an overwhelming love for her nana. She didn't know the silent battle her nana had fought after losing a child. She could never comprehend the racism her nana had endured from growing up in Aotearoa in the seventies and living among rich Pākehā after Ponsonby was gentrified. She could never truly understand what it was like for her nana to see the world shift before her eyes – spending decades living in survival mode and hiding who she was in order to give her granddaughter what she thought was the best life – and suddenly the world had reversed. Now her nana had permission to reveal her true self after masking it for so long.

Her nan would always tell Māreikura, 'stand up straight', 'stop slouching', 'use your words'. She marched to her own beat, her head always high. Everything Māreikura had gained – not just her education but also her resilience and determination – it came from her nana.

When Māreikura arrived home, her nana was asleep in front of the TV. Māreikura took the remote from the clutches of her hands.

'Hey,' her nana said, jolting awake like usual. 'I was watching that!'

Māreikura nestled her head on her nana's shoulder.

'What's happened?' her nan asked in a panicked voice. 'What's wrong?'

'Nothing's wrong,' Māreikura said.

Her nana shuffled in her seat, unsure what to do about Māreikura being overly touchy-feely. She lifted her hand up and patted Māreikura on the head.

'I love you, Nan,' Māreikura said, rubbing her head against her nana's woolly jumper. 'Thank you for everything you've done for me.'

•

Jordana was not expecting Māreikura to show up at her house. It was 10.30 on a Sunday night.

'I thought you were up north?' Jordana said.

'I had an epiphany,' Māreikura announced. 'The world we live in was not designed for us to succeed in, it was designed for us to fail.'

'Is that your epiphany? Capitalism?'

'Capitalism, colonialism. Everything. It's a broken world and a broken system.'

Māreikura walked past Jordana and fell down on the couch.

'Are you hungry?' Jordana asked. 'I can order food.'

She shook her head. 'When I was driving down here, I was thinking about how Māori are not broken people, but we think we are so we go to therapy, do mediation, go to yoga, thinking it's going to fix this yearning we have, but all those things are just a cover-up. Maumau te wā. It's a waste of time if we don't address the real issue.'

'Which is?' Jordana put the jug on.

'Being away from our marae, our land, our whānau. It makes us feel broken.'

Māreikura stretched her legs out.

'I have been thinking about my responsibility to my marae. My aunty is so tau, so at peace. Like, do you think my aunty cares about the things David Seymour says? She don't care, she's too busy living her best life, planting kūmara in the māra, speaking the reo, looking after our marae. Knowing my whakapapa, who my ancestors are, filling the empty gaps of my family tree, fulfilling my responsibility as a descendant of Ngāpuhi means more to me than anything. Does that make sense?'

'Yeah,' Jordana said. 'It does. Do you think that's what Toni Morrison meant when she said racism is a distraction?'

'I think I understand what she means by that, that we spend all our time arguing our existence and not enough time nurturing our intergenerational gifts.'

'Ka tika,' Jordana said.

'I need to respond to the letter,' Māreikura said.

'What, like on our podcast?'

'Yeah,' she said. 'Like a bonus podcast episode.'

Māreikura wanted all of this to disappear, to sweep it away with a broom. But she had an obligation, a responsibility to say something. People were messaging her, asking her. *What did you think of the letter? What's your response? When's your next podcast coming out?* She never wanted any of this. She wished Jordana had never asked her to do the podcast in the first place.

Māreikura had her phone in front of her, notes app open, a speech prepared. She stood up and sat over by the podcast equipment.

'Are you sure you want to do this?' Jordana asked. Her eyebrows were creased in a concerned look.

'I'm ready,' she said. 'I know what I need to say.'

Jordana sat down next to Māreikura and took a sip of her drink. She pressed record.

'Kia ora e te whānau, welcome back to *Wahine Chats*. I'm Jordana, and today we have a bonus podcast episode for you. A response to an open letter that was published online a couple of weeks ago. Māreikura, I'm going to hand the mic over to you.'

•

'When I was seventeen years old, I turned down the role of deputy head girl. I did this because I felt like my school did not hold a student to account for her racist behaviour. I felt that the role I was offered was tokenistic. As a result, I ended up losing my scholarship and having to leave school.

'I was standing up for what I thought was right. I did not expect my speech to go viral or that I would suddenly be on TV, on the news, people coming up to me on the street. I was all over social media. I suddenly had thousands of followers. I didn't ask for any of this.

'No one talks about the burden of intense pressure and responsibility on young activists. No one talks about the hate and criticism that comes from people all over the internet who think they have a right to you. No one talks about the impact on your mental health. No one talks about the danger you put yourself in. You speak up, you tell the truth, but no one talks about how lonely it is. Sometimes, I wish I could turn back time and not do that speech because it ruined my life. That's how I feel.

'I spiralled into deep depression. Mostly because of what was happening but also I had my own struggles, trauma in my own family, my best friend leaving on a mission. Trying to be a regular teenage girl and fit in.

'An open letter was written and although my name wasn't mentioned, I wish to address it as I feel the letter was for me. There was harsh language used and there were accusations of trampling on the mana of the many trailblazers who have come before me, some who signed the letter.

'I was shocked to hear that I had hurt and upset many of my heroes. I mihi to all the long list of activists, scholars, writers, critical thinkers, storytellers and pioneers who have spent their lifetimes explaining, justifying, defending, advocating for us and our culture. I'm sorry I did not acknowledge you sooner. I also want to apologise to my friend Troy, and will apologise when I see him in person.

'I have thought deeply about my actions, and I no longer wish to continue this podcast.

'I don't want the spotlight. I don't want to be viral on social media. I don't want to be successful in the Pākehā world. It means nothing to me. I desire to be a good descendant of my iwi, to be on the marae with my Aunty Lois in the māra, harvesting kūmara and speaking my reo.

'I learnt te reo Māori because I thought it would save me. I wanted to fill the emptiness I've felt my whole life. I yearn for my reo but I have learnt that learning te reo Māori is not learning anything new. It's simply the awakening of my soul. I have spent my whole life searching for something that has been there all along.

'I didn't want to start a podcast, but my friend Jordana convinced me that there were many people struggling to reclaim their Indigenous language. We wanted to offer a safe space for those who were struggling with language trauma, with grief, with all that comes with learning your ancestral tongue – because it's not just about the language, is it? Te reo Māori is expansive and there's so many layers, so much to learn. But it all came at a cost.

'I shared publicly my feelings on our podcast and I unknowingly disrespected many people along the way. It was never my intention, but I also know the intention doesn't matter if the impact is harmful – which it was. I want to apologise for the harm my actions have caused.

'But there are things I am not sorry for.

'I am not sorry for being outspoken. I am not sorry for being a disruptor. I will not apologise for being who I am, for speaking my truth and having hard conversations. I will never apologise for that. I was named after my tipuna Māreikura, who was a noble warrior. She was fearless and strong. I long to live up to her name and I will continue to speak up.

'Yes, we have a responsibility to give back to our marae, to our iwi, but often the biggest barrier comes from the judgement in te ao Māori that further isolates Māori from our culture, language, identity. The irony is that this is exactly what colonisation intended.

'We have all been colonised. We have all been misplaced. We all have a collective responsibility to help each other home.

'Te reo Māori is my rongoā, my medicine. Like Stacey Morrison said, no one gets left behind. Remember that you can't shame people into reconnection. You can only love people where they are.

'You ask me if I know my maunga? Can I stand before the world, not as a Māori but as a proud descendant of my tribe?

'The answer is yes. I now stand proudly – ngākau titikaha – and I can tell you who I am. But I do not need to prove this to you. I do not need to prove this to anyone.

'My maunga knows me. To all those who are listening to this, I want you to know this. Your maunga knows you too. Kaua e whakamā. Hoki atu ki tō kāinga.

'We are all just trying to find our way home.

'Kaua e mate wheke me mate ururoa. Ka nui te aroha e te whānau. Ko te reo te mauri o te mana Māori.

'Nā, Māreikura.'

CHAPTER THIRTY-SIX

The Guardian published Māreikura's podcast episode as an essay and it was read by thousands of people. #IstandwithMāreikura started trending on Twitter.

We never know the brunt of being an activist today, left-wing commentator Crystal Haywood wrote. *I stand with Māreikura and all activists.*

It's the Māori and Pasifika who are often burdened with the heaviness of activism that they don't ask for, activist Mare Kōwhai tweeted. *Kia kaha, Māreikura.*

Messages began to flood into her inbox.

Brave!!!! Māreikura, thank you. And just so you know so many times I wanted to quit because the reo wasn't sinking in, but tuning in and listening to you made me feel like it was normal and that I was part of the journey. I wouldn't be on this reo journey if it wasn't for you. Aroha

Māreikura, I don't always agree with everything you say but I always appreciate your whakaaro. I realise now how much pressure we put on our young ones. We expect you to uphold a future, to break the cycles that come from us older ones. There's so much expectation and I just want to apologise. Please keep speaking your truth. You deserve all the happiness in the world e hoa. Kauri Rogers

Since you began writing and expressing your yearning for te reo, your experiences, feelings, fears, I have cried many tears as you express so well how I've felt for so long. Twenty years of reo classes on and off and still not sticking. Oh the taniwha . . . all of them. Your words have been the needed push, it's time, and I know it will be hard but I've made the call. Moana

Māreikura,

Kiingi Taawhiao said, 'Mehemea kare kau ana he whakakitenga, ka mate te iwi.' If there is no vision, the people will perish. I believe our vision is the same. I believe our vision is for the betterment of all Māori.

I acknowledge you and your beautiful words. May we move forward and work towards a restorative future for us all.

E tū e te rangatira. Ahakoa te aha, ahakoa te uaua, e tū! Kia mate ururoa, kei mate wheke.

Ngā manaakitanga,
Jaz Te Huia

•

Troy was still not talking to Māreikura so at lunchtime she followed him out of class.

'Troy.'

He flinched when he heard her voice but carried on walking.

'Troy!' Māreikura yelled and then she yanked his bag until he almost fell backwards. 'Can you stop ignoring me? I want to say sorry.'

'For what?'

'For doing what I did.'

'What did you do? Maybe be specific.'

'For bringing up your parents in the podcast when I told you I wouldn't, for going off at you when I shouldn't have, for putting you on the spot like that, for . . .'

He broke into a smile and she punched him on the shoulder.

'That's the second time you've hit me,' he said. 'I'm telling Whaea.'

'You just think this is funny. You're not taking this seriously.'

'I am taking this seriously. You used me.'

'What?'

'Yeah', said Troy. 'You just wanted me on your podcast because of my famous parents.'

'It wasn't like that.'

'Yeah, it was,' he said. 'People know me as Jaz Te Huia's son. They love the idea of me just because they want to get close to my mum.' He shrugged. 'I didn't think you were like that but you are. You see me like everyone else sees me.'

'That's not true,' she said. 'I don't care that Jaz Te Huia is your mum. Sometimes things come out of my mouth, and I can't help it, and maybe since starting the podcast, the more validation I get, the more I just don't think about what I say. I know I need to be more careful.'

'I don't think you need to be more careful,' Troy said. 'I love that you speak your truth. You're not afraid to say it for how it is, call people out. But I just didn't think I was anyone. I try my best to uphold Te Tiriti, to do my best for whānau. I just hoped that if you ever had a problem with me, you wouldn't publicly call me out like that. I thought we were friends.'

'We are.'

'You don't call friends out like that in public. If I was really your friend, you would tell me in a private conversation if you had a problem with me. I feel like every other random person on Instagram you call out.'

'You aren't a random person to me,' said Māreikura. 'I love that you care so much about improving health outcomes for whānau Māori. I just don't tell you because your head will grow big and you will get more whakahīhī but I think what you're doing, how you are studying medicine, is amazing – that you're trying to change the health system even though you have a phobia of blood. It's the best thing about you.'

He sighed and unfolded his arms. Words of affirmation were definitely Troy's love language.

'There's a reason I don't want to speak about my mum, Māreikura,' he said. 'I want to be my own person. I don't want to ride off the back of Mum's work.'

'I know,' she said. 'And you are your own person.'

'Everyone loves Jaz Te Huia,' he said. 'But it's hard when you see your parents for who they are.'

'Like what?'

'It's not like she was a bad mum,' he quickly explained. 'But she was never around. Activism comes at a price and for Mum it was at the expense of her own kids. Like, I know Mum loves me and she did her best – all of them did – but when you're a kid and you just want your Mum but she's away for months at some protest and she leaves you with random families . . .'

He paused. 'I was just a kid and I wanted my mum. I didn't care about some dumb protest. She gave everything to te ao Māori and all I got was her leftovers.'

'I'm sorry,' said Māreikura.

'I didn't know my mum was going to write that letter,' said Troy. 'She didn't tell me. I told her off about it, but you know my mum, she does what she wants. Kind of like someone else I know.'

'It's okay.' Māreikura reached into her bag and pulled out a framed photo. 'I got you a present.'

Troy stared at the photo of a hypodermic needle. 'Are you serious?'

'It's the only way we can confront our phobias,' she said. 'If we see them all the time, we get used to them. You can put it by your desk when you're studying. That way, when you have patients, you can confidently use the needle. I don't want your phobia to get in the way of your purpose.'

He was staring at her in disbelief and then she showed him her framed photo of Edward Scissorhands.

'Tāua, tāua,' she said.

He doubled over in laughter.

'You should keep yours by your bed,' he said. 'That way, if you ever meet a white man, you can confidently—'

'Hey.'

They didn't hear Jordana come up behind them. She had a grim look on her face.

'Have you checked your phone?' she asked.

'No?'

Māreikura looked at her phone. There was a missed call from Chloe and five messages in the group chat.

'Chloe's grandma,' Jordana said before Māreikura had a chance to read the messages. 'She passed away this morning.'

•

Māreikura had only been to one Pākehā funeral before. Serena, a girl from school, who died from cancer. The service had been so stiff, like they were at an office meeting. They sang a few songs, said a speech, and that was it. It felt like Māreikura blinked and the funeral had finished. When she went to a tangi at her marae up north, it had lasted for three to four days.

A small boy handed Māreikura a pamphlet with Grandma Simpson's face on the cover and the words 'IN LOVING MEMORY OF MOLLY SIMPSON 1925–2024'.

The whole class was there and when they all walked in, Chloe's face lit up. They sat on the left. People were piling in and now standing by the door because there were no more seats. Everyone stood and sang along to 'Amazing Grace'. It was the opening hymn that played while the men carried Grandma Simpson's casket inside. Chloe was wearing black shades, her body trembling as she followed the casket to the front. The pastor read out his eulogy describing Grandma Simpson's character. He told a story about how Grandma Simpson used to give people hugs and invite them over to her house to the point where it got dangerous and he had to intervene. He once went over and she was making tea while a man was talking to her and robbing her at the same.

Chloe walked up to the mic and read a poem she had written. Her voice was shaking. No one went up to comfort her. Māreikura wanted to. She saw the box of tissues on the piano so she walked over and passed them to Chloe. When she sat back down she realised she was crying. Jordana was crying too.

Afterwards, Chloe invited Māreikura and Jordana to the boat club and Māreikura wasn't sure because it was usually for close friends and family. Jordana said they should go to pay their respects but Māreikura knew it was because Chloe mentioned there would be alcohol. When they got there, a man was walking around with a plate of cheese and olives, and Jordana went looking for the wine. Chloe was holding a wineglass in her hand already and was standing next to a woman who looked like she could be her mum. Chloe waved at Māreikura and then whispered something to the woman. Māreikura called for Jordana and they walked over.

When they got closer, the woman said, 'Thank you for coming. I'm Alexis, Chloe's mum.'

She held her hand out but Jordana leaned in and kissed her on the cheek and then hugged her. 'Ka nui te aroha. I'm so sorry for your loss.'

Māreikura did the same, and when she let go of Chloe's mum, she saw she had the same glassy blue eyes as Chloe.

Māreikura turned to Chloe and, when she hugged her, she could smell her coconut moisturiser. It felt like they both held on longer than they needed to. Chloe was the first to let go.

'It's so nice to meet some of Chloe's friends from school,' Alexis said, smiling. 'Sad circumstances, however. You'll both have to come over for dinner.'

Māreikura found an envelope in her pocket and handed it to her. 'This is from me and Jordana,' she said.

Alexis stared at the envelope, confused, so Chloe said, 'Mum, it's a koha. Can't say no to koha,' and her mum said in a trembling voice, 'Thank you so much,' and clutched the envelope with gratitude even though it wasn't much money.

It looked like she was about to cry again so Jordana said, 'This is a nice place, I like the view of the harbour.' And Alexis said, 'Yes, it is, isn't it?'

While they were talking, Māreikura kept looking at Chloe, waiting for her to start a conversation with her, but she stood back shyly, holding her glass of wine in both hands.

'Oh,' Alexis said. 'Have you given it to Māreikura yet?'

'Not yet,' Chloe said. She turned to Māreikura. 'Gran left you something. You can come over or I can drop it off. Whatever's easiest.'

'Oh, it's okay, I don't want to t—'

'You must take it,' Alexis said. 'Māreikura, Grandma Simpson loved you. Didn't she, Chlo? She talked like you were her own granddaughter.'

'I adored her too,' Māreikura said. Her voice choked up so Chloe instinctively placed her hand on Māreikura's back.

An elderly couple approached them and Chloe took her hand away. Māreikura and Jordana moved back and hovered by the food.

'Have you got grief goggles on?' Jordana asked.

'What?'

'You know, 'cause you're grieving the grandma.'

'What are you on about?'

Jordana tipped her empty wineglass in Chloe's direction. 'I thought you hated her.'

'Jordana, I'm just being a good friend. Her grandma just died.'

'M'kay,' Jordana said and then she picked up another glass of wine.

CHAPTER THIRTY-SEVEN

In their next therapy session, Catherine recommended Māreikura start dating again. 'It will be good for you,' she said. 'Often the best way to learn is through experience.'

When Māreikura got home from therapy, she downloaded Bumble. Jordana said that was a good idea because Māreikura had been lowkey depressed since breaking up with Kat. Māreikura didn't have any good photos for her dating profile. All she could find were screenshots of quotes from Instagram and unhinged videos of her crying. She'd recorded herself crying to remind herself never to go back to Kat but in hindsight that was a terrible idea. She cringed watching back videos of her ugly crying. So she chose old photos from when she was a younger and happier version of herself and hoped she wasn't being a catfish.

Here goes, she said to herself, thinking of her ancestors navigating the Pacific Ocean so she could manifest some of their courage. She started swiping through all of the women in Auckland. She mostly swiped left, occasionally swiped right, and then she dropped her phone because she saw the worst possible thing in the world. Kat's Bumble profile. Māreikura picked her phone up and stared at the photo of

Kat. She was sitting on a boat wearing a black silk dress and holding a wineglass.

Māreikura tapped out of the app in a panic and called Jordana.

'I just saw Kat's Bumble profile.'

'Huh?'

'I just saw Kat's Bumble profile.'

'Send it to me.'

Māreikura screenshot and then sent it. There was a pause and then a gagging sound.

'You're crying over this? Girl. I bet she has no matches.'

'No, but she looks so good.'

'It's the eyes,' Jordana said. 'She has crazy psycho eyes in all the photos. Any sane person can see that, even if she is hot.'

'I can't compete with any of these women,' Māreikura said. 'I should just swap to men and date one of the white guys holding a fish.'

'Māreikura,' Jordana screeched down the phone. 'Stop that. You're talented, smart, hot, a podcast host, a TV star. You're better than any of these mother-truckers on here. Wait, hold on.'

A horn blasted and then heavy breathing.

'Fark. I just passed Macca's.'

'What day are you on?'

Jordana had just started the 75-day Hard Challenge. She was always doing some random challenge she found on the internet.

'Day three,' Jordana said. 'Distract me 'cause I'm about to go into Macca's for some chicken nuggets. Any potentials?'

'There's one.'

'Who?'

'Leslie, but she's white.'

'So is Margot Robbie.'

'Jordana—'

'Māreikura, just chill. You're not looking for a wife. Go on a date with Leslie.'

•

Leslie was a 23-year-old retail manager who loved coffee, walks on the beach and fresh sheets. She said kia ora on her profile, which told Māreikura she wasn't racist. She also wrote the best way to ask her out was to simply 'ask her out' so Māreikura asked her out and she said 'name a place and time' and Māreikura wrote, *Pacific Inn?* She couldn't think of anything else. Leslie wrote back, *omg that's my fave place*, with a heart-eyes emoji.

Leslie was running late and Māreikura had already finished her gin and tonic. The waitress came around and said, 'Same again?' and Māreikura replied, 'Sure, why not?' That was one of the benefits of having money now – she could say yes to another drink without thinking about it.

Leslie showed up thirty minutes late. Māreikura didn't care that she was late, but she did care that Leslie looked super young, even though she was older than Māreikura. She looked like a baby compared to Kat, which Māreikura found widely unattractive. If she walked past her on the street, she probably wouldn't look twice. Leslie wore jeans, Air Force 1s, a white silk singlet and gold earrings. She was also short – shorter than Kat.

'Māreikura?'

'Leslie?'

'Yeah, sorry,' she said. 'Parking is a mission on a Friday night.'

'It's okay,' Māreikura said. 'I'm usually late because of my ADHD.'

'Maybe I should get tested,' said Leslie, taking off her jacket. 'I just have the other ones. Anxiety and depression.' Her eyes slid down to the glass. 'That looks good, what is it?'

'Gin and tonic.'

'I need one of those.'

The waiter came around and asked what Leslie wanted to drink, and she pointed to the glass and said, 'I'll have the same.'

Leslie was studying environmental science at university and wanted to start a non-profit organisation that helped combat climate change. 'Interesting,' Māreikura said. What she did not tell Leslie was that there were plenty of Indigenous people doing it already so really there was zero point in starting her organisation. Leslie liked climbing and asked Māreikura if she wanted to go sometime and Māreikura said sure, though she couldn't think of anything worse than climbing up a wall for fun. Leslie was talking about her travels somewhere and then she asked Māreikura about her last relationship.

'What about her?' Māreikura asked. Her tone was defensive, though she did not mean for it to be.

'Ah,' Leslie said. 'You're still healing.'

Māreikura looked away and Leslie let out what sounded like a disappointed sigh and took a sip of her drink. It felt weird to talk about Kat like she was some random person she once knew and not a person who was very much the love of her life.

Leslie's relationship had ended last year. She started telling Māreikura about her ex, although Māreikura did not ask. They met while travelling in France but the distance was too hard so they both decided it was best to part ways.

'It was mutual,' Leslie said. 'We're still on good terms.'

Māreikura could never imagine breaking up like that, where you're both on good terms.

'That's really mature of you,' she told her, and Leslie said it was still hard.

'When two people aren't right for each other, nothing will make it work,' she said, and then she flipped her phone over and checked the time.

'I broke my rule,' she said. 'I'm only supposed to stay with my first date for an hour.'

'What's the time now?'

'Almost nine.'

'How does that rule work when two girls are on a date?' Māreikura asked. 'Women can just talk and talk.'

'Especially when the woman is hot,' Leslie said.

Māreikura studied Leslie's face and wished she was Kat. This was not a good sign.

'Should we go back to yours?'

'I live with my nana so it's awkward.'

'Auckland house prices, eh?' she said. 'At least you're saving money. That's why I still live at home too.'

Māreikura wanted to tell her that's not how it works in the Māori world, that you actually help out and pay rent, but she was four gin and tonics down and she couldn't stop staring at Leslie's mouth. She had really nice lips. Maybe it was the cherry-coloured lipstick she was wearing.

They ended up in the back seat of Māreikura's car. Jordana would be proud and Eru would tell her it was not a good idea. They were kissing and then Māreikura moved her head away.

'I'm not saving money.'

'Huh?'

'Living with my nana. I pay rent.'

Leslie slowly nodded and wiped her mouth. 'That's kind of you.'

'It's actually a responsibility as Māori to help our whānau out.'

'Okay.'

'Would you ever learn te reo Māori?'

'Um.'

'Yes or no.'

'I haven't really thought about it.'

'So you don't want to?'

'I never said I didn't want to. It just hasn't come up.'

'Well, it's the native language of our country, isn't it?' Māreikura's arms were folded. 'I'm not feeling well. Do you mind if—'

'I'll just go,' Leslie said.

'Okay. Nice to meet you. Thanks for tonight.' Māreikura gave her an awkward side-hug in the cramped back seat and then Leslie opened the door and left.

Māreikura was too drunk to drive home. She was about to order an Uber to Jordana's when she remembered Jordana was also on a date tonight and not home. She saw on her phone a message from earlier she forgot to reply to.

Chloe: *Hey, just seeing if you're free tomorrow so I can drop off Grandma's present for you*

Māreikura: *Hey, I can come get it now*

Māreikura: *Only if you want*

Māreikura: *Hope you're ok*

CHAPTER THIRTY-EIGHT

The door at Chloe's house was half open. Māreikura knocked, took off her shoes and walked in. A shirtless white man with shaggy black hair was hunched over a frying pan and watching what sounded like TikTok videos on his phone at the same time. Māreikura assumed this was the vegan flatmate Oliver who Chloe had mentioned once. He was cooking what looked like bacon but smelled like something else entirely. Māreikura waited for him to look up but he didn't, so she coughed.

'Oh,' he said, glancing up from his phone. 'Hey.'

'Hey, is Chloe home?'

'Yeah, think she's in her room.' He walked down the hall and tapped on the door. 'Chloe? Chloeeee?' He shrugged his shoulders at Māreikura. 'Dunno where she is, sorry, man.' He went back into the kitchen.

Māreikura pushed the door but it was locked. Māreikura heard Chloe grunt and then the door unlocked. Māreikura pushed it open. Chloe was sitting on her bed, fidgeting with a cube on her lap.

'Nice room,' she said, stopping to examine the stack of books in the corner.

'Sorry for the mess,' Chloe said. 'I don't usually have people in my room.'

'How come?'

'I don't like people.' She looked Māreikura up and down. 'Where did you come from?'

'I was on a date,' Māreikura said, taking her jacket off.

'Oh,' Chloe said, then she asked reluctantly, 'How was it?'

Māreikura reached into her bag and pulled out a bag of salt and vinegar Harvest Snaps. She took a handful then passed them on to Chloe, who said thanks and took them without looking at her.

'She had zero interest in learning te reo and it made me think,' Māreikura said. 'I wish more white people were like you.'

It was the nicest thing Māreikura had ever said to her. Chloe didn't know what to say. Māreikura sat cross-legged on the floor.

Chloe reached over by her side and handed Māreikura a bag.

'It's from Grandma.'

It was a book – *Guerrilla Days in Ireland* by Tom Barry. There was a note in between the pages.

Dearest Māreikura,

Sometimes God will put people in our path to remind them they are loved. That is what you have done for me. Remember, dear, you are loved dearly. Sometimes doors need to shut, but in time another will open. Keep strong. You have been an angel who has blessed my life in a very short time. Love always, Grandma Simpson.

'She told me this story about you,' Māreikura said, wiping her eyes. 'How when you were five, you used all your money to buy her flowers.'

'She always tells that story.' Chloe groaned but Māreikura could see a hint of a smile. 'I don't know why. My grandma was the most generous person ever. You met her – she was always giving.'

'You're just like her.'

'I wish.'

'Nah, you are.'

Māreikura paused, looking at a photo of who she assumed was Chloe's dad, hanging by her desk next to photos of a group of white people with nice-looking teeth. Grandma Simpson was standing in the middle, her toothy smile the biggest of them all.

'She's beautiful.'

They were looking at each other as if seeing each other for the first time. Māreikura studied Chloe, lying on the bed in grey trackpants, a black hoodie, knotty hair, panda eyes – a right mess grieving her grandma and now stuffing her face with chips. She was so awkward, so annoying, but for a moment, a split moment, Māreikura thought about the possibility of loving her.

'She collapsed and hit her head at her apartment,' Chloe said. 'That's how Grandma died.

'I was always trying to get her in a rest home, so she could have the help, but she was so stubborn. I'm not a horrible person, Māreikura. I wanted to put her in a rest home so this wouldn't happen.' Her voice cracked.

'She lay there for hours and wasn't found until the neighbours came. This wouldn't have happened if I'd put my foot down, you know? I should have forced her to go to a rest home. She is, was, so stubborn.'

Māreikura sat down on her bed. It was a single bed and there wasn't a lot of room for two people.

'I'm sorry, Chloe,' Māreikura said. 'I really am.'

'Whatever you do, don't read me a grief quote from the internet. I know what grief is. I don't need to read a badly written quote from some anonymous person on the internet who has no clue.'

'Did someone send you a quote about grief?'

'My friend Tracey.'

'Is she white?'

Chloe didn't answer. Māreikura lay down and Chloe rested her head next to Māreikura's shoulder. Chloe wriggled for a bit.

'The thing with grief,' Chloe said, 'is that it never ends, it just becomes more manageable. It shows up all the time. You'll be going about your day and out of nowhere it comes and hits you all over again.'

'But if you don't talk about them,' Māreikura said, 'they die all over again.'

They both didn't say anything.

'Yes, she is,' Chloe said.

'What?'

'My friend Tracey. She's white and annoying AF. Grandma Simpson didn't even like her.'

CHAPTER THIRTY-NINE

Jordana was standing by the bar shouting at everyone to come up for shots. They were celebrating their final assignment, the last one for the year.

'Tahi, rua, toru whā – mauri ora!' she yelled, right before she tipped a tequila shot down her throat.

While Jordana was distracted with tequila, Māreikura tried to slip out of the club quietly without anyone noticing. But Troy did. He stopped her just outside the door.

'Who are you running away from?' he asked.

'Nothing,' she said. 'No one, I mean. I just don't like clubbing. I just don't find it fun.

'It's not our culture,' Māreikura carried on. 'So why do we pretend it is? I find it jarring being around drunk people. It suppresses us, it takes away our rights, our sovereignty – the very thing we fought for. It doesn't make sense to have a graduation where we feel the wairua so strongly and then waste it away at a club where everyone is drunk and acting stupid.'

She sighed. 'I know, I sound boring.'

'You're not boring,' he said. 'You're anything but boring. Alcohol is a tool used by the colonisers to suppress us, I know.' He pointed across the road at Little Turkish Cafe. 'You hungry?'

'I could eat.'

Māreikura was in fact starving. When they got to the counter, she ordered a large falafel on rice, extra-large chips and a large Diet Coke.

Troy whistled, impressed. 'I'll get the same.'

'You can get meat, you know,' she told him. 'I'm not gonna start a protest if you do.'

'I've been trying to give up meat anyway.' He shrugged. 'Good for the environment, nē?'

He was grinning like he was waiting for a compliment and then the man behind the counter asked, 'What salads would you like?'

'All except tomatoes,' said Māreikura.

'You hate tomatoes too?' Troy asked. 'They are like little soggy aliens that ruin everything.'

'Except for tomato sauce.'

'Except for tomato sauce,' he repeated. 'Ka, tika e hine.'

They sat down at the table nearest the window. Troy took his hat off and ran a hand through his hair.

'You still with that wahine, what was her name? Kylie?'

'Kat.'

'Yeah, that's the one.'

'We broke up a while ago.'

'That's good. Mum doesn't like her. Said she was fake or something.'

'Your mum doesn't like me either.'

'My mum doesn't know you. Yet.'

'What about you and Lucy?' she asked. 'You guys are cute. You two could be the next Scotty and Stacey. You with your flash reo and her with her pretty eyelashes.'

'Lucy's my mate.'

'Does she know that?'

'Well, I think I've made it pretty obvious.' He shrugged. 'And if she has a crush on me, that's on her. Can't blame her – it's my Ngāti Porou looks.'

Māreikura rolled her eyes. Their food arrived and she started squashing her falafel with her fork.

'Man, can't believe a year has almost passed,' he said. 'Do you think you've changed heaps?'

'I don't think I've changed at all,' she said. 'I'm becoming who I was meant to be.'

He let out a low whistle. 'We are becoming who we were always meant to be. You should trademark that quote before someone tries to steal it.'

'It's gonna be hard without kura,' Māreikura said. 'It felt like such a safe place and now we have to go out into the world where it doesn't feel safe anymore. Everything feels polarising. My friend sang a waiata tautoko in a restaurant and the waiter told them to be quiet because someone complained about the loud Mowry singing. People angry with te reo Māori added to street names, people fighting over co-governance. It doesn't feel safe to speak Māori, let alone actually be Māori.'

'It means we have to be intentional about seeking out those safe spaces, eh? Like it's up to us now to go into the world with the armour that kura has given us.'

'I get tired of fighting though, don't you?' she asked. 'Like, yes, hello, we would like te reo Māori on street signs please because it was a language that was literally beaten from our ancestors. Can we please have this small thing?' She sighed and pointed to his last falafel, his fork resting on the side of his plate. 'Are you gonna eat that?'

He pushed his plate towards her and she stabbed the falafel with her fork and popped it in her mouth.

'I can order more food, you know.'

Nah, I better not,' she said, looking at her phone. 'I think I'll go home now anyway. I'll order an Uber.'

'We can share one,' he said, standing up. 'I'll get him to drop you off on the way to mine. I just want to make sure you get home safe.'

They said thank you to the owners and then jumped into the back of the Uber, their knees slightly touching, Troy holding onto the door rail. The car whizzed through Karangahape Road and past the street art that read 'Whakaako kia whakaora – Educate to Liberate'.

'What're your plans?' he asked.

'Go home and sleep.'

'No, I mean after kura. Like next year.'

'Oh. I should probably look for a job.'

'You'll get a job anywhere,' he said. 'You're talented like that. I'm gonna take two months off for summer, go back home to Gizzy.' He paused. 'You should come.'

'Why? That place is filled with drunk teenagers over summer time.'

'Is that what you really think of the mighty Gizzy?' He placed his hand on his chest like she had just shot him. 'Maybe I'll take the invite back then. Maybe you're not worthy.'

'Okay, what else does Gizzy have to offer then?'

'The beaches, the surf, my marae . . . me.'

Her first reaction was to burst out laughing.

'Is the Uber driver lost?' she asked, changing the subject. 'It feels like a long way to my house.'

'It feels short to me,' he said, moving his face closer to her.

'Troy.'

'Māreikura.'

'I can smell kebab on your breath.'

He didn't break eye contact, but with his hands he felt in his pockets until he found Mentos. He popped a mint in his mouth. His fingers were playing with the right strap of her dress and then he leaned in and kissed her. Māreikura was taken aback for a moment and didn't move. He was gentle and not what she expected. She kissed him back and the more she gave, the more he matched her energy, like he was waiting for permission. She liked the feeling of being wanted, being desired, the feeling of his lips on hers.

And then she stopped.

'Troy.'

He moved his hands up to her face and then Māreikura pulled away. The Uber driver was staring at them through the rear-view mirror. The car had stopped.

'Thank you for the falafel,' Māreikura said, and then she kissed him on the cheek and got out of the car.

•

Troy followed her out of the Uber and was now standing in front of her house.

'You can't come inside,' she said. 'I'm not having sex with you. Even if I wanted to, my nan is at home and I don't want to wake her up.'

'I'm not trying to come inside,' he said. 'I just want to know if I'm going to see you again.'

'You'll see me again.'

'What, on TV? I mean, I want to see you again. I want to spend time with you.'

Māreikura sat down on the grass in front of her house.

'You just don't give up,' she sighed. 'You truly are the definition of whakahīhī. Imagine if more Māori had your confidence. The things we could achieve together. We could tackle racism, take down capitalism, change the world.'

'I just know what I want,' he said, sitting down next to her.

'How many girls do you tell that to?'

'Only the ones I like.'

She punched him on his shoulder. 'You're wasting your time, anyway. I'm messed up,' she said.

'You're not messed up.'

'Yes, I am,' she said. 'Ask my therapist. Apparently I have an avoidant attachment style, a mother wound and I'm an aggressive communicator. Oh, and I have an abandonment wound too because everyone leaves me. You're studying medicine so you probably just want to fix broken people. Maybe that's some childhood trauma you need to work on.'

'You're not broken.'

'I have things I need to work on,' said Māreikura.

'Not everything has to be so deep. You need to learn how to have fun.'

'So this is all it is, then? Fun?

'The most beautiful thing about you is your mind,' Troy said. 'The way you think, the way you observe the world. I liked you ever since you gave me pūkana eyes in class and called me whakahīhī. Then I came home and looked you up and saw your speech and, from then on, that was it for me. You're unashamedly Māori, but not in a way that's whakahīhī; in a way that you don't care what people think. You speak the truth.'

'Your mum—'

'My mum and I disagree on a lot of things,' he interrupted. 'We wānanga all the time at home but that's te ao Māori. It's multifaceted and expansive because we all come from and offer different perspectives. That's my favourite thing about being Māori. And Mum doesn't know you. She doesn't feel your wairua because she hasn't met you yet. You have a soft side to you, Māreikura. A beautiful side. That's the part I want to know more of, that's the Māreikura I want to love.'

The light turned on and Troy jumped to his feet. It was her nana.

'Tēnā koe,' Troy said. 'I was just making sure Māreikura got home safely.'

Her nan grunted something about being an ungodly hour and went back inside.

'Sheesh,' Troy said, turning back to Māreikura. 'Now I know where you get it from.'

Māreikura didn't say anything.

'Sorry,' he said. 'I'm sure your nan is a nice lady.'

'It's not that,' she said. 'It's late. You should go.'

'But Māreikura—'

'Troy,' she said. 'I have a lot of healing to do. But it's not with you.'

He looked at her like she had just punched him in the gut. She was certain this was the first time he had felt rejection, had his heart broken. But when she looked closer, she realised that this was not the first time, and that the visible hurt in his eyes was the rejection resurfacing from his mum who chose kaupapa over him for the betterment of all people. Her fight to keep te reo Māori alive. It had come at a cost. Those were Troy's own words.

Māreikura wanted to hug him, to kiss him. But she couldn't.

'You think everyone leaves you,' Troy said. 'But you're the one who pushes everyone away.'

'Pō mārie, Troy,' Māreikura said, and then she turned around and walked into the house.

CHAPTER FORTY

The government announced Matariki was to be made a national public holiday while Māreikura was in high school. Māreikura didn't know anything about Matariki back then. For so long, she had celebrated 31 December as the new year, making fake resolutions, getting drunk, counting down and all for what? It wasn't even the real new year.

Jordana was standing outside her apartment wrapped up in a beanie, scarf and jacket, and holding a KeepCup in each hand. It was four thirty in the morning.

'Ngā mihi o te tau hou!' She climbed into the car, tossed Māreikura's drink bottle in the back and jammed her KeepCup in its place.

'Do you think our ancestors ever went to therapy?' Māreikura asked.

'Girl.' She unwrapped her scarf and placed it on her lap. 'It's too early for this.'

'It's a Pākehā whakaaro, though, right? It's the same as the idea of self-love, to put yourself first? Like what, we are supposed to pour ourselves a glass of wine and run a bath and that's the secret to happiness? Did my tīpuna do that? No, they did not. They looked after each other.'

Jordana had the window down, vaping.

'I thought you said therapy is supposed to make you feel better,' Māreikura went on. 'Tell me why I sometimes leave my therapist's office feeling worse.'

'Do you think a one-hour therapy session can undo hundreds of years of colonisation?' Jordana shook her head. 'You have to keep going. Weekly. Anyway, have you got your wish ready for Hiwa?'

'Hiwa-i-te-rangi is a star, not a genie,' Māreikura said. 'And why are you dressed like we're going to Antarctica and not Bastion Point?'

'The correct name is Takaparawhau, not Bastion Point,' Jordana said. 'And it's gonna be freezing out there.'

'I already know your wish,' Māreikura said. 'A tall Māori man with green eyes and a man bun, who speaks fluent Māori, plays guitar and is loyal.'

'You're wrong, he doesn't have to play guitar. I've lowered my standards.' She took a drink of her coffee. 'We need to give our raru to Matariki. We need to let go.'

They parked and Jordana took off her shoes and socks and made Māreikura do the same. Then she held out her pinky finger like they were five years old and at primary school.

'That's what Matariki is about,' Jordana said. 'It's time for us to leave behind the old and bring in the new. What are you leaving behind for Matariki? What are you taking with you into the new year?'

•

There was something healing about welcoming in the new year at Takaparawhau, where a 506-day occupation took place to protect the land. Where hundreds of people were handcuffed in a struggle to make their wishes come true.

Māreikura grounded her feet in the whenua, land that was almost taken, that could have easily looked like something different today if it wasn't for the fight of Ngāti Whātua.

The hautapu ceremony had begun and Chloe stood next to Māreikura. The karakia started.

Matariki was a time to acknowledge the dead, to call out the names of those who died to the star Pōhutukawa. Māreikura held Chloe's hand as they called out 'Grandma Simpson'. It felt like the field was filled with people, not just the living but those who came before them. When Māreikura spoke her wish to Hiwa-i-te-rangi, she asked for guidance to help her turn her pain into good, to help other Māori not have to go through what she went through, to end the cycle of language trauma, of intergenerational trauma,

'What wasn't normal for us, it will be normal for our kids. For the next generation,' Māreikura said, looking out at the crowd of people – all different ethnicities and backgrounds – celebrating Matariki. 'This is just the beginning.'

Māreikura pulled out her phone to take a photo and saw she had four missed calls – two from Eru Senior, two from her nana. She called her nan immediately.

'Nan,' Māreikura said. 'Did you call?'

'Can you hear me?' her nan shouted, and then there was a muffled sound.

'Yes, Nan. What's wrong?'

More muffled sounds and then she heard a voice, a voice she had not heard for a long time.

'Māreikura.'

Jordana sensed something was wrong and began mouthing, 'What? What is it?'

Māreikura thrust the phone into her hand.

'Hello?' the voice on the phone said.

Māreikura could not find her words so Jordana put the phone on speaker.

'Sorry, Māreikura is busy, we'll call you back.' She glanced at the screen and then back at Māreikura. 'Wait, sorry, who is this?'

'It's Elder Johnson. I mean, Eru. It's Eru.'

CHAPTER FORTY-ONE

'Wait, was that *Eru* Eru?' Jordana's mouth gaped open. 'Is he home?'

'Who is Eru?' Chloe asked.

'He's the guy you asked about when Māreikura said you had autism.' Jordana answered.

'Oh. The Mormon?' Chloe asked.

'Yeah.' Jordana said.

'Your ex?'

'No,' Jordana and Māreikura said at the same time.

'I'm confused,' Jordana said. 'I thought he's not meant to be home for another three months.'

'Something bad must have happened,' Māreikura said.

'Like what?' Chloe asked.

'Why does it have to be something bad? Maybe he got sick of his mission?' Jordana suggested. 'Maybe he just wanted to come home?'

Māreikura shook her head. 'It doesn't work like that. You only come home early if you are disobedient or have an accident. I remember Eru Senior telling me.'

'Well, you better go and find out,' Jordana said.

Māreikura didn't move.

'Want us to come?' Chloe asked.

'Yeah, I do,' Māreikura said. 'But you better not. I'll see you later on.'

•

Māreikura had not prepared for this. For Eru to come home three months early. Why had no one told her? By the time he got home, she was going to have a glow-up and greet him at the arrival gates speaking fluent te reo Māori. Eden and Eru Senior would be holding one of those Mormon signs that families hold up when missionaries come back that would say 'Mission accomplished'. There would be people there from church, all of Eru's friends, including Kayla. Māreikura would try to blend in the back but Erana would declare loudly in front of Kayla that Māreikura was part of the family and make her stand with the Johnsons.

Eru would arrive in a black suit and tie, his hair gelled back. Baby Te Atarangi would run up to him and wrap her arms around his legs and he would scoop her up and say, 'You're bigger than uncle now.' He would juggle her on his right hip as he made his way through the line, giving each person his time, thanking them for coming. When he got to Māreikura, he would have to put Te Atarangi down because he was so overwhelmed with emotion seeing Māreikura again. They would both be crying as they embraced, until Eru Senior had to intervene, pulling Eru off her, reminding him there were others at the airport too, in case he forgot.

•

When Māreikura got to her nan's, Eru was sitting on the couch, his right leg in a cast and perched up on a chair.

'Don't get up,' were the first words that came out of Māreikura's mouth. She knelt down and hugged him. There were no tears. It was nothing like she expected. It was nothing like the airport scene she had imagined.

'It's so nice to see you again,' he said.

He was talking to her like she was an acquaintance.

'You too,' she replied with the same energy.

'I was just filling boy here in on all your endeavours,' her nan said. 'He didn't even know, did he? You had a radio show, and been on TV . . . That's our girl, she's famous now. Might be too big for us now, eh, boy?'

'We all knew it was a matter of time, eh, Nan?' Eru replied. He was smiling but Māreikura could see right through it. She hated how much she knew him, how much she could read him when no one else could.

'I can't believe you're here,' Māreikura said.

'Yeah,' her nan carried on. 'Well, it was a surprise to me too, girl, got the shock of my life. I open the door and hullo, what's this handsome boy doing on my doorstep? I thought I was seeing things. Thought I better go back to Specsavers, ha! Anyway, such a shame that you weren't able to finish your mission. Hope the driver was punished because look at you, poor thing. Now, what's going to happen with all that?'

Māreikura snuck a look at Eru. He was broader, his face had filled out. He was browner, like he was the colour he was meant to be.

'What happened?' Māreikura asked him.

'Yes, well, I was shocked when he told me,' her nan said. 'Who knew this could happen on your mission, I always thought the missionaries were being looked over by God—'

'Nan,' Māreikura said. 'I'm asking Eru.'

He used to look at her like she was the most important person in his life but now he couldn't even look her in the eye. He scratched behind his ear.

'A car came out of nowhere,' he said. 'It hit me on the left side and I broke my leg.'

There was an uneasiness in his voice. If there was one thing Eru could not do, it was lie.

•

They were on the way to Macca's. Māreikura was driving. The top of Eru's head kept grazing the roof. He was too big for her car and his cast took up most of the room. She had never seen him so anxious. He was doing that thing where he was shaking his leg. He did that when he was nervous or when he needed to go to the toilet.

'Do you need to go toilet?' she asked him.

He shook his head.

'Are you happy to be home?'

'Yeah. I guess.' He was looking out the window.

'I'm happy you're home.'

'Thanks,' he said. 'How you been anyway?'

That was not an Eru question. Eru did not ask basic questions like that. They hadn't spoken for almost two years and he was talking to her the way Māreikura would talk to the shopkeeper at Countdown, just to be polite, to make conversation while she watched her items being scanned.

'Eru, why didn't you tell me earlier?'

She was hurt that he didn't call her when he had his accident. Hurt that she wasn't there at the airport. Hurt she was only finding out now, like he was excluding her from his life and she wasn't important enough.

'I didn't want to make a big deal,' he said. 'I didn't want anyone to know. It was just Mum and Dad who came to the airport. Not even Erana came. You're the first person I've seen.'

'I was worried about you. Since you sent me the email with the number three. What number are you now?'

He did not answer.

'How did you break your leg?' She asked him again.

'I told you, a car came out of nowhere,' he said. 'It hit the left side of my leg.'

'Was it at night-time or something?'

'Why?'

'Because how did you not see the car coming? Isn't Hawai'i slow-paced? What were you doing? Was your companion there?'

'Yeah, he was there.'

'Did he get hurt too? Where is he now? What about the driver?'

Eru closed his eyes for a second and then opened them up again. 'Māreikura, I'm really tired. It was a long flight and I haven't slept.'

'It's not the long flight that's making you tired,' she said. 'It's the lying.'

She was driving along and then she pulled over to the side of the road, turned the engine off and faced him.

'Remember when we were like twelve and you tried to organise a surprise party for me but you ended up telling me all the details?' she said. 'You can't lie, Eru, you don't know how to. You can't keep anything from me, I know everything . . .'

She stopped talking because she could hear him sobbing. His head was cradled in his hands.

'I had to leave,' he said. 'I had no choice.'

'Why?'

He sighed like he was frustrated at her for not understanding him, not reading between some imaginary lines.

He then pulled out his phone and opened up the email app. He placed the phone on her lap.

'Just read it.'

To: kaleo345@gmail.com
Subject: I'm sorry

Kaleo,
From the moment I met you, I felt intense feelings of attraction that I've never felt towards anyone before. Every day it feels like a war is raging in my head in trying to align my mind with my heart.

This weekend, I prayed and fasted. I felt intense clarity and confirmation through quiet whisperings to my soul of my purpose on Earth. We cannot progress things further. I want to be an instrument of God through the gifts I've been given and bless and help the lives of many people.

This leads me to say that we can no longer see each other or pursue things further.

I know we have a connection but the happiness and love I have with you or could have with any person cannot compare with the love I have experienced in following what God's plan is for me and what my heart knows to be true.

For me there is nothing in this world that comes close to having a relationship with divinity. I love the gospel so much and I have an obligation to keep my covenants.

I hope you find happiness and the love that you deserve with someone who can give you their whole and true self. Thank you for showing me parts of who I am.

Elder Johnson

To: erujohnson@ldsmail.net
Subject: Not forever

Hi my love,

By the time you read this we will have said goodbye. I know this is hard for you, for both of us, so I am trying not to think about it as a goodbye forever but a goodbye for now. I know Heavenly Father has plans for us to meet again either in this life or the life to come.

When I first met you, I thought you were the most handsome missionary I had ever seen. Little did I know that I would develop real emotional feelings for you beyond anything I have felt before. I found myself thinking about you, wanting to be near you. The more time we spent together, the more you were no longer a missionary to me, you became my Eru.

I know our connection is real and it feels heavenly when we are together. What if Heavenly Father's plan was for us to be together? What if you can be an instrument of God and bless and help the lives of people while being with me? Why does it have to be one or the other?

I know the answers to these questions seem impossible to understand and maybe it's something we will never be able to understand in this life. How a loving Heavenly Father could make us this way, allow us to feel so strongly for each other, and yet there is no pathway that allows us to be together.

I pray with all my heart that this will change but I have lost hope that it will. I pray that we can find a way to make this work, Eru, either together or on our separate paths.

Always remember, you are perfect. Heavenly Father loves you and made you just the way you are.

Until then I will always think of you, my love.

Love,
Kaleo

CHAPTER FORTY-TWO

Māreikura had so many questions, so many things she wanted to understand.

'Did you love him?' she asked.

'I think so,' said Eru. 'I've never experienced that feeling before, a real emotional connection with another man. I've had impure feelings to do with physical intimacy, but these were spiritual feelings. They were romantic, and when we were together it didn't feel like sin.'

'Together?'

'I mean, next to each other. The connection felt like it was from heaven. A holy feeling, I can't explain it. It didn't feel bad or evil like I thought it would. I didn't understand what was happening. I just wanted to be near him, Māreikura. I found myself making excuses to be near him, inviting him to teach and come out with us, visiting his home, just wanting to talk with him. We never broke the rules or anything – but then he started messaging, calling.'

Eru cleared his throat. 'I started having impure thoughts. And then I felt physically sick. I couldn't eat, I couldn't sleep. I couldn't think. I couldn't do anything. So I knew we had to break up – I mean, we had to stop seeing each other, and the only way I could do that was to go home.

'I loved my mission,' Eru told her after she handed back his phone. 'I loved the people in Hawai'i and I can't even describe the love I had for my investigators. I was baptising many people and I was senior companion, district leader, and Kaleo was assistant to the president.'

'What's that?'

'It's a calling from the Lord – like a bishop, you know. Every missionary wants to be the assistant to the president. You get to help make decisions – it's kind of like a 2IC. I think the best part was that I was so busy on the Lord's errand that I didn't have time to think about anything – about home, about being, you know . . .'

'Gay?'

'Yes,' he said. 'Gay.'

It was the first time Māreikura had heard him say that word, admitting openly who he was.

'Did you think the mission would change your sexuality?' Māreikura asked him.

'I didn't think it would change it,' he said. 'But I thought it would heal me.'

She wanted to reach over and grab his face and knock sense into him.

'Eru,' she said. 'You don't need healing.'

'I thought Heavenly Father would reward me for my efforts by taking it away,' he said. 'The Lord can move mountains, He can part the sea for Moses, He allowed Peter to walk on water. So surely He who has all power can take this from me.'

'Maybe that's the whole point, Eru? If God didn't take this away from you then don't you think there's a reason for that? That He made you the way you are for a reason?'

'I guess so,' he said, wiping his eyes. 'Like the saviour, when He was at Gethsemane, He asked for the bitter cup to be taken from Him. It must have been hard for God to see His son suffering but choosing not to take it away from Him. That's how I imagine God sees His children, sees me, sees those who are going through suffering. He wants to help us but He can't, not because He's cruel, but because it's part of His plan, because this life is only temporary in comparison to eternity.'

'So what happened to your leg then?' she asked.

He paused. 'I stepped in front of the car. On purpose.'

The very thought of Eru hurting himself made her want to simultaneously throw up and throw her arms around him and love him. This was what kept her from believing in God. Because if God was all-loving, how could God let this happen to her best friend? Eru lived his life in service of God, always doing his best to please God and even going on a two-year volunteer mission that he paid for himself.

When Māreikura was at the Johnsons' house, it was like she was wrapped in a korowai of love. Eru Senior, Eden and Erana all loved so freely and would give the jacket off their backs to anyone who asked – and they always did. They cared about Māreikura, they loved her like their own daughter. Which was why it was so difficult for her to understand, to comprehend how they could belong to an institution that was the cause of suffering for her best friend. Did they know how much pain their son and brother was going through? Eru believed that he was not enough, that he was unworthy, to the point where he would risk his life and harm himself on purpose.

Maybe God didn't agree with this at all. Maybe if God was real he would be just as enraged, if not more, by what was happening to her best friend. Maybe he would feel most enraged at the fact that what was meant to be a safe space, a place of worship, a place of belonging, had now become a place of suffering for so many.

Maybe none of this was God's plan at all.

CHAPTER FORTY-THREE

Jordana's racist dad was coming to the graduation and she was taking it out on Māreikura's hair. She was yanking the brush like a weapon.

'Can you not project your trauma onto my hair?' Māreikura asked her.

The last time Jordana had seen her dad was at their family Christmas party when she punched him in the face at the dinner table.

'I didn't know that you punched him,' Māreikura said. 'You left that part out.'

'Yeah, well, obviously,' she said. 'I'd just met you, I didn't wanna seem crazy.'

'It would have made me like you more,' Māreikura said.

Jordana stopped, still holding the brush in her hand. 'I thought he was gonna hit me back, but he just went inside and got an icepack and ignored me for the next week.'

Māreikura asked if she was drinking and Jordana didn't answer. She yanked Māreikura's hair for the second time.

'I think it's cool that Māori graduations don't have a limit on how many people you invite,' Jordana said. ''Cause how can you put a limit on family?'

'Yeah, true,' Māreikura said. 'Not everyone has a nuclear family. I remember when we used to have the "Bring your Parents to School Day" and it would just be my nana.'

'Don't worry, my dad never came to anything and when he did, he would go on a rant about immigrants taking all the jobs.' She shrugged.

Jordana took a bobby pin from her mouth to hold Māreikura's fringe back.

'It's nice your mum and dad are coming all the way from Aus anyway,' Māreikura said.

'Not like he can't afford it,' she said under her breath and then she patted Māreikura's head to signal she was done. 'Are you ready for your speech?'

'Whaea Terina just said to speak from my heart,' Māreikura said. 'To speak with the wairua.'

'Well, you're good at that,' Jordana said. 'Are you gonna cry? If you are, I won't put mascara on.'

'Nah, it's all good,' Māreikura said. 'Put it on.'

After Jordana did their makeup, they took selfies in the bathroom mirror and did shots, and then Jordana poured the rest of the vodka into a flask and tucked it underneath her bra, and another one in her pocket and another in her shoe.

'Don't look at me like that – you ever been to a Māori graduation? Every mother-trucker will have their aunty doing a waiata and karanga. It's gonna be long, bro.' She was eyeing Māreikura's chest. 'Have you got room in there for another one?'

'No.'

Jordana took another look in the mirror, smoothed her hands over her dress and then put her arm around Māreikura.

'Girl, look at you, look how much you have grown. You couldn't even say the colours in Māori and now you're about to give a whole speech today.'

•

Eru was standing by the gate, dressed in a black suit. The Johnsons were there too with Māreikura's nana.

'Oh my, is that Eru?' Jordana whistled. 'He is something else. And is that his dad? I didn't think I could do over forties until today.'

Māreikura went to hit her but instead she found herself hugging her. She loved Jordana so much. And Jordana was right – Eru was something else. He radiated. It was more obvious when he was around others. He made other people seem ordinary. Like Troy. Troy was so sure of himself, of his identity, of his culture, and yet he seemed dull compared to Eru.

Māreikura followed Jordana out of the Uber. A tall, lanky, white man and a Māori woman were waiting for them, who Māreikura assumed were Jordana's parents. They were carrying a korowai, and the woman told Jordana to turn around while they placed the korowai on her back.

'You look beautiful,' her dad said. He was choked up.

'Oh no, Jords,' Māreikura said. 'My mascara is gonna run.'

When she turned to look, Jordana was crying too.

•

The last time Māreikura gave a public speech, it went viral and had twenty million views on social media. Years had passed since that talk. Now when she looked out at the audience, she realised how different life was. She no longer saw suspicious eyes waiting for her to say something radical. She was not there to protest, to fight for a cause, although she would always fight for te reo Māori. She was there to celebrate, to honour and mihi and pay her respects to her language, to her culture, and to all those who made it possible.

'My tīpuna were storytellers,' she began. 'I ngā wā ō mua, back in the day, my tīpuna would see a manu. Like a tūī, or a kākā, or a kererū. And they would tell a pūrākau – a story so deep, so rich in mātauranga, in knowledge, in wisdom. Our Indigenous intelligence can be found in the form of a whakataukī.

'E koekoe te tūī, e ketekete te kākā, e kūkū te kererū. The tūī chatters, the parrot gabbles, the wood pigeon coos . . . for we are diverse people.

'The stories of my people don't begin in prison cells or in gang headquarters. The stories of my people, the flight of my tīpuna, began when they navigated across oceans of water to this very whenua we stand on today. In the words of Professor Rangi Mātāmua, "Māori have always been scientists, you don't navigate that expansive ocean on myths and legends."

'And so from then, we flew and we flew and we flew.

'My tīpuna were kaitiaki. Kind of like *Guardians of the Galaxy*, except we were guardians of the moana, of the taiao, the natural world around us. The trees were like gods, descendants of Tāne Mahuta, living and breathing, and valued for the breath they gave us each day.

'Our connection to the whenua runs deep through the veins of our whakapapa to our eternal mother and father. Papatūānuku, our mother earth, and Ranginui, our sky father. Ko au te whenua, ko te whenua, ko au – I am the land and the land is me.

'Our wāhine, our women. We were sacred, we are sacred, we are powerful. Held in high regard because we have power over life and death. Descendants of Hineahuone, the first woman formed from soil at Kurawaka. We were matakite. We prophesied, we foresaw, we foretold. We spoke to our tīpuna as if they were still alive. Because they are still alive. Me tiaki i te whare tāngata – we must look after our wāhine. Because mā te wāhine, mā te whenua, ka ngaro te tangata. By women and land do our men perish.

'But then our wings were clipped, we were trampled and torn down. Our stories lost from generation to generation. Our reo Māori cut from our throats until we were mute. Our people taken from our whenua, forced to speak a language that doesn't belong to us. We went from protectors to prisoners. On our own land.

'And so here we are. People are dying, the world is on fire, the islands are sinking, and our infinite knowledge and wisdom is still offered, like a taonga, and yet still we are refused.

'With everything against us, we still fly.

'We took flight when Dame Whina Cooper marched over a thousand kilometres at seventy-nine years old to protect the whenua.

'We took flight when a group of rangatahi marched to the steps of parliament and demanded our reo Māori be seen as a taonga. Ngā Tamatoa.

'I stood up for the first time this year and recited my pepeha. Ko wai au? He uri tēnei nō Ngāpuhi. I am a descendant of Ngāpuhi.

'When I speak the reo of my tīpuna, I'm putting my feathers back on, one by one.

'I remind you about the flight of our tīpuna, who navigated across expansive oceans of water because I am no ordinary person. I am not broken. I am a descendant of greatness. We are descendants of greatness.

'My name is Māreikura Pohe and we will continue to fly.'

Māreikura walked off stage to a standing ovation. She could speak Māori now. She walked with power, with mana, a descendant of greatness, of Ngāpuhi. She could do everything she had always dreamt of doing,

The approval, acceptance and validation she had been searching for all along came from herself.

CHAPTER FORTY-FOUR

Māreikura fell asleep on Eru's bed. She did not want to leave his side. When she woke up, he wasn't there. She walked out to the lounge and he was sitting on the couch, the corner lamp on, a book in his hands.

'What time is it?' she asked.

'I think 2 a.m.,' he said. 'I couldn't sleep.'

'You can have your bed back. I'll go home.'

'I was thinking about what you said, about same-sex attraction not being a weakness,' he said.

'Eru, don't worry.' It was 2 a.m. and Māreikura was too tired to argue.

'It's not a weakness,' he carried on. 'Because God loves me and he created me in his image. So I started pondering about what you said and I got on my knees and prayed. I came to the conclusion that if it is not a weakness, then what could it be? God answered my prayers and he told me it's a strength.'

'It is a strength,' Māreikura said. 'But it's also normal. I'm pretty sure your church and other churches are still the only places left in the world that act like being gay is this big sin.'

Eru looked at her as if she had said a bad word.

'It's not the church that's the problem,' he said. 'It's men.'

'Look at the damage the men in the church are doing, though. If you have these thoughts, there must be so many in your church who feel the same. How many young men and women are killing themselves because your church is telling them it's a sin to be who they are?'

'No one is saying that, Māreikura,' he said. 'It's acting on it that's wrong. When you understand the plan of salvation and our purpose here on Earth—'

'So if you're gay, you can't act on it? So every gay person in your church has to die alone? Are you going to live your life alone, Eru? If you find someone you fall in love with, it's that simple? Don't act on it?'

Eru's face stiffened. She could tell her words had cut him and maybe that's what she was wanting. To hurt him.

'Without God, without the church, I wouldn't have the family I have,' he said. 'My parents wouldn't have the relationship they have.'

'Yeah, and the same God that helped your family is the same God that colonised mine.'

'Māreikura—'

'Eru, it's true,' she said. 'I prayed for my mum to come back and then she died. How come God answers your prayers and not mine? What about all the kids in the world who are dying, who are getting abused? Does God just ignore their prayers too?'

Eru Senior was standing in the hallway. Māreikura didn't know how long he had been standing there or how much he had heard.

'Kei te pai kōrua?'

'Yeah, we're just talking,' Eru Junior said.

Eru Senior glanced at Māreikura, who was looking away from him. She was afraid he would look into her soul. He was good at doing that.

There was a quote stitched in a frame above the TV. 'Remember the worth of souls is great in the sight of God.'

Māreikura pointed to the quote. 'Does your worth stay the same if you're gay?' she asked and she felt Eru's anxiety. 'I mean, because I'm queer. What does God think of me?'

Eru Senior sat down on the couch opposite them. 'God will move mountains for one person. Do you know what I mean by that?'

Māreikura shook her head and he carried on.

'Remember, son, when we were living in Tauranga? Must have been about fifteen years ago now. We had a pretty sweet life. Surfing in the morning, good job, kids were at school – they loved it, eh, son? You remember? And then one day we had this strong prompting to move to Auckland. We didn't know why, but when the Lord asks us to do something, we do it. We found a house, a job, it all worked out. Now, girl, why do you think God would make us pack up everything and move to an entirely different city? You know I don't believe in anything random. Why? It was for you, Māreikura,' he said. 'You were the missing part of our family.'

He reached into his pocket and pulled out a $20 note.

'This note here, it's worth $20,' he said, crumpling up the paper. 'The value of the note stays the same no matter what.'

He stomped on the paper with his feet, picked it up and then squashed it in a ball.

'Just like the note, your worth doesn't change. It doesn't matter who you are, what you do, all the mistakes you make, your worth in the sight of God is infinite. It's eternal. That's what it means—'

'I'm sorry, Dad.'

It was Eru Junior.

'I've tried so hard,' he said. 'I've tried so hard to do the right thing.'

Eru Senior's face softened, searching Eru's eyes as if trying to understand what he was meaning.

'I love you, son,' Eru Senior said. 'You know that.'

'I will never marry in the temple,' Eru said. 'I will never have a family like ours. I won't be sealed to you and mum for eternity.'

'Why—' Eru Senior still wasn't getting it.

'Because, Dad,' Eru said, 'I have same-sex attraction. I mean, I'm gay.'

CHAPTER FORTY-FIVE

Eru was accepted into Brigham Young University, the Mormon university in Hawai'i. He was going to study sports science and play basketball for the BYU team. Māreikura thought she would be more angry. He only just got home and soon he would be gone again. He would come back but as a different version of himself. Unlike his mission, there was no set date for his return. It could be a year. It could be three years. It could be never.

'It's not forever,' Eru said. 'I'll be back soon.'

Eru had told his family he was gay and it was not as bad as he had expected. After he told his dad, Eru Senior started crying and asked Eru for forgiveness for not providing a safe enough space for Eru to be himself.

'It's not your fault, Dad,' Eru told him. 'It's the church.'

'It is,' Eru Senior said. 'I've spent the last decade in service to others, being there when people need me. But I've failed you. No other success can compensate for failure in the home.'

On Sunday, Eru Senior shared a thirty-minute talk on creating spaces of belonging for queer people in the church. He then asked to be released as bishop, effective immediately. He became Eru's greatest advocate. He emailed the president of BYU University and asked, 'What measures will the university undertake in making sure students with same-sex attraction are safe and cared for?'

Erana told Eru she always knew he was gay. Matt shook Eru's hand awkwardly and said love is love. Eden cried as if it was the most devastating news she had heard. She was mourning grandchildren, and Erana said, 'Mum, you know Eru can still have children, right?'

There was a shift in the way Eru conducted himself now. He was still the same Eru, still the most loving and selfless person Māreikura knew. But he was free now. He used to have this permanent crease in his forehead, but now Māreikura was sure that was gone too. He even asked her about how to start a podcast.

'I want to share my story one day,' he said. 'So I can help others. I'm just not a very good speaker.'

'You don't need to be a good speaker,' Māreikura replied. 'Look at you. Just start talking and the whole world will stop and listen.'

He laughed and Māreikura asked him, 'So will you go on dates? There will be so many cute boys at BYU.'

Eru shrugged his shoulders. 'My heart is still with Kaleo . . . and there's the BYU honour code.'

'Excuse me?'

'There is a rule in the honour code about abstaining from same-sex behaviour.'

Māreikura put her hand up.

'I'm not going to say anything, out of respect, but when you decide to start a revolution and overhaul the whole institution, I'll be there.'

Later, she went to Jordana's house and they ate Pad Thai and listened to the Pātea Māori Club. Jordana told Māreikura she felt inspired to move home to Taranaki and live out her dream of becoming a green fairy.

'You can come down and visit,' she reassured Māreikura. 'It will just be me and my plants. And I will be happy living by my maunga. That's my dream.'

'I know,' Māreikura said. 'But I'm going to miss you. You're the best thing to happen to me this year.'

•

They were on the way to the airport. Eru had asked if she could take him, and his family would meet them there.

'I'll message on WhatsApp,' he told her. 'Or I'll get Instagram. The time difference isn't even that bad.'

'Eru, you can't even text here.'

'It will be different,' he said. 'Promise you'll visit.'

'The Indigenous people have asked us not to visit Hawai'i. Tourism is pushing the Indigenous people out of their homes.'

'We could go to Mauna Kea and support Standing Rock. We could support Indigenous people. I'll protest with you.'

Māreikura had never heard him say that before.

'It's always easier for the person going,' she said. 'And it's always harder for the person left behind.'

He didn't say anything, as if processing what she just said.

Māreikura pulled up at the drop-off area of the airport. Eru was leaving but it didn't hurt as much as before. She loved him, but it was never in a romantic way. She had let go of trying to convince him that his beliefs were wrong. She had learnt to love him with no conditions.

Eru popped his head up and his eyes were red.

'I need to tell you something,' he said.

Māreikura could feel the parking warden staring at them, but Eru was hiccupping and ugly crying. She hadn't seen him cry like that since they were young.

'When I was seven and we were living in Tauranga, I wanted to end my life,' he told her. 'I hated who I was, I hated being me. I felt so alone, like I was living with this dirty secret. I was only seven years old, Māreikura. Seven. I didn't even know if God was real but I went into the wardrobe and got down on my knees, and I was crying to God for help, Māreikura. I prayed for someone who would understand me, who would get me. I'd never prayed so hard before but I felt like God was there, right in front of me. Then two weeks later, we were moving to Auckland because Dad got a prompting. And then we met you.'

He reached around his neck and untied his pounamu.

'You saved my life.'

'Eru, no.'

He put it in her hands.

'You are the reason I know God is real,' he said. 'I know God loves me because he gave me you. You are and always will be the greatest miracle in my life, Māreikura.'

•

The sight of Mount Manaia was now Māreikura's favourite view. It never used to be. She used to feel dread sitting in the back seat of her nana's car as a child, knowing that beyond the mountain was an unknown world, a world in which she never felt like she truly belonged. Now it was different. Now when Māreikura sees her maunga, the words of Aunty Lois come to her mind. *Your maunga knows you. You are healing the generations who came before you. You are the bridge.*

Māreikura had asked if her nana would come with her up north and was surprised when she said yes. *Might as well*, her nana said casually, as if they were going for a quick trip to the supermarket and not three hours home.

Māreikura wasn't sure what had happened that made her nana receptive to the journey, but she'd quickly packed the car before she could change her mind.

Eru sent Māreikura two photos. A selfie at the airport and a blurry photo outside the university to let her know he'd arrived in Hawai'i safely. She love-hearted the photos then sent a selfie back of her and her nana sitting in the car. *Going home*, she texted him. He responded, *Māreikura, you're doing incredible things that generations after will be grateful for. You are a blessing. Tell nan I said hi!* She smiled when she read that. It was such an Eru text. She replied, *Love you, be strong. Nana said hi.*

The last time her nana saw Aunty Lois was when their brother died. That was over ten years ago. Māreikura didn't need to ask her why it had taken so long. Māreikura didn't need to interrogate her. There was a mutual understanding of a colonised past, a whakapapa they shared, pain they had both felt and yet could not put into words.

Her nana opened the mirror and checked her lipstick for the last time as Māreikura drove up the driveway to Aunty Lois's house.

Aunty Lois came out wearing a baggy shirt with the tino rangatiratanga flag stitched on the chest.

'That you, girl?' Aunty Lois asked, peering into the car. 'Didn't expect to see you back so soon—'

For a moment, time seemed to stand still.

Her nana opened the car door and Aunty Lois didn't hesitate. She rushed towards her. Before her nana could even speak, Aunty Lois's arms wrapped around her.

Māreikura blinked back tears as she watched her nana and aunty embrace, feeling like, for the first time, she understood what was meant by the power of forgiveness.

'Well, you must be starving,' Aunty Lois said, finally letting go of her sister to wipe away tears. 'By the looks of it, anyway. Gee sis, don't they feed you in Tāmaki? I'll tell you what, that won't last long here. Give me a coupla days, they'll be mistaking us for twins.' She cackled, hitting Glennis on the shoulder before turning to hug Māreikura.

'What did I tell you, girl?' Aunty Lois whispered in her ear. 'We didn't give you your name for nothing.' She touched Māreikura's face, hugged her again and then put her hands on her hips. 'Alright now, must be hungry after the long trip. Gee, how long did it take you to get up here? Heard they closed the roads up by the Brynderwyns. Is that true? Anyway, got some scones in the oven. Not as good as yours though, eh sis? Wait until everyone knows you're here. I'll get Kris to bring the mokos over . . .'

They started walking inside, Aunty Lois talking away while Māreikura's nana nodded and listened. Māreikura followed them and then her eyes caught on Mount Manaia. *Your maunga knows you.* She finally understood what that meant. She finally felt it.

'I'll be back!' she yelled out as she climbed back into the car. She started the car up and headed towards her maunga.

AUTHOR'S NOTE

The idea for *All That We Know* came to me one day while out for a walk back in 2020. I came across a news article involving an Auckland high school student who had done blackface. The photo was being shared all over social media. I was struck by the actions of the young girl and the courageous voices of the students who dared to speak out, and I was disappointed by the school's failure to address racism. What made this event even more poignant was its timing – it coincided with the murder of George Floyd by white police officers in the United States.

I pondered the idea of reconciliation and grace and whether there could be a way for this girl to learn from her actions. I reflected on the reality that, despite being applauded all over the world for our race relations, our country has a long way to go.

Around this time, I saw several young activists in Aotearoa propelled as voices for entire communities. While we need the powerful voices of rangatahi, I began to wonder about the personal cost to our young people. Asking them to address centuries of colonisation and treating them as pawns in political discourse on national television felt more like exploitation. I was also noticing a trend in online activism culture where the incessant pursuit of validation through social media seemed to overshadow the very causes that these online activists were advocating for.

This is where the inspiration for the story came from, my trying to make sense of the world I was living in. I had no idea what was to come in my own life. I embarked on a full-immersion course in te reo Māori, began dating a woman for the first time, and went through a massive crisis of faith. Experiencing all of this at the same time turned my entire world upside down.

I was trying to reconcile my faith in God while simultaneously struggling to comprehend the role of Christianity in not only the slaughter and devastation of Indigenous people worldwide, but the personal ongoing impact of colonisation within my own family. Colonisation is not a one-time event that happened a long time ago. It has deeply traumatised my family for generations; from land loss to language loss, the loss of our gifts, the loss of mātauranga or knowledge.

I was grappling with the harm that religion has caused, and continues to cause, to queer people. In my own life, I was experiencing a deep internal conflict of self-hatred and shame for not living up to what I felt was God's plan for me. I was also witnessing two of my close male friends battle suicidal ideation as they too attempted to reconcile faith with their sexuality.

I could not understand how a loving God could do this. I could not comprehend how the very place I sought refuge with was no longer a place of safety. My soul was yearning for answers, but I could not find peace.

These were some of the most difficult times of my life but they were also the most formidable.

The isolation of writing meant getting to know myself again. I began to understand the meaning of writing being a gift or a form of rongoā. It was as if a mirror was placed in front of me and wounds were opened and exposed, forcing me to examine the deep yearning of my soul.

I was in awe of how much the story of Māreikura began to mirror my own life. I began to find answers to my questions but not in the way I thought. The observations in my writing meant I was able to confront my own grief, reconcile burning questions and hold space for the ongoing pain and confusion I was feeling.

Emily Belle Freeman describes grace as 'radical generosity'. It's a generous act when God gives us grace to grow, and it's even more beautiful when we are able to offer that same grace to ourselves. Love, hope and forgiveness began to show up in my own life. I forgave the others, but more importantly I forgave myself.

This book is about the hope of light in the midst of darkness. It is about how friendship, love and connection will always withstand the test of time, even in a world that feels more polarising and more divisive than ever before.

All That We Know is a mihi to those who have had to dismantle the roadblocks of colonisation in order to forge the paths our ancestors envisioned. The power lies in our reclamation of ourselves and in claiming back our intergenerational strengths.

We have the power to give back to ourselves and to others what we were once denied: our language, our culture, the healing of our whānau for generations. To give what we have been denied is perhaps the greatest manifestation of love.

Reconciliation cannot exist without truth, and we cannot heal without truth. Our country cannot heal without knowing who we once were, so that we can understand who we are now, and where we are going.

Knowledge is infinite. Knowledge is a burning power within us. It is a declaration, an experience, a deep belief. There is power in knowing. No one can take what you know away from you.

I hope you are able to find solace in this book, no matter where you are on your journey. Remember that healing is feeling, and it is not yours to carry alone. In the end, we are all trying to find our way home.

Toitū Te Tiriti, Toitū te whenua, Toitū te reo Māori! Ka rite ki ō tātou tīpuna te maia.

Arohanui,
Shilo

HE MIHI WHAKAKAPI

ACKNOWLEDGEMENTS

This book could not exist without the many activists, scholars, writers, critical thinkers, pioneers and reo champions who have spent lifetimes advocating and fighting for our culture, our land and our rights to simply exist. There are far too many to name.

The writings of Moana Jackson, Margaret Mutu, Patricia Grace, Witi Ihimaera, Leonie Pihama, Rose Pere, Linda Tuhiwai Smith and Ani Mikaere have all been fundamental in my career and life. Thank you for allowing me to learn from the mātauranga that you have all generously offered to the world.

Hinemoa Elder, thank you for gifting me your time while I wrote this manuscript and for reminding me of my ancestral gifts and power. To be in your space and presence was an honour.

Miriama Kamo, thank you for always being supportive of my mahi, and for always offering the gift of your time. They say you should never meet your heroes but I'm so grateful I met you.

Hinemoa Key, thank you for reminding me that we have been and always will be powerful people. Thank you for letting me soak up your wisdom, my friend. You are formidable and I learn so much from you. Nōku te hōnore.

Karlo Mila, thank you for your beautiful words, for your ongoing support and for permission to use your poem in this book.

Stacey Morrison, thank you for inspiring me to reclaim my reo and for helping so many of us take our language back.

Thank you to Hachette, the team at Moa Press and especially to Kate Stephenson for your encouragement, your kindness and for loving Māreikura and her story from the beginning. Thank you to Dom Visini for all of your help throughout the process of publishing!

Thank you to my agent, Cara Lee Simpson; Dianne Blacklock for her editing; and to Antonia Rayne Tangatakino-McIntyre for the beautiful cover artwork.

Mahia Minogue Harrison, thank you for being the Jordana in my life, for our walks, deep kōrero, calling me out when I needed to be called out and going into the moana with me everyday. These small moments had huge significance in my life and were healing me day by day. Ka nui tāku aroha i a koe, tāku hoa pūmau. Aroha mutunga kore.

Kimberley Hurley, thank you for coming into my life at the right time and for always holding space for me. Thank you for being patient with me and for your kindness. Thank you for keeping my plants alive! Thank you for cooking me dinner all those times so I could write this book. Me uaua ka kite ngā tāngata pēnā i a koe. It is hard to find a person like you. Arohanui, my friend. I love you so much.

Taylor Aumua, you are my soul sister and you enrich my life in so many ways. Thank you for inspiring me, for pushing me to be better and for loving me. Thank you for always taking me to the moana! I'm so grateful we both get to navigate uncharted territories and forge our own paths together.

Lizzie Jurisch, thank you for giving me permission to be me, for never thinking I'm too much, and for always encouraging me to wānanga and think more deeply about the world. Love you, love your big heart and love our hearty kōrero.

Talisa Kupenga, thank you, my friend, for your limitless talents, for reading back my drafts and for always being there for me. You are an amazing human being and I am in awe of you. Thank you for always being there for me.

Thank you to Becky, Kate, Astley, Tom, Maurice, Lauretta and to the connections, friends and whānau I have met over the years.

Thank you to my Heavenly parents. My faith has taken me places far beyond anything I could have ever imagined.

Thank you to my mum and dad. I honour you both in the work that I do, knowing how hard it was for you both at a time when society worked so hard to erase you. The courage and resilience of my mother and the work ethic, generosity and humour of my father, I carry throughout my life. I'm so proud of you both for what you overcame to give me the life I have today.

Thank you to all my whānau, my siblings, nieces, nephews and future mokopuna.

I pray we can continue to heal the ripples of colonisation that have wounded our family for generations.

I pray for love.

And I pray for forgiveness.

Nā aroha,
Shilo

HISTORY

This is a brief overview of history in Aotearoa relevant to this book.

1835 He Whakaputanga o te Rangatiratanga o Nu Tireni, also known as the Declaration of Independence of the United Tribes of New Zealand, was signed by Rangatira throughout the North and Waikato areas, and by Ngāti Kahungunu. The declaration of He Whakaputanga served as a foundational assertion of tino rangatiratanga to both the country and the world – that sovereign power and authority would remain with Māori and no foreign powers could make laws for Māori. Many still consider He Whakaputanga to be the founding constitutional document of Aotearoa.

1840 Te Tiriti o Waitangi, the founding document of Aotearoa, was signed. Te Tiriti has a significantly different meaning to the English version, the Treaty of Waitangi. Te Tiriti is evidence that Māori did not cede sovereignty, as it guaranteed Māori tino rangatiratanga and gave Queen Victoria permission to exercise kāwanatanga over her own people. The Crown has continuously failed in their obligations to uphold Te Tiriti, and the consequences have been devastating – both to the whenua and to the people of the land.

1863 The New Zealand Settlements Act was passed to enable the confiscation of land from Māori tribes deemed to have 'engaged in open rebellion against Her Majesty's authority'. Pākehā settlers would occupy the confiscated land.

1865 The Native Lands Acts were designed to remove land from Māori ownership for purchase by settlers as part of settler colonisation. The devastating impact of land loss is still felt today.

1867 The Native Schools Act was introduced by the government, requiring all schools to teach in English. As a consequence, students were punished and beaten for speaking te reo Māori, and te reo Māori was not passed down through generations. The language almost became extinct.

Because of the revitalisation of te reo Māori and the pioneers, activists and reo champions who led the charge, the number of Māori reclaiming te reo Māori is rising.

According to the 2021 General Social Survey, almost a quarter of Māori now speak te reo Māori as their first language.

1907 The Tohunga Suppression Act was introduced, resulting in Māori experts, who are called Tohunga, being banned from using spiritual gifts and traditional healing practices. This has led to the suppression of spiritual gifts in the modern day and a lack of knowledge around traditional healing practices.

The Doctrine of Discovery was a tool used since the fifteenth century to justify Christian colonial conquest, following the belief that European peoples, culture and religion were superior. It resulted in the genocide of millions of Indigenous people worldwide. Moana Jackson called the Doctrine of Discovery a 'crime against humanity' and highlighted how modern states continue to exploit this doctrine to assert dominance over Indigenous peoples today.

Shilo Kino (Ngāpuhi, Ngāti Maniapoto) is an award-winning author. Her debut novel *The Pōrangi Boy* won the Young Adult Fiction Award at the New Zealand Book Awards for Children and Young Adults in 2021.

All That We Know is her second book. She currently lives in Tāmaki Makaurau.